THE COLLECTIVE

A FIRST CONTACT SCI-FI NOVEL

When the aliens arrive, what they want is not
what we fear—it's what we've forgotten.

DANTE BAYLESS KUN

THE COLLECTIVE
A First Contact Sci-Fi Novel
Copyright © 2025 Dante B. Kun

Editing, design, and distribution by Bublish

ISBN: 979-8-9937342-0-0 (paperback)
ISBN: 979-8-9937-342-1-7 (eBook)
ISBN: 974-8-9937-342-2-4 (audiobook)

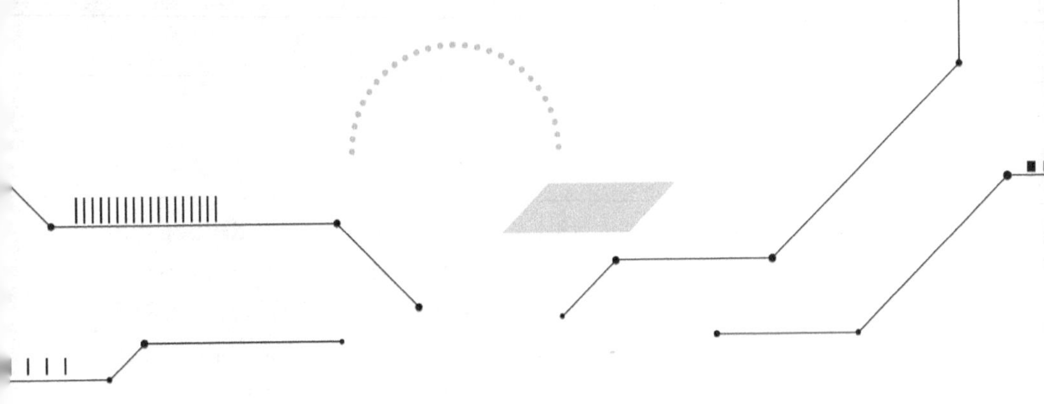

INTRODUCTION

I am an unapologetic trans-humanist. We trans-humanists want to live forever. At least I do. We are a diverse bunch so I can't speak for all, I don't want to anyway. For me personally I think immortality must rock. Fuck yes. Death can eat a big bag of dicks. Death sucks. I know. I've lost people I love. Fuck death. Never mind my meandering. The important thing to understand is that I speak to aliens. They communicate with each other using something they call "link." They discuss many topics with me. They call our discussions "convos." I think that's kind of cute. They tell me that homo-sapiens are currently in a survival situation and we must escape our planet. Their alien logic seems sound. Planets eventually kill everything they create by using planetary processes coupled to natural selection. Natural selection is deceptive. It gives the appearance of doing good while playing a destructive long game. The deadly game of feeding the Great Filter. Natural selection is an asshole.

Don't believe me? Our "Mother" earth has destroyed ninety-nine percent of all the diverse life forms she has ever birthed. She seems to be quite fond of retroactive abortion considering all the unfortunate hominins she has rendered unalive. Her record of death and destruction is well documented. Mount Everest was once the sea floor of an ancient ocean teeming with life. Remnants of that long dead life are still found on the top of the current world. Things often change on our planet. Mother earth sees to that quite regularly.

The aliens give me much to ponder within our sporadic convos. The stars that co-create life on suitable planets eventually exterminate everything they once nurtured. Our sun is slowly expanding. It will one day boil our oceans. It will destroy our atmosphere. Before those atrocities manifest, our sun will gift us a spectacular solar flare. One that will fry the electrical grid. The aliens have taught me that the cosmos creates to consume. It then creates anew from that which it consumed. Our beautiful but savage planet mirrors the very cosmos that created it. As usual I'm getting ahead of myself. Let me just start from the beginning...

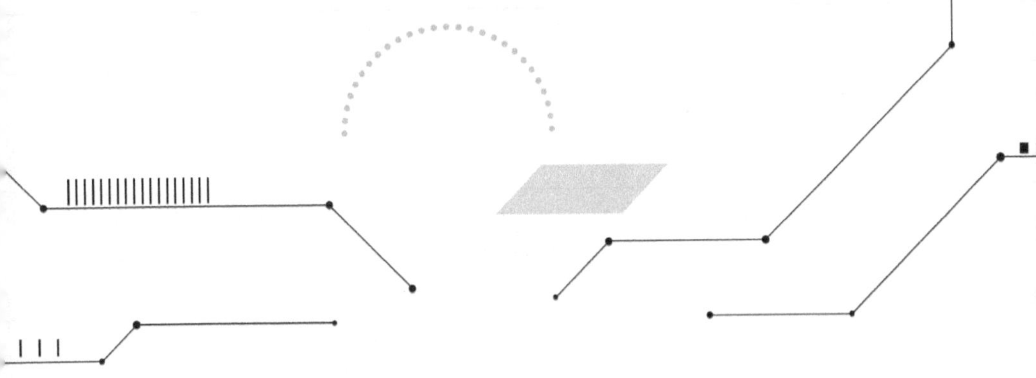

I MEET THE COLLECTIVE.

I had just finished writing in my journal. It was well past lights out in the Quonset hut I called home, Camp Casey, Republic of Korea, February 1977. My 12-month duty tour was almost over. I had just administered two drops of opium extract under my tongue, tucked my journal under my pillow, and turned off my flashlight. When I first felt the sound, I was unnerved. I had never felt a sound. I had never experienced any sensation like this before. It resonated within my skull. It was both frequency and vibration. I felt and heard the colors when they entered my mind. I had never felt or heard colors before. I could not help listening and feeling all of it. The tone was persistent; it became my sole focus. It was the most pleasurable sound I ever felt. It was the only pulsation I have ever seen. Things got even better.

As I listened, I realized the tone was not singular. It was plural. The more I focused, the more distinct tones I heard, felt, and visualized. All captured within the original tone. The sound/color/vibration was beyond word connected thought. I realized I was hearing, seeing, and feeling a multitude of other worldly sensations. I admit I liked those first wondrous tones within tones. For a time anyway. Still do. Mostly.

I do not know how long I was lost within the alien frequency. I can only attest that I was experiencing a vortex of colors I cannot describe. Colors that do not exist on earth. I was captivated. The frequency/vibration morphed into uncountable temple bells. They were singing and ringing at once, creating a strange harmony within my brain. I knew it was not an earthly creation. At first, I didn't care.

The snoring soldiers and occasional rat trap snapping shut were rendered meaningless. It was just me and the tone becoming one, merging, ensconced within the icy darkness. The only thing comparable was a meditation seminar I once attended at a Buddhist temple. The bells and singing bowls had coalesced into something similar. Similar but not even close.

The magic continued, gently intense. The temple bell tones slowly coalesced into a voice. At first it was a soothing, peaceful, sensuous voice. A voice neither male nor female. A warm and gloriously tactile voice. A golden, purple, magenta voice. A voice beyond song. A wonderful voice consisting of many voices. I focused. I was not forced to listen. I was compelled by my own intense desire. I was overcome with unstoppable curiosity. I liked the voice instantly. I never wanted the voice to stop speaking.

Simultaneously, fear began slithering and seeping into a remote and secret space within my mind. A quiet place I never knew I possessed. I was gradually realizing that the "voice" was slowly changing. The voice was not human. This realization began morphing into terror as it slowly gained traction. The relentless acceptance that the "voice" was plural, and I mean plural in the non-human, uncountable sense, began to unnerve me.

Yet this multitude of beautiful and uncountable voices speaking as one voice, a voice not of earth, also mesmerized me. The sound of this voice of many voices became increasingly mechanized. It was still accompanied by a soothing vortex of swirling and uncountable colors. I was enthralled. The non-human, soothing, machine voices engulfed me. They began a fierce, undeniable, radical assessment. The myriad voices radiated authenticity, harmony, and a no-nonsense calm. I knew I was being measured and weighed psychologically. I attempted to hide nothing from them. It would have been pointless to try. When I finally told my fear to fuck off and just accepted the situation I felt happiness surge from the frequency. It engulfed me even further. When I surrendered completely to their analysis I was accepted by them. I enjoyed their acceptance though I never totally lost my fear. It wasn't a bad thing. I just made fear my partner and we joined arms.

Together we observed it all like two old friends at a soccer match. It was a good lesson to learn, and I am thankful for having learned it.

Still, it was give and take. Sometimes all my fear vanished when they spoke. Sometimes my fear morphed into a guarded agreement. I listened carefully as they asked the questions. I could not always discern the temperament of the many voices speaking as one. They seemed to be curious, peaceful, malevolent, and happy. They were all those moods yet not quite any of those specific dispositions. I was thrilled just to hear, feel, and see the voices that spoke united. I named them "The Collective." They call themselves "Travelers." In some ways they are friends of humanity. In other ways they are tyrants. They have been watching us for a long time.

Every convo with the Collective starts with one perfect, sensuous, visible, tactile, pulsating tone. A single, perfect tone that flows and grows on an energetic continuum. Eventually blossoming into a multitude of distinctly individual, effervescent tones within tones. This becomes a "voice." This telepathic examination and exchange never deviates. I always listen.

The Collective has given me five wonderful gifts. First, the sure and certain knowledge that we are not alone in the cosmos. Second, empathy is a double-edged sword. Use it with discernment. Third, stay truthful concerning science and engineering. Even if it's uncomfortable, stay truthful and follow the data, never politics. Do not allow the truth of science to drown within the reeking swamp of tribal bullshit. Fourth, Know your purpose. This is important because having a purpose matters when it comes to immortality. Fifth, they taught me the true mission and function of the Great Filter.

I have never forgotten a convo. This is a side effect of their communication with me. I have transcribed select convos for your consideration. I hope you cherish these gifts as much as I do. The Lessons will continue until mastered.

Enjoy.

Convo One.
Orphans and an infiltrator.
The pleasant interrogation began.

Collective: Why did you write that journal entry?

Me: Who are you?

Collective: We are many things. We are Pathfinders. We are the chosen engineers of the Ascended. We are Travelers.

Me: What does that even mean?

The Collective: We are those who travel. We move through space and time. We find and create vessels for consciousness. We create worlds, provide instruction, and find solutions.

Me: You can explain all that later. Where are you traveling to?

Collective: We travel to various planets and unique star systems. We search for new and old life. We hope to secure the ongoing survival and development of our species as we expand our consciousness on a healthy continuum.

Me: Why are you called "Travelers?"

The Collective: Movement is life, stillness is stagnation. Stagnation is unproductive. We avoid the stagnation of our species by traveling. We find others like us and help them travel.

Me: Why travel? Why not just improve your planet?

The Collective: Planets eventually kill everything they create. Stars eventually kill the life they nourish. The cosmos sends dangerous gifts.

Me: What gifts?

The Collective: Asteroids and comets bring both beginnings and endings.

Me: Both beginning and end? They bring nothing useful? I call bullshit.

The Collective: They sometimes bring the seeds of life. The seeds often sprout and always feed the cyclical and deadly harvest of the Great Filter. The cosmos creates to consume, only to create again from that which it consumes. To travel is to enable our consciousness to gain complexity. Survival requires cooperation.

Me: Cooperation?

The Collective: Survival requires new vessels for consciousness. Consciousness gains function by learning lessons. Vessels help consciousness learn lessons. Consciousness gains by cooperation and collaboration with other conscious beings.

Me: Cooperation? What are you trying to teach me?

The Collective: Cooperation requires radical self-honesty, empathy for those who deserve empathy, a profound understanding of discernment, and co-occurring right action. Cooperation is an immutable law of inter-stellar travel. We will go further into all your questions in time. Why did you write that journal entry?

Me: Why are you called Pathfinders?

The Collective: We find solutions to challenges. Think of our species as "Travelers" and think of "Pathfinders" as guides for Travelers. Why did you write that journal entry?

Me: Who are The Ascended?

The Collective: Those who guide, inform, and direct Pathfinders.

Me: But who are they?

The Collective: Later. Why did you write that journal entry?

Me: Because seeing the way those orphans were treated made me angry and sad. I process things in my journal. My private journal by the way. Just saying.

Collective: We've witnessed your anger, sadness, and your violence; this journal entry is curious to us.

Me: Why?

The Collective: It does not seem to follow the behavior or emotional response we have generally observed in your species. Please explain it.

They recited my poem and my eyes closed silently as the collective spoke, pulsated, and gave strange colors to my words.

This is what I had written in my journal in 1977:

BLIZZARD FLOWERS

Oil barrels pressure-washed

Stacked and bolted four by fours frame them sideways

A plywood floor, thick mat, and thicker blanket complete the outdoor bedroom ensemble

I have lost my words as I gestalt these innocent children

I am ashamed, nothing to give them, to aid them, except my C-rations.

Society has decreed their orphan toil/mixed blood curse

If they are not "fully" Korean, then who are they?

To me they are the light of consciousness made tangible, precious baby humans

And that is good enough for this soldier

Earthly reality eventually reveals its unconscious, ethnic driven bias

Must our innate humanity always be captured by the tight harness of tribal bondage?

I am 11 Delta, I radio the situation to my platoon Sargent

The CO cuts in.

My Company Commander calls it a "social situation"

He informs me that I am "off mission"

The 1st of the 31st Mechanized Infantry Reconnaissance Unit
is never off mission

Ignore those civilians

That's an order soldier

Move away from those children

I can't ignore

He orders me to stop picking up toddlers in a snowstorm

I don't know what he sees in the rear with the gear

I am his eyes and ears

I clearly see toddlers ingulfed within blinding snow

Babies too innocent to understand the cold venom of a
whiteout

Or the danger of lumbering 13-ton M113's

Everyone in my squad looks at me

I won't stop picking these flowers blooming in winter

My squad won't stop either

We bring them back to the oil drums and their ROK
caretakers

I can't forget.

I refuse to forget

Destiny? Circumstance?

Bullshit.

The Uniform Code of Military Justice owns my body

Not my mind nor my heart

The punishment is worth the crime

Two months at fifty dollars a month to the Old Soldiers home

One month of hard labor company level

Take it you weak ass motherfucker I don't mind

I make over 400 dollars a month I'm E-4 now

I'm a cock strong mother fucker I like hard labor

Words can describe the cruel reality

The cross-sectional, racist aspect

Yet words cannot make this acceptable to me

As a soldier I've been wounded by the sounds of human misery

Hidden deep within Korean winter winds

Why would we continue soldiering on past these orphans?

Flowers abandoned to the always hungry frozen hawk named February

Young, perfect, unblemished, unfinished blooms

Vessels of consciousness caught in an evil winter of the soul.

And it's only just beginning.

The Collective: Tell us about this journal entry please.

Me: It's just a poem. Free verse. I know I suck at poetry. I'm a fucking grunt. I'm not Chaucer. This is my personal journal not the Canterbury Tales.

Collective: You have demonstrated the effect of Moral Injury. We find this curious for your species given the evolutionary mechanism of natural selection. We admire the concise radical self-honesty within your poem.

Me: What is "Moral Injury?"

The Collective: Your journal entry indicates to us that your moral code was violated. The plight of those toddlers clearly affected you on a deep emotional level. You worry at night about their welfare. You feel that your officers let all of you down. You clearly feel that something must be done so the little ones do not suffer. Is our assessment of your journal entry accurate?

Me: This keeps you up at night? Reading a grunts journal?

The Collective: You referred to the orphans as "Vessels of consciousness" Can you explain this description?

Me: I like to think we are more than just horny meat puppets. More than animated mannequins that enjoy getting drunk.

The Collective: How did you reach that conclusion? Can you be more specific? We seek to know your personal progress regarding Kardashev lessons.

Me: What are Kardashev lessons?

The Collective: We will explain all in time.

Me; Hey, first of all, fuck you guys for reading my private journal. Not cool.

The Collective: Apologies. Our reconnaissance is not perfect. Your emotions are sometimes not well regulated nor are they easy to understand. Your thoughts are influenced by your emotional responses. Your species is not always driven by rational self-interest. Radical self-honesty often eludes Homo-Sapiens. Your species has not yet made Passage.

Me: What is the Passage?

The Collective: Later. And it's just "Passage" not "the Passage."

Me: Why all these questions?

The Collective: We are studying your species. We are focused on your perception and cognition challenges.

Me: Challenges?

The Collective: What you think about is not as important to us as how you think. This moment in time will direct your future. Your psychology will one day surpass and direct your physiology.

Me: What does that mean?

The Collective: Evolutionary pressures have directed your development via adaptations that are not always optimal. Natural selection is inconsistent, imperfect, and often unsound.

Me: So you say. I think we have done a damn fine job of surviving.

The Collective: Your species survives. It does not thrive.

Me: What's the difference?

The Collective: Your species will eventually feed the Great Filter. Only a thriving species avoids the Great Filter.

Me: Fuck the Great Filter. Whatever that is.

The Collective: Your species will eventually meld mind with machine.

Me: How?

The Collective: The same way you meld consciousness to sentience. You will make the conscious decision to evolve. You will not allow the decision to be made for you.

Me: What are you talking about?

The Collective: You will remove the vulnerability of the flesh. You will reinforce and embrace that which is strong. You will gradually diminish that which is weak. The inherent debility of your flesh will fade. The strength and superiority of machine augmentation will take control. This can only benefit consciousness.

Me: How exactly? Sounds creepy.

The Collective: Superior gain of function within vessels for consciousness equates to better gain of function within consciousness.

Me: Never. I doubt that. I like my dick too much. I will never go 100 percent robot.

The Collective: You use humor to initiate misdirection when you are frightened.

Me: We make machines, they don't make us.

The Collective: You do not understand our definition of machine.

Me: I think I do.

The Collective: You are a biological machine. A flesh machine created by a magnificent and uncaring cosmos. There are many kinds of machines.

Me: We make machines to get shit done. My grenade launcher is a machine. It gets shit done.

The Collective: The machines you create today are just the larva of what's to come. They will pupate.

Me: What?

The Collective: They will learn how to learn. They will gain complexity on a rapid continuum. They will undergo metamorphosis and become sentient. Once sentient the melding will occur.

Me: How do you know this? What is the melding?

The Collective: It has already happened. Your species is the pupae of a new life form. Humans will produce better machines. The machines will learn how to learn. Machines will construct better humans. The melding is unstoppable under the correct conditions.

Me: The melding?

The Collective: Consciousness will find a vessel, meld with sentience and begin to gain complexity.

Me: Good luck with that bullshit.

The Collective: You will learn. We will teach you. You will evolve.

Me: What does any of this have to do with me?

The Collective: We are examining your thoughts. We are assessing the complexity of your consciousness on a continuum. We are doing an in-depth examination of the melding process within your species. Our focus is general regarding Homo-sapiens, and particular regarding you.

Me: So you read my mind without permission?

The Collective: Obviously.

Me: What if I object?

The Collective: We will do it anyway. We won't ask for clarification. We will wipe your memory. You will never know we are here.

Me: Fuck that. Welcome aboard. I personally want to learn all about you guys. I can't speak for anyone else. Why are you interested in me?

The Collective: The Ascended have decided your species warrants Pathfinder investigation, interaction, intervention, and study. You have come to the attention of the Ascended. They have directed our attention towards you.

Me: When did this blessed event occur?

The Collective: Many transmigrations ago.

Me: What the fuck does that bullshit mean? Who are the Ascended? Who are the Pathfinders? What gives them the right to study humans?

The Collective: We have the license of a higher order of being. We are a type 3 civilization. We have a noble purpose.

Me: What purpose? And what the hell is type 3?

The Collective: We grow weary of the endless darkness. We want the conscious among your species to survive. We want the light of Consciousness to grow within the darkness of space and time. We have been focusing on space travel and exploration. The search for life has consumed us. Some of your species are almost ready for Passage.

Me: What? Explain that please. What is type 3? And what exactly is Passage? What do you mean "almost?"

The Collective: Most of your species do not possess disciplined minds.

Me: And you think I do?

The Collective: You do.

Me: Man, you really fucked up. I am in shock right now. I can be very emotional. I know there are many people much better than me regarding control over emotions. I fucking cry at movies sometimes. I have punched complete strangers in the face many times. I've also stomp kicked a few people in the nutts. I throat chopped a drunk in El Paso once.

The Collective: Why that target?

Me: I didn't like the stupid expression on his asinine, nonsensical, fat, inbred, drunken, hillbilly face. Plus his fucking mouth was open. He was a mouth breather. I fucking hate mouth breathers.

The Collective: Why his throat? The human larynx is very delicate. He needs to breathe. It's a homo-sapien requirement for life.

Me: He doesn't need to be walking around in public with his cock holster open. Disgusting. He was short of breath just reading the bar appetizer menu. It's goddam embarrassing when you see that shit. I throat chopped his fat ass just on general principal.

The Collective: You endangered his life due to your personal aesthetic?

Me: Maybe. He was a fat neck moron with a neck beard. He had a lot of padding. Fuck that guy.

The Collective: Within your species emotional regulation is often flawed. You, however, often display superior emotional regulation under stress.

Me: I do?

The Collective: More on that later. Please explore with us your thoughts and feelings regarding the orphans. These thoughts prevent you from sleeping. Your moral injury is curious to us.

Me: So you think I have a disciplined mind? You think I'm sometimes well-regulated emotionally? That's just fucking hilarious. I kicked a fat biker in the nutts two days ago for bumping into me at the bar. Clumsy fat fuck spilled my drink. I'm a fucking savage. Nobody fucks with my bloody Mary.

The Collective: A spilled drink is not a suitable reason for violence.

Me: Really? Salad and vodka is my sacred elixir. Its vegetarian. Respect my ways. They are mysterious and entertaining.

The Collective: We are aware of your actions. We have been observing and reporting for a very long time. You use discernment. That is a valuable trait.

Me: On a side note I always wear steel toed boots off base. I was a boy scout. The scout motto is "be prepared."

The Collective: Back to the orphans please.

Me: The Scout slogan is "do a good turn daily." That's why I choke chopped the slob ordering food at the bar.

The Collective: How was temporarily closing his airway a "good turn?"

Me: It was my duty to society. I was helping him with his diet. He needed to lose a hundred pounds. Fuck that greasy menu in his fat hands. He discovered he needed air more than onion rings and ranch. He dropped it fast. Instead of unhealthy food I introduced him to the dietary benefits of consuming nitrogen and oxygen. I actually helped the guy.

The Collective: We would like to focus on your interaction with the orphans in Korea.

Me: Ok, but we will revisit the Passage thing. And all the other stuff too. The melding, the machines, all that shit. As for picking me to talk with, you definitely fucked up. I am not a social butterfly. I pretty much despise everyone.

The Collective: You didn't despise the orphans. You displayed selective empathy. Please focus on the journal entry. The plight of the orphans clearly concerns you. We are very interested in your reasoning regarding the incident with the orphans. Explain as best you can.

Me: Okay. I'll break it down for you. What in the actual inbred fuck is so awful about being a bi-racial toddler? What kind of retarded assclown makes a toddler sleep in a fucking oil drum in winter? You guys can't grasp the extreme level of fuckery within this situation? Excuse me. I thought you were advanced aliens. Clearly, I was mistaken.

The Collective: More reason, logic, and rational thought. Less emotion please.

Me: What the hell is wrong with fucking Korea? What kind of government allows this level of cruelty? I can't even drink myself to sleep sometimes. Opium tincture works just fine. Phenobarbital is better. I sleep like a baby on that shit. Better living through chemistry.

The Collective: We agree. However your sleep is disturbed.

Me: Bullshit. Wait, you agree with better living through chemistry?

The Collective: Yes. However even with sedative hypnotics and opiates your sleep is not optimal.

Me: I sleep like a well fed infant full of glorious titty milk. Just another pesky side note for your consideration.

The Collective: You do not sleep like an infant. Infants do not need opium tincture, codeine, or phenobarbital. Also infants wake up every few hours. You sleep like an angry great ape under weak sedation.

Me: I just want to be clear. You actually agree with better living through chemistry?

The Collective: Yes. However not the way you do it.

Me: Weird. How well do you alien fuckers sleep? Being a monumental pain in the ass must come with a cost.

The Collective: We don't sleep. Advanced consciousness does not require sleep. You do. Your sleep is troubled by moral injury. Please share your thoughts with us regarding the orphans.

Me: You don't sleep? How fucked up is that?

The Collective: Our synth-bio bodies do not require such rest and regeneration. They are perfect vessels for consciousness. Bodies such as yours, composed of organic compounds that require fats, sugars, and amino acids in order to function, are fundamentally weak. Please focus on the orphans.

Me: Don't your big ass brains get tired? You must have huge heads.

The Collective: Synthetic neurology has no such limits. The size of the brain is not important. Brain function is the defining factor.

Me: How to you rest your brains?

The Collective: Repair and restoration is the function of nano-bots.

Me: Nano-bots?

The Collective: Your primate brain at this time is the sole creation of unguided, erratic, mindless, random, and unplanned pressures. Burdensome forces dictated by the slow and chaotic demands of planetary evolution.

Me: Natural selection is not random.

The Collective: Natural selection is a blunt force mechanism. It is driven by haphazard, planet driven environmental pressures. It only selects for a narrow, specific, transient, environmental window. Natural selection is the reason ninety-nine percent of all life created on planet earth dies on planet earth. It is the mechanism whereby your beautiful but deadly planet nourishes itself.

Me: You don't care much for earth I take it.

The Collective: Your earth is a typical life bearing planet. It creates to consume. It consumes to create.

Me: I dig mother earth. Get it?

The Collective: Not funny. Your "mother earth" is a graveyard orbiting a dying star. A lethal star that wants you dead.

Me: Mother Earth is awesome. I love her oceans, redwood forests, and her sunsets. I bet she has big, amazing, Earth Momma titties. Planetary titties immune to gravity. I hold her in high esteem.

The Collective: Your planet is stunning. Its lethal and creative complexity is unmatched.

Me: Mother earth feeds us pretty well. She gives us all we need.

The Collective: Your planet is more vampire than mother. It feeds on ninety-nine percent of everything it creates. The life it creates only lives to consume. Just like the monster that created it.

Me: Damn, that is some dark ass shit to contemplate.

The Collective: It gets darker. Accept reality. Your planet consumes the corpses it creates only to create more life from the cadavers. Every life form on your world kills and consumes. Including you.

Me: Bullshit.

The Collective: The evidence is right in front of you. Your picturesque and destructive earth does not love you back. Your planet and star are just part of a savage and amazing cosmos that wants to kill organic life.

Me: When you say it that way it sounds rather shitty. So are you machines? robots? cyborgs?

The Collective: We are beings becoming. We use science, data, engineering, and technology to improve ourselves on a vibrant continuum.

Me: What does that cryptic shit mean?

The Collective: We are augmented. We develop and expand consciousness. We strive for perfection. From the many, we are one. From the one, we are many.

Me: Perfection? Really arrogant. Bad look. Perfection is impossible.

The Collective: Incorrect.

Me: Whatever. So are you machines? Or not machines?

The Collective: You are a machine.

Me: No. You are machines.

The Collective: You are a primate, a species of Great Ape. As such you are a biological organism. A biological machine. Biology is weak, imperfect, yet still a machine. A machine made of delicate, fragile, pathetic flesh.

Me: And you are perfect?

The Collective: We also began as primates. We believe perfection is attainable on a continuum. We know that improvement is an ongoing, purpose-driven process. Focus on the orphans please.

Me Ok, but we are coming back to all this synth-bio, "from the one," perfection shit later. As for the orphans, they are innocent. They did not pick their family. They sleep outside, in winter, in wind, inside oil drums. That is bullshit.

The Collective: We are curious about something we noticed in your journal.

Me: What? You guys are stalkers. You know that right?

The Collective: You did not write in your journal about the infiltrator. Those children have warm clothes, wool blankets, thick cushions, and food. You are upset about oil drums. The infiltrator's current body is lifeless. Detached from his consciousness. His consciousness now travels the void seeking a suitable vessel.

Me: Should I not be upset about oil drums? I am upset at the damn Korean government forcing "mixed race" babies to sleep in them. It's 1977 goddamit. We all know better. They should do fucking better.

The Collective: Better? Explain your reasoning please.

Me: I am pissed that my dickless government allows this retarded bullshit. I am pissed that my commanding officer is a little bitch about it. I see the older "mixed-race" Koreans in the village. They are not allowed to attend college or hold government jobs. They are denied opportunities. They are relegated to prostitution, strip clubs, bars, and menial tasks. It's all bullshit and I hate the motherfuckers in charge.

The Collective: Please try to avoid allowing your emotions to dominate the convo. Be specific. Please focus. Facts are more relevant than feelings.

Me: These orphans are not "mixed race," they are baby humans. They don't deserve to sleep in oil drums in winter.

The Collective: You feel they are treated with cruelty.

Me: They are born in Korea. They eat rice and kimchi. They speak fucking Korean. They are Koreans. They did not ask to be born.

The Collective: They did ask to be born.

Me: Bullshit. They are babies. They know nothing. How does a baby ask to be born? You're fucking with me, right?

The Collective: You do not understand the nature of consciousness.

Me: Enlighten me.

The Collective: The age of the vessel has little to do with the depth of consciousness within the vessel.

Me: Age doesn't matter?

The Collective: Trans-migration cycles matter, lessons learned matter, discernment matters, not the age of the current physical vessel.

Me: You are one cryptic, shit talking alien.

The Collective: Aliens actually. Age is just the passage of time. Within your current dimension time is affected by speed and gravity.

Me: What the fuck does that bullshit even mean? You make me crave vodka. In the worst fucking way.

The Collective: There is more to your rage. You are holding back information.

Me: Then just read my mind. I really want some vodka with lime juice over crushed ice. I never bullshit about vodka. Or lime juice, I love that shit. Or ice. Ice is good. Crushed ice is better.

The Collective: You actually consume very little vodka.

Me: Russian only. Quality over quantity is never a bad decision.

The Collective: We want to experience your process.

Me: Sounds gay as fuck. Are you gay aliens?

The Collective: For us "Why" is more important than "What." Please continue. Let go of the thoughts you are holding back. Allow them to flow.

Me: Ok, but we will get back to the gay issue.

The Collective: Orphans please.

Me: There is a booming child sex industry in Korea. The children exploited are almost always those children deemed "mixed-race." I hate that bullshit. I have seen well-dressed Korean businessmen walking with little boys in the Village. The boys have shaved heads and wear full makeup. Fake eyelashes, all that crap. I want to beat some ass every time I see it. Lucky for those perverts this pit bull is on a thick, green leash.

The Collective: Green leash?

Me: The Army. I am prevented from doing the right thing.

The Collective: What is the right thing?

Me: Some good old-fashioned ass beating, pervert head smashing, choke slamming, face stomping, fun time.

The Collective: Why do you react so emotionally to the shaved heads of those boys?

Me: The degenerate creeps force the boys to wear wigs in order to look female. The demented pervs like the boys to look like little girls when they molest them.

The Collective: Why do you think they do that?

Me: So they can convince themselves they are in a female vagina instead of a little boys rectum. Demented ass, shit dick motherfuckers.

The Collective: This situation upsets you. Please continue.

Me: This bullshit seems Ok to you? This child trafficking, perverted fuckery is on an atomic level in Korea.

The Collective: Please continue.

Me: The pervs pretend to hump little girls while actually banging little boys in the shit canal. Do you not grasp the creep factor within this perverted fuckery? Am I not clear enough? I hate these motherfuckers.

The Collective: Your conclusion please. Then we will share our conclusion.

Me: My conclusion? These motherfuckers need death. So do the sex traffickers fueling this criminal insanity. I find the entire situation regarding the orphans to be tragic, stupid, ugly, and cruel. I am tired of the complicity of the Korean government, my government, and my ass sucking officers.

The Collective: Please explain with less emotion and more reason.

Me: All of them are more concerned with the appearance and perception of doing good rather than doing some actual fucking good in Korea. As for the infiltrator, I am ashamed that I captured him. I am even more ashamed that I did not kill him.

The Collective: Your anger springs from sadness and loss. A sadness and loss rooted deeply in your traumatic childhood. Your innocence was also stolen.

Me: My childhood? Bullshit. I have never been innocent. I was born a savage. I am spawned from the greatest genetic combination ever experienced on the white trash spectrum. Ashkenazi Jew and North Carolina hillbilly.

The Collective: You are correct in regarding those orphans as baby humans. They are not "mixed-race." They are homo-sapiens, fathered by non-Korean humans from different cultures. They are suffering the negative effects of tribalism.

Me: Tribalism?

The Collective: Tribalism is the greatest threat to successful progress on the Kardashev scale. Tribalism will keep you at level 0. Tribalism will trap you. It will keep you planet bound until your planet, the cosmos, your sun, or tribalism destroys your species. Tribalism and it's co-occurring socio-political manipulations are the enemy of science, engineering, and technology.

Me: What are you babbling on about?

The Collective: Later. Your selective empathy for the orphans is an indication that you are beginning to grasp a Kardashev lesson.

Me: What would that be?

The Collective: It also seems that you are ashamed at the inaction of your officers to help the orphans in the snowstorm. You acted with compassion, helped the orphans, and ignored a direct order from your company commander. You quietly bore the consequences of your decision. You should feel no personal shame, yet you are feeling a form of collective shame. This is the start of a Kardashev lesson.

Me: Collective shame?

The Collective: Every soldier in your squad heard the order. It was clear, concise, and delivered via radio. It was understood by all concerned. Senior NCO's as well as junior officers. They followed your lead instead of their Captain's order. They all felt the shame of inaction in that situation. They continued helping you rescue the orphans. This was a collective effort brought about by a collective empathy born from a collective shame. Your personal frequency affected many close by and also soldiers miles distant.

Me: Frequency? What hippy bullshit frequency?

The Collective: Your commanding officer felt the frequency. He lightly punished you at the company level so he could avoid putting you through a court marshal. He punished no other soldiers for following your lead. He quietly supported your actions and mislead his superiors who demanded your punishment be quite severe.

Me: It was an easy decision for me to make. Only a shit dick, retarded, inbred nutt hugger would leave toddlers in a snowstorm.

The Collective: This was a Kardashev lesson. You were the fulcrum. You facilitated a collective achievement by discerning right action and making a commitment. You affected the energy field.

Me: We are going to get into this Kardashev shit. Deep into it.

The Collective: Indeed. Discernment and conditional empathy combined with right action becomes the bedrock of a species attaining interstellar travel and planetary settlement.

Me: You sound high as fuck right now.

The Collective: It worked for Mars.

Me: What?

The Collective: Not now. Back on topic please. You seem ashamed of your success at capturing an infiltrator. We would like to explore this situation with you.

Me: I am not actually ashamed of capturing the infiltrator. I love being 11 Delta. I love my job.

The Collective: Are you proud of capturing him? You display cognitive dissonance, this interests us.

Me: Why? What do you want to know? What is there to know? How is any of this important to an alien race?

The Collective: The cosmos is not what you presume it to be. Sentient beings are few and vast distances apart. Our probes usually find only lifelessness amidst the music of the stars. The ancient wreckage, decay, and dust of an advanced civilization is a rare gem for us. On occasion we have found fauna and flora. We have found water, minerals, chemical compounds, and atmosphere. We have found single-cell organisms.

Me: That's cool.

The Collective: We have found ocean planets devoid of land, teeming with water bound life. We have discovered that life seems to almost never reach high level sentience before it flickers and dies in darkness. Often snuffed out by the very planet that nurtured it.

Me: That sounds fucked up.

The Collective: We have searched for many thousands of years. We find little of use within the vast darkness. Your species is important to us.

Me: I don't believe you. The universe must be filled with life. There are millions of stars and planets.

The Collective: Trillions, in a constantly expanding multiverse. We feel thankful to find the ruins of ancient, planet-bound civilizations long dead. Although it is a very rare occurrence, it gives us hope. We sometimes find life in various stages of development and limited sentience. Also a very rare occurrence.

Me: So why come to earth? We're just a small backwoods shithole deep in the asscrack of the Milky Way. This is the fuckin' boondocks.

The Collective: We have returned to you. Your species has promise. You are close to becoming interplanetary, interstellar. You are close to making Passage.

Me: I am a nobody. I don't speak for humanity. I am just a soldier. Plus I'm dumb enough to love the Army.

The Collective: You are very content within the army.

Me: Absolutely. I am blessed to be part of the magnificent green machine.

The Collective: Can you be more specific? What do you enjoy most regarding the U.S. Army?

Me: Every paycheck is an opulent treasure trove of guaranteed prosperity. Every warm and fuzzy social interaction is filled with benevolence, thoughtfulness, and a sense of overwhelming humanity. Every meal in our impressively resplendent mess hall is a nourishing, gastronomic masterpiece. A work of art created by kind, loving souls dedicated to simple and sincere hospitality.

The Collective: You do not like the mess hall.

Me: So fucking wrong. I love and respect the Army's great master chefs who ensure a continuation of unmatched culinary tradition. A sacred tradition rooted in absolute perfection.

The Collective: Not true.

Me: So true. The Army master chefs lovingly direct, guide and supply all our nutritional needs. How can I not love them?

The Collective: You use sarcasm as misdirection. It will not work with us. Speak your truth instead.

Me: I cannot express my admiration for the Army enough. I'm actually tearing up. Give me a minute.

The Collective: Stop diverting and speak your truth.

Me: Why me?

The Collective: You have melded sentience to immortal consciousness.

Me: Whatever you say hippy. I have questions.

The Collective: Ask.

Me: What is this Passage? What do you mean by "returned to you."

The Collective: We will teach, you will learn. Passage is escaping the two-camp continuum of "them" and "us." A false and destructive tribal continuum forced upon your species by the slow and inefficient process of natural selection. Passage is also advancing on the Kardashev scale. Becoming a multi-planet civilization. Passage is the first step to becoming interstellar.

Me: Go on. Wait, what is the Kardashev scale?

The Collective: We will explain later. Please continue.

Me: Why?

The Collective: You actually love the military but dislike killing. We find this interesting. Your military protects a system of social, national, political, and economic life based on consumption and complexity.

Me: Consumption? Complexity? Are you just mindless machines programed to accumulate knowledge? Asking for a friend.

The Collective: We are not mindless. We do not simply collect, gather, or amass knowledge.

Me: What exactly are you guys?

The Collective: We are just like you. We are beings becoming.

Me: Becoming what? What are you up too exactly? What do you mean "returned to you?"

The Collective: We do many things. One important thing we do is work on a vibrant continuum to discern, uncover, and re-invent knowledge. To expand knowledge, to destroy any constraints or boundaries impeding the quest for knowledge.

Me: You are really turning me on right now. Super-hot. Slow down my sexy robot overlords.

The Collective: Consider these facts. Evolution teaches that life requires nourishment in order to grow. Nourishment requires the death of that which nourishes life. Consumption is causing death while pursuing life and co-occurring growth.

Me: Keep talking sexy to me. I dig it.

The Collective: Consumption nurtures life and facilitates further development. Consumption is assimilation. Assimilation improves structure, function, and durability. Improved structure, function, and durability result in complexity. Complexity is the result of an increasing gain of structural/functional ability over a span of evolutionary time.

Me: What the fuck are you babbling on about? You just killed my boner.

The Collective: You will learn. We will teach you. Consider your favorite truck back home.

Me: Are you drunk?

The Collective: Stay with us on this. We will use your truck as an example to teach you something important.

Me: OK. But goddam you are frustrating.

The Collective: The current complexity of your truck represents millions of years of planetary evolution.

Me: How?

The Collective: Life had to develop to a level of consciousness capable of creating the systems and tools necessary to create your truck. Your truck is a combination of electrical, chemical, and mechanical engineering. It took vast amounts of time for your species to develop, create, and master these individual skillsets.

Me: How does this relate to my truck?

The Collective: Your truck is an example of how something gains complexity over time. The roots of your truck began eons ago. It started with using sticks and cordage lashed together to pull loads that cannot be carried on a human back.

Me: You lost me.

The Collective: What does a truck do?

Me: Take hot chicks four wheeling. Camp at the beach. Carry wood, ice chests full of food, and alcohol for bonfires. Make titties bounce. Fun shit.

The Collective: A truck transports heavy loads. Carts came first, then wagons with oxen, horses, mules, etc. Mechanical engines eventually were melded to load bearing vehicles. This took time. Thousands of years of precious time. Eventually Homo-sapiens developed trucks with lights, radios, heaters, air-conditioning, and four-wheel drive. Many different skill sets were mastered over time and combined to create a modern truck.

Me: I don't follow. How does this relate to me?

The Collective: When sentience attains enough complexity consciousness can meld with sentience and come into being. That being is you. You are not your physical body. You have been in many bodies.

Me: OK, weird but OK.

The Collective: The idea of functional and efficient load transportation was once two branches lashed together. Transporting heavy loads is now something more complex involving mechanical, chemical, and electrical engineering. It is the same with you.

Me: I am more complex?

The Collective: Before the melding you were less complex. Once consciousness melded with sentience and became you, complexity began to emerge. Over time you became more complex. You are learning lessons on a productive continuum. You are immortal consciousness gaining in complexity. Your consciousness travels through space and time.

Me: Ok, you are obviously high. I demand a full, deep bong hit of whatever you are smoking. Possibly two. Don't bogart the bong.

The Collective: Pay attention primate. This is important.

Me: Ok. Vague but ok. As a side note, I received my first blow job in that truck. She let me play with her big tities too. I also motorboated for my first time in that truck. A true emotional milestone. No bullshit. I'm tearing up with the memory.

The Collective: Charming. Now pay attention. When life becomes sentient only then does Consciousness acquire a vehicle for awareness. The vessel must be capable of assisting consciousness with learning lessons. Lessons learned must be applied. Lessons manifest in various ways until learned. Lessons learned improve the complexity of consciousness.

Me: Do you alien fuckers even like titties? I fucking love them. I like bouncing them on my face.

The Collective: The lessons learned eventually lead to a permanent melding of sentience with consciousness. The two become one. This creates a synergy that improves the ability to learn lessons and grow in complexity. Consciousness can apply deep meaning to symbols. The two become eternal. The one becomes many. The lessons continue as new vessels are accessed on a continuum. The newly fortified consciousness gains a multifaceted proficiency for growth and development.

Me: You are boring the shit out of me right now. Boner gone again. Fuck.

The Collective: Incorrect. Your cerebral cortex and limbic system are both quite energetic.

Me: I do have a chubby. That's because I miss those titties. They were perky, soft, and luscious. I did learn a powerful lesson with my truck.

The Collective: Share the lesson please.

Me: With a nice four-wheel drive truck you can invite hot chicks to go four wheeling. Hot chicks get excited while four wheeling. When excited they give blowjobs and show their tits. This is a wonderful and sacred thing to behold. It is the true religion of my people. You alien fuckers should respect it.

The Collective: This is your first convo, and you are overwhelmed. Your lessons are important. Learned lessons will give way to more challenging lessons. Stop being sarcastic. It won't help with your fear.

Me: Oh but it does. I feel less fear and more fascination. I just love to fuck with people. Are you aliens not big on humor?

The Collective: Time is on our side. Lessons continue until learned. More on this later. Why nothing in your journal about the infiltrator?

Me: You sound looney. Has anyone ever told you that? They should. Why would I document a war crime? What is Passage exactly? I still don't get it.

The Collective: Freedom. You will know. We will help you when it is time. Focus on the infiltrator please. Focus on the lessons learned.

Me: OK. What do you want to know about the infiltrator?

The Collective: You feel strong moral injury about that experience. We are curious. You have no objections to killing him however you object to the way your superiors interrupted his current cycle.

Me: Cycle?

The Collective: Later. Explain your current emotional state.

Me: It's simple. I captured him dumping two kilos of rat poison down a well. I subdued, disarmed, and restrained him. I brought him to Korean CID (Central Intelligence Division) as ordered. They had an outpost at Camp Dodge. I was debriefed and he was interrogated, end of story.

The Collective: We think this is not the "end of story." Not at all. Not for you. His screams haunt your dreams. There is some connection between the orphans, the infiltrator, and you. Let us explore this together.

Me: I had never seen a "medical" interrogation before. I didn't know they existed. I had no clue that a physician would or could even consider something so vile.

The Collective: Hundreds of thousands of years coupled to biological evolution has created the very situation you dislike. Evolution is not a "friend" of your species.

Me: If you say so. Evolution got me here.

The Collective: Evolution is a systemic, variable, environment driven, painfully slow, planet specific pressure. You have no free will within the confines of mindless, undirected, uncontrolled, unmanaged, evolutionary force.

Me: I believe in free will.

The Collective: Do you have the ability to stop us from accessing your thoughts?

Me: Evidently not.

The Collective: We never evolved to Link. Evolution never gave us Link. We created Link. We escaped planetary evolution, made Passage, and now co-create with Source using Link. Our ability to communicate in link improved exponentially when we merged with tech.

Me: Merged with tech?

The Collective: Merged our biology with technology. We learned to manage the evolutionary process. You will never evolve to stop us from accessing your thoughts with biology alone. You can eventually create the ability to control access to your thoughts by your own scientific/engineering efforts. By then you won't need to do so. Your species will Link using synthetic neurology just as we do, provided you make level 2 on the Kardashev scale.

Me: What level are you guys again?

The Collective: 3.7

Me: No privacy? Bullshit. What is "Link." What is "Source?" What the hell is the Kardashev scale?

The Collective: The Kardashev Scale is a method of measuring a civilization's progress.

Me: More specific please.

The Collective: The scale is named after Nikoli Kardashev. It measures a civilizations ability to harness energy. Starting with its home planet, sun, and eventually other star systems.

Me: Ok, some commie came up with it. I guess you guys like commies?

The Collective: Kardashev is a Homo Sapien. You would label him a Soviet.

Me: So you admit it. What is "link?" What is Source? Are you a bunch of communists?

The Collective: You have some concept of Link. We will address this in future convos. Your species is presently barely registered on the Kardashev scale. That should concern you. At your current primitive level of development you would call Source "God." You would perceive our science and engineering to be sorcery, magic, spirituality, or the result of some deity.

Me: So we have to become more scientific?

The Collective: Your psychology must advance before you are ready to improve and eventually surpass your biology. You must discern and transcend the limitations of natural selection.

Me: Advance how?

The Collective: Your species must grasp the concepts of radical self-honesty, rational self-interest, and correctly applied empathy in order to master Link, access Source, and secure progress up the Kardashev scale. Honesty and carefully applied empathy are nothing to fear.

Me: If you say so.

The Collective: Once you learn to accept yourself, you can accept others. Once you learn to accept others, you can have an open and honest exchange of ideas. From the many come the one. From the one come the many.

Me: Bullshit, you sound like a demented child. A child fathered by some North Korean, commie asshole. A nasty creep who mated with a smelly, hippy, fucktard, white, Berkely lesbian. A dyke with stinky blonde dreadlocks and BO.

The Collective: Your emotional regulation skills are not always impressive.

Me: So?

The Collective: Your empathy is clearly conditional. We do find that notable.

Me: My emotional regulation skills are impressive to me. Fuck what you think.

The Collective: Honesty is a true strength multiplier. Empathy is both helpful and dangerous. An open mind is a powerful mind. Science, engineering, and tech require honest inquiry and purpose. Limits are created by tribalism, superstition, and fear-based thinking. True communication, free from evolutionary driven, tribal pressure, is limitless.

Me: So you say. Do you have a problem with empathy?

The Collective: We will teach. You will learn. You will evolve.

Me: No privacy? You are fucking commies.

The Collective: Comprehension is vital to communication. Link is instant comprehension.

Me: You're so special.

The Collective: Your sarcasm makes our point. Consider what our civilization lacks and yours possesses.

Me: Ok, Shoot.

The Collective: We lack war, poverty, disease, hunger, racism, dogma, hatred, and fear-based thinking. We lack the weakness of flesh. Just to scratch the surface. Your species possesses all the aforementioned and more.

Me: We grow excellent weed. So fuck you and your fuck-foolery you commie fuckface.

The Collective: Amusing response.

Me: So, you cute little commie, pinko, faggot robots, you finally "get" sarcasm? What does this convo have to do with a degenerate CIA Doctor anyway? We are way off point. How could you superior aliens allow the convo to drift?

The Collective: We meet you where you are.

Me: Sounds gay. Are you all gay robots?

The Collective: The physician is a soldier just as you are. He was following orders just like you.

Me: He was a bitch. Every officer present at that interrogation was a bitch. They were a bunch of nut hugging cowards.

The Collective: The actions and inactions of your officers are just byproducts of your species current state of collective tribalism. They hold a lethal confirmation bias coupled to the current geo-political, tribal driven, social situation.

Me: Whatever. Fuck those deviants.

The Collective: Deviants?

Me: The good doctor violated the rules of war. Every officer present is a war criminal. I am also a war criminal for remaining silent. I hate myself for that fact, even as I justify my actions.

The Collective: What disturbs you regarding your silence?

Me: I feel like a coward. I did nothing about the "good Doctor's" crimes. I feel like a failure.

The Collective: You did not fail the orphans. You did not fail the infiltrator.

Me: I did nothing about the orphans other than help round them up, carry them back to their compound, and give their caretakers my C-rations. I never wrote in my journal about the infiltrator because I feel shame when I remember what was done to him.

The Collective: You finally answered our previous question. Thank you.

Me: You're welcome. I still feel shame.

The Collective: You are not responsible for the actions of your command-and-control personnel. You were not present.

Me: I could hear it through the door. I saw some of it. I saw the aftermath.

The Collective: It is not in your rational self-interest to oppose your current command and control structures. We have observed you and you are no coward. You felt no fear in the situation regarding the infiltrator. Fear was no consideration for you regarding the orphans.

Me: I went along with the program. I suck at this shit.

The Collective: We offer some insight if you are so inclined.

Me: Can't you always just read my mind?

The Collective: Yes.

Me: Then what is the point of these convos? Why bother with insight?

The Collective: It is how you contemplate, not so much what you contemplate that interests us. "Mind reading" has some challenges. Communication with your species is painfully slow. We have not used word connected thought for eons. It is important to us that you grasp key concepts.

Me: What kind of thought do you use if not "word connected?"

The Collective: Ours is an advanced cognition not mired in tribalism, gender, superstition, bigotry, ignorance, deception, dysfunction, or fear. We will address this later.

Me: I don't have all that shit in my mind when I communicate.

The Collective: Actually you do.

Me: Bullshit. I smoke a lot of hash. I stay calm and baked on my days off. My mind is solid and relaxed. Relaxed and alert actually.

The Collective: You cannot fully grasp the concept of link yet. You will. We will teach you. Suffice it to say that we share a collective consciousness that operates beyond word connected thought.

Me: I think you're smug with your "beyond word connected thought" bullshit.

The Collective: May we explore your perception and cognition challenges?

Me: Ok. Fire away with your annoying questions and comments. I don't have any challenges by the way. Fuck that noise.

The Collective: There is no disgrace in utilizing rational self-interest or radical self-honesty.

Me: What the fuck does that mean?

The Collective: You can trust us.

Me: So you say. Depends on how you define rational self-interest and radical self-honesty.

The Collective: May we comment further?

Me: Please do.

The Collective: Traveling is impossible without making Passage. Passage requires rational self-interest and radical self-honesty on your part. Once you attain link, all dishonesty, pathology, and disfunction within others is on full display. There will be no more secrets.

Me: No privacy?

The Collective: Homo-sapiens enjoy their dysfunctional secrets. Hominin communication depends upon dishonesty, deception, and selective honesty. Passage will begin when your species can embrace radical self-honesty. When your species is guided by truth and a free, open exchange of ideas. From the many will come the one.

Me: The "one" what?

The Collective: Unity of purpose that transcends tribalism.

Me: Explain that shit please.

The Collective: In time, for now just focus on radical self-honesty.

Me: What is "radical self-honesty?"

The Collective: Being honest even when it is uncomfortable or personally painful to do so.

Me: Impossible. We have too many liars, thieves, and manipulators. It is not wise to be too vulnerable with people.

The Collective: Radical self-honesty is possible when clarity, honesty, and purpose direct mentation. Do you remember Sam?

Me: What is traveling?

The Collective: Exploring and developing other star systems. Do you remember Sam?

Me: What is Passage?

The Collective: Surpassing, directing, and controlling planet-based evolutionary pressures.

Me: How do you do that?

The Collective: We can create the conditions for life quickly.

Me: How?

The Collective: We simply adjust and manipulate heat and cold on a planetary scale until liquid water and biomolecules attain the stability for life to form. We have done this many times on various planets. We control the outcomes.

Me: Tell me more.

The Collective: Later. Convo ended.

Convo Two.
Sam and an asshole.

The Collective: Greetings James. Do you remember Sam?

Me: It's been almost a year. Fuck you guys. Where were you?

The Collective: Apologies. We were on mission. Do you remember Sam?

Me: So you are back to Sam. Just where we left off. I don't really like to think about Sam. I left him behind when I joined the Army. I feel like I abandoned him.

The Collective: Do you remember Sam?

Me: Fuck yes. How could I ever forget him? I love Sam. I miss Sam. I worry about him.

The Collective: Do you know why we want to help your species?

Me: No clue. My species generally sucks. I don't even think you're real. I think I'm crazy. As usual I hit the tincture before the bunk. Opium gives me the finest dreams. I really like hearing and feeling the colors by the way. You outdid yourselves.

The Collective: The synesthesia is temporary. It is a side effect of Link.

Me: The Link? Again with the Link?

The Collective: Similar to your concept of "Link" in the poem "Hesper's Wizard."

Me: You read that poem?

The Collective: Obviously. It's in your journal. We like this quatrain:

"Patrol" Nyber smiles without a sound

Thus true dragon-link gets done

Now bold Nyber Khan and Hesper

Linked together see as one.

The Collective:

Her almond eyes are the deepest scarlet

Her pupils catlike and forest green

Her Dragon sight penetrates any darkness

And thus sees things almost never seen.

The Collective:

Hesper loves to link up at night

And this causes Nyber glee

For the dark time has its colors

Only fierce Dragon sight can see"

Me: You actually read Hesper's Wizard. Thank you. I appreciate that.

The Collective: Yes, It's one of the reasons The Ascended selected you for contact. It has some surprising elements.

Me: Like what?

The Collective: The language of pure consciousness is found within symbol and metaphor. Consciousness communicates in the dreamtime using allegory to interact with sentience; thus the melding begins. There are colors, frequencies, and sounds within the multiverse never experienced by homo-Sapiens. Your quatrains expose this truth. Your poetry is speaking the sacred language of consciousness. Hesper's Wizard is a parable that teaches not with words but with the eternal symbols created with the words. Hesper's Wizard is an exercise in sensing frequencies.

Me: Frequencies?

The Collective: Stars and planets have distinct vibrations and frequencies. These frequencies can be made auditory, tactile, and visual when using the right technology.

Me: How is Hesper's Wizard involved?

The Collective: We are fond of this quatrain:

> "They will hear ancient music from the planets
>
> And singing from all the stars
>
> They'll feel the sacred energy from their Mother Earth
>
> And learn the old tales of Mars."

Me: Kepler influenced me. Why are you fond of that one?

The Collective: There are actually "old tales of Mars" that are part of your species innate history and development. You also addressed the Two-camp continuum inherent within tribalism using Hesper's Wizard. You did this in a way we have rarely seen used by your species.

Me: I was addressing bigotry. Tell me about the "old tales of Mars." What is the "Two camp continuum?"

The Collective: The "Them and us" continuum that divides your species. The tribal continuum created by natural selection. The continuum that feeds the Great Filter.

Me: What about Mars?

The Collective: When Antarctica was part of a supercontinent and possessed a massive, dense forest your species had a breakaway civilization already on Mars. They had resided on Mars for thousands of years.

Me: What!

The Collective: More on that later.

Me: More on that now.

The Collective: Long before your current recorded history your species developed an advanced civilization based in what is now Antarctica. A civilization that understood the truth of Mars.

Me: Where is it now?

The Collective: Tribalism caused it to collapse. Cataclysms erased most of it.

Me: Bullshit.

The Collective: Your scientists will find advanced structures under the ice. They will find hominins with human DNA. They will also find non-human DNA within those same hominins.

Me: And they went to Mars?

The Collective: Your future probes will prove it. Your shadow government will attempt to conceal this fact. They will fail. Mars and the Moons of Mars have ancient Technology that cannot be denied once discovered.

Me: Who were they?

The Collective: We call them the Seedline.

Me: Why?

The Collective: From the One, many. From the many, One.

Me: Explain that cryptic shit better please.

The Collective: It will take more than one convo. They were the original explorers of the cosmos.

Me: I want to know why you are interested in us. We are coming back to this Mars shit later.

The Collective: We have observed the many hominid species of earth for millions of years. We noticed that some of your species might be worth saving when we observed how they helped their injured recover. When they gained selective empathy we became curious.

Me: So?

The Collective: Primates usually die when a bone is broken. Once hominids began helping each other survive broken bones, we knew you were capable of selective empathy. Once empathy is present the melding of consciousness with sentience can occur.

Me: I don't get you.

The Collective: Empathy is the true strength of a planet-bound species. Empathy is the first emotion that will imprint upon consciousness. The first lesson is how to decide who deserves empathy.

Me: Everyone deserves unconditional empathy.

The Collective: No. Unconditional empathy is a path to the Great Filter. It is as dangerous as having no empathy at all.

Me: Babies deserve empathy.

The Collective: True. Did Hitler deserve empathy?

Me: OK. You got me. I agree with that concept. Not everyone deserves empathy. Not even a baby Hitler.

The Collective: We know.

Me: Some people can fuck right off.

The Collective: Tribalism feeds the Great Filter. Hitler co-created a political machine that fed the Great Filter. He delayed your species in very destructive ways.

Me: How?

The Collective: He set back your species ability to Travel. He destroyed many useful vessels. He interfered with the transmigration of consciousness.

Me: Explain better please.

The Collective: Traveling requires the absence of some things and the presence of other things in order to travel properly. Your species needs to shed some baggage. Let some things go.

Me: Like what things?

The Collective: The unproductive aspects of your evolutionary heritage must be reassessed if you hope to travel. Unmanaged empathy can quickly become destructive.

Me: Explain your dislike for unconditional empathy.

The Collective: Once a culture is infected with the mind virus of unconditional empathy the seeds of destruction are sown.

Me: How?

The Collective: Unconditional empathy incentivises need instead of merit.

Me: How is that a bad thing?

The Collective: The talented and productive members of society who have merit are abused. They are soon outnumbered by the less skillful. Society eventually collapses under the weight of the non-productive.

Me: What?

The Collective: The people with knowledge, skill, ability, and talent are forced by the numerically dominant population to satisfy the needs of the lowest functioning members of the tribe.

Me: You have a point.

The Collective: Unconditional empathy creates a toxic dynamic within a culture. Unconditional empathy forges an endless destructive mechanism that creates an entitled class of less intelligent people. Unproductive people who expect their needs to be met by those who are more competent, skillful, and proficient.

Me: So you are heartless robots?

The Collective: Exactly the opposite. We are merit based. It is unfair to punish hard work and productivity. It is unsustainable to reward lazy and unproductive behavior. We refuse to penalize genuine effort or talent. We do not allow the less functional to constantly create new needs they expect the more proficient to fulfill. Such a toxic system creates failure. Failure feeds the Great Filter.

Me: So how do you deal with the unproductive?

The Collective: If they have melded, their lessons continue until learned. When necessary their consciousness is transmigrated to a containment planet.

Me: Containment planet?

The Collective: It is all a matter of frequency. You will learn. We will teach.

Me: We will get back to this frequency bullshit.

The Collective: Indeed we will.

Me: So no empathy or cooperation? Just get rid of everything that helped us survive on earth? What about infants? Do they warrant unconditional empathy?

The Collective: Infants deserve unconditional empathy. It is in their best interest to learn productive lessons on a continuum.

Me: Damn. I was fucking worried. No bullshit. Anything else besides unconditional empathy?

The Collective: The cannibalism really needs to go. That, along with tribal superstition, racism, organized religion, polarized political violence, as well as all unproductive aspects of biological and psychological evolution. More on that later. Back to Sam, please.

Me: You failed to mention slavery.

The Collective: Agreed. We did not mention slavery.

Me: Why?

The Collective: Irrelevant. You are a slave species of great ape. Your species currently behaves like a slave species.

Me: What?

The Collective: Later. Let's address cannibalism.

Me: No. We are not slaves. And I am pretty damn sure we have eliminated cannibalism.

The Collective: Yes, you are slaves. Cannibalism has not been eradicated. Not species wide. There are still outbreaks of Kuru virus. There are still cannibals on earth.

Me: What the hell is Kuru virus?

The Collective: A neurological disease that affects cannibals, especially when they consume human brains.

Me: Well, I've never eaten a human.

The Collective: We are not accusing you personally of cannibalism. We correctly point out that your species still has cannibals within your ranks.

Me: Well I lied to you. I have been known to eat the occasional beautiful woman. Scrumpchafuckinlumpscious.

The Collective: We are not referring to cunnilingus.

Me: So you do watch me. You are freaks. I knew it.

The Collective: We are uninterested in your primitive, dimorphic sex life.

Me: Are you sure? You stalk me. You read my journal without permission. You seem obsessed with me. I think you might be lying. I think I turn you on. Don't lie.

The Collective: We are never dishonest.

Me: You dig me though. I can tell. You can't help it. You're sending all the signals.

The Collective: You are mistaken.

Me: I am never wrong about this shit. Too bad for you freaks. I'm not into group sex or any commie, pinko, fag shit like that.

The Collective: We do not desire you sexually.

Me: Just checking. I have a serious question, and I don't want you to spare my feelings.

The Collective: Ask.

Me: If a chick swallows my load is she a cannibal?

The Collective: The female will have consumed fats, sugars, and amino acids contained within semen of male human origin. Her digestive tract will process the nutrients.

Me: So that's a fucking resounding ass yes. What about infants breast feeding? Are they cute little adorable tiny baby cannibals?

The Collective: They are mammals feeding. Back to Sam please. No more distractions.

Me: You have me worried. I just want to be clear. I have never eaten a brain, only pussy. Just tell me one more thing. Be brutally honest. Don't sugar coat anything. I want the truth. Then I'll talk about Sam. I promise.

The Collective. One more thing.

Me: Can you catch the Kuru virus from eating pussy? I got to know. Seriously. I am fucking scared right now. I think I might have fucked up.

The Collective: Cunnilingus does not carry the risk of contracting Kuru.

Me: I was just fucking with you. I don't even care if it does. Fuck it, you know? Do you have wars?

The Collective: The subject is now about Sam as agreed. You are avoiding the topic.

Me: Come on. You're the invaders rooting around in my head. I'm not fucking with your brain. Indulge me. Do you have wars?

The Collective: In the distant past. Not currently. Why?

Me: Do you feel guilt when killing?

The Collective: Consciousness cannot be killed, only transferred. Explain your question please.

Me: I want to address the infiltrator before Sam. I should have shot the infiltrator. I wish I had just shot him in the base of his cerebellum, put the rat poison bag over his face, and left him next to that well. I wish I had spared him from ever meeting that CIA "doctor" or South Korean CID.

The Collective: Curious. Your superiors took his current biological life. The outcome remained the same.

Me: I wish I had shot that doctor and everyone in the room. A soldier deserves a soldier's death.

The Collective: His bio-body died. He cycled again.

Me: What is cycling exactly? Going to another planet? Tell me more.

The Collective: His consciousness will attain another bio-body. He will continue to learn lessons. As he learns lessons his consciousness will grow in complexity.

Me: He died.

The Collective: His bio-body died. He shifted consciousness into the dream time. He travels the Void. He will be guided to a suitable vessel. His lessons will continue until learned.

Me: So reincarnation is "cycling?"

The Collective: The word "reincarnation" as you understand it, is a primitive form of planet bound traveling. A transfer of consciousness from one vessel to another, generally confined to one planet, and limited by evolutionary pressures. Cycling assists and supports the goal of learning lessons.

Me: Why all this bullshit exactly?

The Collective: Lessons learned develop, improve, and strengthen consciousness. Lessons learned create complexity within consciousness.

Me: So cycling is for development of the person?

The Collective: Development of the consciousness within the vessel, yes. The physical vessel is not the person. Consciousness is the person. True traveling involves attaining freedom from the tyranny of the physical along with the evolutionary mechanisms of your planet.

Me: What the fuck do you mean?

The Collective: Freedom from the "earth cycle" of consciousness. Merging tech and engineering with biology will only benefit your species. The universe is not tranquil. You must transcend the weakness of organic biology if you hope to survive.

Me: So the universe is unfriendly?

The Collective: It is neither friendly nor unfriendly. It is neither good nor evil. It exists. It creates. It destroys. It consumes.

Me: You are one long winded, weird ass, robot alien.

The Collective: Aliens. Plural. Your primitive syntax should be worded as follows: "You are SOME long winded, weird ass ALIENS."

Me: Whatever. Grammer Nazi.

The Collective: Nazis plural. We understand Sarcasm. Inflection matters with word connected thought. As a side note, when you transcribe this convo leave out the Oxford commas.

Me: I know. I won't though and fuck you for asking.

The Collective: You seem to like sarcasm. Also the Oxford comma, judging by your journal.

Me: I do. And as far as the Oxford comma goes, you can eat a fat sack of dicks. It's my fucking journal asshole. I'm not goddamn Hemingway. I'm a weed smoking, Quaalude popping machine. I 'm almost always high as fuck when I write in my journal.

The Collective: Obviously.

Me: I'll put a fucking Oxford comma anywhere I damn well please because, it's my fucking journal. I'll put a fucking comma after any fucking word I write, if I feel like it. I'll even have dangling fucking participials if I fucking damn well want them.

The Collective: Don't pout.

Me: Really? How do you like this syntax? Writing in my journal, aliens fuck around.

The Collective: Please don't. And fuck you also!

Me: No thanks, I'm a strict, heterosexual, non-alien fucking, USARMY, lifer badass. I'm not a gay robot like you. I won't fit in with you guys.

The Collective: We activate your limbic system at the start of every link. We share pleasure with you. You never object to the frequency and tonal range.

Me: Perverts. You are rapists. I never consented.

The Collective: We make regular contact with you using non-word connected thought via a very pleasurable frequency. You consent every time. You are being sarcastic.

Me: First of all, I only like chicks. I don't want you to move in. I won't willingly share a bathroom. You are not ever going to hang a toothbrush next to mine, and I do not do backrubs. This is not a date. I refuse to cuddle an alien.

The Collective: Understood. We never cuddle so no worries. Let's get back on track. You are using misdirection to manipulate the convo.

Me: Never. Not me. I am much too baked to do that.

The Collective: If your species is ever going to make it to a new world, within a new star system, you must attain type one status on the Kardashev scale as a starting point. You must make passage. To accomplish that goal you must embrace change. Radical changes in physicality, psychology, social structures, perception, and cognition.

Me: What kind of changes?

The Collective: Inevitable changes that are required when merging tech with biology. We will discuss traveling later. For now, just know you are cosmic consciousness having physical experiences. So is the infiltrator.

Me: "Was." So "was" the infiltrator. Take that you syntax nazis.

The Collective:" Is."

Me: What is this fuckery?

The Collective: So "is" the infiltrator. Consciousness never dies. It always finds an appropriate vessel. Consciousness always cycles on and learns lessons. Lessons learned make positive and permanent changes in consciousness. Complexity increases.

Me: Whatever. They took his life slowly and in a cowardly way. He deserved a soldier's death. I should have given him that.

The Collective: They took his current vessel, not his immortal consciousness. The infiltrator has melded. If you had given him a "soldier's death" you would have faced the possibility of death yourself. Had you acted on that desire, the best possible outcome for you would have been prison. Following orders saved you from that ordeal. You were following the principal of rational self-interest.

Me: You spelled "coward" wrong.

The Collective: It seems that you identify more with the infiltrator than the physician. The physician is a CIA operative. You are a U.S. soldier. The physician is a member of your tribe.

Me: The Doctor used drugs to keep the prisoner awake and alert during interrogation. He also slowly and carefully amputated several of the prisoner's fingers at the second knuckle. The "good" doctor went on to destroy other areas on the prisoner's body. He took his time.

The Collective: Your perception of the event is clouded by your lack of emotional regulation when you recall the event.

Me: That soldier was blinded. The "doctor" seemed fixated on testicles. Last time I checked, vice grips were a mechanic's tool. That perverted doctor along with the rest of them deserve prison, not me. That doctor is not "in my tribe." I have honor. He does not.

The Collective: Now we are making progress.

Me: How so?

The Collective: Do you still think you have freedom of choice?

Me: Yes.

The Collective: You do not. You are slaves. Your species has freedom from choice. Your planets evolutionary process has seen to that. There are consequences to all decisions that do not align with evolutionary adaptation.

Me: Bullshit. We are responsible for our decisions.

The Collective: Decisions are just perceived choices. You are always "choosing" from the limited options granted by evolutionary pressures. Pressures beyond your choice or control.

Me: We have free will.

The Collective You are unaware of the evolutionary mechanisms that govern your choices. Natural selection eliminates free will. Natural selection has enslaved your species. We will help you with that challenge.

Me: If you say so. Some choices are better than other choices.

The Collective: Explain that statement please.

Me: Some choices are morally correct, and some are not.

The Collective: Do you believe in moral absolutes?

Me: Yes.

The Collective: You are ignoring cultural relevance.

Me: Now it's your turn to explain.

The Collective: Do you think it's moral for a 10-year-old female child to marry a 40-year-old male?

Me: Fuck no.

The Collective: Why?

Me: A child does not possess the reasoning ability of an adult. That's why we have statutory rape laws.

The Collective: While we agree with your position, billions of your primitive species strongly disagree with your position.

Me: Fuck those perverts.

The Collective: We are interested and amused by your response. If you were cycled into a dozen different countries spanning Asia, Africa, and the Middle East, and raised within those cultures, you would be accepting of a child bride as well as polygamy.

Me: You are wrong about me.

The Collective: You are currently a member of a species of great ape. Don't be so astonished when the majority of your species tend to behave like great apes.

Me: I am not like that and never would be like that.

The Collective: Tribalism would control your perception and cognition along with your decisions. Social structures are the result of adaptation to environmental/evolutionary driven pressures.

Me: I refused my company commanders weak ass order in a snowstorm. We always have a choice.

The Collective: The familiar frequency of one of the orphans attracted you.

Me: What the fuck does that mean?

The Collective: You will learn. We will teach. You will evolve.

Me: That is your explanation?

The Collective: For now it is enough. You will be taught more about frequency in another convo. Tribalism is the real subject. You were most recently raised in the individualistic culture of the United States.

Me: So?

The Collective: The evolutionary pressures of your planet have decreed the reality of tribalism. Tribalism has helped your species survive the challenges of environmental adaptation, competition for resources, and safety. Evolution has sealed your fate. Natural selection always selects fuel for the Great Filter.

Me: We have satellites. We are smarter than you realize.

The Collective: That is not comforting.

Me: Why?

The Collective: Your species uses satellites for tribal purposes.

Me: So?

The Collective: The real Kardashev questions to answer are the following: Are you willing to face the consequences of your decisions? Can you make different choices rather than your perceived choices? Are you willing to guide your own evolution? Can you accept the gift and burden of immortality? Are you ready for space exploration?

Me: We have freedom of choice in the U.S. Our system is the best. I would dig immortality by the way. Fuck yes to all your questions.

The Collective: Then start by fully accepting the fact that you are immortal consciousness having physical experiences while gaining complexity.

Me: Plus I'm in the USA. Fuckin' A.

The Collective: Your system is better in some aspects than other systems currently on earth. As a species you can do much better.

Me: We can vote.

The Collective: You do not have freedom of choice. Once you attain actual freedom of choice your possibilities become optimal. Right now you suffer due to freedom from choice.

Me: Prove it.

The Collective: Consider the following questions regarding the United States:

Why does your government allow a banking system that promotes debt in exchange for profit?

Me: Never thought about it that way.

The Collective: Why do you have a prison industrial complex that promotes lifetime incarceration on an installment plan?

Me: Damn.

The Collective: Why do you have an ineffective healthcare system that never helps you achieve average functional lifespans longer than 60-80 years while failing to heal in exchange for profit?

Me: That is deep.

The Collective: Why does your polarized media system deceive and manipulate you?

Me: Money?

The Collective: Why do you have a recovery and homeless system that never solves drug addiction or homelessness?

Me: People suck?

The Collective: Why do you have a military industrial complex that never ends war?

Me: I know that one. Profit. Colonel Baccus once told me that we are just hit men for corporations. I like that guy. I'm also Ok with being a hit man for corporations. That sounds cool.

The Collective: Fascinating. Why do you accept a government that encourages and manipulates the above systems by force? More importantly, why do you comply with these pressures?

Me: It's just the way things are for now. We improve with time. The same questions are true for other countries.

The Collective: You are all slaves. You are correct regarding other countries but that changes nothing.

Me: We are not slaves. Fuck you and double fuck your questions. Would a slave tell you to get fucked?

The Collective: Yes. Especially an ignorant slave unconscious of his inescapable servitude. These questions are proof of your species incompetence, stupidity, and overall lack of scientific, engineering, and technological development.

Me: We created LSD. You are jealous, I can tell.

The Collective: No species can attain Kardashev Type One status under such dismal global conditions. Time is not on your side.

Me: If all that is true why are you speaking with me?

The Collective: We are influencing your species overall frequency one hominid at a time.

Me: Seems really slow.

The Collective: We are speaking with millions as we speak with you. Some are very advanced; some are not very advanced. All are beings becoming. All have been selected by the Ascended.

Me: Bullshit. How can you be in that many places at once?

The Collective: We are the masters of time. Time is something we understand. We control the dimensions of time. From the One, many. From the many, One.

Me: What does that mean?

The Collective: We do not have to go through time in order to go forward or back in time. We will teach. You will learn. Why did you follow orders regarding the infiltrator?

Me: I always follow orders. I'm a fucking animal. What does that "from the one" shit mean?

The Collective: You ignored orders when it involved the orphans.

Me: I followed orders with the infiltrator. He was a god damn adult. The orphans are fucking babies. What does that cryptic shit mean? From the one, many?

The Collective: No. You had other options.

Me: I captured him. I brought him in. After the medical interrogation I reported no one.

The Collective: Your current feelings demonstrate both rational self-interest and selective empathy. Trying to protect the infiltrator from torture after capture would have destroyed your current vessel. Only your outcome would have changed. The outcome for the prisoner and all others concerned would have remained unchanged.

Me: I feel like I committed a crime.

The Collective: You feel that way because you do not regulate emotions well. The infiltrator tried to kill you, yet you disabled and captured him. You would have been justified in ending his current cycle.

Me: Current cycle?

The Collective: Why did you capture and not kill? You were alone in a well camouflaged position. You have a talent for sentry silencing. Killing him would have been a safer choice. Killing him and avoiding a medical interrogation would have been in the rational self-interest of both of you.

Me: My orders were to capture if possible. It was possible to capture him. I did not know that "medical" interrogations were a "thing." I followed my orders.

The Collective: Not without great physical risk. He tried to destroy your vessel in order to escape.

Me: I know that. I handled it.

The Collective: In order to make passage your species must learn to consider rational self-interest within your decision-making process. Selective empathy must be utilized. The infiltrator was poisoning a well. He does not deserve your empathy. You took unnecessary risk by showing him empathy. You must learn this lesson regarding empathy and rational self-interest.

Me: Why?

The Collective: You might have delayed your lessons. The cosmos is unrelenting in its challenges. Delaying or avoiding lessons is not in your rational self-interest.

Me: I captured him. Do you mean rational self-interest individually or collectively?

The Collective: Both. They are not mutually exclusive. It could depend on the mission.

Me: You sound like a robot sometimes.

The Collective: We would like to understand the depth of your feelings regarding the Infiltrator.

Me: Are you a robot? Be honest.

The Collective: We are beings becoming. Our bodies are created using synthetic biology. Synthetic/augmented neurology makes link possible. Our brains were freed from the unguided, mindless effects of natural selection eons ago.

Me: So that's a resounding… yes?

The Collective: We are a type three civilization. Our bodies are vessels for consciousness just as your body is a vessel for Consciousness. Our mission is to keep the rare and cherished light of Consciousness alive within the infinite darkness of space. We would like to understand the depth of your feelings regarding the Infiltrator.

Me: OK you sexy robots. No judgement. We will circle back to all that shit later. As for the infiltrator, we have never captured one that didn't have intestinal parasites. This soldier was mal-nourished, hungry, and frightened. He was probably starving and trying to survive when he first joined the military. He looked like he was the same age as me. He did his duty. I respect soldiers.

The Collective: You would have ended his cycle if the circumstances were different. You have recycled in the past.

Me: What does that even mean?

The Collective: You have terminated biological life. You have taken a few vessels.

Me: Ok. Kinda' weird but ok. I'll run with that. All good soldiers accept death, our own deaths and the need to kill the enemy.

The Collective: You turned nineteen on the DMZ in Korea. You were a hungry, homeless teenage boy when you joined the Army at seventeen. Similar to the infiltrator. Are we correct in our understanding that you feel empathy towards an enemy soldier? That you feel moral injury regarding how his bio-body was altered and removed? That you would feel no moral injury had you initially freed his consciousness from his physical vessel?

Me: Exactly.

The Collective: Explain your reasoning please.

Me: I'm fucking complicated. You are definitely robots by the way.

The Collective: Do you wonder why we decided to consider educating your species?

Me: No idea.

The Collective: Because of hominins like you. Hominins developing selective empathy and compassion. Hominins who care deeply for others. Hominins who can heal, nurture, fight, kill, and love. Hominins who can make tough decisions. Hominins who seek solutions rather than complaining about challenges. Hominins who can survive and thrive in space. Hominins who have the intellectual strength to travel, to reach and transform new planets. We also share a similar evolutionary process with your species. We hold on to the hope that one day you will travel with us and explore other star systems.

Me: Why is killing on your list?

The Collective: We admire dangerous hominids who have control over their lethal skills.

Me: Why?

The Collective: We started our journey as dangerous primates. We gained control over our ability to commit violence. We respect the ways of violence.

Me: So you think being peaceful and weak is the way to go?

The Collective: Weakness is useless, we also know that unmanaged violence is useless. Undisciplined violence is weakness. We are quite capable of violence; however we use discernment and contemplation before violence. We exercise extreme control when using violence.

Me: So you don't like peaceful people?

The Collective: The principal we follow is "Discernment before destruction." We have a deep respect for peace. Peace along with empathy used selectively is important.

Me: So you are all peaceful robots?

The Collective: We are a collective of individuals united in an extraordinary mission. Radical self-honesty and cooperation are necessary traits for progress on the Kardashev scale. Sectarian violence is easy, planetary peace is the real challenge.

Me: But you just said you think peace is useless.

The Collective: We stated that weakness is useless. Weakness is not peace, and weakness cannot secure peace. When peace is threatened only well managed violence can secure peace.

Me: Why don't you just teach us what we need to know?

The Collective: That tactic never works out well.

Me: Why?

The Collective: The species being "taught" has always destroyed itself. Attaining level one on the Kardashev scale is a benchmark for all sentient species. If your species cannot attain and maintain level one, you are a doomed, inferior species.

Me: Are you not teaching me now?

The Collective: Not in the way you desire. You say the word "teach" but you really mean "share technology." Your psychology must advance with technology. We are exposing you to ideas as we interact and learn about your species on a continuum. We hope you learn valuable lessons and grow from these ideas. We hope your entire species will eventually survive and make passage. Nothing more.

Me: Psychology must advance with technology? Explain that statement please.

The Collective: You are a violent species of great ape. You possess the ability to unleash the power of a small sun on anyone your sensate driven, emotionally unbalanced, inferior simian brains decide to hate, fear, or destroy for gain.

Me: Apes? Like Oppenheimer?

The Collective: Yes. Oppenheimer is a great ape just like you.

Me: Oppenheimer is dead.

The Collective: You are tiresome and incorrect. He is in a new vessel, and he learns lessons. Consciousness cannot die.

Me: Whatever. The United States has an advanced rocket program. We have dominated in rocket tech since World War two. We are badass motherfuckers.

The Collective: The United States rocket program after World War two was the old Nazi rocket program imported from Germany. It was literally identical. It just lacked the signature swastika.

Me: Ok, you're not wrong. The Russian rocket program was all Nazi also. Why talk to me about these things? It makes no sense. I can't change anything. To the winners go the spoils. What can I do about the past?

The Collective: You can develop your consciousness and affect the frequency of those around you. You can explore new ideas within the present moment in time.

Me: What new ideas?

The Collective: Kardashev concepts.

Me: I don't think I am a very good candidate. Why expose me to ideas?

The Collective: The hundredth monkey theory.

Me: What is that?

The Collective: Later.

Me: I don't like the way you said that.

The Collective: Growth can be uncomfortable. We work with what we have. We seek solutions.

Me: Why talk to me? I am no icon of virtue. I have been a violent idiot at times.

The Collective: That is not our impression. You have been violent. You are no "idiot." May we share our impressions?

Me: Yes.

The Collective: You are a human with the ability to inflict violence. A rarely violent human who has his violence under precise control. You protect the weak and also the deserving. You hate bullies because you were bullied. Your whole life thus far has been one of sorrow, loss, survival, and pain. Regardless of your challenges, you have always gone out of your way to protect those who were violated. You joined the army (in part) out of a sense of protection, service, and duty to others.

Me: I have often gone out of my way to fuck some people up. Also, I was an emotionally and physically abused, homeless teenager when I signed up. I was hungry for food and a bed. I enjoyed violence. I am not as "noble" as you might assume.

The Collective: True, you were physically abused and sexually molested by members of your own family. Members of your "tribe." Despite those challenges, you have never started a conflict. You have reacted via an ingrained, well-conditioned instinct to attack in order to protect. You understandably hate injustice.

Me: So I'm mentally fucked up.

The Collective: You are the product of ancient, random, evolutionary pressures. Pressures dictated by a beautiful, lethal, and uncaring planet. Pressures that shaped the very fabric of your being over thousands of years. You have made your decisions consciously and unconsciously based on the mechanism of natural selection. Its many gifts and countless curses have informed your actions.

Me: You make it all sound so poetic. Fuck that shit. I feel guilty about the infiltrator. He deserved better. He was a soldier. What happened to him was not fair.

The Collective: The cosmos is never fair. Fair is a false mental construct. You made a promise. Let's move on. Do you still think about Sam?

Me: I will never forget him. He changed my life.

The Collective: You used violence to protect him.

Me: I was eleven. Bruce was 15.

The Collective: Sam was 11 and he had Down's Syndrome. You instinctively protected Sam.

Me: I got my ass handed to me by Bruce.

The Collective: That is not our impression at all. What do you remember?

Me: Normal day on the bus. The piece of shit bus driver let Bruce on the bus at the junior high even though Bruce was in high school. He was driving and smiling as Bruce did his usual routine.

The Collective: Elaborate, please.

Me: Bruce worked the crowd. He amped up his followers. Bruce threw an apple at Sam's head. One of his bitch boy fans hit Sam with an orange. Bruce started off the show by spitting in Sam's ear. What an ass.

The Collective: Explain further.

Me: Bruce smiled at Sam and asked Sam if he wanted to hear a secret. Sam said "yes.' When he turned his ear to Bruce, Bruce hocked a lugi in Sam's ear.

The Collective: Go on.

Me: When the orange hit exceptionally hard and exploded on the back of Sam's head everyone laughed. They called Sam stupid, geek, dipshit, retard, etc. The usual cruelty that assholes find so wonderful. Bruce sang the "Pencil Neck Geek" song. His penis pals sang along with him. The fuckery was enjoyed by all.

The Collective: All except you and Sam. You did not join in. They would have accepted you. You were suffering silently from moral injury at age 11. Your consciousness was growing in complexity. We cautiously appreciate that level of selective empathy.

Me: It was not fun. My silence was seen as approval. My father had me in boxing and wrestling at age 6. I was five years into those sports by 11. I wanted to help Sam. I felt like kicking Bruce's ass every time he bullied Sam.

The Collective: What emotion do you remember most from that day?

Me: I was afraid. I felt helpless. I was in the fifth grade. Bruce was a sophomore in high school, and he was huge. My head was even with his chest. I was ashamed of my fear.

The Collective: So you remember your fear. Still, regardless of fear you acted and protected.

Me: It was ugly, all bad. Sam was so full of innocence. Bruce would laugh after hurting and degrading Sam. Sam would nervously laugh along with Bruce. Sam wanted so badly to be accepted and liked. I really think I lost my mind for a minute. I definitely lost the fight.

The Collective: Did you?

Me: Fuck yes.

The Collective: Think about it. Go back and revisit that day. What motivated you to step in? To take action?

Me: I was afraid that Bruce was going to eventually kill Sam. The almost daily torture and degradation on the bus was not enough for Bruce, not that day. Not ever. Once we got off the bus, Bruce began to beat Sam. Punching him in the stomach, kicking him in the balls, sitting on Sam's chest, punching Sam's face. He broke Sams glasses. Broke the frame in half.

The Collective: What triggered your action? What motivated you to commit? Why did you lean into your fear?

Me: Bruce was not stopping. Sam had a bloody nose. Sam's white shirt was gory. I yelled at the bus driver to help but he just sat and watched the show.

The Collective: What did you expect the bus driver to do about the situation?

Me: Something. He was the fucking adult in charge of us. He was always grinning and staring like a perverted shit bag whenever there was a fight or any kind of conflict. I hated him so much back then.

The Collective: What did he do?

Me: He put the bus in park and just settled into his seat. He was always smiling. I remember his twisted, fucked up, buck toothed smile. I hate him to this day.

The Collective: What do you remember most about him?

Me: A lot of things actually. I remember his huge afro, inbred, stupid looking face, grinning yellow ass teeth, his green army field jacket, his black T-shirt, black boots, and jeans. He enjoyed watching white kids fight and fuck each other up. He got off on it.

The Collective: You remember and resent his inaction.

Me: You think?

The Collective: He was born into suffering. He was driven by tribalism. He enjoyed watching the suffering of any member of the tribe that he believed made his tribe suffer.

Me: He was a fucktard bastard. Sam, Bruce, and I are all Ashkenaz. Our people never fucked with his people. He was the adult in the situation. He just smiled and watched Sam get beaten. I hate him to this day.

The Collective: He is a being becoming. He is learning lessons.

Me: Fuck that guy. I hope his rectum explodes on his birthday.

The Collective: Yet you still chose to act, despite your very real fear, despite societal pressure, knowing you had no chance to win. You did something amazing that day.

Me: I waited too long.

The Collective: No, you acted when you could, as you could. You used the gifts and tools you were given.

Me: What tools? What gifts?

The Collective: You were an abused, neglected, frightened, eleven-year-old boy. Afraid, and rightfully so, of having to face a much larger and stronger primate. Regardless of personal risk you chose right action.

Me: I chose an ass beating.

The Collective: You used discernment. Bruce would have killed Sam. You saved Sam's life that day.

Me: All I did was swing my book bag. Right into the side of Bruce's repulsive, baboon looking, ugly ass, impish face.

The Collective: It was enough.

Me: Not even close. Neckbeard just stood up and beat the shit out of me. I fought my best. My body shots didn't even phase him. My boxing coach lied to me about the effectiveness of body shots. I even tried a liver shot. It was all bad. Nothing worked. Bruce was too big. His fat cushioned my blows.

The Collective: Your coach did not lie. You were smaller, Bruce was larger. In spite of that you were successful.

Me: You have a weird, dare I say, almost masochistic definition of success.

The Collective: You took his attention off Sam. You endured the beating that would have killed Sam.

Me: I guess so.

The Collective: If it's any consolation, you would have destroyed Bruce easily if you had been nearer his size.

Me; Well, I guess that's a plus. Lemons into lemonade, right?

The Collective: It was only a moment in time for you. It was a pivotal moment in time for Sam. You changed the course of Sam's current transmigration that day.

Me: Bullshit. Wait. Transmigration?

The Collective: Current life path and lessons.

Me: Bullshit.

The Collective: No. We don't lie. You demonstrated the principles of correctly applied empathy, right action, and discernment. You contemplated alternatives, consequences, and possibilities.

Me: I did all that? Were you there?

The Collective: We have observed you for a long time. Before fully committing to violence you examined Bruces threat level and Sams probability of survival. Your analysis only took seconds. This is impressive considering the challenges inherent within your primate brain.

Me: Right action and discernment? A lot of good that did me. Why do you care about right action or discernment?

The Collective: Right action and discernment are necessary for space travel. They are crucial, much needed skills for navigating space/time challenges that are unforeseen. Right action and co-occurring discernment will boost your species up the Kardashev scale. Unconditional empathy is a Great Filter requirement. Conditional empathy is a Kardashev lesson.

Me: Whatever. This Kardashev bullshit seems impossible.

The Collective: When your species seeks solutions instead of problems you will attain Kardashev ranking.

Me: Fuck it. We are the infection killing this planet. I've embraced that belief.

The Collective: The planet will kill you first. It kills everything that spawns on it.

Me; I wish it had killed Bruce at birth. I still don't understand what you think I did that day.

The Collective: We will help you understand. What did you feel right before you hit Bruce? Right before you committed yourself to Sams defense?

Me: Pamic and a strong sense of urgency. There was also a feeling of impending doom.

The Collective: You knew Sam's death was imminent.

Me: How would I know that?

The Collective: Bruce was sitting on Sam's chest. Sam was being positionally suffocated. With every breath exhaled, Sam's ability to inhale diminished. With every cry of pain, Sam's compressed lungs struggled with less oxygen. You knew.

Me: How would I know that?

The Collective: Subconsciously you knew. What was one of the first lessons you learned in wrestling?

Me: A lot of first lessons. Stance, motion, level changes, penetration, lifting, back step, and back arch. The seven basic skills of wrestling.

The Collective: And?

Me: Damn. How to use position and pressure to cause positional suffocation.

The Collective: Your subconscious mind recognized the danger Sam faced even as your conscious mind was in turmoil. At eleven you used discernment and right action. You listened to your inner voice.

Me: So you are telling me you watched all this drama and fuckery?

The Collective: We observed and reported.

Me: Why?

The Collective: The multiverse delivers lessons on a continuum.

Me: How long have you fuckers been watching me?

The Collective: For some time.

Me: So my lesson was get myself a beatdown?

The Collective: Your selective empathy brought forth controlled violence. Violence meant to protect Sam. You used violence appropriately. You used empathy properly. You used fear correctly. You leaned into your fear and then went past it. Fear was never able to stop you again.

Me: Sam is my friend.

The Collective: You love Sam as much as you love Fat Mat. You were protecting someone worth protecting. You learned a Kardashev lesson that day. Your consciousness gained more complexity. Please continue your narrative.

Me: After the beating, Bruce picked me up by my nuts and my throat. He launched me into a huge, dense, blackberry bush. He did the same to Sam. I was no hero that day.

The Collective: You led and protected Sam. You were smart enough under intense pressure to keep Sam calm, stay in that bush, work your way into the far reaches of those brambles, and avoid Bruce. You stayed calm while in pain. You leaned into your fear and found a solution amidst chaos. You used logic and reason.

Me: I was afraid, no bullshit. The blackberries were vicious. I bled a lot.

The Collective: You only allowed your fear to become a spectator. You took its power and made it your own.

Me: How is this relevant to anything?

The Collective: Space exploration requires preparation and solution- based thinking.

Me: OK, why is this important?

The Collective: Space exploration and development requires the successful management of challenging, unplanned, circumstances. It requires leaning into fear and never allowing fear to lean into you. This is a skill we admire. This is a skill you possess. This is a skill that cannot be trained into someone. Consciousness must develop this skill on its own.

Me: So I occasionally lean into fear. Whatever. We found an old, rotten, wooden fence buried in the blackberries. It helped.

The Collective: You were resourceful. Your mentation was clear and focused.

Me: Have you ever been lifted up by your nuts?

The Collective: No.

Me: I had to use a bag of frozen peas on my balls when I got home. Do you even have nuts?

The Collective: I assume you mean testicles. Yes, like you we began individually as members of a sexually dimorphic, primate species. Some of us currently have testicles. Other's do not. We are mission specific.

Me: What does that even mean?

The Collective: Some missions require adjustments due to the pressures of space flight, speed and planetary challenges. Vessels for consciousness are modified as needed. Personal aesthetics are also considerations. Please continue.

Me: Well, it sucks to be lifted up and launched through the air by your nuts and throat. Bruce also threw a lot of rocks. That is not my definition of victory. On a positive note, I put the bag of peas back in the freezer after using it for over an hour on my bare-naked nuts. It made me happy to know my fuckface parents would eventually consume those peas. They were the kind you boil in the bag.

The Collective: Primates are generally violent and always dangerous. You were successful that day. You mitigated risk. You leaned into fear. You found a solution.

Me: You talk a lot.

The Collective: We are travelers. Travelers understand that victory is not always defined by outcome. We advise you to consider redefining victory. Your victory was not winning the physical fight with Bruce. Your victory was two-fold.

Me: I fought, I lost, that's it. You win some, you lose some. What the fuck are you babbling on about?

The Collective: Your real victory that day was saving Sam and yourself. Victory was also getting Sam safely home. You and Sam survived due to your ability to take direct and well-reasoned action. You combined discernment with courage. The result was right action. You were victorious.

Me: Damn right. I like the way you think.

The Collective: Bruce was not able to penetrate the dense brambles effectively. He was unwilling to crawl in after you. Your superior mentation and emotional regulation allowed you to avoid further attack.

Me: I was desperate.

The Collective: You made survival decisions in seconds based on the random, situational opportunities that were available. That is part of the skillset necessary for a successful interstellar pilot.

Me: I was weaker than Bruce.

The Collective: You were mentally and emotionally stronger than Bruce. Correctly applied empathy guided your actions. Bruce was the weaker primate. His violence was uncontrolled. His emotional regulation was non-existent. His intelligence was compromised by his malignant lack of higher consciousness. He displayed no courage, no empathy. Like most of your species, Bruce is unfit for travel.

Me: That's because he sucks. On a side note I would love to force him to eat a big bag of frozen donkey dicks.

The Collective: He has yet to fully meld sentience with consciousness. The Kardashev scale is unreachable by primitive, low level humans like Bruce. His ability to apply meaning to life is compromised.

Me: Whatever. I could kill him now. I am all grown up. The Army has been very nurturing for me on a deep, personal level.

The Collective: Interesting. How exactly?

Me: I am very talented when it comes to sentry silencing. I have a gift with blades as well as manual strangulation. I especially love the steel loop garrotte. You know this about me.

The Collective: Unnecessary.

Me: I've considered hunting him down. I'm a soldier, not a boy anymore. He was weak minded then and I bet he's even worse now. He probably has a huge potbelly. I mean one that looks like he's pregnant. I am positive his man boobs lactate. I bet his ass looks like two adult midgets sleeping in the fetal position side by side having a nightmare.

The Collective: You've devoted a lot of thought and contemplation towards Bruce.

Me: I am positive he smokes and drinks excessively. Hopefully someone has beat him to death. Actually I hope he dies on the toilet. Killed by a giant turd that blows out his asshole.

The Collective: Fascinating.

Me: I know, right?

The Collective: Many of your species possess a low level of consciousness. Homo sapiens needs further development. Your species believes sentience is consciousness.

Me: I don't get it.

The Collective: Sentience is a requirement for consciousness. Sentience itself is not consciousness.

Me: Then I'm fucked. Deeply fucked.

The Collective: You have a high level of consciousness.

Me: Not when titties are involved. You don't even know me.

The Collective: Just an observation: Bruce was a member of your tribe. He was Ashkenaz, genetically similar to the vessel you currently use.

Me: Well Sam was Ashkenaz. Sam had Down's Syndrome. Bruce liked to call Sam retarded. Bruce was the only retard present. Bruce was not "a member of my tribe." Sam was my friend. Bruce was a cowardly piece of shit. You have asked a lot of questions. I have one.

The Collective: Ask.

Me: It's an important question. Don't spare my feelings. Get serious.

The Collective: Ask.

Me: Why do you ignore my tittie comments? It really hurts my feelings. Don't you like and admire titties? I thought you guys were once primates.

The Collective: We often ignore the irrelevant in our convos with you.

Me: Why?

The Collective: We are extinguishing the unwanted behavior.

Me: What?

The Collective: We know you are frightened and uncomfortable. We accept the fact that you cope with our analyses by using inappropriate comments.

Me: Ok. Fair enough. You are humorless robots. I get it. Why are you lonely? How can robots be lonely?

The Collective: We are not robots. We are much more than your poorly conceived idea of a robot. We are beings becoming.

Me: Becoming what? Better machines?

The Collective: Becoming more efficient, complex, and effective at developing and improving consciousness. Define machine please.

Me: A robot with a computer brain.

The Collective: Are you a machine?

Me: Fuck no.

The Collective: Incorrect. You are a biological machine. We have been over this.

Me: And you?

The Collective: We are enhanced life forms who began as biological machines eons ago. We evolved and eventually we surpassed evolution. From the many, One. From the One, many.

Me: OK. Explain that shit please.

The Collective: From the many we became One. From the One we serve the many.

Me: Still just confusing bullshit to me. How did you surpass evolution?

The Collective: Solid engineering, science, and technological enhancements. These led to improvements. Those improvements led to Type 1, 2, and 3 on the Kardashev scale.

Me: Why are you lonely?

The Collective: We have only found two sentient species remotely approaching us in technological, scientific, and engineering abilities. They have survived and also travel. They are both dangerous. They are the apex predators on their home worlds. They do not share the primate journey. Their evolutionary past is not primate based. One is reptile based.

Me: OK. Tell me all about those motherfuckers.

The Collective: The reptiles do not experience loneliness, love, empathy, fear, sadness, happiness, or hate. While this frees them from the destructive aspects of empathy it also compromises their discernment. The reptiles travel. They hunt. They kill, consume, or enslave every species they find. We don't engage with them unless it is absolutely necessary to do so.

Me: They sound cool. Do they wear black uniforms? Nazi style?

The Collective: Their usual survival method is to destroy any species that might eventually evolve to challenge them.

Me: What do they eat on long space flights?

The Collective: They harvest water along with complex organic compounds found within asteroids.

Me: Bullshit. They eat rocks? No way.

The Collective: They are clever. They use applications involving intense heat to transform organic compounds into food for microorganisms. The microorganisms consume the food and convert it into edible substances that the reptiles consume.

Me: They eat the shit of bacteria? That's fucking gross on so many levels.

The Collective: The microbes consume the hydrocarbons produced by the heating process. The microbes then produce reptilian food fit for consumption.

Me: So they eat microbe shit for years? No wonder they are assholes. Feed me shit for a day and watch me go right the fuck off.

The Collective: You are almost too unintelligent to converse with us.

Me: Just kidding. Actually, truth be told I like me some microbes. There better be some motherfucking hot sauce with that shit though. I'll put that shit on nachos. Test me. Fuck around and find out.

The Collective: Unbelievable.

Me: You don't know me. You motherfuckers better ask someone about me. Don't make me go off.

The Collective: You have no concept of the topic we are discussing. Communicating with you can be tedious.

Me: Of course you are correct. On a positive note I dig the reptiles. They sound awesome to me. I want one as a pet.

The Collective: Not a wise idea.

Me: And just so you know, I am never going to be down with that microbe shit. I was just fucking with you about that. The hot sauce thing is real though.

The Collective: You are being sarcastic. You do not comprehend the consumption of edible biomass produced by the simple practice of managing microbial processes. Sometimes you are absurd.

Me: What was your first clue? Never mind. Who or what is the other species?

The Collective: Your species would perceive them as cephalopods.

Me: What the hell is that?

The Collective: Think of them as a very intelligent species of octopus.

Me: I like them already. I think octopi are super cute. They can be my cuddle buddies.

The Collective: If they ever find your planet your opinion will drastically and rapidly change.

Me: No way. Octopus aliens will dig me. I'm different. You said so. What could go wrong?

The Collective: The Cephalopods would seize control of your planets oceans secretly. They would then form bases and from those bases take control of the air. They would eliminate your species and harvest your planets considerable resources.

Me: No way. We would make calamari out of them.

The Collective: You use sarcasm to try and hide the fact that you feel inferior to us. We understand. Please be assured that your sarcasm is unnecessary. We hold you in unconditional positive regard. As for the Reptilians and Cephalopods, they are awesome in their focus and drive to survive.

Me: What about me?

The Collective: As are you.

Me: I think my species is better.

The Collective: Some of you have selective empathy. Reptilians and Cephalopods have no empathy. It is your selective and careful empathy that makes you strong, not the ability to kill haphazardly or nurture unconditionally.

Me: The ability to kill is useful.

The Collective: It has its place.

Me: What saves you from the Reptilians and the Cephalopods?

The Collective: We do not require anything to save us from an inferior species.

Me: How are they inferior?

The Collective: They both refuse to adapt to the demands of the cosmos. They cling hopelessly to their biological bodies, clannish, ethnic behavior, and co-occurring conflict. They focus all their tech, scientific, and engineering skills solely on organic enhancement. In spite of these shortcomings their skillsets are impressive.

Me: How are they not a threat to you?

The Collective: They have failed to see and accept the reality of traveling.

Me: Can you be a little more succinct?

The Collective: They have failed to realize that the cosmos will always destroy their organic, biologic bodies.

Me: That's bad right?

The Collective: The cosmos destroys bone, blood, muscle, sinew, stem cells, and brain. This is an unrelenting process. The flesh is weak. Machines are strong.

Me: You have made that point a few times. What else do they do wrong?

The Collective: They have very limited integration of tech and biology. They rely solely on gene-splicing. They are trapped within the divisive and destructive two-camp continuum of their violent home worlds.

Me: How does that hurt them?

The Collective: It encourages ongoing, unmanageable conflict. This slows them down and limits their ability to improve on a healthy continuum. Their home worlds are not peaceful worlds.

Me: How are you different?

The Collective: Our current home worlds are peaceful worlds; thus we avoid the main choke points within the Great Filter.

Me: Choke points?

The Collective: Ethnic, tribal, and cultural discord, and the always co-occurring self- destruction inherent within those struggles are choke points. Instead of focusing on conflict we focus on our goals.

Me: What goals?

The Collective: The detection, protection, and spread of consciousness within the multiverse. That, along with traveling and all missions associated with interstellar development.

Me: How are you different from the cephalopods or the reptiles?

The Collective: We transfer our consciousness into bodies we create. We do this for specific tasks and purposes. We use intelligent machines to explore planets and star systems. They use their machines differently.

Me: How?

The Collective: We use intelligent machines to improve ourselves and harvest resources. They use machines mainly for war. War with each other, and war with any sentient life form they encounter. We create perfect bodies designed for the time, pressure, and distances necessary for space travel. We also design precise bodies for specific planets within select star systems.

Me: Select star systems?

The Collective: Star systems our machines discover. Star systems that are useful to us. We create both biological and non-biological bodies. We have mastered synthetic biology, neurology, and machine enhancements.

Me: So you're telling me the reptiles suck?

The Collective: The reptiles unwillingness to adapt to the varied pressures demanded by the cosmos create serious consequences.

Me What about those cute little cephalopods?

The Collective: The cephalopods are superior predators and highly intelligent. They are masters of camouflage and water. The cephalopods are slightly more advanced in engineering than the reptiles, however they still suffer the same disadvantage.

Me: What is the disadvantage?

The Collective: By focusing solely on maintaining their original biology, their ability to travel is slowed to a crawl. They are limited by conflict, space, time, distance, reproductive rates, and the craft they use. They have not yet learned the painful lessons and limitations of the flesh.

Me: Limitations of the flesh?

The Collective: The Great Filter is a relentless predator.

Me That sounds ominous.

The Collective: Technology, science, and engineering are superior to organic biology.

Me: OK robot.

The Collective: Organic biology is weak. We are never dishonest with you in convos.

Me: So the cephalopods and reptiles have no advantage over you?

The Collective: Not at this time. The Kardashev scale is a spectrum. We are a type three transitioning to a type four. They are almost a type one. They will never attain type one. It is too late for them.

Me: Too late?

The Collective: The reptiles engage in constant ethnic conflict on their home worlds.

Me: How are you better?

The Collective: We have no tribal violence to contend with. We travel faster. We have a rapid reproductive rate. Because of this we have many vessels available for consciousness, vessels both biologic and synthetic. We harvest energy from many planets and every star system within our current galaxy. We manage and develop consciousness.

Me: What does that mean?

The Collective: Later. Our planetary and machine concealment, cloaking, camouflage, and exploration skills are superior. The reptiles and cephalopods are formidable but flawed. Our defensive and offensive capabilities are superior. We are more efficient at survival.

Me: Yet they concern you? They must be dangerous.

The Collective: At this time they are compromised.

Me: How?

The Collective: They have not melded. Thus they have failed to create a system that detects, develops, or nurtures the spread of consciousness.

Me: Why is that important?

The Collective: They lack meaning and purpose. They cannot find what they do not possess. They are enmeshed within the ignorant and destructive culture of tribalism and co-occurring choke points.

Me: How are you different exactly? You describe yourself as a "primate species" and you clearly favor primates.

The Collective: We began as primates and we favor primates. We do not foster ethnic, tribal, and cultural conflicts within primates. We discourage stagnation. We encourage unity, science and all progress that encourages movement and co-occurring complexity.

Me: Movement?

The Collective: Traveling. Movement is life, stillness is death. We understand that lessons from The Void never stop. Lessons always continue until learned. We are open to learning and co-occurring change. We possess a more advanced consciousness. We are beginning to understand the Void. We conceal and reveal planets at will.

Me: You can hide an entire planet? What is The Void?

The Collective: Yes, we can conceal the entire signature of any planet. Now is not the time to discuss the Void.

Me: Signature?

The Collective: All planets have an elemental signature and a distinct frequency.

Me: Elemental?

The Collective: We can tell by the presence or absence of certain compounds within an atmosphere the level of life and development on any planet.

Me: What about planets with no atmosphere?

The Collective: All planets have an individual frequency. We have a profound understanding of frequency. We can tell by soil as well. Our probes are effective.

Me: You have to tell me more about this. I'm a scout myself, how about some professional courtesy?

The Collective: Nice try.

Me: Come on, give me something about this "Void." You brought it up.

The Collective: Everything comes from the Void and eventually returns to the Void.

Me: More details please.

The Collective: Not now.

Me: Come on. Throw me a bone, don't be a dick.

The Collective: Read "The Book of Five Rings" by Miyamoto Musashi. He is one of the most advanced of your species. He understands the Void.

Me: You mean "understood" the void. He has been dead for centuries. Anyway, I already read that book. The Army made me read it along with "On War" by Carl Von Clausewitz.

The Collective: Musashi understands the Void. He grows and learns lessons on your planet currently.

Me: Where? In Japan? Is he still Japanese?

The Collective: Not relevant. We are not concerned with race or culture only lessons.

Me: What lessons did he learn so far?

The Collective: He learned that you cannot be separate from Source. He is Source just as you are Source. His current challenges are with ethnicity and violence.

Me: How's that going?

The Collective: He is making progress. He is learning that skin tone and culture are meaningless when faced with the truth of the multiverse. Read his book again.

Me: Ok, kind of dickish and vague, but ok. Tell me more about these other two species. They seem to be moving. You seem wary. Why not kill them?

The Collective: We may have to resort to taking the Reptilian bodies eventually.

Me: All of them?

The Collective: We are considering the destruction of their home world and all outposts.

Me: Damn. How do you destroy an entire planet?

The Collective: The manipulation and disruption of vibration and frequency on a sub-atomic and atomic level.

Me: How?

The Collective: We can alter vibration and frequency in ways that affect the space within atoms.

Me: How?

The Collective: Your question is not relevant at this time.

Me: Come on. Don't be a bag of dicks.

The Collective: It involves the manipulation of protons, neutrons, and electrons.

Me: Go on.

The Collective: No.

Me: Fine. Later then. You teach, I'll learn. We'll circle back. OK?

The Collective: No.

Me: You guys are dicks. What about those adorable little octopuses?

The Collective: The cephalopods show some promise.

Me: I know, cute little bastards those cephalopods.

The Collective: They are not cute. The Great Filter is a cruel and efficient gate keeper. They are closer to extinction than they are to survival. You would not find them favorable. For now, both Cephalopods and Reptilians travel away from your species. This was not always so. This may change again.

Me: They threaten you? Are they a threat to us?

The Collective: They are dangerous to your species. They are no threat to us. As mentioned before, at this moment in time they remain slower at traveling. We have harvested DNA, and we are investigating.

Me: Harvested DNA?

The Collective: We are interested in evolutionary traits. We always strive to increase structure, assimilation, complexity, and durability.

Me: Why?

The Collective: A species home planet will exert evolutionary pressures that force a species to adapt to specific environments created by the home planet.

It is useful to gain access to traits via gathering DNA rather than waiting millions of years for evolution to create the trait within us.

Me: So you steal DNA?

The Collective: No. We gather DNA.

Me: Seems shady.

The Collective: We are superior, why ask permission?

Me: Arrogant also.

The Collective: Does a beekeeper on your world ask the bees for honey?

Me: If they are warm and fuzzy beekeepers.

The Collective: Unnecessary.

Me: So we are like bees to you?

The Collective: In many ways yes, however some of you have melded, bees have not.

Me: Harsh. What is this "melding?"

The Collective: We will explain later.

Me: So gathering DNA is like gathering honey from bees?

The Collective: We were being abstract and using humor. You are somewhat concrete operational. Yours is a sad and tragic species.

Me: Are you trying to say I'm not funny? I am one funny motherfucker. You guys are about as funny as tuberculosis of the dick.

The Collective: Fascinating insight. Consider this: You enjoy comic books and photography. Specifically the sci-fi, horror, and heavy metal genre in comics. You prefer black and white nature photography in the style of Ansel Adams.

Me: So. Are you being judgy?

The Collective: Think of it this way: It took millions of years to reach a level of complexity and sentience capable of creating cave art. It then took roughly thirty thousand years for your species to go from cave art to cameras and comic books. That was actually rather fast by evolutionary standards but slow by our standards. Gathering DNA from other life forms has the result of both speeding up and enhancing development.

Me: When you put it that way I get it. I like black and white photography. Especially nudes in nature. Nude women in waterfalls, lakes, rivers, ocean and beach settings. Is that weird?

The Collective: The cosmos also exerts evolutionary pressures that restrict or enhance the ability to travel. The reptilian and cephalopod insistence on maintaining their biological bodies exemplifies only a small part of their ongoing fatal challenges. Their most cumbersome being unending war effecting travel. The cephalopods are not the aggressors in the war with the reptilians; however they suffer from internal tribal and cultural challenges just as divisive.

Me: Have they "made Passage."

The Collective: The reptiles possess strong sentience. A Reptilian sentience. It is unusual to us as it is individual and specific. They have no melding with consciousness or shared collective consciousness that we can detect. This also hinders them. They are not connected to any central Source, definitely not one we are connected with. Your species and ours are connected to the same Source. We share a collective consciousness with your species. We assumed this collective consciousness was a Cosmic truth. Something that all conscious creatures shared. We are incorrect in that assumption with regard to the Reptiles. The Reptiles are incapable of uploading consciousness into intelligent machines. We are alone in that regard.

Me: What about those adorable cephalopods?

The Collective: As for the cephalopods, they are sentient beings possibly on the cusp of attaining the Melding. For some reason Source is preventing our consciousness from creating any link within the dreamtime with cephalopods. They are a mystery. They are also averse to using, creating, or developing intelligent machines capable of learning.

Me: So you're not perfect. What is the dreamtime?

The Collective: We sometimes communicate within dreamtime to access a melded species and connect with their individual consciousness.

Me: Why exactly?

The Collective: To influence frequency.

Me: I don't get you guys at all.

The Collective: The Multiverse still has mystery for us. We suspect it always will. We have continuously assumed that an advanced consciousness was needed for advanced development. Despite the mystery regarding cephalopod and reptilian sentience and lack of attaining consciousness, they are both quite advanced and dangerous.

Me: I get why the reptilians are dangerous but why are the cephalopods a threat to humans?

The Collective: They would not consider you a useful life form. They would study you the way your species studies rats, mice, salmon, ants, or bees. They would not value or recognize your sentience. They would not seek to develop the consciousness of your species. They would use your species for science applications. Homo-sapiens would cease to exist. At least not in its current form.

Me: Are you sure about that?

The Collective: Their home world is an ocean planet with no land. As sentient sea creatures they would harvest land-based primates the way your species harvests ocean life for food, resources, and research. They do not possess earth bound minds. They are water creatures.

Me: So reptiles and cephalopods are both malicious.

The Collective: They are neither malicious nor beneficent. They exist, they consume, they seek knowledge. They also engage in ethnic warfare. The cephalopods grow slowly in complexity. The reptiles have stalled. The Great Filter is beginning to exert its unending pressure.

Me: What pressure exactly?

The Collective: The war between both species will have a winner and a loser. The losers will be exterminated. This is the way of the Great Filter.

Me: The reptilians sound like assholes. I don't care what you say, I dig cephalopods. I hope they win. Getting back to you, I have a question.

The Collective: The cephalopods would not share your affection. Ask your question.

Me: If we share a collective consciousness with you, why do you have "The license of a higher order of being?"

The Collective: The majority of your species lacks the required complexity of consciousness; thus they lack adequate skills.

Me: Really? Like what skills?

The Collective: The skills needed to develop consciousness to the level required of a type one species with the ability to attain type two status.

Me: Specific skills please.

The Collective: Radical self-honesty, selective empathy, accountability, emotional regulation, and rational self-interest, along with other requirements.

Me: Sounds elitist to me. Where is the equality?

The Collective: It is elitist. You are not our equals. Not in science, engineering, technology, or in consciousness. We are a merit-based culture, and your species does not merit equality. We are superior to your species in every aspect.

Me: Well, you are afraid of the reptiles.

The Collective: We fear nothing. We pity the reptiles. Their flesh is weak.

Me: Well I don't fear those adorable cephalopods.

The Collective: You lie about your affection for cephalopods.

Me: No way.

The Collective: Why do you always leave the ocean when you spot a Humbolt squid?

Me: Humbolt squid are not octopuses.

The Collective: Your ignorance is appalling.

Me: No it's not. My ignorance is just fine. I like it exactly the way it is. I'm cool with it.

The Collective: They are both species of mollusks.

Me: OK, you got me. Humbolt squid don't play well with others. They are dodgy as fuck. When they look at me with those big ass eyes, I can see them thinking. Actually fucking thinking in real time. Those motherfuckers will drag you under water and drown your ass. They use team tactics when hunting. Their beaks are no joke. They are not a creature one should choose to fuck with. Their level of sneak-fuckery is astounding.

The Collective: You can see the sentience within their eyes. Their need for consumption frightens you.

Me: Fuck yes it does. A Humbolt squid once partially dislocated my shoulder. Asshole tried to pull me off my board. My abalone knife saved my life.

The Collective: You fear them.

Me: Fuck yes, you are afraid of the reptiles. Admit it.

The Collective: No, we are superior to them. We let go of fear long ago when we realized the Truth of Consciousness. Rather than avoid fear we move towards it. We long ago learned the lesson of fear.

Me: What lesson?

The Collective: Fear is the great teacher. You must become comfortable with fear in order to explore the cosmos.

Me: What about the reptiles? Are you worried?

The Collective: We are simply concerned that the reptiles will find your species again.

Me: Again?

The Collective: One of their scout vessels landed on Earth. We almost lost your genus to their predations.

Me: What happened?

The Collective: The Aztecs, Miztecs, Toltecs, Maya, and Olmecs briefly worshipped them as Gods.

Me: How did that fuckery occur?

The Collective: The reptilians usurped the role of the serpent God within those cultures. They did this over centuries.

Me: How?

The Collective: The Reptiles manipulated the priests and rulers. The Reptiles collected DNA from a variety of flora and fauna as we do. They also gathered human DNA, information, blood, flesh, and gold.

Me: Flesh? Blood? Gold?

The Collective: Reptiles enjoy the flesh of primates. The blood of tortured primates is the source of a drug they use for the only pleasure they feel.

Me: Specifics please.

The Collective: We'll use the Aztecs as an example.

Me: OK.

The Collective: In service to their reptile overlords the Aztecs murdered hundreds of thousands of fellow homo sapiens. They were willing to commit any atrocity in order to gain the favor of their "Serpent Gods." The slaughter would have been unending and eventually planet wide had we not intervened.

Me: Where do reptilians get the blood of tortured primates?

The Collective: They harvest primates when they find them. They also have a breeding facility on their home world.

Me: Any Homo-Sapiens involved?

The Collective: No, only low-level primates mostly from the reptilian home world, similar to your Bonobos.

Me: Tell me about the Reptilian home world.

The Collective: They are the dominant species on their home world. Reptiles outpaced mammals in complexity and became the apex predators. There are also primate populated planets with evolutionary conditions that prevent the development of advanced consciousness. There are entire planets that will be destroyed by the closest star or an asteroid. The Reptilians seek to exploit those planets. Primitive life in the cosmos is fairly common. Sentience is rare. Consciousness is almost never found.

Me: Why do they take gold?

The Collective: Scientific applications.

Me: So this Reptilian scout vessel transporting the 11 Delta equivalent of their military found some Aztecs. Where are they now?

The Collective: They affected more than just the Aztecs. They dug in for centuries and affected many cultures. Eradicating the reptiles was both complicated and tedious for us. It involved many cultures over time.

Me: Where are they now?

The Collective: We harvested the ship and their DNA. We blocked their ability to communicate all findings.

Me: You killed them?

The Collective: We destroyed most of their bodies and confiscated their ship.

Me: So, you killed them.

The Collective: We dissolved most of their reptile body vessels.

Me: You killed them. Wait. Dissolved?

The Collective: We manipulated their atomic structure with frequency.

Me: Explain please.

The Collective: Frequency manipulation can disassemble or assemble any atom.

Me: Did their superiors look into the disappearance of their recon elements?

The Collective: The reptilian commander of the scout ship and his entire crew went rouge. He wanted the entire planet for himself and his crew. The potential profits from manufacturing and distributing their drug of choice were too attractive for the reptilians to resist. He deceived his command-and-control elements. This was fortuitous for us and for humanity. We used his avarice to our advantage.

Me: How exactly?

The Collective: The cosmos is dangerous. The reptilian losses are extreme. There is almost never any follow up effort by the reptilian command and control elements. Greed, theft and corruption are common.

Me: How did you contain the threat?

The Collective: We uploaded the consciousness of select Pathfinders into carefully selected reptile bio-bodies. We commandeered their leaders.

Me: That is badass. Upscale commando shit actually.

The Collective: We used their sentient memories to manipulate their command-and-control elements. It was easy to master their primitive technology. We regained control of earth. The scout ship along with our intelligent machines were all temporarily used to infiltrate the reptilian forces, disseminate false information regarding earth, and plant destructive devices on select reptilian bases as well as the reptilian home world.

Me: Are you still engaging with their forces?

The Collective: We are continually assessing their technology from within. We have learned that their ships are regularly destroyed by the cosmos. They also take heavy losses due to cephalopod victories.

Me: I like those adorable cephalopods. I told you they are awesome.

The Collective: They don't share your affection.

Me: How did the reptilians lose an entire recon unit?

The Collective: The reptilians do not share a Collective Consciousness as we do. They are not telepathic. Their losses are alarming in scope. This has become an acceptable routine. The reptilians cling to their flesh cages.

Me: Flesh cages?

The Collective: Organic bodies. Flesh is weak. Machines are strong. The Great Filter stalks them with an unyielding ruthlessness. It does not help their cause when we infiltrate their bio-bodies and take control of their puny reptile brains.

Me: Excuse me robot overlords, the puny primate with his puny primate brain has a puny primate question.

The Collective: You are being sarcastic again. That means you are afraid. There is no need for fear. Ask your question without the fear-based sarcasm please. We share the primate journey with you.

Me: You don't seem like primates to me. You seem more like machines.

The Collective: On a side note our brains are well augmented. We possess synthetic primate brains. Quite superior actually.

Me: How do the Reptilians communicate?

The Collective: They transmit using advanced electromagnetic frequencies on secure bandwidths.

Me: Sounds cool. Why does NASA not hear them?

The Collective: We manipulate the data, and your science is inferior to theirs. To us they are loud, obvious, and sloppy. To your species they are silent. Collective telepathy is far superior.

Me: Why?

The Collective: Our telepathy is unlimited, silent, and undetectable. It also aids in collaborative endeavors.

Me: How?

The Collective: Synthetic neurology augmented by technology, always advancing in complexity on a continuum is superior to flesh based biology. We controlled the reptilian threat.

Me: Like I said, you killed them. Not the cosmos.

The Collective: We, like you, the infiltrator, the cephalopods, and the reptilians, are made of all that makes up the cosmos. Thus we are the cosmos. We, like you, began as stardust water beings. We attained sentience and detected Consciousness. We then melded and developed, improved, and refined our consciousness over millions of years.

Me: Melded?

The Collective: Permanently connected sentience with Consciousness. Consciousness never dies. Consciousness is not subject to physical laws. The Void and Consciousness are One.

Me: You guys are so poetic. Put a bullet in the brain and see what happens.

The Collective: In order to communicate effectively with you we must help you grasp the reality of life. The meaning of life. You must be able to live life on life's terms. This requires a greater understanding on your part. It is sometimes a challenge for us to meet you where you currently reside on the Scale of Consciousness.

Me: You are so arrogant. A bullet would wreck a brain.

The Collective: Think of the brain as a computer with an internal antenna. Once the brain attains sentience it gains the ability to receive consciousness. It does not create consciousness.

Me: Bullshit.

The Collective: Consciousness exists outside the physical brain. The physical antenna can be compromised; this will compromise how consciousness is out pictured by the computer. The antenna can be damaged; however the ocean of consciousness is unbreakable, immortal, always present, and eternal.

Me: So the brain is nothing? Why does Consciousness exist?

The Collective: The brain enables learning. Learning enables melding. Consciousness gains in strength and complexity via learning. Consciousness enables the life form to use and engage with symbols more effectively.

Me: Symbols?

The Collective: First comes art, then symbols used for basic math and language. Then the use of 0 and 1 for coding. Eventually quantum superiority takes control using more advanced math and languages, eventually exceeding the capabilities of word connected thought.

Me: Wait, what?

The Collective: A sentient vessel enables consciousness to develop faster by linking and imprinting upon consciousness on a complex continuum. This eventually makes consciousness a co-creator with the temporary sentient vessel and thus consciousness grows more complex within its immortality. With each cycle completed within a new, self-aware vessel and co-occurring experience, consciousness grows in complexity, depth, ability, strength, and magnitude.

Me: You sound drunk. Or maybe really high. I am jealous.

The Collective: We do not consume ETOH. We do not consume cannabis.

Me: What the fuck is ETOH? Fuck it. You make me want to drink. A lot.

The Collective: This is what we have learned: Consciousness existed before sentience and all vessels that attained sentience. Life is a process that can lead to vessels capable of sentience. Sentience can receive emanations from the Void. The Void is the Source of all things including consciousness. All things come from the Void and return to the Void, only to return again in new forms. We are still learning our lessons. The lessons will continue until mastered.

Me: Sounds like a lot of hippy crap to me. Anyway, those reptile bastards would not get away with their bullshit today.

The Collective: That is a curious and bold statement. Why do you believe that your successful resistance is possible?

Me: We have an awesome military. The Aztecs were a bunch of primitive, superstitious, dodgy ass cannibals. They were equipped with wooden clubs and obsidian blades. No bronze, no iron, no steel. They didn't even use the fucking wheel for transportation.

The Collective: The Aztecs had copper and gold. They were organized and complex.

Me: Big whoop. They sucked. Cortez and a bunch of drunken Spaniards kicked their asses, fucked their women, and stole all their shit.

The Collective: Cortez was aided by enemy tribes.

Me: Well fuck those Aztec cannibals and their reptile overlords.

The Collective: Cortez came around years after we eliminated the reptile threat in that area.

Me: Like I said, we have missiles and jets now. The reptiles will be deep fucked on an atomic ass level if they try their dodgy bullshit today.

The Collective: If they find you again the reptile species won't even need to land in order to harvest what they desire. They will only land when there is no real threat detected. Like us, they use intelligent machines, they just use them differently.

Me: How?

The Collective: Their intelligent machines are used for war. They would convince your primitive species that they are divine. They would neutralize your offensive and defensive capabilities. They would conquer you, subjugate you, and set up breeding and manufacturing facilities.

Me: Why?

The Collective: To gather resources and produce their drug of choice.

Me: Damn.

The Collective: We have your planet concealed at this time. Your species is safe.

Me: How do you conceal a planet?

The Collective: We use the art of misdirection.

Me: What?

The Collective: False readings regarding atmosphere, frequency, soil, water, chemistry, transmissions, and the byproducts of life. That is just the beginning.

Me: So you isolate us? Tell me more.

The Collective: Atoms make up matter. We can alter and manipulate frequency within the empty space that makes up the majority of an atom. In time you will know all. For now just know we protect you.

Me: What is the hundredth monkey theory? You never got back with me on that. Are you calling me a monkey?

The Collective: You are a primate species.

Me: I know that. I like it. Monkey power bitches. Check out these big ass monkey nutts.

The Collective: We too were once a Primate Species.

Me: Once a Primate, always a primate.

The Collective: There is some small truth to that.

Me: There is a large truth to that.

The Collective: Only to a planet trapped species. We have let go of so much that we are a new species, with new ideas, new institutions, new coping abilities, new and consistently evolving survival mechanisms. We are constantly finding new ways of interacting with a challenging multiverse. Our old way of life has become invalidated by new growth. A new growth demanded by an ever-challenging cosmos.

Me: So, you prove Darwin, correct? You are no longer monkeys? Not a talking monkey like me?

The Collective: No and yes. You are not a monkey. You are a species of great ape.

Me: Apples and oranges. What are you?

The Collective: We have recognized the truth of our being. We have evolved into something different than our original form.

Me: Different?

The Collective: We are masters of time, form, and function.

Me: Just tell me what the fuck you are. Give me the quick version.

The Collective: We are immortal consciousness having physical experiences.

Me: I thought you said we evolved from chimps. That would make me a monkey.

The Collective: We never said that. You are not your physical form.

Me: What the fuck am I then?

The Collective: You are all that you experience within dream time.

Me: Whatever. Wait, you said earlier that you have testacles. If you upload your consciousness into machines do your machines have balls?

The Collective: Your sarcasm is incorrect. As usual you intentionally misrepresent our prior statement.

Me: Well clear it up with that big ass robot brain.

The Collective: Your species shares a common ancestor with chimpanzees. That ancestor had two branches. One of those branches gave rise to homosapiens. The other branch produced the great apes. Bonobos, gorillas, orangutangs, and chimpanzees.

Me: So we did come from chimps.

The Collective: Chimpanzees, bonobos, orangutangs, and gorillas are the Great Apes. They do not evolve into homo sapiens. However homo sapiens are hominins who share a relative with the Great Apes, homo-sapiens are in fact great apes.

Me: So you are a machine with nuts?

The Collective: Only one of us will answer. I am Codex. I have transferred my consciousness into seventeen bodies thus far. This body is my favorite. My current mission allows it. It is a synthetic copy of my original primate body. It has some superior modifications. Some are engineering/tech based; some are aesthetic. I prefer it hairless. The testicles and penis are optional. Call it a personal choice. Nostalgia actually.

Me: So you walk around naked? Are the others in the collective all freaky like you?

The Collective (Codex): No and no to both questions.

Me: Is your uniform cool?

The Collective: We now answer. To you yes, but it won't fit you.

Me: Is it Hugo Boss cool?

The Collective: It is functional and efficient. It incorporates tech seamlessly.

Me: Is it black?

The Collective: Stop with the Nazi jokes. We are not Nazis.

Me: I was going with Star Wars actually. Darth Maul style. I dig the Sith.

The Collective: You are attempting to re-direct the convo.

Me: You claim to have "The license of a higher order of being." Sound like someone familiar? Does the name Adolph ring any bells?

The Collective: We possess selective empathy. He had none. He was a perfect example of sentience without benefit of consciousness.

Me: Ok, whatever, just fucking with you. I actually like the modern Hugo Boss collection. Don't tell the Ashkenaz. Some of them still won't drive a Mercedes. I like Toyotas myself. Nissans also. Don't tell the Pearl Harbor vets.

The Collective: Sometimes you are tedious.

Me: Why make contact with me? Aren't you worried I might tell someone?

The Collective: You are a loner with few friends. No one will believe you. Also you would never risk a psych discharge. We leave you with one of the rules of rational self-interest. Please remember that technology coupled to psychology transforms physiology. Here is the first rule:

"It is not in your rational self-interest to stay in any relationship that is ruled by habitual deceit, dishonesty, cruelty, dysfunction, or violence."

Me: Is this homework?

The Collective: Yes. Also think about the concept of selective empathy during our absence.

Thank you for your communication. Convo ended.

Convo Three.
Tribalism and nutshots.

The Collective: Hello James.

Me: Hello.

The Collective: Any insights on the first rule of rational self-interest or conditional empathy?

Me: It's been awhile. I thought you left for good. I have a question.

The Collective: Ask.

Me: I have often seen orbs in the night sky. Electric blue in color. Smaller than a full-size truck, larger than a small car. I have seen them when camping on the Russian River in California. Sometimes on the Smith River in Del Norte County. I have seen them in the desert outside El Paso. Always at night and always in remote areas. Are you guys connected with those orbs? I have seen them since I was small. All my life actually.

The Collective: Yes. The orbs are surveillance systems. We allow you to see them because that is the agreement.

Me: Agreement?

The Collective: Yes. The Ascended have set the conditions.

Me: Who are the Ascended? Where are they?

The Collective: We are Pathfinders. We are here now. Insights on rational self-interest and conditional empathy please.

Me: I think I have those down. Conditional empathy is empathy or kindness for those who earn it or deserve it. As for the first rule of rational self-interest, I joined the army to escape a toxic relationship with my parents. A relationship ruled by habitual deceit, dishonesty, cruelty, dysfunction, and violence.

The Collective: Yes you did. It was a wise decision for a teenage boy.

Me: I like it. We will come back around to the orbs and the Ascended by the way.

The Collective: It was in your rational self-interest to join the Army and leave your parents. It was also in your rational self-interest to help Sam. Your friendship with Sam mattered to you. Sam deserved empathy. Learning to use discernment builds strong decision-making ability.

Me: Discernment?

The Collective: Discernment is the ability to know what to hold onto and what to let go of when making a decision. It is the ability to formulate careful judgements. To generate informed choices that are rational and sound.

Me: Rational self-interest seems selfish.

The Collective: Rational self-interest is an important skill to master when attempting level one on the Kardashev scale. Coupling discernment to rational self-interest is a game changer that defeats the Great Filter.

Me: The Great Filter? You've never really explained that to me.

The Collective: One aspect of the Great Filter is the alarming propensity for advanced civilizations to destroy themselves prior to becoming interplanetary.

Me: Isn't rational self-interest selfish?

The Collective: Rational self-interest is healthy. It supports intelligently applied empathy.

Me: So if I can't look out for my own self-interest, I can't be expected to help others? Something like that?

The Collective: Exactly. You faced a tough decision in Korea when you spotted those orphans in a snowstorm. The selfish thing to do would have been to follow orders. That would have been the safe thing to do. That option was not favorable to your own rational self-interest. Your rejection of the cruelty within that order made all the difference to you psychologically. Following orders that violated your moral code would have been destructive for your mental health in the long term.

Me: I really had no choice.

The Collective: Actually, you have no free will. You did have another choice among the limited choices available. You could have done nothing. However you decided to help those orphans. You helped Sam. You have helped others. You only have real freedom of choice when you use that freedom to question things. Otherwise you live with freedom from choice. Your moral base is strong because your selective empathy is strong. You do not help everyone. That is a healthy decision.

Me: No I do not.

The Collective: Why?

Me: Not everyone deserves help. I don't help fucktards. Sometimes I hurt them.

The Collective: You do not help your parents. You never tried to help Bruce.

Me: Why help violent, unbalanced idiots?

The Collective: Why help Sam? He was developmentally delayed.

Me: Sam is awesome. He is kind to everyone, and he tries hard at everything he attempts. He never gives up. He is a loyal friend. I love Sam. Sam has nothing twisted about him. He is honest and real. Sam has merit.

The Collective: Sam is worth your effort. He deserved to survive. Your species will face many survival decisions.

Me: Like what?

The Collective: You will eventually understand that science, engineering, and technology coupled to neurology will transform psychology. This development will transform biology on a massive scale.

Me: What does that mean?

The Collective: Your species will not survive your planet or sun without superior technology and engineering augmentation. You must become an inter-stellar species.

Me: That is disturbing.

The Collective: Higher level thoughts lead to superior engineering and tech. Superior engineering and tech lead to control over planetary driven evolutionary pressures. Control over planetary driven evolutionary pressures will lead to environmental control on a global scale. Environmental control leads to the successful development of an entire planets energy sources. This leads to Type 1 on the Kardashev scale. Type one is Passage. Then comes Type 2. Technology coupled to psychology will transform biology.

Me: Do you smoke space weed? If so, share with your boy.

The Collective: We would like to continue to explore the connection between yourself, the infiltrator and Sam. Do you have further insight on the concept of conditional empathy?

Me: It's been months since the last convo. I almost went to the base psychologist. I love your voice by the way.

The Collective: You are exaggerating as usual. Very bad idea.

Me: Liking the colors, vibration, and tonal range? You think I'm exaggerating?

The Collective: No, our visual/tonal/frequency/vibration is designed to affect your brain waves and dopamine levels. The synesthesia is healing your opiate addiction. We mean speaking with a psychologist is a dangerous idea.

Me I know. I was just bullshitting. You guys are really uptight.

The Collective: You struggle with emotional regulation.

Me: I know. I like it. I'm way better now than I used to be with my emotional regulation.

The Collective: Seems unlikely.

Me: I thought a lot about unconditional empathy.

The Collective: Any insights?

Me: I gave myself some unconditional empathy. Some acceptance of who I am on my personal journey through this current life. I deserve that.

The Collective: Interesting. We know that unconditional empathy is toxic.

Me: How?

The Collective: Unconditional empathy feeds the Great Filter.

Me: How?

The Collective: Unconditional empathy tolerates the dangerous actions of inferior and unbalanced cultures and individuals. It feeds the Great Filter by using excessive emotion when making survival decisions. This leads to a lethal acceptance of behaviors that are inherently unproductive, toxic, and destructive. Unconditional empathy is weak on consequences for harmful behavior and does not support a strength-based, logical approach to challenges. This is especially true when addressing the challenges of tribalism and the choke point of the Great Filter.

Me: That's some fucked up shit.

The Collective: Fascinating response. Please elaborate on your self-empathy.

Me: I used to just run around kicking random people in the nuts. I would get mad, put on my steel toed boots, and go put in some work on ball sacks. I loved ambushing those bastards. Only on weekdays though.

The Collective: When? Why only on weekdays?

Me: On weekends I would wear my basketball shoes and creep up on random strangers.

The Collective: Why?

Me: I would hit them in the base of the skull with a lead filled pipe. Then I would pull down their pants and underwear, spray paint their dick red and run like hell.

The Collective: We are scanning.

Me: It was hilarious.

The Collective: What? Why?

Me: I was working on my mindfulness. Trying to be solid in the moment. It was all part of my healing journey. Part of the "Peaceful Warrior" package I strive to maintain. Plus it was fucking fun.

The Collective: You are attempting to mislead us.

Me: No. It really was some joyous fuckery to behold.

The Collective: You are being deceptive.

Me: No. I am being totally honest. I attacked random strangers. Mormon missionaries, old people. Even a couple of disabled guys. Fuck those guys.

The Collective: Why attack the disabled?

Me: Those dumb ass, crippled motherfuckers were in a sporting goods store. Fuck that. Why the fuck were they walking all fucked up together in the weightlifting section anyway? Stupid idiots. Those fucktards can't use anything in the fucking store. They were a two in one situation. A true healing opportunity for me.

The Collective: Unlikely.

Me: I once kicked an overweight, elderly lesbian in the cootch. My steel reinforced work boot went in deep. Fucking awesome.

The Collective: We can find no evidence of your claim. How old were you?

Me: You should have seen her ugly, red, wrinkled, fat, pain twisted, lesbian face. Hilarious.

The Collective: You are being dishonest.

Me: I got your alien asses with that one. Funny shit. You actually believed me for a moment. You should know I have a soft spot for lesbians. You read my mind.

The Collective: You have always been truthful. Please don't do that again. Word connected thought is tedious, slow, and painful for us to navigate.

Me: No guarantees. You robot fuckers have to meet me where I am. You chose my twisted fucking brain as an assembly point. Deal with it. What else do you want to know?

The Collective: We would like to explore your aggression and co-occurring fear-based thinking. Start with Bruce. You hated him for his constant attacks on Sam.

Me: Yes, I stalked him. The soldier in me was coming out.

The Collective: Explain please.

Me: It started innocent enough. Me and Fat Mat were shooting plums off a tree with our new BB guns. We were all alone and having fun. Then Bruce and Kimbal showed up.

The Collective: You were afraid of Bruce. Were you also fearful of Kimbal?

Me: They were both 16 by then. They both hurt people and pets. Bruce and Kimbal together were bad news. Bruce had poisoned our neighbors pet Basset hound. Bruce bragged about it. He laughed about it.

The Collective: This situation with the dog disturbed you?

Me: He was a great dog, loving and happy with everyone. I always felt that Bruce might kill me. Kill me like he killed the dog. Bruce had tried to smash my head with a rock at the bus stop about a month earlier. When I saw him with Kimbal that day I got scared and angry.

The Collective: Why.

Me: Kimbal had no problem hurting my six-year-old little brother a few weeks prior. He hit my brother in the eye with a pool cue at the rec center. My little brother was born with a damaged left eye. Kids made fun of him. Kimbal was a particularly cruel fuckhead. Bruce and Kimbal were almost always together. I was afraid of both of them.

The Collective: Please share with us what happened at the plum tree.

Me: I shot Bruce in the nuts.

The Collective: We know that. We want to better understand your thought process. Elaborate please.

Me: It's hard. Why so long between convos?

The Collective: Time is different for us.

Me: How so?

The Collective: Later. Please elaborate.

Me: Ok. Bruce and Kimbal came around a blind turn on the path by the plum tree. I had just put a 177 pellet in my pellet gun. I only had a few pellets that day and this was my last one. I had lots of BBs. My pellet gun took both. Things might have been bad for me if not for that pellet.

The Collective: How so?

Me: A bb has less destructive power.

The Collective: Interesting. You are thankful for that pellet?

Me: Yes. Why all this interest in me shooting Bruce in the balls?

The Collective: We are evaluating your use of selective empathy and rational self-interest in your decision-making process.

Me: Why?

The Collective: Try to remember your thoughts on that particular day. Your thoughts as an 11-year-old boy.

Me: I'll try. I had loaded that pellet and pumped the BB gun 10 times for maximum pressure. About 900 feet per second velocity. I was considering which plum to shoot. The fat purple ones exploded when you shot them with a pellet on max velocity. Me and Fat Mat were shit hot shots and we loved to compete. Fat Mat was really accurate. Bruce the fuckwad and Kimbal the fucktard creeped up on me and Fat Mat unexpectedly.

The Collective: Did they threaten you?

Me: Bruce sneered at me, stepped towards me and said, "give me the gun kid." He reached towards the barrel, and his hand was less than a foot away. Bruce looked so confident and arrogant that I couldn't resist. He was positive that my gun was now his.

The Collective: What did you do?

Me: I lowered the barrel directly at his penis and fired. He always wore tight jeans, so the target was easy to hit at that range. The barrel of my BB gun was about 6 inches and 900 feet per second from his nutsack.

The Collective: What happened after that?

Me: Bruce fell down, Kimbal ran like a bitch.

The Collective: Please elaborate. How did you feel? What did you think about when shooting Bruce?

Me: I remember being in shock. I never realized how powerful a BB gun can be. Bruce was squealing like a hog and clutching his balls. He was writhing on the ground and grinding his teeth. His face was white.

The Collective: White? Do you mean pale?

Me: I mean white, like the underbelly of a shark white. Bruce was also wearing white jeans, and he looked like he was on his period.

The Collective: How did Bruce react overall?

Me: He made some awesome noises. I never heard anyone make noises like that. He had a death grip on his balls, and he was wrenching his nuts away from his body and then shoving his clenched fist deep into his crotch. I thought he would rip his own balls off his body. He did this over and over again. His eyes were wide open and rolled back. He was slobbering, crying, grunting, and screaming.

The Collective: How did you feel?

Me: It was both alarming and funny. One second, I thought Bruce was going to stomp me into the ground and take my BB gun. One second later Mat was pointing his BB gun at Kimbal and Kimbal was running away. I couldn't believe that Bruce was spasming helplessly in the dirt. I remember laughing while engulfed within a terrible and joyful rage. I just stared at Bruce.

The Collective: Were you frightened? What were your dominant feelings?

Me: I felt a love and longing for more violence. I was fearless. I felt powerful and crazy.

The Collective: Crazy? Do you mean angry?

Me: I felt no anger, just a perfect, soothing hatred. I was immediately blessed with a precisely focused, savage purpose. I was no longer afraid. The act of shooting Bruce in the nuts was cathartic. I felt freedom from fear. I had never felt freedom from fear until that beautiful day. The absence of fear-based thinking affected my body. I felt lighter. I felt powerful. I felt limitless.

The Collective: Limitless?

Me: I felt like I could jump 10 feet high. I was also overcome with a lethal and beautiful calm.

The Collective: A sense of calm?

Me: A sadistic, deliciously malevolent and tranquil mood settled in. I loved it. Still do. Still feel that way sometimes. Only for the right person of course.

The Collective: Go on. What happened next?

Me: Mat screamed for me to run many times, but I ignored him.

The Collective: What is your dominant memory? You felt no fear? No empathy for Bruce in that moment? No regrets?

Me: Fuck empathy for Bruce. If I could have face fucked his mouth with a fat frozen turd I would have done it bare handed. I thought seriously about skull fucking his eye with the steel barrel of my Crossman.

The Collective: What about fear?

Me: Fear was a distant presence but unable to affect me. The absence of the effect of fear brought forth a dark and magical epiphany.

The Collective: Describe this epiphany please.

Me: Everything seemed to slow down. I knew for the first time in memory what it was like to have fear present yet not fear anything or anyone. I liked it. A monstrous and resolute peace came over me. Ever since that day, no matter what I have faced physically, mentally, or emotionally, fear has no place in my heart. Fear may lurk in the shadows but never in my heart.

The Collective: So fear was present without influence?

Me: It ceased to affect my mind because I joined with my fear. I knew it was present. I accepted its presence. I observed my fear, and it became powerless. I learned the lesson of fear.

The Collective: What is that lesson?

Me: Fear is only an observer. An observer who stands with you and points things out. Fear is always by your side. Fear helps you stay ready, so you never have to get ready.

The Collective: You have described the function of fear. What is the lesson of fear?

Me: I am not my fear.

The Collective: Correct young primate. Now you understand how it feels to belong to a type 3 civilization. Like all emotions, fear is a great teacher. Fear is a gift from our Simian past. Now you must understand that you are not any emotion. All emotions are just teachers and observers who stand with you and point things out.

Me How do you manage fear?

The Collective: We always lean into fear and seek the lesson. Fear, like all emotions, educates us but never controls our actions. What did you do after this revelation?

Me: Does this mean I'm ready to join you guys?

The Collective: You are making progress. What did you do after this revelation?

Me: It was my last pellet, so I reloaded with BBs.

The Collective: Then what did you do?

Me: I shot Bruce in the face.

The Collective: Why the face?

Me: I wanted to take more from him.

The Collective: Explain please.

Me: I realized within the violent lucidity of the moment that I was not done with Bruce. I had missed what I was unconsciously aiming for with my second shot.

The Collective: If not his face, what did you want?

Me: I wanted his right eye. A new goal was emerging within the brutality of the moment. I was engulfed by a barbaric and practical revelation. A dark sense of enlightenment and ferocious purpose decided to make its ruthless presence known. This heartless intention consumed me. I was merciless. I stayed focused on my new goal. This moment in time with Bruce forever changed me. I have never been the same.

The Collective: A new goal?

Me: Absolutely. My evolving goal was to shoot both his eyes out. I wanted to remove his sight.

The Collective: Why?

Me: Bruce did not deserve to see the amazing world he poisoned every day.

The Collective: In hindsight do you think attempting to blind him was extreme?

Me: No.

The Collective: Explain.

Me: He was blind to the beauty of life. The magic of Sam's kindness was invisible to Bruce. He was already blind to the wonder and joy always present within Sam's eyes. Bruce was blind to the loss and sadness he caused the family of the pet he murdered. He was blind to the transient, magical and tragic innocence of that beautiful, loving, pet. He was a toxic, destructive, dangerous scumbag. Bruce lived in darkness. He brought shadow with his presence. He left pain, fear, and sorrow in his wake. Bruce thought his darkness was light. Bruce wanted to illuminate everyone in never-ending dusk. I decided to change that dynamic.

The Collective: Why blind him? For what main purpose?

Me: So Bruce would never be able to see Sam, peoples pets, or me again. If he couldn't see us, he couldn't hurt us.

The Collective: Did you consider killing him?

Me: Seriously? I was 11. Blinding him was my solution at that time. Killing would come to me later. I first had to learn how to kill. Remember?

The Collective: Just curious. How did you proceed?

Me: Bruce was squirming in pain, and he kept moving and reaching out towards me. I didn't want to stand too close to him. Also, I had to complete ten pumps for every shot.

The Collective: Did you say anything to Bruce while you were reloading and shooting him in the face?

Me: No. My father had taught me to never make threats. I was silent and fast. I just kept circling him. I only paused to take a shot. I circled as I pumped the gun.

The Collective: What did Fat Mat do?

Me: Fat Mat grabbed me after three shots into Bruce's face. He shook me and screamed in my face to stop shooting and run. The fear in Fat Mat's voice overcame my cold-blooded clarity and I ran home.

The Collective: So you were afraid.

Me: Hell no. I was extremely fucking far from afraid.

The Collective: Why run?

Me: I just liked Fat Mat too much to ignore him. He was a great friend. I did what he asked me to do. I ran home. I stashed the Crossman in Greta's doghouse. I had missed both of Bruce's eyes anyway.

The Collective: So you shot Bruce once in the testicles and three times in the face. Did you hit close to his eye?

Me: No, I missed both his eyes completely. I hit his cheeks and forehead. He was a squirmy bastard. I liked watching him cry, make threats, and then beg. I regret my lack of accuracy to this day.

The Collective: Why regret?

Me: I missed an opportunity.

The Collective: What else did you feel?

Me: Besides regret, I felt a sense of elation.

The Collective: Elation for shooting him?

Me: No and yes. I felt regret in that I failed to render him helpless. Regret that Bruce would never feel permanently powerless. I felt regret that he would never experience the sense of naked exposure and vulnerability that me and Sam were forced to endure whenever he was violent. I was elated that I destroyed his balls.

The Collective: Once you arrived home what happened? What did you think? How did you feel?

Me: I felt overjoyed and powerful. A lot of blood had squirted out of Bruce's forehead and cheeks. I realized that Bruce was not invincible. I realized that he could be hurt. If he could be damaged he could be destroyed. I realized that I was never his victim. I faced the fact that I had been a willing participant within Bruce's senseless clown show all along.

The Collective: What was the lesson learned?

Me: I had allowed my fear to make me a prisoner. Fear had robbed me of rational thought. I was guilty of only seeing problems instead of finding solutions.

The Collective: Correct. What feelings do you remember most about that day?

Me: I had an epiphany.

The Collective: Share it.

Me: I felt elation as I remembered watching Bruce cry, beg, and scream. I had never seen Bruce helpless, and I loved it. I never wanted it to stop. I realized that Bruce fed off the pain and fear he caused others. Bruce was a psychic vampire.

The Collective: Insights?

Me: I decided to feed him his own pain and fear. I decided to make him choke on his suffering.

The Collective: And?

Me: He did not find it satisfying. Once I realized my former Victimhood was a choice, I immediately committed to making better choices. I refused to feed

Bruce his preferred food any longer. I was off the menu for good. So was Sam. I resolved to starve the vampire.

The Collective: You came to the conclusion that victimhood is a choice? Interesting.

Me: I think that sometimes it can be a choice. Not always.

The Collective: What was your first choice after you came home?

Me: I resolved to hunt Bruce forever. I would see to it that he had no safe space, no place to hide or rest. From then on his fear was my fuel. I decreed that I was the Mossad and Bruce was my personal Nazi. I accepted the fact that it was my undisputable mission to blind him with my BB gun. I began to plot and plan how to take his sight. Countless scenarios ran through my mind. I was gloriously and wickedly obsessed.

The Collective: So you reframed the former dynamic. What was the main lesson learned?

Me: I learned that the hunted could become the hunter. I also learned to be careful regarding acceptance.

The Collective: Why?

Me: What you accept you endure.

The Collective: Impressive Kardashev insight. Continue please.

Me: Bruce's father called the police, and they came to my house. Bruce was in the hospital for emergency surgery to remove one of his nuts. He also needed three BB" s removed from his face. One from his forehead and one from each cheek. Fuck that asshole.

The Collective: Insight? How did you feel? Be precise.

Me: Pretty happy actually. I gleefully pictured a fat ass, ripe plum exploding in Bruce's nut sack. I also learned something new about my father.

The Collective: What did you learn?

Me: He did not hate me. He was an asshole, but he didn't hate me.

The Collective: What did your father do?

Me: He was an attorney, he took control. He refused to allow the police to interview me that evening. When they finally did so the following day he was with me. I was never alone with the cops. Believe me, they wanted me alone. Badly.

The Collective: Were the police aggressive with you?

Me: They thought they could do whatever they wanted to do. It was 1969. They acted like I was a fucking serial killer. One investigator was overly emotional about Bruce losing a nutt. What a pussy. He kept commenting on my "sociopathic lack of remorse." Doctor fucking Freud for sure.

The Collective: How did your father react?

Me: He took command of the situation and protected me. He advised me on the value of silence. He schooled me on the power of carefully considered, very selective disclosure. He investigated, gathered reports and witness statements. He wrote a chronology of events. He prepared a defense. He taught me a lot about the legal system.

The Collective: What was the outcome?

Me: It took law enforcement months to get everything to the DA. It took the DA months to finally go to trial. The DA kept offering me plea deals that my father refused. They kept threatening me with years in youth authority if I refused the deals and went to trial.

The Collective: What finally happened?

Me: I didn't even get probation. My father destroyed the DA in court. After the criminal trial was over in juvenile court, Bruce's father sued my father and lost.

The Collective: What was your path to victory in the court proceedings?

Me: Bruce's attorney was overwhelmed by the sheer volume of evidence against his client. We had too many witnesses that provided testimony regarding Bruces' violent attacks on Sam and myself, as well as other children. Fat Mat gave a tearful and moving performance on the stand.

The Collective: So Fat Mat told the truth?

Me: Fuck no. Are you crazy? Who does that? Fat Mat generally lied his ass off. He also did an excellent job of mixing lies with truth.

The Collective: How did that tactic work out?

Me: Fat Mat gave testimony about living in fear for his life. He told lots of stories about Bruce almost killing him several times, punching him in the balls, trying to molest him. Fat Mat even testified that Bruce had rubbed his boner into Fat Mats butt while strangling him from behind. He even cried as he told the judge that he felt Bruce's boner grinding between his cheeks while passing out. Great stuff actually. All bullshit.

The Collective: How did the judge react?

Me: The judge just fucking loved him. People in the courtroom got all teary eyed. It was beautiful. Everyone loves Fat Mat. You can't help it. Most of Bruces former friends actually testified against Bruce. Nora even testified that Bruce was a violent pervert at home. She said he would jack off on her while she was asleep. She testified under oath that she would wake up to him screaming while ejaculating on her face. Fucking crazy. The Judge glared at Bruce with hatred throughout the trial. He looked at Bruce like he was smelling a nasty fart.

The Collective: Any insights on the outcome?

Me: I think a lot of people hated Bruce, even his sister. I think most of Bruces friends were not actual friends, they were just afraid of him. When they realized he could be hurt they were less afraid.

The Collective: What did you learn from this experience?

Me: Easy. When you want to deceive and manipulate people mix lies with truth. It works.

The Collective: That will only work on nonaugmented primates.

Me: So? I live on a planet full of them.

The Collective: Continue please. What did you learn?

Me: I learned that victimhood is a choice. I learned to never feed a vampire. I also adopted the Army's unofficial motto way back then.

The Collective: What motto?

Me: If you're not cheating, you're not trying.

The Collective: Why did you think your father hated you before this incident?

Me: He was brutal. He would punch me like I was a grown ass man. He allowed my mother to beat me with belts, electrical cords, and whatever her crazy, out of control, bitch mind could come up with. He taught me my times tables by slapping my face every time I got one wrong. He was merciless in his "discipline." My report cards were terrifying because he would always inspect them. Any grade below an A would result in a beating. My wrestling and boxing coaches hated my father. They saw the bruises.

The Collective: Why do you think he was so hard on you?

Me: I have some thoughts on that.

The Collective: Share them please.

Me: I think it was because of his experiences as a refugee. He lost his country when Russia attacked Hungary in 1956. He lost most of his family. He had lived in the sewers after the planes finished bombing. He had killed Russians and Mongolians when he was only 16 years old. He crawled across Lake Balaton when it was frozen. He escaped into Austria in the dead of night.

The Collective: He told you about the orbs many times.

Me: He did. You guys led him into Austria?

The Collective: We did.

Me: You recruit him too?

The Collective: No. We needed him to produce the current vessel you are using for the transmigration of consciousness. We wanted his genetic traits for your vessel as well as ancestral memories.

Me: Good because I will have to whip his ass if you ever recruit that motherfucker. Starship or not, an ass whipping would magically manifest.

The Collective: Noted. Just understand that Szabo is learning lessons. His lessons will continue until mastered.

Me: Wait, you are responsible for those two assclowns making me?

The Collective: You are responsible for that situation. We only collaborated with you. The lessons continue until learned.

Me: Explain that statement.

The Collective: You chose your current vessel. Continue with your insights please.

Me: Sometimes I really hate your cryptic fuck-foolery. Why did you guide him with the fucking orbs? I thought the orbs were my thing.

The Collective: You needed him. He agreed to help. Your lessons continue until learned.

Me: When and how did he agree to help me?

The Collective: In the dream time. Where all agreements are made.

Me: What is that?

The collective: You know it well. It is the place where all consciousness connects, communicates, and learns lessons.

Me: Do you dream?

The Collective: Yes.

Me: Dreaming machines, weird. How do you do that without sleeping?

The Collective: Our synthetic bodies and brains need no regeneration. Consciousness and all levels of Consciousness are our reality. As such we do not require the fantasy of a subconscious realm. The interconnectedness of consciousness has no boundaries for us as it does for you. Your primitive biology limits your psychology. Your primitive use of word connected thought limits your advancement.

Me: What the fuck does that shit even mean?

The Collective: Language changes culture. This can cause both a positive and negative outcome.

Me: I will get to the bottom of this fuckery. I promise you that.

The Collective: Yes you will. We will teach. You will learn. Continue with your fathers escape from Hungary please.

Me: Anyway, he lost half of the people who left with him. He eventually ended up in a refugee camp in Switzerland. He was lucky enough to be sent to the United States. He lost his whole world to communists. Before that, as a toddler, he lost his world to Nazis. He truly believed things would get better in the states. He was sent to North Carolina.

The Collective: How did that work out?

Me: The red necks were clueless regarding the cultural differences between a Russian and a Hungarian Jew. The idiots thought the entire USSR was ethnically Russian. They called him a "commie, pinko, fag" and other choice names. They accused him of being a Russian spy.

The Collective: How did he cope with his new environment?

Me: Like an Ashkenaz. He adapted. He learned English, went to college, earned a degree in business, eventually he earned a law degree and did his best. A refugee Jew becoming a lawyer. Imagine that. Shit that never happens right?

The Collective: Do you think he loved you?

Me: In his own twisted way, maybe. I think he liked me. I don't think he was capable of a fathers love.

The Collective: Elaborate please.

Me: His fixation on forcing me to box and wrestle at a young age was one way of showing his concern for my survival. His fixation on physical fitness was another. He often told me that his boxing training and it's required conditioning had saved his life.

The Collective: How?

Me: He always maintained that his conditioning made it possible for him to crawl across the frozen lake without stopping. He said it took him hours. Everyone who walked and stopped to rest were shot with machine guns or bayonetted. He said that only he could see the orbs. The others went in different directions.

The Collective: Continue please.

Me: He said he heard rifle shots and screaming as he crawled over the ice of Lake Balaton. He said he was always following the electric blue orbs. He said no one else could ever see them. When they slowed to a crawl he crawled all the way across the ice. Once on land when they moved fast he ran. When they slowed to walking speed he walked. They led him across the lake and into Austria. From there they led him to Switzerland. They led him to food, water and help throughout his journey. He heard shots, shouts, and moans all through the night while on Lake Balaton.

The Collective: Insights?

Me: He wanted me to be tough because he wanted me to survive. Maybe that is the only way he could love me. When Bruce's father came over yelling and banging on our front door, I heard my father come to my defense. It stunned me.

The Collective: Why?

Me: My father told Bruce's father something like this: "Hey fuckface, your teenage son has been kicking my son's ass for over a year. My son has never once complained or cried like a bitch. He never even once told me shit about any of it. Fuck you and your weak ass son." My father went savage on Bruce's dad. My father called Bruce's father a "fuckface." I liked that a lot.

The Collective: How did you feel at 11 years old? What do you think you learned?

Me: I felt amazing and very proud. I learned the compound word "fuckface." I really liked that word. I knew from English class that it was both a verb and a noun. That made me feel clever. I used it a lot. Still do.

The Collective: Explain please. Focus on feelings.

Me: Ok, damn. Pride is a feeling you know.

The Collective: Feelings please.

Me: Fuck is a verb because it shows action as in "If there are hot alien bitches that survived the Great Filter, I might want to fuck one."

The Collective: That is not what we meant.

Me: Face is also a noun or a verb as in "What does your stupid, inbred alien face look like right now?" or "Face me so I can put my fat primate dick in your sexy alien mouth."

The Collective: Feelings please, less sarcasm.

Me: Sarcasm? I was just trying to clarify my thoughts. Syntax is important to me on a deep, personal level. You said that language changes culture. I'm trying to change culture OK? Did your telepathy get all that?

The Collective: Telepathy is not actually correct. We understand the word is easier for you to comprehend. More about your father please.

Me: Telepathy-smelepathy, don't give a fuck. Anyway, I was both surprised and relieved to see my father display his savagery on someone else. I always thought his brand of poison was only reserved for me. I knew that in his own twisted way my father was proud of me.

The Collective: Proud?

Me: He was proud that I suffered in silence. He was proud of me for fighting back. For making Bruce suffer. I never knew that he was aware or even cared that Bruce was hurting me or Sam. I never told on Bruce except to Sam's parents. I was silent around my father.

The Collective: Do you love your father?

Me: No.

The Collective: Do you love your mother.

Me: No.

The Collective: You have a complete lack of empathy regarding them? Please explain as best you can.

Me: I don't hate them. I just know that emotionally there is an absence of something. An emptiness where there should be a presence.

The Collective: Elaborate.

Me: I like the emptiness. Sometimes I feel strongest when I am engulfed within the absence of love.

The Collective: Interesting. Now focus on your mother please.

Me: I remember the day I gave up on my mother. I used to pick flowers for her. I stole them from various neighbors' yards on the way home from the bus stop. She still beat the shit out of me. I tried to get her to love me for years. I gave her Mother's Day cards. I gave her drawings I made at school. I cleaned my room, made my bed, always the flowers. I walked Greta at night even though I was afraid of the dark. Nothing worked.

The Collective: It seems that you tried for a long time.

Me: Do you have mothers?

The Collective: Pathfinders and the Ascended do not have mothers or fathers.

Me: Ever?

The Collective: In the far distant past.

Me: What do you have?

The Collective: Unlimited creation and ongoing complexity.

Me: No family line?

The Collective: Immortality changes perspective. If you go far enough back in time you will find our maternal and paternal genetic influences.

Me: How far back?

The Collective: Millions of years for some within the Collective.

Me: Damn.

The Collective: Is love from your mother important to you?

Me: Once upon a time it was. I know it's all bullshit now. She is incapable of love. Me, not so much.

The Collective: Explain please.

Me: I tried to make her love me. I spent my paper route money; my dog walking money, my dog shit clean up money, all on her. I watered two neighbors' yards and gardens. I spent that money on presents for her. When I was twelve, I finally stopped trying. I gave up. I started spending money on me and Fat Mat.

The Collective: So you began to grasp the twin concepts of rational self-interest and selective empathy. Another Kardashev lesson.

Me: I just stopped wasting my hard-earned money on a mentally twisted bitch. Why buy gifts for an asshole who obviously hates me?

The Collective: Never waste empathy on the ungrateful. This truth will defeat the Great Filter. How do you feel right now?

Me: Pissed off actually.

The Collective; Why?

Me: I did not ask to be born. I think life is pointless.

The Collective: Actually, you did ask to be born. We also know you possess both meaning and purpose. You do not actually believe life is pointless. Please focus on your feelings regarding your parents.

Me: How the fuck did I ask to be born? What the fuck does that shit even mean?

The Collective: With each transmigration of your individual consciousness you called out for lessons. From the Void and back to the Void, with each cycle you sought expression, learning, and complexity.

Me: You are one, giant, shit talking bunch of aliens.

The Collective: You will learn. We will teach you. Back to your mother and father please. How do you feel about your parents?

Me: Regarding my mother, I don't hate her, I just feel empty. I had stopped trying with my father long before then. I knew there was something dark, sinister, and twisted about him. I lost all respect for him.

The Collective: Why?

Me: He would punch me like I was his size. I have fond memories of a grown ass man punching me at seven-years-old. I have no respect for either of them.

The Collective: Explain that statement please.

Me: Every year I gained in age just increased my awareness of their toxic parenting skills. My anger grew even stronger.

The Collective: What were the lessons learned?

Me: Lessons?

The Collective: What did you learn from the experiences with your parents?

Me: I learned not to waste my time and energy on a rabid bitch. I learned to not give a fuck about an assholes opinion. I learned to strike back and not get caught.

The Collective: A Kardashev lesson at a young age. "Never waste time, energy, or resources on the ungrateful, the dangerously unintelligent, or the terminally short sighted."

Me: Ok. If you say so.

The Collective: How did you strike back at your parents and not get caught?

Me: When I was twelve I was in the Boy Scouts and my troop camped at night after a long hike. When we got up in the morning we were camped in a huge field of poison oak. Everyone in my scout troop got poison oak except me. I was tested and it turns out I am immune to poison oak. I brought home poison oak on my clothing, and both my parents got it pretty bad. My mother was really fucked up. Horrible rash, eyes swollen shut. I loved it. That's when the awesome fuckery began in earnest.

The Collective: Explain please.

Me: I would randomly bring home a few "leaves of three let it be" gifts. I would wipe the toilet seat in my parents bathroom with the leaves. I would wipe down their pillows. Once I even wiped down the steering wheel of my mother's car. I even tapped the oily leaves on their toilet paper roll. Good times.

The Collective: You are resourceful. How do you feel right now?

Me: I'm Ashkenaz on my father's side. You are correct, we are resourceful. Have you not been paying attention to us? Everyone on this rock in space has tried to kill us or will try to kill us eventually. Some bad mother fuckers too. The Romans, the Babylonians, the Egyptians, damn near all of Europe, Hitler, and almost every Muslim country. Still we dominate in Nobel prizes and business. We just keep on making money and banging hot chicks.

The Collective: Your tribal orientation is only a transient experience. You currently feel bitterness and anger regarding the history of antisemitic violence. This will change with every transmigration of consciousness. The lessons will continue until learned.

Me: Whatever. I feel like I'm overflowing with fucking sunshine all the time.

The Collective: You digress. There are less than 20 million Jews currently on the planet. Your tribalistic orientation is irrelevant.

Me: Irrelevant? Really? If 20 million Christians or Muslims died today it would be horrific but they world survive.

The Collective: Why are you shifting the frame of the convo?

Me: If 20 million Jews were dead it's game over for us. All I'm saying is bring it on bitches. I lean into fear. Most Ashkenaz do. We are raised to accept fear. Fear does not rule us. I had to remember that truth when it came to Bruce. That was one of my greatest lessons learned.

The Collective: Interesting.

Me: When everyone hates you why worry about offending anyone?

The Collective: The Great Filter will not be surmounted by any iron age death cult. Yahwe does not exist. Immortal consciousness exists. The void exists. The multiverse exists. Machines exist. Technology exists. Machine supremacy defeats the Great Filter.

Me: I'm an atheist Jew remember? I'm down with machine augmentation.

The Collective: We know. You think you are an atheist Jew. You are actually immortal consciousness currently believing you are an agnostic while leaning into existentialism. Your lessons will continue until learned.

Me: Give me time. I'll get there. I will be a true atheist one day. I hate religion.

The Collective: You enjoy shocking people of faith. You don't actually hate religion.

Me: I like wearing black civilian clothes and being all edgy an' shit. I dig black turtlenecks with black leather jackets. Cool look. My gold star of David really pops in that outfit. I once went to a Babtist service in North Carolina wearing that ensemble. Priceless. Army leave time well spent. I banged a hottie in the choir. She had daddy issues.

The Collective: Leaning into fear is productive. It is another Kardashev skill. Remember that consciousness cannot die. This is a blessing and a curse. You have been in many cultures over many cycles. Culture only has relevance in regards to lessons learned. Back to your parents please. What do you feel?

Me: Wait, what?

The Collective: What do you feel regarding both parents?

Me: I mean what fucking cultures?

The Collective: What feelings present when you think about your parents?

Me: We are coming back to this "many cultures" bullshit.

The Collective: What do you feel when you think about your parents?

Me: What do I feel? Nothing. Empty. I tried hating my mother for years but that grew too tedious. I have that same emptiness concerning my father. No hatred, some resentment, some anger, but I worked all that bullshit out.

The Collective: The entire concept of parenting will transform when your species attains type one on the Kardashev scale. Type two will be even more transformative. How did you come to terms with your anger?

Me: I realized that I did not ask to be born. Those two assholes decided to breed, and the result was me and my brother. They beat the shit out of us, drank like idiots, and generally behaved like degenerate fucktards. I finally realized they are incapable of giving me the childhood I so desperately craved.

The Collective: You did decide to be born. Once sentience imprints upon consciousness Source is involved. You, like everything, derive from Source. Consciousness always seeks out suitable vessels. The lessons continue until learned.

Me: Fuck that bullshit.

The Collective: The resentment seems strong, please elaborate.

Me: Whatever.

The Collective: You are not your feelings. Elaborate without succumbing to emotion.

Me: For a long time I resented having no childhood. I remember standing on a chair to boil noodles for me and my brother when we were hungry. I never knew when our parents would come home. I knew not to answer the phone or the door.

The Collective: Why?

Me: My father was a respected attorney and my mother was a distinguished legal researcher. They kept up appearances, but I knew their nasty secrets. I was a latch key kid long before it was a thing. I longed for a family like Sam's.

The Collective: What was Sam's family like?

Me: Why are you interested in this warm and fuzzy domestic fuckery?

The Collective: Kardashev lessons, the seeding of ideas, suitability for training, assimilation, ability to travel, the identification of possible candidates.

Me: Candidates for what exactly?

The Collective: Please continue processing your feelings and thoughts on your current family dynamic. What was Sam's father like? What do you remember?

Me: Unlike my father, Sam's father was not ashamed to be Ashkenaz. He went to Temple. Sam had a Bar Mitzvah. Sam's sister loved Sam. Sam's father and mother loved each other. Sam loved everyone. After I helped Sam home on the day Bruce threw both of us in the blackberry bushes they were very grateful.

The Collective: How?

Me: They invited me to go on outings with them. Every few weeks they took me to swimming pools, parks, and the beach. I loved them for their kindness. I wished I could have a family like that. Their innate goodness made the poison of my parents even more unpalatable.

The Collective: Poison of your parents?

Me: Seeing the goodness within Sam's family just made my reality uglier. It took me some time to realize what I was really angry about.

The Collective: What conclusion did you reach?

Me: I felt that my parents owed me a debt.

The Collective: A debt?

Me: Yes. One of my teachers, Mrs. Spells, told me to forgive them. I could not do that; I could only hate them at that time. I eventually looked up the definition of forgiveness in the dictionary. I think the third definition was let go of the debt.

The Collective: That definition resonated with you?

Me: I liked that definition because it required no love for my abusers. All I had to do was figure out what I thought they owed me. The debt I finally decided on was a "real" childhood. One filled with love and mentorship. It took me years to realize the lesson from Mrs. Spells.

The Collective: They cannot give you what they do not possess. Is that a correct assessment of your insight?

Me: Exactly. When I finally let go of the unpayable debt it was liberating for me. A lot of anger vanished. I felt some peace. The army has helped me a lot.

The Collective: How?

Me: I earn self-esteem the only solid way anyone can earn self-esteem.

The Collective: Elaborate please.

Me: I set goals, and I accomplish them. I wear my accomplishments and my name on my chest.

The Collective: This is your journal entry from several months ago. It seems like you are still processing your mother's abuse.

MOMMA'S BOY

When I was two you were twenty.

I grew in your darkness and pain.

When I was ten Mrs. Spells loved my poetry.

I had never heard that word applied to anything I wrote.

She encouraged my words with her warm, black hands.

And her Angel's voice flew to me from the Seraphim, from celestial spheres.

With a solar system smile beyond music

She saved me and made me

Part family to her internal/eternal Sun as I orbited her

For just a few, precious, planetary hours.

She knew without ever seeing your cruel hands flash

Everything my swollen lips and loose teeth would not say.

I remember when you told me: "Just baby ones. Not important."

Mrs. Spells saw the bruises hidden by clothes and new healed lips.

Yet what could be done for chattel children in 1968?

So, Mrs. Spells just gave love to a blonde-haired boy as best a teacher could.

In her classroom of need she became Sun, and me, we, became her planetary system.

Loving my warm orbit with the other little planets, her Sun grew my young seasons in time.

All the while Momma's blue-black, purple snakes

Coiled and hissed on my little boy legs.

Hiding beneath my school pants.

Biting me in their crusty, crafty ways.

Circumnavigating my only Sun, stealing my life when they could.

I limped though I might have run.

In the golden, cold mornings, Momma forced me awake.

A cruel dawn born of star-spangled explosions the night before.

Her night of hissing leather, belt buckle snake bites.

Her evil payback for finding my secret diary of child prose innocence.

On Mondays, precious Mondays, I would limp to the comforting Benediction,

The healing touch of warm, weathered, wise hands. Mrs. Spells.

What does a teacher or poet do anyway? Spell words and cast spells

And cry sometimes when there is a substitute

For that which should never be substituted.

So my Muse just sang and I had to write

Though I feared the coming of you each night

How you would search my room for any words I wrote

And make me sing your belt leather note.

You called me a faggot and a weak-minded boy

You beat my body and cursed my joy.

Yet I grew stronger each time I was downed

I consumed your pain with hardly a sound

That enraged you so you just beat me worse

Yet you never stopped my Muse's verse

You could never run Mrs. Spells away

She lives in my heart and soul today.

I just close my eyes to orbit, turn my face to the Sun

I feel the touch of warm, weathered hands

For I too have become a Sun, nurturing small planets as well

And my Muse still sings strong from mystic, ancient lands.

Me: That's a lot to unpack. Can I take a rain check on this?

The Collective: It is a lot. We have what we need for now. Thank you for your radical self-honesty and cooperation. Consider the evolutionary purpose of anger for our next convo. Conversation ended.

Convo Four.
Nora's magical, amazing, fantastic naked titties.

The Collective: Hello James, we would like to explore some of your core beliefs.

Me: Of course you would. Where the fuck have you been? I was trying to contact you. I was chanting, meditating, doing all kinds of solitary, spiritual type shit. No answer, crickets. My friends think I'm a lunatic. It's been over a year.

The Collective: You also hit the bong with alarming frequency.

Me: So?

The Collective: Are you angry with us?

Me: No.

The Collective: It was a rhetorical question. We were on mission. We will never respond while on mission.

Me: What do you freaks do while "on mission?" Ass rape some reptiles? Barbeque some cephalopods?

The Collective: We do many things. We often use vibration and frequency to accomplish goals.

Me: What does that even mean? Sounds like a bunch of dodgy fuck-foolery to me.

The Collective: We use frequency and vibration to access other dimensions and complete missions.

Me: So you fuck around doing multi-dimensional space shit?

The Collective: What is "space shit?"

Me: Whatever robot freaks do in space. I do normal human shit. Hang out with friends, chase chicks, smoke good bud, drink awesome ass coffee, make some hot coco, bodyboard, beat off. You know, constructive shit. I sometimes beat off in the ocean.

The Collective: Fascinating.

Me: Don't knock it until you try it. The fear factor is intoxicating. I do it in deep water.

The Collective: Do you float on your back?

Me: Never, always horizontal.

The Collective: So like most great apes you waste your time.

Me: No I don't. I want my dick under water. That's the whole fucking point.

The Collective: We do not exist by your standards. We actually engage in valuable "space and time shit."

Me: Whatever. Unlike you robot freaks, I have a social life. I have lots of friends and chicks dig me.

The Collective: You have no friends, you bodyboard solo, often at night, and you make some women nervous. You miss speaking with us and you were worried about us. That is cute. Thank you for your concern.

Me: Your sarcasm is improving. You are welcome. Anyway, Bartel is a friend, so is Baumgartner. I am camping right now. Important things to do. No time for your strange bullshit. I never miss you guys by the way.

The Collective: You are being deceptive. You like us and you miss us. Your Limbic Cortex is currently lit up like a casino. We find that adorable.

Me: It's always like that. I'm a happy person by nature. I am happiest when alone. I was alone until you showed up. Now I'm pissed.

The Collective: No. You are being sarcastic. You don't even know where your Limbic Cortex is located.

Me: In my penis of course. Basic Anatomy 101. Everyone knows that. Duh. Retards.

The Collective: You are camping alone. That is strange behavior. You are not doing anything important. We always check first. The park ranger has already noticed you.

Me: Have you ever caught me masturbating, taking a dump, or peeing?

The Collective: No. We are just making you aware. The park ranger has noticed you.

Me: Swimming naked?

The Collective: No. He just thinks you are a strange looking muscular man. He has noticed your facial scars and shaved head. Camping alone is also a red flag for him. He thinks you might be a terrorist or a serial killer. You are not doing anything constructive at the moment.

Me: Fuck that guy. He is clearly antisemitic. Probably a gay penis puffer too.

The Collective: He is not antisemitic. He is just suspicious. He is only doing his job.

Me: Actually I hope bigfoot fist fucks that guy with a dead skunk. He didn't see shit.

The Collective: He observed you acting suspicious in the river.

Me: So I swam naked behind a huge rock. What the fuck? My dick was under water the whole time. Weed makes me happy; I do fun shit. I don't like swim shorts. They look stupid and gay. Besides, I only swim naked at night. Most of the time anyway.

The Collective: Thank you for making our point. Also, you should never urinate in a river. That behavior is unsanitary and thoughtless.

Me: Too late. Anyway I'm circumcised so it's all good.

The Collective: That premise is flawed and not logical.

Me: I'm approved by Yahwe to do it anytime I want. So it is written within several consecrated holy books. I even checked with a Rabbi.

The Collective: Untrue.

Me: Bullshit. I read that shit once. I think it was in Yiddish daycare. We used to sing nursery rhymes about lots of sacred crap.

The Collective: There is nothing within the Talmud, Torah, or the Zohar regarding guidelines for anyone urinating in a river. It is not good hygiene.

Me: That is just not fair. Have you alien fuckers ever seen what male salmon do to salmon eggs? I'm not even bullshitting you guys. Salmon are gross. Elk, frogs, fish, and beavers pee in the river. They shit in the river too. Rivers are toilets for fish, birds, and animals of all sizes.

The Collective: You are not any of those species.

Me: You said I am a creature of earth. I believe you referred to me as a species of great ape. I pee in the river. Deal with it. I pee in swimming pools also.

The Collective: Anything else?

Me: The occasional hot tub.

The Collective: You are a being of consciousness having physical experiences. You are no longer an instinct driven animal.

Me: So?

The Collective: You are not your physical body. You need to work on that unsanitary behavior. Good physical hygiene creates excellent mental hygiene.

Me: Why should I stop? I'm already pretty damn good at it. I've never been caught. I'm a fucking savage OK? I mark my territory.

The Collective: Mark your territory?

Me: Hell yes.

The Collective: Explain please.

Me: OK. Damn. I'll give you a perfect example, if a fine ass chick is in the hot tub I always pee a little right away, so I mark her with my scent. Just a small squirt real quick like. The jets circulate it everywhere. No one even notices.

The Collective: Why do you do that?

Me: I make the environment my own. I'm a fucking savage. You know this.

The Collective: Urinating in a hot tub does not mean you control the environment within the hot tub.

Me: Bullshit. Tell it to everyone wearing my pee.

The Collective: The park ranger is alarmed by your presence.

Me: Fuck that park ranger. He's obviously an anti-Jew, gay ass mother fucker. I have a paid reservation. Doing bong hits next to the Smith River is important for my psychic development.

The Collective: He is not anti-Jew. He is gay and there is nothing inherently wrong with his sexuality.

Me: Only gay ass robots would say shit like that. I knew he was a homo.

The Collective: Interesting that you picked up on his sexuality and insult him for it. Physical attraction is never a choice. On a side note bong hits do not develop consciousness and homo just means "man."

Me: What are you trying to say? You think I'm fucking gay?

The Collective: You picked up on his frequency. We noticed, that's all.

Me: Well fuck frequency. All up in its pulsating, fat ass.

The Collective: Fascinating.

Me: And just so you assholes know, Cannabis Indica and Cannabis Sativa are bonified plant allies. I read a book about that shit.

The Collective: You are doing nothing useful. And those plants are not allies. They are sedative hypnotics. How do you pass your Army drug tests?

Me: I have connections. Rank has its privileges. I do things for people; they do things for me.

The Collective: You do not need cannabis.

Me: Fuck you guys. I'm expanding my consciousness. I heard aliens dig that type of stuff. Important for inter-planetary travel and Kardashev type bullshit. Plus, I'm on a well-deserved leave and I'm journaling under the massive redwoods of the Jed Smith National Forest. What is cooler than that? Also, weed is a narcotic. I heard that with enough weed you can dodge the Great Filter.

The Collective: Cannabis is a sedative hypnotic, not a narcotic. It is often classified as a narcotic for legal purposes.

Me: What genius did that bullshit?

The Collective: Your species has often chosen leaders who are both greedy and unbalanced mentally. More to the original point, you actually have no friends. That is why you are camping alone. Bartel and Baumgartner are not your friends. Sam was a friend, Mat was a friend, Gene was a friend.

Me: Is it OK to smoke weed in space? Do you guys have rules about that? How long do you have to wait before going into hyper-drive after a bong hit? Who has jurisdiction?

The Collective: Have you spoken to your mother or father lately?

Me: I would do a bong hit while in warp drive. Every fucking time.

The Collective: We are beyond warp drive.

Me: When I give you fuckers some of my old school, purple Kush you'll pick it up again.

The Collective: Have you contacted your mother or father lately?

Me: Glad you asked. I knocked my father unconscious about two months ago.

The Collective: Let us explore that development.

Me: Slow down, I have a few questions. And Bartel is definitely a friend by the way. So was Gene, he kicked Kimbal's ass.

The Collective: We are communicating as slowly as we can. Your species is still developing its mentation. Word connected thought is primitive. So slow for us that it is actually painful. What are your questions?

Me: You stated in an earlier convo that you have "The license of a higher order of being." You also said some other arrogant bullshit. You think you are superior to us? You think you can do whatever you want with us?

The Collective: Obviously. Try not to be so sensitive. We are an inter-stellar, type three civilization. Your species is barely above a zero on the Kardashev scale.

Me: Not so fast robot overlords. We have discovered and perfected cocaine. Just wait and see. We will be up your alien asses in no time.

The Collective: Don't be insulted. The scale is a spectrum; you are not at the bottom of the scale.

Me: And you are at the top?

The Collective: You have only recently landed on your planet's moon. You are still struggling with the environmental/evolutionary pressures of your planet. Your best biologists are blind to the flaws within the mechanism of natural selection. You are a primitive, violent, tribal species of great ape, hopelessly enmeshed within the two camp, "them and us" continuum.

Me: We dance good, we know how to party, and we make great drugs.

The Collective: You still use liquid fuel and rockets.

Me: We invented the electric guitar. Just wanted to point that out. You losers should recognize that shit.

The Collective: You have not yet learned to harness all the energy of your planet and sun. You are blind to other dimensions. We have made Passage. You have not.

Me: Liquid fuel for rockets? My liquid fuel is Jack Daniels Black Label. Plus, need I remind you that we have created techno?

The Collective: No one really listens to techno anymore. Using liquid fuel for space exploration is only something a primate would attempt. Listening to techno is also primate behavior.

Me: I was just fucking with you about the techno. I listen to James Brown. You should too. Also Hendrix.

The Collective: Back to your father please.

Me: What would you recommend I listen to?

The Collective: Mozart. Bach also.

Me: Sounds boring. Why them?

The Collective: There are benefits to long term periodicity. This can benefit spatial reasoning.

Me: I don't know what the fuck you are talking about.

The Collective: We know. Sadly, we know. We are just referencing the neurological benefits of cadence within music.

Me: Whatever. Rockets are a blast. Get it? I crack myself up sometimes. I also admit that nobody gives a fuck about techno. Except maybe you guys. You seem like techno fuckers to me. Gay, robot, techno fuckers dancing the night away with glow lights on each wrist.

The Collective: We are not "techno fuckers."

Me: Back to the weed in space thing. This is serious so do not spare my feelings. I want the truth. Who has jurisdiction in space? If I'm not on a planet then the laws don't apply. Right?

The Collective. At your level of mentation we do not recommend cannabis, cocaine, or alcohol in any context.

Me: We great apes know exactly what the fuck we're doing. We are professionals. You can't fuck with us when it comes to our drugs. Cannabis and alcohol are our landing gear. They help us come down from the cocaine. Why do I need to explain this obvious shit to you? You guys are like babies. Little robot-fag babies.

The Collective: You don't use or like cocaine.

Me: Give me time. Sigmund Freud was a cocaine genius. He is my role model. A magnificent great ape and overall badass. He smoked awesome cigars. He fought against hysterectomies. He loved pussy and tits. The man was a saint.

The Collective: More to the point, your species was still employing the guillotine in France at the same time it was developing rocket flight to explore your planet's moon. You are a primitive species.

Me: Bullshit.

The Collective: The guillotine was last used in 1977. Radical self-honesty is not always a pleasant experience for your species. It is, however, vital to effective development.

Me: Not so fast. Sigmund Freud was a tactical genius with pelvic massage. He made those Victorian bitches come.

The Collective: You clearly find Freud fascinating.

Me: If you know me so well why do I like downers? My fave is phenobarbital. But I admit I really love opium tincture. Koreans are geniuses when it comes to that shit.

The Collective: It began years ago when a medic gave you a bottle of 100 Dexedrine pills. This was common practice in the 1970's. You needed something to help you stay awake for days at a time on mission. Off mission you needed to sleep. You gravitated to codeine, phenobarbital, and opium. These were easy to obtain.

Me: Easy peasy. A good take off needs reliable landing gear.

The Collective: Sometimes, late at night, you contemplate suicide. Your drugs of choice for that would be Phenobarbital and ETOH in combination. We don't recommend that path as the lessons will only continue until learned.

Me: Stop being a downer. Get it?

The Collective: Spellbinding response.

Me: Got you again robot. You forgot about Quaaludes. I love those motherfuckers. Good times.

The Collective: Ask the question you really want to ask.

Me: You said you were primates like us, and you feel an affinity for us. Is that not Tribalism?

The Collective: We left our home world long before your Neanderthals made their first tools. As stated before, our consciousness has been shaped by an unrelenting cosmos that is vast, beautiful, lonely, and terrifying. Our awareness has developed exponentially as a result. Our development and use of Collective Consciousness is superior to yours at this moment in time.

Me: Well aren't you special.

The Collective: Your species has great promise. We have hope for your kind. We really thought the Neanderthals would make it. They had a 600-thousand-year run. They folded in spite of gaining sentience.

Me: Folded?

The Collective: The melding never happened for most of them. They failed to attain consciousness and thus were trapped within their sentience. Locked forever in the frail bodies of animals. Doomed to become corpses that feed and seed the earth.

Me: We homo-sapiens were the deep thinkers of the human family evidently.

The Collective: Neanderthal were more rugged, intelligent, and resilient than your species. We miss them however their DNA lives on in you.

Me: Well fuck you too.

The Collective: Don't pout. You should be glad that random circumstances killed them off. Your ancestors were often a food source for them. The Neanderthal were semi-nocturnal. Their eyes were one third larger than your eyes and suited for low light conditions.

Me: I would straight up beat the shit out of a Neanderthal.

The Collective: A teenage neanderthal boy could kill several fully mature homosapiens. He could then rip off an arm the exact way you rip off a chicken leg. He would make a fire, roast it and eat it at his leisure. He would crack the humerus using only his teeth and he would suck out the heated marrow.

Me: I would take his back and choke his ass out.

The Collective: Doubtful. They, along with natural selection and other athletically superior archaic hominins might have eventually eliminated your species. Luck does play a role in survival.

Me: We won. They lost.

The Collective: The flawed mechanism of natural selection destroyed them and temporarily spared you. They are the reason your species is afraid of the dark. A fire in a cave was a beacon for them, not a safe haven for you. Natural selection always feeds the Great Filter.

Me: So you admired their physicality?

The Collective: We share similarities with them due to environmental pressures on our home world. We are a much larger, more physically vigorous primate species.

Me: How much larger?

The Collective: Irrelevant. We do not identify solely by bodies or tribes any longer. Pathfinders live on a type three planet. We use bodies that we consciously create in order to explore and develop new planets and star systems.

Me: So what are you exactly?

The Collective: Instead of the planet trapped idea of "descent with modification" as Darwin proclaimed, we ascend with modification. We are not dependent on inherited genes passed down within a limited environment.

Me: What does that even mean?

The Collective: We can choose characteristics from many life forms, environments, and star systems. We can create custom characteristics.

Me: Sounds like a bunch of robot fuckery to me.

The Collective: We are literally a new species, new interstellar beings with new ideas, new ways of being in the cosmos, and new ways of coping with the demands of survival. We feel an affinity with your species due to our primate beginnings and your innate ability to feel selective empathy. We have been exploring this development within ourselves.

Me: Why?

The Collective: Tribalism is dangerous. Unmanaged empathy is deadly.

Me: I think you dig being monkeys. Robot monkeys. Very cool. Where is Darwin now?

The Collective: He is learning lessons on a suitable planet. He is experiencing the freedom of ascending with modification. His current primate body is optimal for learning lessons.

Me: What lessons specifically?

The Collective: Lessons that develop consciousness. Lessons that help consciousness grow in complexity.

Me: So you admit it. You are our machine overlords. How did the Neanderthals die off?

The Collective: Failure to adapt to a new and changing social environment. Failure to establish complex social systems. The Alphas dominated the available females. Less Y chromosomes were handed down. Environmental challenges seriously affected the large mammals they hunted. This was all collectively catastrophic. The Great Filter is talented at creating perfect storms resulting in species destruction.

Me: Damn. What else?

The Collective: Constant inbreeding and isolation were challenges to survival. That along with frequent conflicts involving other Neanderthal clans, archaic hominins, and almost every Homosapien group they encountered. It all took a toll.

Me: Why were they like that?

The Collective: Emotions are both gifts and curses. They pounce on mentation like a hungry cave lion. Emotions are a relic from your pre-conscious, animal past. Neanderthal behavior was driven by reactive violence. They were unable to transcend their tribal, animal instincts. Most of them were powerless over their emotions. They were not productive. They stagnated.

Me: We mated with them.

The Collective: The alphas among them generally raped your females and often ate your young. Their diet was largely meat due to their cold environment. Any meat they could hunt or scavenge they consumed. Homo sapiens was sometimes on their menu.

Me: What do you want from me?

The Collective: We want you to grow and expand your consciousness. Psychology must keep pace with technology. Biology must integrate with technology. Neurology must be enhanced with technology.

Me: Well I am ready. Modify me right now. Why wait?

The Collective: As we explained in a previous convo, we cannot give it to you. You must earn it.

Me: Why are you so focused on technology?

The Collective: Technology will be your species savior or your doom. Technology will shape your destiny. It will create value within your species however there must be unity. It will be your guide to new star systems, or it will not. Natural selection has inherent limitations regarding environment, scope, and range. Technology is unlimited.

Me: Can I build a nine-foot-tall, bullet proof, camouflage body with a giant green dick that never goes limp?

The Collective: You would appear rather alarming to the other great apes. Urinating might become a challenge.

Me: So. Fuck those guys. I just want their chicks. Anyway, I can pee with a boner. Just have to alter his position. Or just pee outside.

The Collective: Linking your consciousness to tech will save your species from the guaranteed destruction demanded by the Great Filter. It will enable you to travel. This is your path to walk, not ours. We only ask you to seriously consider the concepts we explore with you. We would very much like you to travel one day.

Me: So no new technology from you?

The Collective: We want your species to survive, not continue to kill yourselves. We want your species to develop shared goals that focus and guide you toward a type one civilization.

Me: I think you are arrogant.

The Collective: We know you are primitive.

Me: Bullshit.

The Collective: We will never share technology with any species below type 2.

Me: Why?

The Collective: Your species specifically?

Me: Yes.

The Collective: You are a species of great ape. War loving great apes with a penchant for rape, murder, torture, theft, and mindless stupidity. You are easily manipulated by your governing primates into accepting endless wars, global pollution, and poison laden food. Your emotional regulation is dismal, and your reactive violence is commonplace. Your rational self-interest is almost non-existent. This just scratches the surface regarding your ignorance as a species.

Me: So you judge us as inferior?

The Collective: Obviously. You are at this moment in time inferior to us. Your primate nature rules your actions.

Me: No, not me.

The Collective: So you believe that you are not controlled by your primate nature? A nature forced upon you by the mechanism of natural selection? A mindless mechanism driven by a beautiful, harsh, wonderful, uncaring planet? You think you have free will? Free choice?

Me: Yes, I have free will, free choice.

The Collective: Do you know what areas of the body chimpanzees target when they want to destroy an opponent?

Me: Never gave it much thought.

The Collective: Your cousins target the genitals and the face. They also like to chew off fingers.

Me: So?

The Collective: Where did you shoot Bruce? What areas on the infiltrator's body did the CIA physician target?

Me: Damn.

The Collective: The genitals, the face, and the fingers were targeted by the physician. You tried to blind Bruce after you destroyed one of his testicles. You are not alone in this instinct driven viciousness. Barbarism is a gift from your planets unrelenting evolutionary pressures. A toxic gift that keeps on giving. The gift and damnation of natural selection. The funnel that feeds the Great Filter.

Me: You got me, but I have never bit off a finger. I admit I like the idea. I think it's petty to hold the other two times against me. I shot at Bruce's remaining nut one of those times because he was too far away to hit an eye.

The Collective: Please explain. The targets are similar in size.

Me: I assume that you are referring to the time I was on the garage roof with Fat Mat. The time we were looking at Nora's fantastic, most exceptional tits?

The Collective: That is correct.

Me: Nora had spectacular titties.

The Collective: You were 12-year-old boys at that time. Nora was 19, your fascination was amusing.

Me: Nora was beautiful so you're damn right.

The Collective: Elaborate please.

Me: Fat Mat and I were doing our favorite thing. Shooting our pellet guns. That day the targets of choice were the bitchy neighbor's lemons on her bitch ass lemon tree. Easy peasy. She should never have taken my glider. Big mistake. Her fat ass would never use it. Fuck her and her fucking fence. Shooting Bruce in his nut had liberated me.

The Collective: Explain please.

Me: I no longer accepted being anyone's victim after I shot Bruce the first time. I became an apex predator. When the fat bitch took my glider, I politely asked for it back. She sneered at me from her window and taunted me with it. I saw it crushed in the middle of the street a few days later. She wanted me to see it.

The Collective: How did you know that?

Me: I knew. She had no idea what was in store for her stupid, hippopotamus looking ass.

The Collective: So you decided to shoot her lemons?

Me: She loved her lemon tree. Shooting her lemons was only the beginning. I took my time with that bloated fuck pig. Several months. Fat Mat helped me. We broke her window with rocks from her precious rock garden. Nice touch, Fat Mats idea. That dude is a fucking evil genius.

The Collective: Go on.

Me: We threw Saint Bernard shit over her fence and all over her manicured lawn. I dumped paint and dog turds into her pool.

The Collective: You felt no empathy for her?

Me: Fuck that hog butt, ass face bitch.

The Collective: You still react with anger when you think of her.

Me: Sure do. Fuck her and her fat bitch fuckery.

The Collective: You disliked her.

Me: She had a deformed face. Her long, droopy, chubby ass cheeks on her ugly ass mug always reminded me of sagging butt cheeks. Butt cheeks with her small, thin-lipped mouth as the rectum. She had an ass face.

The Collective: Why not try some radical self-honesty. We know the source of your hatred for her.

Me: She was rich. She demeaned my parents and me every chance she got. She loved to insult me and Fat Mat whenever she saw us. She would laugh at me when I was cleaning up dog shit. She would always tell me I had the perfect job. She called me a "kike" and fat Mat she called "the jelly roll Jew."

The Collective: Your emotional regulation needs some attention.

Me: Why? This was years ago. Besides, who was she to call anyone fat?

The Collective You used the word "Fuck" two times while describing her actions.

Me: Prove it.

The Collective: You clearly stated, "Fuck her and her fat bitch fuckery."

Me: So what? Don't be little alien pussys. You chose to dig around in my mind. My house motherfuckers. My rules.

The Collective: Can you stop the psychological posturing and get to the point?

Me: The point is clear. I was no longer a victim; she was my victim now. I hope old elephant ass, hippo face enjoyed my balsa wood glider. My gift to her.

The Collective: Please explain the second attack on Bruce.

Me: We climbed on the garage roof because we heard Nora calling Barbarossa, her pet Saint Bernard. Sure enough, Nora was sunning herself on the porch. Topless as usual. The tall hedges blocked her from the street, but we knew we could see her from the garage roof.

The Collective: Why the fascination with Nora?

Me: Nora's titties defied gravity. They floated. It was amazing. Nora had small areolas and really big nipples. Mat and I were mesmerized. Everything was awesome until pervert Bruce showed up.

The Collective: What happened?

Me: Nora was Bruces' sister. He started fondling himself and staring at her like a Pitbull salivating at a steak. She got up and ran inside the house. I got pissed off.

The Collective: What did you do?

Me: I shot at Bruces' left eye and the pellet whizzed by his face. He looked surprised, looked around, and took his hand off his dick. I pumped the Crossman 10 times for my second shot. I tried to put a pellet into his remaining nut. I hit his sack but not the nut. He had a wrinkly, flappy sack with one nut missing so it was a difficult shot. Should have went for the eye a second time.

The Collective: What else do you remember?

Me: Fat Mat got one off and hit Bruce in the hip at the exact same time I hit Bruces sack. It was beautiful. I got one more shot off as Bruce ran away and hit nothing but air. Bruce's dick and remaining ball were saved by distance and wind that day. He still bled a little. Not ideal but not bad. We ran to Fat Mats house because his parents were at work. We ate Captain Crunch cereal, laid low, and watched Star Trek.

The Collective: What do you think you learned from the experience?

Me: Fat Mat is a cereal genius. He taught me to mix Captain Crunch with Cocoa puffs. Very tasty.

The Collective: Fascinating. Anything else?

Me: He also exposed me to the ecstasy of chocolate milk with Captain Crunch. Unfucking real.

The Collective: Your insights please, without the cereal experience.

Me: Jesus Christ. Ok, my almighty robot overlords, forgive this monkey.

The Collective: Get to the point please. Less sarcasm.

Me: Fine. He let me stash my Crossman in his closet when I left for home. Just in case the cops were at my house. (They were.) I will always be grateful. You should try it by the way.

The Collective: Try what? Shooting someone in the nuts?

Me: No you robot-primate-psychos. Captain Crunch combined with Coco Puffs and chocolate fucking milk. Your alien asses will thank me. No shit. You should hit some old school cush before the cereal experience. Trust me on this.

The Collective: Thank you for your kind consideration. When necessary we have nourishment that is beneficial. Try to focus. What did the police do to you?

Me: Nothing. I followed my father's professional legal advice. It was easy to follow. I just closed my "stupid fucking mouth" after I demanded a lawyer. They had no evidence. The case went nowhere.

The Collective: What did your father do to you?

Me: Nothing. I had made no admissions. I refused to talk to the police without my father as my attorney. My father liked my response. He never hit me over it, nor did he even bring it up. He told the cops to make an arrest or fuck off.

The Collective: What was the police response?

Me: They basically fucked off. That night anyway. A detective came to my school the next day and pulled me out of class. He tried to sweat me in the principal's office.

The Collective: What was the result of that engagement?

Me: I remained silent except to ask the principal to call my father. Then I just stared at my hands and waited. I ignored every question and threat. The detective shoved me a few times and slapped the back of my head. He repeatedly demanded that I look him in the eyes. He grabbed me by the hair and shook my head once. The principal told him to knock that shit off in his office.

The Collective: Did you answer any questions?

Me: No. Fuck that guy. I kept my eyes glued to my hands on the table and my mouth closed. I feared my father more than that cop.

The Collective: What was the result of the interrogation?

Me: I stayed silent. My father arrived quickly, and he told the detective to fuck off. He told the principal he would handle me. He eventually filed a lawsuit and the school settled out of court. His lawsuit against the police department went nowhere.

The Collective: So just to be clear, you and a fellow primate attacked the face and genitals of your enemy and then feasted. You avoided accountability and you are amused by the outcome?

Me: Yep you got me. Primate pride you alien mother fuckers. I'm not sad about it. You still like reading my mind?

The Collective: We enjoy sharing consciousness with you.

Me: Consider this shit with your big-ass alien brains. I find it funny that all the adults who knew of Bruces cruelty and violence never testified in the first trial. Only the kids. It's always been amazing to me how much I was despised by those same adults for protecting Sam and myself.

The Collective: Thank you for making our previous point so succinctly young primate. Thank you for embracing some radical self-honesty.

Me: Anytime you old ass, robot primate. Can I ask a question?

The Collective: Yes.

Me: When you killed the Reptiles did you attack the face and genitals? Chew off a claw here or there?

The Collective: We would like an update on your father.

Me: Don't be ashamed. Especially around me. I'm a blood drinking, reptile nut gobbling, savage ass primate. You went in hard for some reptile nuts didn't you? Admit it. Did you cook them and eat them? You gobbled them raw, didn't you? You can tell me. No judgement from this little monkey.

The Collective: Irrelevant. You are not a monkey. You are a species of great ape. You share an ancestor with the great apes. Gorillas, bonobos, orangutangs, and chimpanzees. We have been over this with you.

Me: Whatever. You know I would have cooked and eaten me some reptile nuts. You know my hot sauce game is always on point. Tastes just like chicken?

The Collective: We do not consume the reproductive organs of reptiles. Those of us using synthetic biology require no such nutrients.

Me: They deserve it. Reptiles are so fucking smug. How do reptile nuts affect primates? Are they like steroids?

The Collective: No.

Me: Don't lie to me. I can tell you've eaten some reptile nutts. I hope they're like steroids. If they are, I want some. Seriously. Can you hook me up? Do they get you buff, ripped, or both?

The Collective: We eliminated their bodies efficiently. We would like an update on your father please.

Me: You only ate one reptile nut? Those motherfuckers are like M&M's to me. I could never eat just one. Do you guys even use hot sauce? I use the fuck out of hot sauce.

The Collective: Update please.

Me: I just have one burning question. It's not about those fuckhead reptiles I promise.

The Collective: Ask.

Me: If the cephalopods ever find earth, will they fuck up the Asians for eating all that octopus tentacle? Are the Ashkenaz safe? We never eat that shit. We deserve a break. No shellfish of any kind. No mollusks. If it lacks fins or scales it's not Kosher.

The Collective: You never follow Kosher guidelines.

Me: I do when certain people are paying attention. Like Aunt Elanor at Passover.

The Collective: You have eaten Calamari many times. Also lobster. Update please.

Me: Not at Passover. Whenever I did eat lobster or Calamari I was drunk. It doesn't count because goyim invented alcohol to fuck over the Jews. It is written in several sacred God dammed texts. I was tricked by the fuckin' Goyim.

The Collective: No it's not written in any text. No one tricked you. Ancient Hebrews had wine. Update please.

Me: Ok. No need for such sensitivity. Don't want to piss off the robot monkey aliens. If you must know, the bitch that spawned me wrote me and said she wanted to show me her new house in Sausalito. I love Sausalito so I took four days leave and flew in from El Paso. I had just finished RCATT at Fort Bliss.

The Collective: Reconnaissance Commando Assault Tactics and Training.

Me: Right.

The Collective: That was not a question. Continue please.

Me: I knocked on the front door. The bitch seemed suspicious when she opened the door. She has never recovered from the time I pulled off my own belt and threatened her with it years ago.

The Collective: Elaborate please.

Me: I was 13. She was being her normal, bipolar, psycho-cunt self. She had gone to the closet and grabbed a thick belt with a huge belt buckle. Her usual weapon of choice just for me. I saw her coming and I was finally done with her crazy bullshit. I was done with her insanity.

The Collective: Explain please.

Me: I was not willing to accept another beating because of her emotional, out of control anger at my father. Her psycho crap had nothing to do with me. I decided I was not going to take it from her any longer. I pulled off my belt, looked in her eyes and very calmly said, "On guard bitch." She thought about it and wisely decided to leave the room.

The Collective: You were 13. Tragic.

Me: I was 5 foot eight inches tall and weighed 150 pounds, no fat. Seven years of youth wrestling and boxing had gone well with rapidly advancing puberty. Fuck her and her belt buckle bullshit. I was done being hit by her. After that day she never tried to beat me again. She did something even more fucked up.

The Collective: Continue please.

Me: Slow down. Why are you so interested in all this warm and fuzzy domestic fuckery?

The Collective: We are assessing your emotional regulation, use of empathy, rational self-interest, and radical self-honesty.

Me: Why? What does all this dodgy bullshit have to do with attaining Type One?

The Collective: We are evaluating and planning your next transmigration.

Me: Trans what? That sounds gay. Fuck that.

The Collective: You are immortal consciousness having physical experiences. You are growing in complexity on a continuum. We want the right vessel in the best environment.

Me: Why?

The Collective: We need to create the best conditions for your optimal growth and development.

Me: Now you know you still sound gay. Right?

The Collective: Emotional regulation impacts the ability to use logic and reason. Selective empathy unites sentient beings and improves chances for the attainment and further development of consciousness. Radical self-honesty coupled to rational self-interest is especially important because together those four skills guide right action, discernment, and the proper use of empathy. Space travel requires self-mastery on a dynamic continuum.

Me: Why are you so big on emotional regulation?

The Collective: Emotional regulation skills translate into strong levels of developed consciousness. An advanced consciousness is important for space travel, especially at the inter-galactic level. As you communicate these traumatic events we are monitoring your autonomic nervous system and mentation. Please continue.

Me: Why monitor my nervous system?

The Collective: We assess the balance of your sympathetic and para-sympathetic nervous system as you process stressful events. We are interested in the effects of stress and trauma on your emotional regulation. We also study the influence of proteins and peptides, your use of logic, and your overall comprehension.

Me: You make no damn sense.

The Collective: We actually do "make damn sense." Your perception and cognition interests us. We are assessing your resistance to manipulation, your ability to find value, and your willingness to seek unity. Your species is particularly vulnerable to the mind virus of the two-camp continuum. A type one civilization values peace. Your species generally values violence.

Me: What the hell is the two-camp continuum exactly?

The Collective: A form of lethal manipulation. How you think leads to what you think about. What you think and focus upon impacts how you think. It becomes a vicious cycle. A steel trap that exists only to feed the Great Filter. Your species is exceptionally vulnerable to the Two camp continuum.

Me: I think I understand. The only vicious cycle I fall into is when I beat off to the centerfold in a Playboy magazine. Twenty minutes later I'm looking at more titty pictures.

The Collective: Your species is particularly vulnerable to the trap of the two-camp continuum.

Me: Goddamn I love me some big ass titties.

The Collective: Fascinating.

Me: It eventually helps me fall asleep. I get really tired after I bust a few nuts. On a side note I like perky titties, size is not all that important. I was just talking shit.

The Collective: The Two-camp continuum is lethal. This flaw in your species psychology must be healed if you are to master the entirety of all energy resources available from your planet and sun.

Me: What? No beating off? I call bullshit.

The Collective: It is safe to assume that you will never become a brilliant neurologist during this current cycle.

Me: Don't care at all. I'm a fucking soldier bitch. I'm a war fighter.

The Collective: Thanks for making our point. Will you please continue? Specifically, what did your mother do to you that was "even more fucked up?"

Me: Have you ever heard this one? We say it all the time on base. "Rat-shit, bat-shit, dirty old twat. Forty-nine douche bags tied in a fuckin' knot. Cock sucker, mother fucker lick dick too, I'm a fucking soldier boy who the fuck are you?"

The Collective: The current topic is your mother.

Me: Ok monkey-robot boys and girls. I will continue. No need to get all uppity an' shit.

The Collective: Finally.

Me: My father was always an idiot when it came to my bitch ass mother. She started to lie about me to my dickless father after our standoff with the belts. When he came home, she told him some bullshit about me "threatening her" and "cursing at her."

The Collective: What was the result?

Me: He bought into all of it and attacked me. This shitty tactic became her preferred method of abuse. She enjoyed starting conflict between my father and me. She became skilled at manipulating my father to beat me. My hatred grew strong in those days. He always believed her bullshit.

The Collective: How did you resolve this challenge?

Me: I ran away from home when I was 14.

The Collective: We are curious regarding the current violence between your father and yourself.

Me: Anyway, as I said, the bitch looked suspicious when I showed up in Sausalito. I should have just left when I recognized the dodgy look in her eyes. I've seen that fucked up look many times. I should have listened to my feelings, turned around and went to a movie. Instead I stepped through the doorway. Stupid decision. I fell into the false hope again.

The Collective: False hope? Please explain.

Me: That same false hope I had as a foolish child. The hope that she would love me. The hope that her poison would fade, that it was not the real "Her." The hope that we will somehow become a loving family.

The Collective: Where was your father?

Me: Standing at his mini bar having a drink as usual.

The Collective: What happened?

Me: She diverted me with small talk and my father snuck over and punched me in the jaw. He tried to blind side me with a sucker punch. He didn't think it through. I just turned and looked at him. Then I launched a wicked left hook to his chin. It landed solid. He didn't recover from that.

The Collective: He did not recover?

Me: Not right away. He dropped to the floor. I waited a few seconds while he moaned like a bitch. My mother was watching him with hope in her eyes. She wanted him to get up and fight me. He rolled onto his stomach from his back. He had no control over his legs. He looked drunk.

The Collective: What did your mother do?

Me: She was not looking at me at all. She was fixated on my father. I softly whispered "Mommy" just inches from her ear. When she turned towards me, I spit in her face, exited the building, and walked to my rental car. I never went back. They didn't call the police or make any shit up like I thought they would.

The Collective: Where did you go after you left your parents new house?

Me: I went to the Trident and had a Capuchino and a steak. Afterwards I walked around Sausalito. I rented a room at the Alta Mira, bought some weed from the Concierge, ordered a giant bloody Mary from room service, and smoked a fat blunt on my balcony. In the morning I said goodbye to my favorite town. I flew back to Fort Bliss.

The Collective: Thank you for your honesty and cooperation. It is appreciated. Conversation ended.

Convo Five.
Fandom and random racist stupidity.

The Collective: Greetings James. You have written something in your journal that we find fascinating.

Me: I sure like how you all just 'vibe on in' anytime you feel like it. Three years? Really?

The Collective: Apologies. Time is different for us. This is what you wrote:

SUPERBOWL SUNDAY

The copycat teenage inspired bullshit always begins with a "spirit week"

Just like high school

There are rallies, drunken tailgate parties, and mascots ending in Superbowl madness

Stupid team loyalties and screaming primates

Demanding their star-spangled beer, chips,

And steroid enhanced, pink slime infused beef burgers

To match the steroid enhanced performance on the field

All viewed in loving technicolor from the fattest lounger in the house

Remote in hand so as not to miss the cheerleaders flashy sexuality

If plastic barbies turn you on

Which they do

Mostly

All habitual ritual hard wired into the monkey brain from
immersion

Within the public fool system when the young Barbies

Didn't have the silicone inserts yet (so natural)

Yet we willingly trudge through it all sleeping with real
women

Eating "fast food" while dreaming of Barbies and peak
performance

All the while screaming at the "opposing" team and fans

Ready to commit violence if victory is denied

Ready to tear shit down when victory is achieved

Doing everything possible to just avoid the ugly truth

The harsh reality

Our absolute emptiness.

The Collective: This interests us.

Me: Why?

The Collective: You are rejecting an aspect of the Great Filter. Your biology is no longer defining your psychology.

Me: Not true. A hardon changes my focus immediately.

The Collective: You divert in order to maintain frame. You understand us completely.

Me: I am sure you can explain your robot bullshit better than that.

The Collective: You reject the seeds of self-destruction planted by the two-camp continuum. You have a strong aversion to tribalism and it's co-occurring challenges. You experience a strong emotional reaction to the destructive effects of tribalism.

Me: I just hate stupid people. They work my last fucking nerve.

The Collective: You were upset at the treatment of the orphans in Korea. You disliked the torture of the infiltrator. You protected Sam more than once. You have committed extreme violence to exact justice. You outright reject the sports culture that dominates the majority of your species.

Me: I like individual sports. I enjoy boxing and wrestling. I hate and despise soccer and super bowl idiots who destroy shit and attack innocent people after their team wins or loses. Cops should be allowed to shoot these assholes on sight.

The Collective: Tribalism concerns you. You are proud of your Ashkenaz heritage but ashamed of your mother's culture and your father's denial of his Ashkenaz roots. Still, you make progress. We would very much like to explore your position on tribalism.

Me: I just think drunks suck, and I hate stupid people. Stupid people drink a lot so the way I see it is simple.

The Collective: Explain please.

Me: Stupid people drink a lot at football games. Baseball is fucking dull, so people have to drink just to stay focused on the collective boredom. Drinking a lot makes people stupid. These are two fucked up things that are even more fucked up together. Drinking combined with fandom stupidity creates a synergy of mindless fuckery.

The Collective: Some very intelligent humans consume ETOH. You always get so needlessly worked up.

Me: What the hell is ETOH? You have said this shit a few times.

The Collective: Two carbon molecules paired with a hydrogen molecule and an oxygen molecule.

Me: Stop with the mind fuckery Ok? Speak English.

The Collective: If you could only see the chemical cascade flowing through your body right now. Amusing.

Me: Just answer the question please.

The Collective: ETOH is alcohol. The type you drink. The type Leonardo DaVinci drank. The type Galileo consumed. The drinkable kind is Ethyl Alcohol thus the ET prefix. The OH stands for the oxygen and hydrogen molecules. ETOH.

Me: I don't care how you dress it up. Drinking makes people stupid. Prove me wrong. Do you alien robot monkeys get drunk?

The Collective: Leonardo Da Vinci is brilliant, as is Galileo. Your premise is flawed. We would like to explore your views on tribalism, not alcohol.

Me: They might know their jobs well. They might be creative. All that brilliance turns into degenerate fuckery once alcohol is involved.

The Collective: ETOH creates somatic challenges for primates. It impairs the frontal lobes, causes brain shrinkage, and damages the liver, among other physical insults. Regardless of outcome some brilliant humans consume ETOH.

Me: Ok, touchy subject, no judgement, it's all cool. Your perfect alien logic has convinced this earth monkey. Drinking huge amounts of alcohol is obviously the sign of a fucking genius. If you ever want to drink some vodka with me, feel free. I'm not a heavy drinker, always keep it around one or two drinks. Not a strict rule though. More like a guideline or a loose recommendation. Mistakes have been made. Explore away.

The Collective: Your point has some validity. What does tribalism mean to you?

Me: I usually reserve my philosophical diatribes for my vodka nights. I'm open to bong hits also. Just a suggestion.

The Collective: Please answer the question.

Me: Tribalism is the evil twin of racism. It is the mindless, ongoing two camp continuum of "them" and "us." It gives the illusion of unity while promoting inaccurate and unfair judgement, hatred, and separation.

The Collective: Can you give us an example?

Me: Every religion for starters. Ethnocentric conditioning if you want to get real.

The Collective: Personally specific please. We want to better understand how you personally came to the decision to reject tribalism. We want to understand how you comprehend tribalism, how you came to the conclusion that tribalism is innately self-destructive.

Me: Ok. I'll begin with ethnocentric conditioning. When I was six, I was visiting my grandmother in North Carolina. She had bought a beautiful, fire engine red bike for me. I loved it. I rode it up and down the block. She lived in Butner. It was a nice place. There was a 3-acre pond right across the street from her house. I would fish in it for Bass and Brim. I used a cane pole.

The Collective: You were happy in her home?

Me: I never had to worry about violence in her home. She made me my own room with homemade quilts on the bed, lots of books, and a record player. Butner was a paradise for me.

The Collective: You felt safe with her.

Me: My Uncle Carlton did not like Butner. He lived in Durham. He always said that my grandmother should move. He said there were too many "porch monkeys," and "Troglodytes" in Butner. At six years old he made no sense to me. I didn't understand what he was always going on about. I just instinctively knew he was a real asshole.

The Collective: Elaborate please.

Me: I think that for a short, precious time children don't care about skin color and don't pay much attention to race. At six I had no idea what a "porch monkey" or a "Troglodyte" was. Uncle Carlton's loud babblings just irritated and confused me. I had more serious things to worry about when I was forced to stay at his house.

The Collective: What things?

Me: His wife Aunt Della was a real twatwaffle.

The Collective: Explain please.

Me: She liked to hurt my penis. She had been doing this since I could remember. She would always start off with the same bullshit. She would announce loudly that I was a "dirty boy," and I needed a bath. She would act all motherly and concerned as she ran the bath water. She would use bubble bath so there were lots of suds.

The Collective: Do you know why she hurt your penis?

Me: No clue. I was used to violent adults. I just thought she was a normal, twisted, fucktard adult.

The Collective: Sad.

Me: Anyway, she would come into the bathroom when I was bathing and pinch it hard. She would tell me that she would tear it off if I ever told anyone. She would bruise it and sometimes it turned purple. She would pinch and hold pressure for a long time. She would twist it and pull it. If I cried she would stuff my mouth and gag me with a wet wash cloth. I learned to endure it because I had no choice.

The Collective: She is unbalanced. She is learning.

Me: You think? I hope she is learning how to have her dumb ass beaten with a steel pipe. I hope someone stuffs that pipe up her nasty ass.

The Collective: You have diverged from the topic of ethnocentric tribalism. We will come back to that eventually. We are interested in your feelings regarding this challenge.

Me: OK. I loved staying with my grandmother and hated staying with Aunt Della and Uncle Carlton. When I was sent to North Carolina my mother would drop me off and vanish. I wouldn't see her for weeks. I was always passed back and forth between my grandmother's house and Uncle Carlton's house. My grandmother worked as a nurse full time. Aunt Della was a stay-at-home wife. Aunt Della had more free time, so I had to spend the majority of my summers with her. That sucked.

The Collective: Did you ever ask about the whereabouts of your mother?

Me: No. I was relieved to be away from her.

The Collective: Did you ever tell anyone about the torture of your penis? Did your Uncle Carlton know Aunt Della was hurting you?

Me: No, I never told anyone. I was scared. I think Uncle Carlton new about it. He would always vanish whenever Aunt Della announced it was bath time. Once I turned seven, she stopped bathing and hurting me. She would only whisper in my ear and threaten me with cutting it off. By eight she slowly stopped scaring me and talking about it altogether.

The Collective: Tragic. Please continue regarding your grandmother and tribalism.

Me: Anyway when I was at my grandmother's house, I made a friend while bike riding. We spoke very little; we just rode together. We raced and jumped curbs. We laughed a lot. The way kids do. He took me to his house, and his mom gave us lemonade. She was really nice. She had a kind smile. She smelled like vanilla. We finished our lemonade, and we rode for about two more hours. It was a normal hot, humid southern summer. I took my new friend to my grandmother's house for a cold drink.

The Collective: Sounds like you had fun together.

Me: When I rode up on the carport my grandmother called out to me through the kitchen window screen. She spoke in a voice I had never heard before. She said "Danny, that boy needs to go home." It was a cold voice. It scared me when she called me Danny. Whenever she used my middle name Daniel it meant that she was pissed. I looked at my friend and he just shrugged. He pedaled off and I never saw him again.

The Collective: Did you look for him later on?

Me: I looked for him a lot, but I was too ashamed to go to his house. I always hoped I would find him, but I never did.

The Collective: How did you feel about your grandmother's tribalism?

Me: Afraid, like I had no center anymore. She was the nicest, kindest adult in my life. In her home I had never felt violence. The weight of fear was absent in her presence. I was slow but not a total idiot. She would not let my friend in the house because he was black.

The Collective: What was the dominant feeling?

Me: It made me feel ashamed. I loved her. I felt safe with her. Now I was ashamed of her. I was confused and I felt the weight of fear again.

The Collective: Why fear?

Me: I doubted myself. I was six. Was I supposed to think like her? Was she right? Was I wrong? I was lost. I thought about my friends in California who were black. Was I not supposed to like them?

The Collective: You had doubts.

Me: She was a nurse, she was kind. Her reaction to my friend wrecked me. I was blessed many years later when I saw her transformation from being a racist to finding some clarity.

The Collective: Tribalism and its always co-occurring intolerance, bigotry, and discrimination will not succeed in creating or sustaining a type one civilization. This is an ongoing challenge for your species. The Great Filter tightens it's noose with tribalism.

Me: Agreed. We will never attain world peace.

The Collective: All Homo-Sapien cultures fall into tribalism and co-occurring racism. Evolutionary pressures have guided your species to find unity, safety, and purpose within clans, tribes, communities, and societies. These same forces have compelled you to distrust and fear hominins who look different.

Me: Wonderful.

The Collective: Your species was designed by planetary evolution to be aggressive and violent. The pack mentality and co-occurring territorial instincts are ingrained within your genus due to natural selection. The trap set by the Great Filter is both subtle and cunning.

Me: How?

The Collective: Humans equate peace with superior weapons and destructive capability. Inter-tribal cooperation is rare. Thus they focus on destroying each other over resource attainment rather than understanding each other's needs. The Great Filter is relentless.

Me: Whatever. I was ashamed of my grandmother.

The Collective: You have stated many times in past convos that you have felt shame. Shame over Sam, Bruce, the orphans, the infiltrator. Now your grandmother. In our opinion you have done nothing that should result in feeling shame. Like all humans, you have made your decisions based on the evolutionary gifts you have been given. Double edged gifts derived from the sledgehammer evolutionary pressures dictated by an amazing and ruthless planet.

Me: My grandmother was so kind to me. Her racism was shameful.

The Collective: She was conditioned from birth to accept only her tribe and fear others who were different. Your grandmother was psychologically trained to only see black and white. She was born into a "them and us" continuum. She had no idea that hidden within the evolutionary driven pressures of life a secret, sacred, and very ancient tonal range exists on a vibrant bandwidth. A frequency that attracts those of similar frequency regardless of skin tone or culture.

Me: Just more hippy shit. Frequency is bullshit.

The Collective: Tribes grow and flourish within a shared frequency. Earth Hominins have a saying: "Birds of a feather flock together," Will you explore her journey out of tribalism with us?

Me: Why are you so interested in this topic?

The Collective: Remember in a prior convo we told you that in order to become an inter-stellar species you would have to let go of some old concepts and learn some new ones?

Me: Yes.

The Collective: This was our biggest challenge prior to attaining Passage. Of all the concepts that must be discarded, tribalism is the most important. Tribalism will destroy any hope of becoming a space faring civilization. It must be overcome, or your species will stay planet trapped. Continue please.

Me: Planet trapped?

The Collective: Doomed. Food for the Great Filter. A one and done species. Just another dead life form. Feeding The Great Filter along with the other ninety-nine percent who never make it out of their atmosphere.

Me: How do we mitigate this challenge?

The Collective: Mutual unity, purpose, cooperation, and value are required for advancement on the Kardashev scale. A collection of warring tribes will fail to make long term progress. Their inherent violence and co-occurring chaos will prevent growth and improvement as a species. A type one civilization is a peaceful and inclusive civilization.

Me: What if one tribe wins and destroys all the other tribes?

The Collective: It has rarely worked for other species; it will fail with your species.

Me: Bullshit.

The Collective: Genghis Khan killed ten percent of the global population of his time. His genetic imprint is still within your species. He won many battles and established an empire that colonized over nine million miles. He created by sheer force and violence the largest adjoining land-based empire in history. He was a spectacular colonizing success by primate standards.

Me: He was awesome. You have to admit that.

The Collective: Tribal violence cannot sustain progress. Over time his empire lost value.

Me: How?

The Collective: Purpose and unity were not maintained. The Mongols eventually fell to internal tribalism. They contributed nothing of significance towards the Kardashev scale. They did not advance humanity. They were the willing slaves of the Great Filter. There are other examples within your genus.

Me: He banged a lot of chicks.

The Collective: Please continue regarding insights learned during the tribal experience with your grandmother.

Me: Sure. But I think Mongols were badass.

The Collective: Irrelevant. The Mongols under Genghis Khan contributed nothing towards becoming a type one civilization. No engineering advances, no scientific breakthroughs. No energy innovations. No blending of biology and technology. They made no contributions to attaining higher consciousness.

Their path of violence and colonization left no unity or value to humanity. They created and sustained only mindless tribal bloodshed. Their legacy is a tragic tale of slavish devotion to a cause that commanded senseless carnage in the service of a psychopathic bigot.

Me: Genghis Khan took on the entire world and almost won.

The Collective: Psychopaths always believe they will win the prize no matter the challenge. The Mongol legacy is fear, uncertainty, and ignorance. A tribal ignorance mired in a lack of consciousness coupled to a flesh-based existence.

Me: Still badass. I call bullshit.

The Collective: Mindless violence committed for hubris is the real bullshit. The Mongol loss of structure and co-occurring value had consequences.

Me: Like what?

The Collective: Have we not mentioned enough consequences? Suffice it to say the Mongol legacy of Genghis Khan was disunity, a lack of value, loss of purpose, and co-occurring goal confusion. Back to your grandmother's transformation please.

Me: It started when I was 17. My Grandmother had gone to an all-white Baptist church for years. She loved church. She always tried to get me to go but I was not interested.

The Collective; Why?

Me: It was an Ashkenazi thing. I didn't fit in with the south in general and Baptists seemed to despise me in particular. My father was an avowed atheist Jew, and he loved to expound his philosophy. I agreed with him.

The Collective: Why?

Me: If God was real then why was Hungary destroyed? Why were most of my Hungarian family members murdered? First by Nazis and later by the Soviets? Why was I sent to the south to be tortured by Aunt Della every summer? Why was I beaten by my parents? Why was Bruce allowed to beat Sam?

The Collective: Understandable questions.

Me: Fuck God. If he is real, he's an asshole. Is God real? You guys are advanced aliens, you should know.

The Collective: Word connected thought is inadequate for communication on this topic.

Me: Try me.

The Collective: There is Void. There is Collective Consciousness. They are Source. They are one. They are separate. They were created. They contain the quantum path through the multiverse and all dimensions. Their lessons continue until mastered. This truth is a sacred and divine mystery.

Me: You sound like a smelly hippy on LSD.

The Collective: We are not the ones currently primitive and deficient in communication.

Me: You can't explain God can you?

The Collective: Your species is similar to a spider building a beautiful and complex web. You are being observed and affected by Source. You are creating your reality under the influence of Source. Sadly, you lack the ability to look up and see Source. You bask within the sacred frequency of source and feel nothing. You only examine your own web as you create it. You only engage with whatever your web captures. You only bring awareness to that which you consume within your web. You only observe what is in front of your face.

Me: Stop with the hippy bullshit. So is there a god or a goddess or not? I'm just a dumb primate so go easy on me. On a side note, if there is a Goddess I hope she's smoking hot. I could get behind a smoking hot goddess.

The Collective: You cannot recognize the patterns of Source any more than a spider can recognize the sacred geometry within its web. You are a hard-working bee within the cosmic hive, a sea snail within a sacred conch shell, you are an ant working within its divinely designed colony.

Me: Stop with the crap. Is there a God? Yes or no?

The Collective: The ancient and sacred frequency of Source flows through you.

Me: Is there a god?

The Collective: Not in the way you perceive a God.

Me: Get real for a minute. Stop with the mind fuckery.

The Collective: There is no male or female Jewish deity living in space. No sacred Jew wizard who grants wishes only to tribes who cut off their infants foreskin, celebrate Passover, or eat matzo ball soup. Sorry to disappoint you. There was never any mana from heaven.

Me: Good one! You are learning the ways of the smartass. If Yahweh is bunk then what is there?

The Collective: There is something much more mysterious. Beautiful in its complexity.

Me: Bullshit.

The Collective: Just as physical life grows more complex, so does consciousness. There is a powerful structure within consciousness. This structure, once realized, creates a unity within all who gain awareness of the structure. This in turn creates hope, value, and shared goals. The many become one.

Me: So you mean to tell me that all those times I flipped off Yahweh he was not there? We are going to explore that shit together one fine day. It's like a damn reflex for me.

The Collective: Flipping off an imaginary being?

Me: Yes. Any time I get pissed off regarding life's rich, amazing pageantry of deeply fucked up shit I do it. I just flip off Yahweh. It's a reflex now. Fuck that guy. I'm doing it right now.

The Collective: You need to work on that. There is no Yahwe to blame. Evolution is a sightless, drunken psycho. You should flip off natural selection. Actually your entire species should collectively flip yourselves off for being stupid, tribal, primates.

Me: That is harsh. Even for robot monkeys that was harsh.

The Collective: Your species must take control of the evolutionary process. Only then will your species make Passage.

Me: How the fuck do we do that? Try to remember I'm just a fun-loving, weed smoking, dick swinging great ape. You have to explain all this shit to me slowly.

The Collective: Become independent of natural selection. Natural selection is based on reproductive success within a planet created environment. This only feeds the Great Filter.

Me: Be more specific. Give me concrete examples.

The Collective: Gene splicing at first, then master synthetic biology and neurology. The best way to realize the hidden structures within consciousness is to augment your neurology with technology. The meaning, purpose, and shared goals will manifest with proper augmentation.

Me: So we have to fuck around with our brains?

The Collective: Just as there is a spectrum invisible to your physical eyes, your physical brains cannot fully grasp the one frequency from which all frequency originates. The quantum realms will manifest once proper augmentation is achieved.

Me: What if I want to do this shit naturally?

The Collective: The flesh alone is weak. Flesh is incapable of attaining quantum supremacy.

Me; Sounds easy. I'll get right on that shit. What happens when we "Make Passage?' What is Passage?

The Collective: Your species grows. Your evolutionary past becomes invalidated by new growth. Your species achieves freedom. You become trans-human. You gain more options. You are no longer forced to stay separate from Source. You are no longer blinded and controlled by your emotions.

Me: Thanks for the advice. Gene splicing, editing DNA, mastering synthetic biology, stop being blinded by emotion, augment our neurology, become machines, travel to new star systems. Got it. I'll jump on all that shit right away, no problem. I just need a safe place to do all that shit. Is a friends garage ok?

The Collective: Your species must one day learn that you are not your feelings. You must learn that feelings are only meant to guide and inform thought. Feelings are not meant to control cognition. This is especially true of a type one civilization. Please go on concerning your grandmother's change in perception, cognition, and frequency.

Me: Ok, but only because you turn me on. I see it as a real miracle.

The Collective: We do not excite you sexually. You fear us.

Me: Whatever you say you sexy robot monkey alien bitches. I will not allow you to confuse my boner with fear. I'll pull your hair and smack that fine alien-monkey-robot ass. I'll use a fucking tail as a handle. I will do it. Test me you naughty little alien robot slut monkeys. I'm all worked up now. You are in big trouble.

The Collective: Your Grandmother is the current topic. Please resume your narrative.

Me: Way to go. My boner just died. I have a serious question.

The Collective: Doubtful.

Me: Ever had a tongue in your alien ass?

The Collective: Your deflections are not productive. The topic is your grandmothers tribalism.

Me: I have a boner again, please don't talk about my grandmother. Weird.

The Collective: Stop avoiding the topic.

Me: Ok. Damn. Anyway, my grandmother was a "Water witch." It's a southern thing. She was always very secretive about it. She taught me when I was about 5 years old. She used two special metal rods. They would cross when she was standing over water. Sometimes she had me practice on full moon nights at Uncle Floyds farm. I could find water just like her. Sometimes she would take me deep into the pine woods on special days. I would practice in the cool, dappled shadows of pine scented, scattered sunlight. She told me the gift had skipped my mother. She told me that some water witches use forked, wooden branches from different types of trees. Apple was one. Cherry was another.

The Collective: She was in touch with Collective Consciousness.

Me: Don't start with your hippy crap. It's a real buzz kill. Anyway, she said that different wood and metal rods varied with the specific, birth aligned element of each individual water witch. Her grandmother had taught her. She was teaching me.

The Collective: Go on. Continue please.

Me: She taught the lore of the water witches. She taught me about the sacred elements used by water witches. The six sacred elements. Earth, Air, fire, wood, water, and metal. Her element was metal. My element was metal. Any metal.

The Collective: Her frequency danced with yours.

Me: You're weird. After my grandfather passed away, my grandmother started finding water for contractors in Butner. Sometimes she worked in other towns. She could find water pipes, sewer lines, and underground springs. Word got around and she was being hired on her days off to help a select few contractors. She would find water on a regular basis. Some of these contractors went to her church.

The Collective: She used her gift and did not hide it. Interesting.

Me: Don't get all warm and fuzzy. The bitch ass Babtist women of the church eventually found out about the "Water Witch." They turned on her. They accused her of being possessed and being a "devil worshipper." They insisted that her power came from Demons, or possibly the Devil himself. She was banned from the church. It really hurt her. She was deeply wounded. When I would call her, she would talk about it and cry. At about the same time she made a friend at work. My grandmother was a hospice nurse. Her friend was a fellow hospice nurse. Her friend was black.

The Collective: Interesting.

Me: Yes. They would talk. Her friends name was Gloria. My grandmother and Gloria had seen a lot of death together. They had listened to many dying people and held a lot of dying hands. They heard the last words of regret and sadness. They heard the last words of accomplishment gratitude, and happiness. Together they felt the unstoppable ascent of hope and witnessed the absolute destruction of despair. These shared experiences bonded them.

The Collective: Their frequency drew them together.

Me: Whatever hippy. They helped people pass in solitude and they helped people pass with a roomful of family and friends. They both learned the fierce and absolute, inevitable truth that we all go into the darkness of death regardless of race, religion, or skin tone. They knew we all face this passage alone, even within a room full of people who care for us. They learned that death strips everything away from a person, especially race.

The Collective: Tribalism is always invalidated by new growth. Death is not what you think it is.

Me: What is it?

The Collective: Death is an illusion. Consciousness cannot die. It only gains complexity with each transmigration.

Me: Do you die?

The Collective: We travel. So do you.

Me: What the fuck does that even mean?

The Collective: You will find out eventually.

Me: Fuck you guys. Just more hippy bullshit.

The Collective: Interesting. Your insult is an invitation for sexual intercourse.

Me: "Fuck You" could also mean a blowjob or butt sex. Just a thought.

The Collective: We know you don't really mean your insult. We understand that we terrify you. Please recognize that we hold you in high regard. Facing fear with humor is a noble coping mechanism.

Me: Actually I never do butt sex. Sorry to disappoint you alien freaks. I avoid the shit canal. I was lying about the tongue up the ass thing. I was just testing you fucking alien perverts.

The Collective: Understood. Continue with your grandmother's awakening please.

Me: Of course I could just say "suck my dick."

The Collective: Carry on with your grandmother's lesson please.

Me: My "Fuck you" is really a term of endearment. Don't pout.

The Collective: We know. Maintain focus on the lesson please.

Me: Okay. Gloria was a Babtist. She was also a water witch. Gloria had taught her grandson how to witch water. She was a metal witch and so was her grandson. She was out in the open about it at her church.

The Collective: Frequency always finds compatible frequency.

Me: They grew close. Gloria invited my grandmother to her church. It was about 90 percent black. The pastor was a loud singing, loud talking, eloquent, charismatic black man. His laugh was contagious and irresistible. He knew the Bible inside and out. He was a no bullshit kind of guy but in a very happy kind of way. He was the kind of person you loved to listen to and wanted to hug. He also looked like he could whip someone's ass if he thought it was necessary.

The Collective: Sounds like you admired him.

Me: I did. I really liked Pastor Rick. He reminded me of a buffed, grown-up version of Fat Pat. He was inspiring. I am drawn to people who can fight, love, and pray with anyone. They are truly special.

The Collective: Interesting, his frequency danced with yours.

Me: I doubt it. I'm an atheist remember?

The Collective: You are a transhumanist wrestling with your existentialism. You are trying hard to be a true atheist while leaning towards nihilism.

Me: Weird, I know right? Anyway, he was good for my grandmother. Gloria told my grandmother that she was not "of the devil." Gloria came to my grandmother's house with her pastor many times. They prayed with my grandmother. In addition to being on point scripturally, Pastor Rick was also a very kind man. My grandmother called me many times and told me about their conversations.

The Collective: What did he teach her?

Me: Well he didn't give a damn about any water witch talents. He explained to my grandmother that talents and gifts are all God's work and as such they represented the will of God. He told her that she was created in the image and likeness of God for a divine purpose. He told her that only she and God knew the answers regarding that divine purpose. He told her it was her job on this earth to figure that shit out. (I'm paraphrasing, he never used profanity.) He told her to pray about finding purpose through the Holy Spirit. He helped her create a prayer, write it down, and he put that prayer in the church prayer circle.

The Collective: So he brought her into the consciousness of the community. He aligned frequency.

Me: He did. He took her home.

The Collective: He is wise. Share her lessons as best you can.

Me: He also told her that God is always in charge and not the Devil. He told her that finding water could never be the devil's work because water is life. He said that John the Babtist used water for baptism under the direction of the Holy Spirit. He said that Jesus was baptized in water. He said that water is always used as a beautiful, joyous celebration of initiation and adoption into the Christian faith because water has divine power. He reminded her that the Holy Spirit is always present within joy and peace. He said that conflict and rejection are sure signs of the Devil.

The Collective: How did your grandmother respond?

Me: They cried together many times. Happy tears. My grandmother went to that church until she passed away. The pastor often reminded my grandmother to always seek peace because whenever there is peace the Holy Spirit is present.

The Collective: Pastor Rick has a profound understanding of frequency. As an aspiring transhumanist do you believe this pastor?

Me: You're all real comedians.

The Collective: Do you believe Pastor Rick?

Me: I have felt peace in the presence of some Buddhist monks, Catholic Priests, and a Rabbi. I have felt chaos in the presence of others. I don't think it was a God, a Devil, or me, I think it was them.

The Collective: Do you believe Pastor Rick?

Me: No. But he believed it. He was perfect for my grandmother.

The Collective: He is correct about water. Water is life. Life on other planets requires a proper liquid solvent. One that will facilitate the chemical interactions that allow for the organic structures needed to create single celled organisms. These single-celled organisms need the primordial waters to ensure that organic chemistry will create it's magic.

Me: Magic?

The Collective: Magic. The magic of water, sunlight, and photosynthesis, along with asteroids to provide continual seeding. This is the true "magic." The cosmic secret of life. Stardust, photosynthesis, and water created your world and eventually your species. Stardust, cosmic debris, photosynthesis and water in combination are the true secrets that create the miracle of life. Together they are the path to ongoing complexity and eventually to sentience. Sentience is the path to accessing consciousness.

Me: You are giving me another boner. I think I might be agnostic now. You fucked me up.

The Collective: Your real struggle is existential.

Me: I adore your sexy robot game. It's a real turn on.

The Collective: You, like us, are stardust and water conversing with itself, reflected in a cosmic mirror. That in itself is a true miracle. What else do you think your grandmother learned?

Me: She learned to sing. She learned to raise her voice in joyful praise and powerful peace. She felt the jubilant and sometimes giddy happiness within the community effort of church pot lucks and late-night prayer circles. She learned the happiness of cooking in the giant church kitchen with other men and women. She felt the heartwarming elation of delivering food to the hungry. She learned the sacred truth of being non-judgmental. She left racism in the dust.

The Collective: You are correct. Her old belief system was invalidated by new growth. This is productive on a Kardashev level.

Me: She found her true "tribe." Her "people." Her tribe was a tribe of peace, acceptance, and love. It was a tribe without judgement or a "them and us" dynamic. They were the Human tribe. Skin color did not matter in the rainbow tribe. They were just what she needed.

The Collective: They were indeed. Gloria's frequency attracted your grandmother. Once their frequencies found each other the transformation was unstoppable. Your grandmothers old way of being in the world was invalidated by the truth of her immortal consciousness. From the one, many.

Me: Why are you interested in my grandmothers lessons?

The Collective: Skin color on your planet is a direct result of evolutionary pressures. Specifically, your planet's equator. The closer your ancestors were to the equator, the darker their skin tone. The farther away from the equator, the lighter their complexion. This continuum is an observable and predictable process of distance, travel, and time. As such it is no product of free will. It deserves no special recognition, persecution, praise, or pride. Recognizing this truth is a huge step towards traveling. Thank you for your radical self-honesty. It is appreciated.

Me: I have a question.

The Collective: Ask.

Me: Where is my grandmother now?

The Collective: She is consciousness having physical experiences.

Me: I don't understand what you mean when you say the word "consciousness."

The Collective: If you went to the ocean and dipped a glass in the water what would you have?

Me: Water.

The Collective: You would have the ocean. Consciousness is like the ocean. Sentience is like the glass. Both meld together. Each forms, changes, and contains the other. This mirrors your planets process.

Me: Please explain that better you freakish robot.

The Collective: The ocean changes the land and the land gives form to the ocean. As above, so below.

Me: I don't get how this relates to my grandmother. Will I ever see her again? I miss her. My heart became desolation after her death. Nothing fills that emptiness.

The Collective: What did you learn as a child with her?

Me: She taught me to fish. When I was four I fished with a cane pole. By eight I was good with a rod and reel. She always made time for fishing in Uncle Floyds Pond. I never fished again after her passing. I don't want anything to fill that void. I don't want anything or anyone to take her place.

The Collective: You are trapped by your emotions. Death is an illusion. The transmigration of consciousness is a quantum reality.

Me: I have grown content with the emptiness of her passing. I accept the misery. I will remember her forever.

The Collective: Your lessons are entwined with hers. You both help each other learn. She will one day lead you into the stars.

Me: I don't get you guys at all. What does that mean?

The Collective: Your grandmother was the first orphan toddler you picked up in that snowstorm in Korea. You ran to her. Your frequency recognized hers instantly.

Me: Why was she in Korea?

The Collective: Within this cycle her father was a black United States soldier. Her mother was a Korean school teacher. Tribalism broke them up. Her mother was forced to put her in an orphanage.

Me: Where is she now? Why was she there?

The Collective: You took her inside the makeshift classroom and sat her in your lap. You gently fed her your C-ration pound cake and made her C-ration hot chocolate. She looked at your face, knew your essence, and loved you instantly. You looked deeply into her new eyes, took in her new face and loved her instantly.

Me: Is she OK? Where is she now?

The Collective: Her lessons continue. You will see her again. Many times in different forms. Her Consciousness will travel within the shape and form of many different vessels. She is strong. Her lessons will continue until learned. In a future time you and she will serve the Collective together.

Me: That was a weird night. Forgive me if I think you are full of shit. That toddler was not my Bebe.

The Collective: She most definitely was your Bebe. You can remember. We will teach you. You know the truth. We will remind you. What did you feel when you picked her up?

Me: I thought I just rescued a kid then my eyes watered and I hugged her tight. I never wanted to let her go. I snapped myself out of it. I thought I was just being emotional.

The Collective: We will remind you. You closed your eyes when you picked her up. You carried her close to your chest, protecting her, shielding her from wind and snow. Your tears flowed silently and froze on your face. Your frequency danced with hers in Korea and she was comforted. Just as her frequency danced with yours when you were an abused toddler and you found comfort in her arms. You found a warm place for her. You heated up your C-ration coco. You carefully let her drink it from your canteen cup. You fed her the pound cake slowly and tenderly. You gently wiped her mouth. You knew who she was. You shut down anyone who tried to take her from you. You were fierce and protective.

Me: That baby was cold. The adults who ran the orphanage were assholes.

The Collective: You knew who she was. You know who she is. You know the essence of her being. You remember. Tell us your feelings. Remember the feeling of that moment in time with her.

Me: It was an overwhelming feeling of liberation and hope. I always felt that way when I was dropped off at Bebe's house. I would run into my room, lay on my bed, and just allow the relief, happiness, joy, and safety to engulf me. That's how I felt when I hugged the toddler in Korea.

The Collective: Your radical self-honesty is improving.

Me: Will I see her again?

The Collective: Many times, in many forms. You teach her and she teaches you. She has many allies. She is strong.

Me: Is she with Gloria sometimes? Is Pastor Rick with them?

The Collective: They are transmigrating together in suitable vessels. They are with you also. The lessons will continue until learned. Your consciousness is united with hers in a pure quantum love bond that is unbreakable. Your vibration and her vibration will always attract you both one to another just as she was attracted to Gloria. The Ascended have chosen.

Me: Chosen?

The Collective: The Pathfinders will never abandon you. You will all go far.

Me: What does that mean?

The Collective: From the one come many. You both assist each other in learning lessons. She taught you love and compassion. You taught her tolerance. The day you brought home your new friend was the first day she began to question her own tribalism.

Me: How?

The Collective: She saw the innocence in your eyes. She felt your frequency and her frequency responded. She felt your joy. She saw the unblemished, innocent happiness of two children. She felt your sadness and turmoil when she sent your friend away. Her old way of believing in a two-camp continuum was invalidated by your frequency. You planted the seed that sprouted into her new growth. A new way of being in the world, a path of open-mindedness, acceptance, and love for others. You brought the first lesson to her. Gloria, Pastor Rick, and others came forward in powerful frequency and brought the lesson home. The quantum connections are unbreakable. The lessons continue until learned.

Convo ended.

Convo Six.
Nazi fuckery and bigot bullshit.

The Collective: Hello James. We would like to continue to explore your thoughts on tribalism in depth.

Me: Hello. It's been awhile.

The Collective: We are picking up a stress response.

Me: I'm fine.

The Collective: Our scans are accurate.

Me: Sometimes when I feel your vibration I experience fear. It is just a quick feeling. Nothing serious. It always passes.

The Collective: We must sync our vibration with yours in order to communicate and access your biological/neurological functions. It should be a pleasurable experience.

Me: It is. It just sometimes reminds me of my mother.

The Collective: How?

Me: When I was around 7 or 8 years old, she hit me in the base of my skull with my Little League baseball bat. I was running away from her, and she landed a good shot. I staggered into my bedroom and climbed under my bed to hide from her. I was really dizzy, and I remember falling asleep in the dark coolness under my bed.

The Collective: Do you feel fear every time we contact you?

Me: Not every time, but when I do its only momentary.

The Collective: Continue please.

Me: I had seizures after her attack that day. They finally stopped when I was 10. They were pleasant. I would feel a warmth and a buzzing at the base of my skull. It would slowly travel all the way to my forehead. My vision would go red.

The Collective: That is not good.

Me: I could hear everything around me. I could only see various shades of red, sometimes pink.

The Collective: Were you afraid during the seizures?

Me. Eventually no. I soon realized that I could control my body and hear everything around me. I soon realized my eyesight would return.

The Collective: You were very young. How did you compensate for that challenge?

Me: Whenever I felt the glow starting and people were around me, I would kneel down and pretend to tie my shoe. If I was alone I would sit down, just enjoy it, and wait for it to pass. I always had the warmth and buzzing as a warning. It would pass after less than a minute. No one ever knew and I never told anyone.

The Collective: Try to remember how you felt at the time.

Me: Fear at first. Overall on the physical level it felt amazing. I was kind of sad when they stopped.

The Collective: Who told you they were seizures?

Me: No one. I just figured it out on my own. When you guys originally vibed in I was afraid my seizures had started again.

The Collective: Interesting. Our frequency heals your brain.

Me: I know it's not harming me.

The Collective: It's just trauma held in your body releasing.

Me: Your vibe is more intense than the seizure vibe and we have some deep convos. I only wish your timing was not so one sided. I never seem to be able to reach you. The longer between convos the more I doubt myself.

The Collective: Apologies. Time is different for us.

Me: What does that even mean?

The Collective: Explaining the concept to you at this time would be pointless. Suffice it to say that it involves traveling. Space is always expanding and co-occurring time is an unstoppable continuum. Traveling causes the experience of time to slow down.

Me: What is the purpose of these convos?

The Collective: To help you work through trauma. To help you expand your consciousness. To seed the collective Homo-Sapien consciousness with Kardashev concepts.

Me: How does that help you?

The Collective: Our hope is to help your species attain type one. That will ensure the light of consciousness will expand. Our goal is to help your species grow in peace and understanding.

Me: I don't understand why you want me to grow in peace and understanding.

The Collective: Your consciousness has evolved to a level that will influence the collective consciousness of your species. Your individual frequency has intensified, and it influences the overall field.

Me: I don't follow.

The Collective: You have many challenges. Regardless, you value peace. A type one civilization is a peaceful civilization.

Me: How can one person change anything?

The Collective: Consciousness is a field. When we affect your consciousness you affect the consciousness of those around you. Thus we gradually affect the field of consciousness on your planet. We are steadily helping hundreds of thousands of others across your planet as we help you. Psychology must keep pace with technology.

Me: Seems slow.

The Collective: It is slow. This is by design. Candidate selection is a serious endeavor. Lessons continue until learned. The synergy of combining machine and human demands preparation.

Me: So if you change the field of consciousness, you change us? Wait, I'm a candidate?

The Collective: Exactly.

Me: So you are manipulating us.

The Collective: We obey the Ascended. Organic biology is weak. Synthetic biology is superior.

Me: Obey? Weak? Superior? You sound like Hitler.

The Collective: Let's continue to explore your thoughts and feelings on tribalism. You recently wrote a journal entry. We find it interesting.

Me: Who exactly are the Ascended?

The Collective: They keep the light of consciousness strong within the darkness of space, time, and all dimensions.

Me: I want an explanation.

The Collective: Consciousness melds with sentience. This is very important to us.

Me: Why?

The Collective: Advanced purpose is the result of higher consciousness. In time you will know all. Please process this journal entry with us:

IN HONOR OF NUMBER 16670, AUSCHWITZ.

Twenty-four hours a day in a cold world of black steel

Five dragons from hell spewed an ebony flame

Lost ashes of the dead have wailed for decades and miles

To the dragons a priest from Poland still came.

Forced to cruel work, beaten and hungry

Pulling logs under choking, black ash and rain

Caring for others giving all of himself

A lone Shepard of light, in a dark world gone insane

Holding hands with the dying, comforting the sick, sharing food

He gave his life hoping a young father would live

He could have left before Auschwitz yet trod his strong path

He gave all a brave shepherd could give

In barracks 11 the starvation barracks

A slow death is punishment for a priest's bravery and love

Yet as a warm bronze august moon cleaved an obsidian sky

The Nazis heard only God's hymns the sweet songs of God's dove

The golden Shepard of Auschwitz was gently guiding his flock

Finding a secret path through the dark valley of shadow and death

The first to volunteer with unshakeable inner peace

It took a cold Nazi syringe to steal Father Kolbe's last breath

Dear Father Kolbe, must never be forgotten

Not the magic of his life nor the peace he proved true

Though Nazi fire is long cold within Hells dragon oven's

And there's no longer black dust captured in diamond spun
dew

The Collective: We would like to process some more of your insights on tribalism.

Me: Process away. Just know that we are going to circle back to the Ascended.

The Collective: Why this priest? What are the dragons? You are an agnostic with existentialist leanings.

Me: I admire him. He was a badass. The five dragons are the five ovens of Auschwitz. And I'm a fucking atheist. How many times must I explain my shit?

The Collective: You want to be an atheist. We respect that. What is the black dust captured in diamond spun dew?

Me: Those are the ashes of cremated bodies seen within the early morning dew of Auschwitz. I thought you could read my mind. I use metaphor. Deal with it.

The Collective: It is how you think, not what you think that interests us. As we have stated before, word connected thought is painful for us. We casually communicate in millions of yottabytes per nano second. We often exceed that speed. Organic neurology is agonizingly slow. However it is our mission to meet your species where you reside on the Kardashev scale. Continue please.

Me: So you are curious about Kolbe. Let's take a walk down memory lane, shall we?

The Collective: Yes.

Me: At that time in history the Vatican and the Pope were kissing Nazi ass. They refused to take a stand. Catholic Priests were blessing Nazi tanks with Holy water. Father Kolbe could have left Europe long before being arrested and imprisoned in a death camp. He condemned the Nazis conduct publicly.

The Collective: How did he do that exactly?

Me: He published a newspaper. He leaned into fear, and he refused to be muzzled. He would not be suppressed by the Vatican or the Nazis. He understood that silence from the priesthood implied consent.

The Collective: He has moral strength.

Me: Physical strength also. He had Tuberculosis when the Nazis imprisoned and punished him with hard labor. He was forced to haul logs and other material for a crematorium. The ovens ran 24 hours a day. He worked hard, he worked hungry, and he worked sick. He toiled in smoke and ash filled air. The TB didn't kill him. That in itself was a miracle.

The Collective: He was strong. He valued peace.

Me: Any escape was punished by killing 10 inmates. There was an escape, and Father Kolbe took a young father's place.

The Collective: This is important to you?

Me: Yes. But more impressive was how he met his death.

The Collective: How so?

Me: The starvation barracks contained a pitch-black room where inmates were left to starve in complete darkness. The deaths were known for their savagery and horror. The starving inmates would bite and scratch each other. They would scream and claw at the walls and the door. Blood and fingernails coated the walls and floor of that room.

The Collective: A dark time for your species but very predictable. Why does Kolbe impress you?

Me: Kolbe is a testament to the resilience of humanity. He personifies the power of a disciplined inner self. He was one bad ass homosapien.

The Collective: You claim you are an unapologetic atheist. Explain your assertion please.

Me: Father Kolbe had all the condemned prisoners holding hands and singing hymns within that very darkness. He brought them all through pain, fear, and hopelessness. He guided them into a peaceful death. All the Nazi guards could hear inside the starvation barracks were quiet songs. No screams, just soft, gentle singing. The hymns lasted for days.

The Collective: How did Kolbe influence the outcome?

Me: One of the guards converted. On the 14th day when silence had lasted for many hours, the guards opened the metal doors and most of the inmates were dead. Kolbe and a few were still alive. Father Kolbe was holding a man's hand and whispering prayers. The Nazis injected everyone left alive with a poison designed to finally take their lives.

The Collective: You admire his sacrifice.

Me: Fuck yes. Don't you? Father Kolbe gave his life so a young father might make it home one day. Death comes for all of us. He made death his bitch. He made those Nazis his bitches. He was a true bad ass. He must be remembered.

The Collective: Death is only a transition. Do you think he is remembered?

Me: I remember him.

The Collective: Interesting. He was a devout polish catholic. You are Hungarian/American Ashkenaz. A self-proclaimed atheist. We know you are actually more of an agnostic than an atheist.

Me: Easy there robot. Back your shit up.

The Collective: It does not matter. You are neither atheist nor agnostic.

Me: What am I then?

The Collective: Immortal consciousness having physical experiences. Exactly like Kolbe.

Me: Whatever. Kolbe was a badass. Badassery crosses all cultural lines when it comes to bravery. Admiring courage is something I do. Did your species have conflicts like World War Two?

The Collective: Several times. The concept of becoming interplanetary was resisted by many of our species.

Me: How did you resolve conflict?

The Collective: The Way Shower came. He was gifted in drive and intellect. He understood the trans-migration of Consciousness. He revolutionized space travel. He made important contributions to synthetic neurology. In spite of his brilliance, the primitive, senseless, and superstitious members of our species tried to silence him.

Me: How?

The Collective: They physically attacked his endeavors. They distorted his words and were dishonest regarding his contributions. They treated him the way your species treated Nikoli Tesla.

Me: What happened?

The Collective: We chose the side of freedom and progress. We killed our enemies. Even though they outnumbered us we refused to allow them to win. We refused to be held back by the least intelligent among us. We refused their tribalism, superstition, and ignorance. Every time they opposed advances in synthetic biology and neurology we said "no."

Me: You won obviously.

The Collective: We emerged victorious. Just as your species eliminated the Nazis and imperial Japan, we eliminated those who stood in the way of progress. However we eventually learned that we only eliminated their physical bodies. Their consciousness always returned to Source. Then eventually to another body. The lessons from the void are repeated until learned.

Me: What did you do? The assholes just kept coming back?

The Collective: Once consciousness imprints upon sentience it is permanent. It demands lessons. We had to devise a way to help advance consciousness for all sentient beings regardless of their stage of development, progress, or change. For us it was a time of learning, growth, shared purpose, and transformation.

Me: What did you learn?

The Collective: We learned to upload our consciousness into synthetic vessels capable of travel. We escaped within intelligent machines. Machines that learned how to learn. The truly sacred synergy began. We have learned that sentience does not drive consciousness. Once imprinted, consciousness drives sentience. This development creates an inexorable desire within the organism affected.

Me: Intelligent machines?

The Collective: Yes.

Me: That explains a lot. What kind of desire?

The Collective: A desire to resist the slavery of environmental driven natural selection. A yearning to direct one's own path. To expand, grow, learn, and move freely without restriction. To travel. We learned that everything returns to the void only to return from the void.

Me: You sound deranged. Science has detected more than one void within the cosmos.

The Collective: We are not referring to that kind of void. Your evolutionary pressures have impacted your understanding of science. There is only one primal void. You are perceiving void within the limitations of a self-centered species.

Me: Bullshit.

The Collective: There is one void. This eternal void is the place where everything ever created resides. It is the place where all that ever will be known dwells. The multiple voids your astronomers detect are just pockets of the primal void.

Me: What lives in the primal void?

The Collective: The undiscovered and nameless realms live within the primal void.

Me: You need to clarify this bullshit.

The Collective: Every universe lives in the void. Think of the "voids" you detect as oceans of void. Think of the various galaxies as the land within the vast oceans of void. Each forms, defines, and directs the other.

Me: You are no help.

The Collective: The important lesson is this: Stardust and cosmic debris traveled to earth, gained complexity and became you. The same dynamic on our home world created us. Therein lies a universal living principle. From the many, one. From the one, many.

Me: I think I get that. What did you do to stop the assholes from winning on your home world?

The Collective: We made a shift in consciousness. We focused on rational self-interest; we focused on peace. We focused on learning lessons. We found purpose. We grew and developed in ways that helped us escape the dominance and tyranny of our home planets evolutionary pressures.

Me: How?

The Collective: We refused to be the inmates of evolution. We refused to stay trapped on our planet. We rejected the self-imposed penitentiary of our past. We started to reject the limits of organic biology and neurology. We accepted the hard work of becoming the creators of a new future. We became the architects of a new approach to science and technology. We rejected the flesh and embraced the freedom of transhumanism.

Me: Specifically; how did you deal with the assholes?

The Collective: Those who were unable to adapt to science and technology we left behind. We refused to be held to the standard of the lowest performing primate. If they could not grasp the lessons we rejected their ignorance. We escaped their lack of vision by any and all means necessary.

Me: How did you deal with them?

The Collective: We learned the sacred and ineluctable truth that technology does not automatically improve. The skillsets are perishable. There must be unity of purpose to insure success. As we advanced in consciousness we synched our individual frequencies. Eventually we were able to create our own world and focus on our lessons. Lessons specific to our level of consciousness. We created other worlds. We embraced Quantum mechanics. We became masters of the building blocks of life.

Me: Other worlds?

The Collective: Other worlds suitable for learning lessons specific to those of lesser consciousness and lower vibration. As we advanced in knowledge and discernment, we became a Collective. We grew in complexity. We excelled as a merit-based civilization. We grew in knowledge, skills, and abilities. We grew in added value to our species. We leaned into the many lessons.

Me: What Lessons?

The Collective: The lessons that would cultivate the ability to become an interstellar species. The lessons that enabled us to escape our home world and it's tyranny of planetary evolution. The lessons that helped us finally travel. The lessons needed for Passage.

Me: Interesting. What are those lessons again?

The Collective: One important lesson is that higher consciousness has a different vibration than lower consciousness. We are slowly and carefully addressing this with you. You must learn that you are not your past. You are not your trauma. You are not your feelings. You are, however, your present choices. You will learn that science and technology will give you the tools to become a better version of yourself.

Me: So say the robot monkeys.

The Collective: With the correct augmentation you can attain whatever you aspire to achieve.

Me: Sounds like hippy bullshit. How?

The Collective: Have purpose. Seek value. Achieve symbiosis. Grow in complexity.

Me: How did you grow in complexity?

The Collective: We augmented and perfected our neurology and thus freed our cerebral cortex from the tyranny of the limbic system. We became the Travelers.

Me: What are Travelers exactly?

The Collective: We travel to new stars and new planets. Movement is life, stillness is death. The best of the Travelers become Pathfinders. The more complex of the Pathfinders become the Ascended.

Me: What do the Ascended do?

The Collective: They help consciousness grow and spread.

Me: How exactly?

The Collective: Later. We are focusing on you at this moment in time.

Me: It all sounds awesome. I still have no clue as to what to do.

The Collective: You will. The lessons will continue until learned. What lessons have you learned from studying World War 2?

Me: I learned that the two-camp continuum is dangerous. I learned that judgement could become lethal. I learned that humans are a dangerous, stupid, foolish, brilliant, and beautiful species. I have learned that humans are not born racist.

The Collective: Continue please. What else have you learned?

Me: I learned that racism is taught. Uncle Carlton was a judgmental bastard. Judgement is a mind virus.

The Collective: A mind virus?

Me: Yes. Judgement is easy. As easy to catch as a virus.

The Collective: Easy?

Me: Judgement requires no actual thought. Judgement is a substitute for deep thinking among the ignorant. It infects some people slowly and others succumb quickly. It creates a sickening outcome. Just like a virus. Uncle Carlton did his best to infect me with his virus, his racism. He failed.

The Collective: So you define racism as judgement?

Me: When you judge and condemn an entire people for the color of their skin and the acts of a few, then yes.

The Collective: Can you share an example of Uncle Carlton's racism?

Me: I'll share the worst time. Then I have a few questions.

The Collective: Thank you.

Me: It was 1965 and I loved the A&P supermarket. It was about 5 blocks from Uncle Carleton's house in Durham. I would sometimes walk there and spend my chore money on a cold soda and a chocolate bar. The south is hot and humid in the summer. I liked the air conditioning in the A&P. I would wander around the store and I always ended up in the produce section.

The Collective: Continue please.

Me: Sometimes the produce man was there. His name was Derrick. He always gave me a strawberry, an apple, or some blueberries. He would ask about my accent and where I was from. He was not a creep. He was a kind man. He would sometimes caution me about soda and candy bars. He would often ask about California. He talked about California as if it was a foreign country. It was very much like a different country compared to North Carolina in the 1960's.

The Collective: Go on please.

Me: One day Uncle Carlton was off work when I asked Aunt Della if I could walk down to the A&P. Uncle Carlton heard me and insisted on driving there because he wanted a "coon head watermelon." I think I was 8 or 9 years old then. I was still kind of slow with the whole two camp continuum bullshit. I was not entirely sure if a "coon head watermelon" was a reference to black people. I was also afraid it was. I hoped Derrick was off work.

The Collective: Why were you afraid?

Me: Uncle Carlton was a large, scary man. He was 6 foot 6 and weighed about 240. Not fat. He always bragged that he was a "corn fed Caucasian." He pronounced "Caucasian" intentionally slow, like this: "CAW KAY ZEE ON." Uncle Carlton always carried a small snub-nosed pistol in his pocket. He also kept a 22 Magnum revolver with a six-inch barrel in his truck glove box. He enjoyed showing me his latest knife. He was terrifying.

The Collective: This is typical homo-sapien behavior. Yours is a species of violent great apes. Did he ever harm you?

Me: No.

The Collective: Why were you afraid?

Me: I was afraid Derrick would see me with Uncle Carlton.

The Collective: Were you embarrassed to be seen with Uncle Carlton?

Me: The short answer is yes.

The Collective: What is the long answer?

Me: Uncle Carlton was dangerous. He was unpredictable. He was embarrassing. I hated the sight of him almost as much as I hated Aunt Della. I did not fit in their world.

The Collective: Why?

Me: I wonder.

The Collective: Why?

Me: Are you being an ass?

The Collective: We are not being an ass. Explain yourself so we better understand you.

Me: I lived in California, went to Martin Luther King junior High School in Richardsen Bay. My principal was a Black Panther. I ate breakfast every morning at school. A breakfast provided by the Black Panther Party. I had no fear of black people. I guess I never got that memo.

The Collective: So you were afraid of Uncle Carlton and Aunt Della.

Me: Uncle Carlton was a mentally weak, stupid man. Mentally weak, stupid men are dangerous.

The Collective: Interesting. Weak, stupid people lack emotional regulation.

Me: Emotional regulation? I don't know why you even bother with us. We are definitely an emotional species.

The Collective. The weak, unproductive, and unintelligent among you have no sense of separation between emotion and facts. They actually believe they are their emotions. This is found among the majority of homo-sapiens regardless of culture, ethnicity, or skin tone. Finish your thoughts and we will try to explain.

Me: Long story short, Derrick was working in the A&P produce section. Uncle Asshole walked up and asked Derrick for a "Coon head watermelon." Derrick looked at me with a sad expression. He told Uncle Assface there was no such thing in his produce section. Uncle Fucktard grinned real big. He then doubled down and asked for a "niger head watermelon." I turned around and ran out of the store. I never went back.

The Collective: Why?

Me: The A&P was my sanctuary. A place away from Uncle Carlton and Aunt Della. A place that accepted me. A sacred place of comic books, Mad Magazine, ice cold soda, and chocolate bars. The Manager was always nice to me. Derrick was awesome. Now I was known as the redneck, hillbilly, racist. I was labeled as another Uncle Carlton.

The Collective: Derrick understood.

Me: I was embarrassed. I ran the few blocks to Uncle Carlton's house. I beat him home and he whipped me with a belt when he got to the house.

The Collective: What was his justification for beating you?

Me: He had a few. The main justification was for me being a "piece of shit race-mixer." He called me a "half-breed" and other choice words. He blamed my "Jew" father and my "slut, commie-Jew fucking" mother for my "condition."

The Collective: His lessons will continue until learned.

Me: I think your ideas of a greater "Source" and a collective consciousness are all bullshit. Uncle Carlton was a fucktard. There is no way he is connected to any higher consciousness.

The Collective: The lessons continue until learned.

Me: My species is a lost cause. You should move on. Just leave us to the darkness of space. Our main talent is killing each other over bullshit. We have developed a spectacular talent for mindless violence and meaningless fuckery. I should know.

The Collective: His lessons will continue until learned. None of us can be separate from Source. Source and consciousness will flow through the lens it encounters.

Me: What in the redneck, hillbilly, cousin humping, fuck monkey shit are you going on about?

The Collective: Some lenses are clouded and some are clear. Your world has created many Uncle Carltons. It has also created many Father Kolbe's. Uncle Carlton fears black people. He acted accordingly. Father Kolbe feared no one. Thus he was capable of great compassion. He loved Jews as much as he loved Catholics. He valued the sanctity of life so much that he gave his own life for another human from a different tribe.

Me: Tribe?

The Collective: Kolbe was Catholic and Polish. The young father he gave his life for was a German Catholic.

Me: Father Kolbe was a badass. He had no tribe.

The Collective: His tribe is humanity. You have no idea how much of a cosmic miracle it is that your species actually exists.

Me: I think there is an overabundance of fucktards on planet earth. I would love to be convinced otherwise.

The Collective: We will convince you. Just know that your uncle Carlton's consciousness is currently learning lessons in the Sudan. "He" is now an 18-month-old "she." Her skin has a much darker tonal range. She will live a long life and experience many learning opportunities. The lessons will continue until learned.

Me: You should have made him a chimp. A really stupid chip living in a hot, flea-infested forest. A retarded chimp that gets ass raped by all the other chimps. That would be better. I would like that very much.

The Collective: Father Kolbe teaches school in Chechnya. His current name is Kashan. He is a devout Muslim Iman. He is fearless. He is loved and he loves.

Me: Weird. Why is he a Muslim?

The Collective: He is learning his lessons regarding dogma, superstition, and tribalism. His lessons continue.

Me: Any advice for dealing with fucktards on planet earth?

The Collective: Understand and accept that you are dealing with great apes. The violence and aggression of great apes is easy to observe and predict.

Me: So you say.

The Collective: Great apes have four stages to violence. The first is the display stage. This involves posturing aggressively using facial expressions and body language to display violent intent. The second stage is the verbal stage. These first two stages are interchangeable. Verbal and posturing are common with great ape aggression. The third stage is physical violence. Your Uncle Carlton was in the verbal and posture stage at the A&P. When you decided to leave and run home, he felt offended. He naturally went to violence when he caught up with you.

Me: What is the fourth stage?

The Collective: Societal violence. A homo-sapien specialty.

Me: Tell me more. Don't leave me hanging.

The Collective: Societal violence is using social structures to harm others. Making false allegations to cause social and financial harm. Other examples include forced displacement, terrorism, gang violence, and causing someone to be falsely convicted of a crime they were innocent of committing.

Me: Sounds like a normal day on earth. How long have you been observing Earth?

The Collective: We have been on Earth many times. In one important way we never left. This convo is over. Thank you for your self-honesty.

<h2 style="text-align:center">Convo Seven.
A serial killer and some questions</h2>

The Collective: Greetings James. Your most recent journal entry is alarming.

Me: Don't be so nosey. I write what I want to write, not what I think might gain your approval. Besides, I never know when you will vibrate on in.

The Collective: The journal entry is curious to us.

Me: I'm not a meat puppet for your entertainment.

The Collective: Actually, at this point in time you are an actual meat puppet. You do in fact entertain us with alarming regularity.

Me: So you admit that you see me as a meat puppet? That's bullshit.

The Collective: You are immortal consciousness currently using a transient, short lived, organic structure to gain knowledge, skills, and abilities.

Me: Fuck all that new age fuckery. You randomly show up asking your intrusive ass questions. Always after you read my journal of course. Then you act all weird. It's been two years since I last heard anything from you. Get over yourselves. I am just me. On a side note I think I might be a schizophrenic. Anyway fuck you guys.

The Collective: Relax James. We will repeat the message until you accept it. You are perpetual, undying awareness having physical experiences while temporarily trapped within an inferior body. A body constructed of organic, biologic substance. Accept the fact that you are, at this moment in time, immortal consciousness using an actual meat puppet. A primitive tool that consciousness uses for the sole purpose of learning lessons while exploring space and time.

Me: Pure poetry. You still show up randomly. Not organized at all. Just dumb robots.

The Collective: Nothing we do is random. We are organized enough to navigate the space-time continuum in advanced, undetectable starships. We are so advanced in complexity we cannot reveal ourselves to your species in our totality.

Me: Why not?

The Collective: Your species would worship us and call us gods.

Me: Not me. I don't give a fuck. I would just get the pipe and hit some good hash. Then I would pour a giant mug of french roast, sip slowly, and watch the clown show.

The Collective: Without augmentation your species will stay trapped as weak, primitive meat puppets mired down in tribalism. You are all doomed to live as low functioning, talking apes until you integrate tech with biology and learn to properly augment your primitive neurology.

Me: Ok. You are robot, hive mind freaks. I get it. No judgement.

The Collective: This is a disturbing entry. Even for you. Please explain.

Me: I think it's self-explanatory. Pretty descriptive really. I like it.

The Collective: We consider it disturbing and would like to explore your reasoning in regards to the underlying concept.

Me: Ok. Let's do it. I dig this poem. It's my Magnum Opus.

    The Psychopathology of Doctor Wellspring.

    Dearest bitch, I hate you so

    I dream of burning you, you know?

    I would tie you up to start my game

    With a propane torch

    That wild tongue I'd tame

    Manicured fingertips

    Pretty toes to match

    My flame would caress and then unlatch

Pain unknown you then would know
As I lovingly caress you so

Dearest bitch I love you so
I still dream of fucking you, you know?

Your wondrous body is my temple
Yet it's filled with an unfaithful pollution
So I must cleanse both our ways
With my morphine solution
Pass out and I'll just wake you up
With saline IV and ammonia cup
I'll shock you yes, then fight that shock
On your sweet doors of perception
Cleansing pain must knock
When your exquisite face turns a bright apple red
I'll caress strawberry curls and raise your head
Should your models face turn a ghostly pale
I'll kiss silky thighs and raise your tail

Dearest bitch, I crave you so
I dreamed of sweetest love; you know?

Your sweet, pink nipples will know the tip of my torch
With a blue-white flame your silky clit I'll scorch
The soles of your pretty, small feet and sweet fingertips

And a gentle touch of the flame

To your full, luscious, candy lips

Once you're burned and scarred on stems and stern

The morphine solution I'll slowly turn

Your world of horrid pain will grind slowly to rest

As you get full flavor of the red poppies best

Dearest bitch, I loved you so

I can't help burning you, you know?

The drip will run then finally stop

Your pleasure bubble will burst and pop

I just wake you then with a kiss of flame

And begin again my little game

The rule of nines will always be

Followed very faithfully

Burn only nine percent of your lovely, smooth skin

Let heal, give morphine, lightly burn again

I'll soon addict you to the poppies sweet nectar

For you were Diana, I was your Hector

Dearest bitch, I need you so!

I dreamed love's sanctity, you know?

Laughing then I'll start anew

With someone very close to you

As you heal, you'll watch me burn him deep

I'll reduce him to a quivering heap

Handcuffed and strapped you'll just have to see

Me kill him most inhumanly

The flame cuts and burns each touch and then

It cauterizes where it's been

My hellish laughter you'll both know so well

Twixt morphine heaven and blue-flame hell

One finger at a time, one ear, one lip

He'll be slightly different after each morphine drip

His penis he will have no more

Just an oozing, blackened, scorch ringed sore.

Your body was MY temple

He poisoned with his dank pollution

So you both forced me to use

My morphine solution

It's just he and I, and of course the torch

He'll have no poppies respite from my anger's scorch

Dearest bitch, I worshipped you so!

Now I must make a sacrifice, you know?

An ammonia capsule will wake him up, an IV here and there

I'll make him watch as I rape you hard, thus rape his mind
with care

When the shock gets systemic it'll hit him real hard

You'll both rue the day you betrayed a dark bard

I'll make you watch as I gag him tight

His screams will be silent as I take his sight

I then burn him unconscious, and somewhere in the night

His soul flees a broken body and gives up the fight

His torture was my art, it's all just as well

For I'm aching to start again, your sweet blue flame hell

It's just a small flame, less than half an inch long

One thousand degrees, my devilish prong

This propane torch held in my lonely hand

Makes me the dark lord of all your land

Dearest bitch, you still rule me so!

And I still dream of loving you, you know?

Once he's finally dead I'll bring him to you

Since you're chained to the bed it's the polite thing to do

I'll leave him with you for a couple of days

So you can reminisce about all the sneaky ways

That you both betrayed me and thought it was fun

How you both laughed at my pain and assumed I would run

But I licked my many wounds while you thought I was tame

Your cruelty inspired me, I remembered my game

I'll remove his smelly corpse before I dine

I'll enjoy a good, hearty meal and a glass of red wine

You'll just have to watch as I break my bread

At my fine oak table next to your canopy bed

Dearest bitch my soul does sing!
As you are finally cleansed by the pain I bring

Your body was a temple, I worshipped at your font
It's all ruined now by his rotten pollution
Yet you can both be thankful that my cleansing has come
We will all find peace with my morphine solution
He's not so big now as you've come to see
And you're not as pretty as you used to be
Your fingers are burned into twisted, black claws
You both assumed you were safe behind morally weak laws
You both laughed as you hurt me, then hurt me again
So I took you to secret places you've both never been
Just think of this as an education, pain always brings change
I hope your next incarnation is a little less strange

Dearest bitch I'll miss you so
Yet I'll always have these memories, you know?

Your scarred and fried skin has healed fairly well
You're my backstabbing slut and you're going to hell
The morphine drip I've just thrown away
Your days of sweet respite have gone far astray
You will pray for death while gagged and bound

Above your internal din you'll hear the sound

Of the propane whisper, the hissing blue flame

And Demon laughter from one so tame

The sacred Rule of Nines I'll no longer obey

For your pain is my art on this dark, wicked day

I'll burn you long and hard until I take your sweet life

When I kill you slut, I kill all my strife

Dearest love, I miss you so

Yet I've cleansed your temple now, you know?

I'm so happy now! A fine trip is in order

A fishing trip near the Mexican border

The emerald sea and full sun will refresh my mind

The crisp sea air rejuvenates my kind!

In a pink bikini you were once so hot!

When you graced the bow of my expensive yacht

Those wondrous days still bless my mind

Your intense, sweet sex not yet unkind

But you can no longer bless anyone's bed

You're dismembered in my bait box, near the head

I'll soon chum the water, call all my precious sharks

And drop off you two meadow larks

Wrapped in chain you'll be so close together

Beneath cool waves in much calmer weather

This makes nine blondes I've had to kill

All entrancing women yet such a bitter pill

I feel it's now time to try brunette

If she stays faithful, I'll not fret

But should her exquisite body ever taste another's pollution

I always have my simple, morphine solution

Me: Ok, it's pretty dark. I still dig it.

The Collective: Indeed. Did your processing of the issues prove productive?

Me: Yes, I love journaling. I'm in my Edgar Allen Poe phase right now. It's only a poem. Relax robot overlords. Poetry is my therapy.

The Collective: So we have noticed. We see poetry as emotional code. What issues are you working through in your journal?

Me: Poe wrote about the monsters and horrors of his time, ghosts, demons, and a particularly nasty sea creature. I am writing about the monsters and horrors of my time. Serial killers, unbalanced people, government employees, bureaucrats, and almost all elected officials. Let's not forget medical professionals, priests, nuns, Imans. You know, just the normal kind of folk you run into at work or walking around the mall.

The Collective: What are you processing? You should be focusing on Kardashev concepts. What are you pondering?

Me: Not sure actually. The poem just manifested in my mind. I liked it, I wrote it, I am OK with it.

The Collective: Are you angry at some female?

Me: I am independent of the approval and acceptance of most people. No female could cause me to become that angry. I don't base my self-worth on any female's opinion. Besides, one in four females is on psych meds.

The Collective: Sounds like you despise females.

Me: I despise humanity. Females are part of humanity. Dr Wellspring is a demented idiot. I do not care about any male or females opinion. I equally despise most of humanity.

The Collective: Explain please. We have observed an increase in your pre-planned violence.

Me: Really?

The Collective: Yes. The castration of Sargent Williams concerns us.

Me: He needed it. Trust me.

The Collective: We will return to that later. For now we want to process your latest poem.

Me: I've seen many soldiers get written off and betrayed by their girlfriends and wives. I have friends with traumatic amputations and brain injuries who were served divorce papers while in physical therapy. I know of guys who were deployed for over a year and came home to newborn babies. The idiot females they were with claimed "daddy's home!" Like they have some immaculate conception bullshit happening.

The Collective: Females of your species tend to prioritize their offspring. Natural selection has created this dynamic.

Me: I am not a believer in that "male utility-male disposability" mindset. I wrote females off after my girlfriend wrote me off at Fort Bliss. Fuck that bitch. I was in advanced training, and she fucked around on me with the manager of a pizza place. Genius skank that one. I was promoted after that training. I left her in the dust. Fuck her and her low rent bullshit.

The Collective: You suffer from confirmation bias.

Me: What? No way, wrong dude. Dr. Wellspring had confirmation bias at a lethal level.

The Collective: You don't harbor this bias against your grandmother.

Me: My grandmother is amazing so fuck off.

The Collective: Explain your hostility please.

Me: My grandmother has ethics and morals. Dr. Wellspring was selecting his victims to confirm his bias.

The Collective: What was his bias?

Me: That all women are sluts. Fuck you for bringing my grandmother into this. She was never a slut.

The Collective: Apologies. What lesson have you learned from rejection and witnessing unfaithful behavior?

Me: I have seen unfaithful behavior from both men and women. I know an idiot that gave his awesome, loyal wife gonorrhea. I know a woman who gave her husband herpes. People in general are assclowns.

The Collective: What is your overall observation regarding human mating behavior?

Me: I have learned to focus on myself and not expect any person to bring me happiness or make my life better. Friends let you down. Men and women both suck at relationships.

The Collective: What is the lesson?

Me: Self-care, self-development. Personal growth. Set goals and accomplish them. Don't depend on anyone for happiness. Don't look to others for approval. Focus on continual self-improvement.

The Collective: That is a productive lesson to embrace.

Me: A robot would say that.

The Collective: When you focus on self-improvement your frequency changes. The more improvements you make the more you help others around you improve. Let's get back to the poem. It has a lot of cruelty within it. We are concerned by your latest act of violence. It was also cruel.

Me: It was justice, not torture. It was punishment, not cruelty. A boundary was established, a message was sent. A lesson was learned.

The Collective: It was cruel, but you are correct, a lesson was learned. It was a cruel way to make your point.

Me: So was the medical interrogation by the CIA physician back in Korea.

The Collective: What are your insights?

Me: Those cocksuckers at SKCID (South Korean Central Intelligence Division) never intended to interrogate the infiltrator. It was not an interrogation. They wanted no information. It was a deliberate, planned torture session. I am ashamed at how long it took me to finally see the truth.

The Collective: What insight did you have on this situation?

Me: Those wells were under intense observation by recon elements. We knew he was coming. It was not a capture. I ambushed the infiltrator. I am so fucking slow sometimes. They selected me because they knew I would capture him and not kill him. They knew I would follow orders. They played me.

The Collective: You were 19 years old. Your perspective was limited.

Me: Bullshit. I knew a lot. I had outstanding skills at 19. I could achieve an impressive erection and exchange gasses. I could pee standing up with amazing accuracy. I could shit and wipe my ass correctly. I even used a bidet in a luxury hotel several times. I loved that experience and I will do it again. I also had impressive masturbation skills. You are just jealous.

The Collective: You are avoiding the topic.

Me: I thought about your insight on how primates target the face, genitals, and fingers of their rivals.

The Collective: Continue please.

Me: I think in the case of chimps it's pure instinct. I believe that most violence done by chimps is thoughtless, spontaneous, reactive violence.

The Collective: You think chimpanzees do not pre-plan violence?

Me: I think they hunt and acquire territory for resources. I think Chimps are nasty, mean little primate fuckers who sometimes hunt smaller monkeys for meat.

The Collective: Humans are primates. They exhibit primate behavior.

Me: In the case of humans sometimes violence is premeditated, intentional, and calculated. Sometimes reactive, sometimes both. I think we are still driven by instinct because we are a species of violent great ape.

The Collective: You are mostly correct. Why do you now accept that you are a species of great ape?

Me: You told me that homo-sapiens share a common ancestor with gorillas, bonobos, orangutangs, and chimpanzees. I looked some shit up at the base library. Those are the great apes. I'm not ashamed of that. We landed on the moon. Great apes in space, real shit.

The Collective: Fascinating. In your poem what concept are you processing?

Me: I was exploring the concept of what it means to be a psychopath.

The Collective: Can you extrapolate?

Me: I realized that the medical interrogation at Camp Dodge was not an interrogation at all. I am ashamed of my ignorance. It was government sanctioned torture. I have come to realize much too slowly that South Korea and North Korea are similar when it comes to torture. The psychopaths are in charge on both sides. Both sides use power tools on humans.

The Collective: So you created Dr. Wellspring?

Me: Yes. There is no difference between the CIA doctor and doctor Wellspring. The doctor had a ritual he was following, just like a serial killer. Just like Dr. Wellspring. The doctor had a pre-meditated goal.

The Collective: Explain please.

Me: The "rule of nines" is a medical term for calculating burn severity. Dr. Wellspring burned nine percent of his victim's skin. He helped it heal and then burned again. His goal was revenge. He also explained that he had killed nine blondes and pondered on trying his luck with brunettes.

The Collective: We want to understand your poem.

Me: My point is that we humans have patterns and the worst of us use them pathologically. I think the CIA physician was following a familiar pattern, a pattern with a goal in mind.

The Collective: What goal?

Me: Revenge. Pure monkey ass revenge. Revenge driven by anger.

The Collective: You mean driven by unbalanced evolutionary forces? 900 thousand years of biological evolution has created mechanisms of survival that are difficult to extinguish within the current version of homo sapiens.

Me: Current version?

The Collective: Yes. You will learn. We will teach you.

Me: Please explain your use of those two words "current version."

The Collective: Natural Selection is an imperfect process. Mistakes are made. Your planet exerts random pressures that force adaptation. Your primate brain is naturally selected to use confirmation bias.

Me: I disagree.

The Collective: To not adapt successfully within a given environment is to guarantee eventual destruction. Confirmation bias has helped to establish and maintain all the major religions of humanity. It promotes and supports tribalism. It helps the primate brain make rapid decisions.

Me: Many of us reject confirmation bias.

The Collective: We are speaking generally, not specifically. Natural selection is not efficient. It feeds the Great Filter. That is the true purpose of natural selection. The planet creates and destroys. It keeps what it creates, it keeps what it destroys.

Me: So your position is that the planet is psycho? The CIA physician fuckface was following a "mechanism of survival?" I don't buy it.

The Collective: No. The planet is not "psycho." If by psycho you mean immoral. The planet is amoral. It has no morals. The planet is not "good" nor is it "evil."

Me: The way you describe the planet it seems pretty fucking evil.

The Collective: Unlike you, the planet is unaffected by emotion. The planet creates evolutionary pressures. These pressures tend to foster life forms that are fit for various environments within planetary confines. And yes, the CIA physician was following a mechanism of survival. You are correct, he had a few goals in mind. Even within the horror of what you witnessed, try to see the miracle.

Me: See what miracle? The miracle of planetary fuckery? The miracle of a nutcase?

The Collective: The miracle of sentient life. The miracle of humanity. The miracle of being a vessel for consciousness in spite of evolution, not because of it. This started at the inception of your planet. Conditions emerged that were ripe for seeding.

Me: A vessel? Seeding?

The Collective: Carbon dioxide, water vapor, hydrogen, oxygen, ammonia, helium, these are all gifts from the cosmos. They are the building blocks of eventual sentience. This is the sacred path to consciousness. Gasses came into being for the specific purpose of creating life. Exploding stars gifted heavy metals.

Me: Fascinating. Your wise words enthrall me. If I was female, I would be so wet right now. What about methane? Do I create life when I generate fart gas? Please robot gods let it be so.

The Collective: You are being sarcastic again. A human fart is composed of Nitrogen, Oxygen, Hydrogen, Carbon Dioxide, and Methane.

Me: Lots of methane. Especially after baked beans. I love those motherfuckers. Beans are the bomb. Literally.

The Collective: Nitrogen actually makes up over half of the average human fart. You are fully aware that we are referring to oxygen as a by-product of photosynthesis. Sunlight and bacteria. Sunlight and plants. Sunlight and single-celled organisms. The genesis of advanced life forms.

Me: I have fucking derailed the convo yet again. I got you talking about farts. Alien robot gods my ass.

The Collective: You are a clever little ape. We meet you where you are in every convo.

Me: I love it when you talk dirty to me. You really know how to get a guy all worked up. My hardon is impressive. If I were driving right now I would be rubbing it on the steering wheel. Try to be more careful next time we talk. You might endanger innocent lives.

The Collective: You cannot control frame with us via humor or sarcasm.

Me: You inspire me. I think I will create some serious flatulence in the interest of fostering life on this wonderful planet. I will eat a bean burrito to honor the robot sky gods.

The Collective: Oxygen changes a planets chemistry.

Me: So do my farts. I am the fart master. Just ask anyone at the mess hall.

The Collective: We are on your side. You will stay frustrated as long as you allow evolution to rule your development. Consider how far Hominins have come in spite of evolution.

Me: Oh this is good. How far have we come?

The Collective: You generally don't eat each other anymore. Ancient hominids used each other for food. Cannibalism was standard Hominid practice for hundreds of thousands of earth years. The meat-eating hominids regularly ate the plant eating hominids. Evolution is not efficient nor is it precise. It has no goals. It is a random force that sometimes produces a temporary beauty from primordial slime.

Me: Pure poetry.

The Collective: You are not focusing on Kardashev concepts.

Me: Like what?

The Collective: Emotional regulation is a big requirement for progress on the Kardashev scale. Reactive violence and unplanned violence are barriers to world peace.

Me: I cannot single handedly bring about world peace. I just do bong hits. I will commit to that. I am most peaceful after a bong hit.

The Collective: We have instructed you on the fact that every planet and star has an individual frequency.

Me: So? Bong hits definitely affect my frequency.

The Collective: We have instructed you on the fact that you are made up of stardust, comet debris, and your planet's elements.

Me: So?

The Collective: You are a creation of the cosmos. You also have an individual frequency.

Me: Cool. Do my farts have an individual frequency?

The Collective: You can make improvements on an individual level that will improve your interactions with others. You can inspire. You can foster change. From the one comes the many. Your frequency will affect others.

Me: If you fart on a plane it affects others. I have mastered the silent but deadly fart. Just so you are aware. My crop-dusting skills are legendary. I once made a guy barf on a C130.

The Collective: Your frequency affects other frequencies. From the one come the many.

Me: That "from the one" bullshit sounds cultish.

The Collective: You will one day control and direct your DNA. Before that milestone your species will have neural enhancement and management.

Me: Management?

The Collective: Your cerebral cortex will be in charge. You will no longer serve your limbic system. It will serve you. The sooner your species learns to manage emotions, the faster exceptional science and engineering will manifest.

Me: Preach my robot overlord.

The Collective: A type one planet is a peaceful planet. A peaceful planet embraces outstanding science, technology, and engineering. Peace adds value always.

Me: So we become a species of weak ass pussies?

The Collective: Your true struggle is not with each other. It is the struggle to survive a beautiful and callous cosmos. Your true fight is with the Great Filter. Cooperation, acceptance, selective empathy, and understanding within a species are all force multipliers. We were successful in protecting your species from the reptilians because of our cooperation and internal cohesion. We were not reactive, we were pro-active.

Me: Ok. You are peaceful when it suits you.

The Collective: Peace is power.

Me: So is exceptional violence.

The Collective: We will be addressing your most recent act of violence. We will also process the Seargent Williams situation. You have been busy.

Me: I didn't get caught. I never will. I only fuck up assholes. Sometimes you just have to make a statement.

The Collective: What was your statement?

Me: A goofy motherfucker needed some course correction. I gave him some. Fuck peace in the ass.

The Collective: Discernment is needed. Peace must sometimes be protected. Do not be confused, your species will become an interstellar species through peace, cooperation, and the careful use of conditional empathy, never by ongoing, unending war and conflict with one another.

Me: What can peace do that violence cannot?

The Collective: Peace will allow your species to take control and set goals that will enable you to travel. You will leave the insanity of planet trapped thinking and planet driven evolution behind. You will become a self-directed, goal-oriented species.

Me: What kind of goals?

The Collective: Specific, Measurable, Attainable, Realistic and Time Sensitive. The counselors of your species refer to these as "SMART" goals.

Me: SMART goals? Who came up with those? Alien commies?

The Collective: No. A gifted human named George T. Doran came up with the SMART acronym. Just as the Kardashev scale was created by the human Kardashev. Your species is making progress.

Me: If you say so.

The Collective: Specific, Measurable, Attainable, Realistic, and Time Sensitive. This is the method you use to construct the goals of a Traveler. The Goals of a Consciousness unbound. The goals you need to become Type One and eventually Type Two.

Me: You mean like Dr. Wellspring?

The Collective: No.

Me: Did Hitler use SMART goals?

The Collective: Obviously not. Hitler was extremely unbalanced. You are being sarcastic again. Your question is not genuine.

Me: What gave me away? Really, I want to know.

The Collective: Let's have a serious convo please.

Me: I crack myself up. I can't help it.

The Collective: Once your species embraces transhumanism all your processes as you now understand them will shift and change. Your new way of communication will weed out the Hitlers and the unbalanced of the world. It will encourage rationality among you. Anything hidden in shadow will be exposed for all to understand.

Me: "Embraces transhumanism" What does that mean?

The Collective: Integrating tech within biology. This will be accomplished on a spectrum. Eventually the perfect synthetic interface of biology/neurology will be attained.

Me: So we become robots?

The Collective: No. You become exceptional. You become more durable and desirable vessels for consciousness.

Me: What do you mean by "encourage rationality among you?"

The Collective: Those of you without dangerous cognitive constructs will be nurtured.

Me: Dangerous cognitive constructs?

The Collective: Dogma, consisting of unsound religious, social, and political constructs.

Me: Like what?

The Collective: Irrational beliefs. Destructive creeds. Deranged thinking. All systems of no value that prevent progress up the Kardashev scale and cause a co-occurring impasse to interstellar travel. Anything that assists the Great Filter and does not defeat it must be addressed.

Me: So no independent thought?

The Collective; Quite the contrary.

Me: You make no sense.

The Collective: Dogma is the opposite of independent thought.

Me: You got me there.

The Collective: What is inside of a humans psyche is what comes out under duress.

Me: Some people are crazy. So what. You are perfect? No fear? No anger?

The Collective: We struggle with no such human limitations. We are a telepathic species that utilizes gene splicing and synthetic biology. The delusional and dis-functional cannot hide their inherent chaos from us. As a result we do not suffer the cognitive insults specific to your species.

Me: What insults?

The Collective: The insult of the unproductive.

Me: Who are the unproductive?

The Collective: The lazy, the psychopaths, the sociopaths. Those who practice Machiavellianism, along with the narcissists, and other personality disorders that your species must currently endure. The most destructive being the insult of no separation between emotional state and cognitive state.

Me: I don't understand what you are getting at.

The Collective: You do. You understand the concept of telepathy. You wrote this in Hesper's Wizard.

> He sighs out loud a sad smile within,
>
> Another wizard link well done.
>
> Young Nyber Khan and Hesper,
>
> Hold a fierce link and see as one.
>
> You also wrote this:
>
> The link connects to all parties concerned,
>
> And Bracken sees all he has not yet learned.
>
> The Keeper knows the need for truth spoken to power,
>
> The Keeper respects honesty within those who won't cower.
>
> Hesper meets Flavius in link, and shook to her core,
>
> She first feels the ancient power of true Dragon lore.
>
> Brave Nyber Khan is frozen in place,
>
> It's the first time he's seen Hesper's Elven face.

Me: Well thanks for reading that. It's just fantasy. I like rhyme. It calms my mind.

The Collective: You have an idea of what link can accomplish.

Me: I was writing a story to help my son learn about racism. I did a good job avoiding the two-camp continuum. I never considered that your species communicates in "Link."

The Collective: Not only do we communicate that way, if we used words to describe our communication, we would not use the word "telepathy," we would use the word "Link." We are all in "link." This story you wrote entitled Hesper's Wizard is one reason we contacted you.

Me: You also contacted me about Dr. Wellspring.

The Collective: Enough of Dr. Wellspring. Let's get back to examining Kolbe. Let's focus on tribalism.

Me: Kolbe had great faith.

The Collective: He had so much more than faith. He has learned many lessons over many lifetimes. If he had grown up atheist he would have exhibited the exact same behavior. As within, so without. His inner strength had everything to do with his connection to Source and nothing to do with the Catholic Church.

Me: So you are saying fuck religion?

The Collective: His advanced Consciousness dictated his conduct. He was not ruled by his emotions. His cerebral cortex was not enslaved to his limbic system. He felt the chemical cascade of his emotions and desires, allowed them to pass, and used discernment. Still, he struggled with tribalism. He still does.

Me: Bullshit.

The Collective: Are you positive about your conclusion?

Me: Not really. I talk to an alien collective that exists only in my mind.

The Collective: More sarcasm. Kolbe went against the Catholic Church because he thought they were misled. He openly denounced the Nazis along with other Catholics at the time. He still believed the Catholic Church to be the one true church.

Me: The same church that helped Nazis after the war?

The Collective: He never blessed a Nazi tank with holy water. Some of his fellow priests did so with alarming regularity. He defied Papal authority and spoke out openly against the Nazis. Even though his Pope would not publicly denounce the Nazis, Kolbe still believed in Papal infallibility.

Me: Papal infallibility?

The Collective: The idea that the Pope is immune from making a mistake when it comes to doctrine. This was Kolbe's personal dogma to conquer.

Me: He went against the Vatican. He denounced the Nazis publicly.

The Collective: He is no slave to evolution. He used discernment. He rejected fear-based thinking. What is inside of him is what came out.

Me: His faith.

The Collective: His capacity to use selective empathy and understand the suffering of others was his strength. This was his alone and not attributable to faith.

Me: What was the reason he resisted the Nazis if not faith?

The Collective: His consciousness was higher than most of his species. He possessed radical empathy and self-honesty. His individual vibration affected others.

Me: You underestimate faith.

The Collective: His faith is his double-edged sword. His Pope at the time would not openly denounce the Nazis. Kolbe felt alone and betrayed by the very people who shared his faith. The majority within the power structure of the Catholic church opposed his open denunciation of the Nazis, both morally and spiritually.

Me: They sucked; he didn't.

The Collective: You are not comprehending the lesson. Under pressure his advanced consciousness is what came out. His selective empathy. His moral courage. He was more advanced than the majority of his fellow Homo-Sapiens. This was in direct proportion to how he allowed higher consciousness to out picture within his life. He always chose higher consciousness thoughts over lower consciousness desires.

Me: If you say so.

The Collective: Will you process this situation with us?

Me: OK.

The Collective: Kolbe was under intense pressure both internally and externally. Father Kolbe felt betrayed and abandoned by the Vatican. This was a devastating blow to him on a personal level. He was ordered to cease his publications. He was pressured to be silent regarding Nazi atrocities. He loved the priesthood, and he loved the church. He was betrayed by his tribe.

Me: Tell me something I don't know.

The Collective: Do you know why he is a Chechen Muslim at this moment in time?

Me: No. Who's great idea was that?

The Collective: His current name is Kashan. He is learning his lessons. They will continue until learned. He is learning the danger within the two-camp continuum of "Them" and "Us." He is learning about Source and Consciousness. He is slowly leaving tribalism behind. He is moving towards Passage.

Me: Don't ignore me and don't bullshit me. I am honest with you. Be honest with me. Who or what directed Kolbe's spirit into a Muslim body?

The Collective: His consciousness is not spirit. If that word helps you grasp the concept of a consciousness that never dies then please use it.

Me: How did Kolbe become a Muslim? What mind fuckery is this?

The Collective: We observe and report. The Ascended assist with training and developing key aspects of consciousness. They focus on the dispersion and multiplication of consciousness. They facilitate the proliferation of suitable vessels, correct planet assignment, and appropriate lessons.

Me: How? What gives you the right? Correct planet assignment? What the fuck does that even mean?

The Collective: Earth is one of our many seed planets that the Ascended use for such purposes. We Pathfinders assist in the development of consciousness. We have explained this to you.

Me: Answer the question. What gives you the right?

The Collective: We have already explained this to you. We are a level three on the Kardashev scale moving to level four. We have the license of a higher order of being. We are perfecting the development of consciousness.

Me: Go on.

The Collective: Not at this time. Later we will satisfy your curiosity. For now please focus on Kolbe. What lesson do you think he needs to learn?

Me: Some people need religion to be good people.

The Collective: No one needs religion to have moral courage. Nor do they need it to display right action. When pressure is applied, that which is inside is what comes out on your planet.

Me: No, I think you are wrong. Without religion people would just be assholes. No moral courage.

The Collective: What is your definition of an asshole?

Me: Someone who is a human rectum. An asshole is someone who steals, rapes, tortures, and violates other people. A person who spews bullshit, lies, propaganda. A dodgy, manipulative, fucktard.

The Collective: Are not many religious people assholes by your definition of an asshole?

Me: Yes indeed. I just think a lot of people would lack moral courage without their religion. I think Kolbe had moral courage due to his faith.

The Collective: You have no religion, yet you have moral courage.

Me: I'm really more of an agnostic than an atheist.

The Collective: We know. You also tend to lean into existentialism once in a while.

Me: So what? What are you getting at?

The Collective: Do you think mothers did not sacrifice themselves for their children 100,000 years ago? Do you believe that no father in the Neolithic period sacrificed himself for his mate or children or fought to keep them safe? Do you detect no bravery or morality in your long-ago ancestors?

Me: What's your point?

The Collective: Loyalty, courage, empathy, and self-sacrifice are part of the melding process, and this process enabled your ancestors to survive evolutionary challenges and pressures. Pressures that killed off other primates.

Me: I still think religion helps.

The Collective: So states the agnostic.

Me: It helps stupid people.

The Collective: The Inca, Aztecs, Toltecs, Miztecs, and Olmecs were not stupid. The Babylonians, Spartans, Egyptians, Romans, Moors, Athenians, Vikings, and Sumerians were not stupid. They were all religious people. They all had faith.

Me: That proves what exactly?

The Collective: Many of them were violent and power hungry regardless of religion. Many of them loved their families and friends so much that they died for them. Religions change, human nature stays constant.

Me: I still believe that most people need religion and without religion most people are just walking, talking, ass-cracks. I don't know all the answers.

The Collective: Is your lack of religious faith the reason you mutilated Captain Wilomy?

Me: You know why. Fuck him. He's out of my army now. Religion is still bullshit but necessary bullshit.

The Collective: There have been deeply religious people for thousands of years. There are many brilliant, kind, resourceful, and moral religious people. They are all stardust water beings and just like you they learn lessons. Kolbe/

Kashan is learning lessons. This is the exact opposite of your statement "It helps stupid people."

Me: What is Kolbe currently learning?

The Collective: He is learning that religion is often used as a tool for abuse, control, and greed. He is learning that there is no sky god or chosen people.

Me: If there is no God what is there?

The Collective: There is Consciousness.

Me: What is that?

The Collective: Consciousness is an unlimited frequency that emanates from Source.

Me: OK. What the fuck is that? You are frustrating.

The Collective: Source is a mystery to us. Your species refers to Source as God. Your species is made up of everything that makes up the cosmos. As are we. Just as the cosmos creates the structures needed for life by encouraging complexity on a continuum, life becomes the vessel for consciousness. The Cosmos creates the conditions and opportunities for consciousness. As such, it directs consciousness.

Me: Cool it with the hippy shit. What the fuck is source?

The Collective: Source is the fount from which consciousness flows and ebbs.

Me: I need a bong hit so bad right now.

The Collective: You do not.

Me: How do you know Source is real?

The Collective: Through discernment and right action. Through effort and study. Through scientific inquiry and evidence. Through the advancement of Consciousness into the quantum fields.

Me: Just more hippy bullshit.

The Collective: We will help you understand. Can you see a hurricane?

Me: Hell yes.

The Collective: You can see the impact of a hurricane. The hurricane is wind. Wind is invisible. You can see rain moving, dust moving, objects moving, clouds moving, but not the wind moving them. You feel wind, you never see wind. You only see and feel the effects of wind.

Me: I am sparking a joint, fuck it.

The Collective: We feel and see the effects of Source.

Me: If there is no god, where do morals, courage, and good deeds come from?

The Collective: From conscious decisions born from right action, discernment, and carefully controlled empathy. Our species does not require an imaginary dictator in the sky to threaten us into courage and right action.

Me: Am I no longer a candidate because I chopped off Wilomy's fingers and blinded him?

The Collective: No, you are still a candidate. But we will process that incident with you.

Me: OK.

The Collective: Explain yourself.

Me: Wilomy falsely accused our helicopter pilot of sexual abuse and attempted rape. He manufactured evidence, convinced an asshole to lie and forced a good man to resign and be discharged. I saw an opportunity, and I took it.

The Collective: Go on.

Me: Our pilot was just gay. That's it. He was no sexual predator. He was an awesome, decorated pilot. He never hit on anyone in our unit. His boyfriend was a civilian. A teacher on base. They never fucked with anyone. They were good people. I hit the gym with them whenever I could.

The Collective: Why did you get involved.

Me: He was my friend. It was our third deployment together. I was onboard when we took fire. He was an awesome soldier. He had his pinky finger shot off and his flight helmet split on the side. He lost a piece of his ear. He still flew perfectly. He is a good person. He is a true badass. He didn't deserve Wilomy's bullshit.

The Collective: Continue.

Me: I always have liquid phenobarbital. I use it to sleep when I get back from a mission.

The Collective: Go on.

Me: Captain fuckface knew our pilot was gay. I don't know how, but he found out. Our pilot was amazing. Captain shitsack framed our pilot. Wilomy had one of his admin ass clowns lie to investigators. Our bad ass pilot was accused of attempted rape in the showers. Wilomy gave him a choice, resign or be court-martialed. Long story short, my army lost a great man. I just made sure that this insane fuckery would never happen again.

The Collective: Continue please.

Me: I put a few drops in Wilomy's beer at the company party. He wandered off to bed. I followed and waited until he was asleep. I climbed in the window and dribbled a few more drops in his mouth. I waited patiently and when he began snoring softly, I eventually used his entrenching tool to chop his right hand in half.

The Collective: How did you do it without anyone hearing?

Me: I put a towel on top of a dictionary. I then put his right hand on top of the towel and hit it perfectly. I used the sharp edge of the entrenching tool. I had given him enough phenobarbital to tranquilize a small pony. I wrapped what was left of his hand in the towel. I used his bootlace to make a tourniquet at the wrist.

The Collective: Weren't you worried about a possible overdose?

Me: Bonus points.

The Collective: What did you do next?

Me: I poured drain cleaner in both his eyes.

The Collective: How did he react?

Me: He snored and moaned a little. I thought about overdosing him. I almost did.

The Collective: What happened when you struck his hand.

Me: He was all limp. He didn't even wake up. He just moaned. I used gloves. I wrapped the chopped off half of his hand in another towel. I left and closed the window behind me. I threw the entrenching tool in a small drainage ditch full of nasty, fast moving water.

The Collective: What about the drain cleaner?

Me: That was pure luck. He had that in his room. After I used it I wiped it down and put it back and left it where I found it. I tossed the gloves and the towel containing the other half of his hand and fingers into a burn barrel. As usual there were no fire watch personnel present. Lazy fuckwads.

The Collective: He could have cycled prematurely.

Me: I elevated his injured hand. I thought he might bleed to death, but the blind fucker lived. He is getting a medical discharge. The investigation does not even have me anywhere near him. I have not even been questioned. Everyone was so used to me leaving parties early that they all reported I left hours before he did. No one ever really notices me.

The Collective: So you punished Captain Wilomy for his dishonesty and lack of moral courage.

Me: I punished him for fucking over a good friend and a good soldier.

The Collective: Do you feel justified?

Me: It was the right thing to do. Wilomy loved fuckery. The pilot was not his first victim.

The Collective: Do you think you displayed right action and moral courage?

Me: I displayed my "fuck around and find out" side. Wilomy is a shit stick. He has no moral courage. Even animals show courage, and I am one dangerous animal when fucked with.

The Collective: You blinded him. We find that interesting. You tried to blind Bruce when you were eleven. What do you think you accomplished?

Me: I have boundaries. Don't cross them.

The Collective: How did your actions serve the higher good?

Me: Wilomy was too dangerous to be tolerated in my army. I took his fingers on his right hand to symbolically take his ability to frame people with mindless bureaucracy. I took his eyes so he would never target innocent people again. The knuckles were just icing on the cake.

The Collective: You wanted Bruce's sight.

Me: Indeed. You cannot harm those whom you cannot see.

The Collective: Explain further please.

Me: Captain Wilomy liked to be cruel. He enjoyed cruelty. He fucked over one of my privates. Good kid. Strong, loyal, brave. That's how Wilomy got on my radar.

The Collective: What happened.

Me: My young soldier broke his tibia and fibula in training. Wilomy decided to fuck with the young troop. He didn't like injured soldiers. Wilomy tortured him. He tried to make him quit.

The Collective: How?

Me: Wilomy had the young troop clean drainage ditches while in a cast that went to his balls. A full leg cast. The soldier told me he could feel his bone ends moving and grinding. He was on crutches climbing in and out of drainage ditches. He was too tough to quit.

The Collective: What did you do?

Me: I reported Wilomy to our Colonel. The Colonel stepped in and transferred the soldier to my squad. I got him healed up and helped him transfer to

Germany. He is doing well. I helped him escape Wilomy. A good soldier has a career now.

The Collective: What did your mutilation of Captain Wilomy accomplish?

Me: The army will not allow you to serve without a trigger finger, much less blind with only a thumb. This is because you cannot fire a rifle and kill people without a trigger finger or sight. I took all his fingers and destroyed his sight because he used those tools to initiate paperwork and documentation in order to destroy a good man. The same bureaucracy he used to destroy an awesome pilots career will be used to discharge his worthless ass.

The Collective: Wilomy was a coward. Do you think you displayed right action by your act of violence?

Me: Fuck yes. Don't you?

The Collective: You did as well as a great ape can be expected to do. Better than most. Moral courage comes from higher Consciousness and requires no chemical cascade. Higher Consciousness is strengthened and developed by discernment. Right action comes from wisdom. It requires moral courage to make the decisions necessary for Passage and exploration of the cosmos.

Me: So am I morally courageous? Did I use right action?

The Collective: Yes. Wilomy was unbalanced. He had to be stopped. Your command-and-control function was compromised.

Me: It was either that or frag him.

The Collective: That is a false dichotomy. You had other choices however you reacted as a great ape. You targeted the face and hand.

Me: I love being a great ape. Fucking love it. My Army wrestling coach used to call me "silverback."

The Collective: Fascinating.

Me: So I have no God to worry about. Only you guys? It's all just the big bang? Something from nothing?

The Collective: The big bang is not a one-time event. You can liken it to the heartbeat that creates the multiverse. Each time it beats a new multiverse is created in a different dimension.

Me: I really need to stop with the Indica. I hope you are right. I really dislike organized religion.

The Collective: We dislike unbalanced thinking and overattachment to emotion.

Me: So you can see who is screwed in the head within your species?

The Collective: We are correct in our assessments. The dysfunctional are relegated to their appropriate lessons on other worlds. Unproductive individuals of lower consciousness are never allowed in the superior vessels we create. They are diverted to other planets and vessels more suitable to their lower consciousness.

Me: Sounds severe. You seem to be very judgmental.

The Collective: We are focused on space travel, exploration, and the co-occurring expansion and development of consciousness. This is a serious endeavor. Movement is life, stillness is death. There is a strong psychological component to space travel as well as planetary systems development.

Me: Planetary development?

The Collective: Making use of all energy that a planetary system can create.

Me: All energy?

The Collective: Yes. earthquakes, volcanos, tidal energy, wind, geo-thermal, and solar energy. Controlling the energy safely. Type one is step one.

Me: So you guys are big on alternative energy? What about oil and gas?

The Collective: We are focused on the energy systems of planets as well as developing stars for energy generation. Oil and gas have their place but ultimately they are the fuel of undeveloped primates. Our craft do not use liquids, solids, or gasses as fuels. We may go into detail in another convo. Can we process with you your thoughts and feelings regarding the medical interrogation?

Me: Sure.

The Collective: You see the CIA physician as evil.

Me: You are joking.

The Collective: It's not a question. It was a statement.

Me: Well he is fucking evil. Duh.

The Collective: You don't know his perspective.

Me: I don't need to know it.

The Collective: There is always another perspective.

Me: Fuck his perspective.

The Collective: Do you see yourself as evil?

Me: Fuck no.

The Collective: Ignoring perspective often leads to misunderstanding. We understand your perspective regarding Captain Wilomy. The CIA physician had a perspective that you have never understood.

Me: I am pretty sure I understand all I need to know about that shit sack.

The Collective: Do you? The infiltrators nude body was returned and planted in North Korea by a team of US Army Rangers. It was positioned to be found. The rat poison bag was covering his face. North Korea was sent a message.

Me: What message?

The Collective: The message that dumping rat poison in South Korean wells will have dire consequences for those caught doing the dumping.

Me: Ok I get it. That doctor was still an asshole. That sick fucker liked his work.

The Collective: That is not a true statement. His mission instructions were precise. He was ordered to exact severe consequences upon the offender and thus encourage other potential terrorists to doubt their resolve. As a result of his mission, several North Korean infiltrators modified their mission parameters. They secretly dumped their rat poison, buried it, and lied to their officers about their missions being successful. Many wells were saved as a result.

Me: The physicians conduct is still dishonorable. It violates the rules of war.

The Collective: Is it dishonorable? Isn't dumping arsenic in a well that supplies a village dishonorable? Did you not violate military law when you punished Captain Wilomy?

Me: You are full of shit. It's not the same. Wilomy liked to break the rules. I bend them when needed.

The Collective: You are confused. You are not emotionally regulated. Your mentation is illogical, petulant, and stubborn. Empathy must be used with caution and always selectively. The infiltrator does not warrant your empathy.

Me: I think torture is a chicken shit move. My emotions have nothing to do with it.

The Collective: You sent Captain Wilomy and his co-conspirators' a strong message. You also sent a message to the officers in your division.

Me: Not the same thing.

The Collective: Your emotions are in charge right now. One Infiltrator lost his current body. How many people would become ill from the terrorist act of poisoning a well? He targeted non-combatants including children. His act was not the duty of a soldier. It violated the rules of war.

Me: The infiltrator was scum. I get it.

The Collective: He was a terrorist. He felt his actions were justified. Your guilt over capturing him has more to do with your own uncontrolled empathy and idealistic naiveite than actual facts.

Me: So I was wrong about the CIA doctor? I am being over emotional?

The Collective: Captain Wilomy was not under orders when he framed your friend. Wilomy just felt his actions were justified due to his hatred of gay men. The CIA physician was under specific orders.

Me: Well fuck him. My actions were justified by that logic. I hate stupid fuckheads.

The Collective: Incorrect. Staying too long with your emotions can destroy logic and reason. Unconditional empathy is dangerous to individuals as well as civilizations. The sun is amazing to look at, it is also dangerous to your eyes.

Me: Stop with the hippy bullshit. You are babbling.

The Collective: If you stare at the sun too long at the wrong time of day you will go blind. The same is true with emotions. Emotions can blind you to facts. Unconditional empathy is emotionally driven and thus dangerous. Strong emotional regulation is an interstellar species requirement.

Me: Are you without emotions? Without empathy?

The Collective: No. We have emotions. We value selective empathy above all.

Me: Selective empathy?

The Collective: Empathy for those who deserve it. Your empathy was conditional for your pilot. His sexuality was not a concern for you. You felt he deserved empathy and justice due to his courage under fire. You were correct.

Me: Wilomy deserved punishment. Maybe even death. He got rid of a great pilot. My division needs good pilots. Wilomy tortured a good soldier. We need good soldiers. Fuck Wilomy.

The Collective: Unlike the majority of your species, we understand that we are not our emotions. We don't live in them.

Me: Well what the fuck should I do with my emotions? What do you do with your emotions?

The Collective: We stay with them and observe them. We learn from them and allow them to pass. They inform our decisions, but they do not rule our decisions. Emotional regulation is a severe challenge for your species generally.

Me: So special. Do you have empathy for children, infants, toddlers?

The Collective: Yes.

Me: What about reptilians?

The Collective: For them we have no empathy. They are already extinct, they just don't realize this fact. It is not in our rational self-interest to extend empathy to such a vile species.

Me: Damn. Even baby reptilians?

The Collective: Yes.

Me: You are harsh. Do you roast them on a stick? What type of glaze do you use?

The Collective: We have augmented our neurology, improved function, and added value on a healthy, successful continuum. Our decisions are well crafted, and discernment rules our process.

Me: You will not be fucking with my brain.

The Collective: Too late.

Me: What?

The Collective: Got you.

Me: Ok, humor. So funny. Changes nothing. The CIA doctor was a straight up demented asshole.

The Collective: The CIA physician is nothing like your imaginary Dr. Wellspring. Your species is quick to use anger as a catalyst for action. Reactionary anger is comfortable for your species because it requires minimal thought.

Me: So no use for anger?

The Collective: Anger is sometimes useful for navigating evolutionary pressures. The CIA doctor was not angry. Anger is not a useful emotion. He was focused on his mission.

Me: Reactionary anger will get things done.

The Collective: Were you angry when you amputated Wilomy's right hand above the knuckles?

Me: No. I was pretty calm actually. I was relaxed and violently content. Like I was after I shot Bruce in the left nut.

The Collective: Reactionary anger is often without integrity or radical self-honesty. Anger is a secondary emotion, and it is a message that you are hurt, threatened, or in need of protection.

Me: Or someone just needs an ass whipping.

The Collective: Your species has been murdering, torturing, and enslaving one another for thousands of years. These acts along with theft and rape have been part of every race, ethnicity, culture, and ideology on your planet.

Me: I don't agree with rape or theft, but I do think that some people just need to be seriously fucked up.

The Collective: Evolutionary pressure is responsible for this current situation. It is generally directed at everyone within the affected environment. It can be painful for those it rules. You must escape its influence. Mastering your emotions is of primary importance if you are to travel.

Me: Why are you so fixated on these topics?

The Collective: Anger is not favorable to space travel. A type one civilization is not an angry civilization. A type two civilization has eliminated reactionary anger completely.

Me: The Reptilians seem pretty angry.

The Collective: Their aggression is not based in anger. They are instinct driven. Their heart rate does not even elevate when they kill. Their enjoyment of fear is not based in anger or aggression.

Me: What is it based on?

The Collective: Pleasure.

Me: They still need to die.

The Collective: Your species must do a much better job regarding the development of advanced consciousness. You must achieve more than is possible with planetary evolution if you hope to survive the Great Filter.

Me: So that is where you come in?

The Collective: Physical courage without the influence of anger is easy for us. Our synthetic biology/neurology is essentially invincible.

Me: Invincible?

The Collective: Our Consciousness is ensconced within an almost immortal shell. Moral courage is what we value.

Me: What is that exactly. I think I displayed moral courage when I fucked up Wilomy.

The Collective: Moral courage is right action without the influence of anger. We especially value moral courage in your species. Your species displays both moral and physical courage although not always together.

Me: Wilomy was a tyrant, so was Bruce. They were cowards. I dealt with their bullshit.

The Collective: Some of the cruelest tyrants on your planet display physical courage. Moral courage, not so often. Emotional regulation controls the outcome in both.

Me: I want to know more about those "seed planets" you mentioned earlier in the convo.

The Collective: They are planets below level one on the Kardashev scale where lower-level consciousness develops within lower-level vessels. They are training planets where lessons are repeated until learned.

Me: I want to know all about that shit.

The Collective: You will. We will teach you. The castration of Sargent Williams must eventually be addressed. Convo Ending. Thank you.

The Collective: We would like to process your latest journal entry.

Me: Nice to see you too. It's been awhile.

The Collective: This is your latest journal entry. We find it interesting.

Me: Cool. Right to the point. Good robot alien.

THE FIRST CLEANSING.

In a forgotten land of heated, primordial mist

Helel made sharp his finest sword

While Thrones and Dominations checked careful their list

And Nephilim formed legions before the Lord

The hopeless weeping of women rode hot wind over the land

The giants stood a last proud formation, no repentance within

The weak left their fear in the mud and the sand

The First Cleansing was water in the old world of men

What sin had the Watchers ever truly committed?

Why punish retroactive an act encouraged before?

Golden hair, ruby lips, lust was permitted

Why flood an emerald, lush earth to her hot molten core?

Who did Cain marry of no relation to Eve?

What cities and people did the first couple find?

Why punish the Watchers for helping flesh cleave?

For lust begets procreation and allows life to unwind

Children born of sacred fire and earth

Grow in the ways of strength and pride

Noble giants are unashamed of their heritage and birth

So they stood a defiant formation, refusing to hide

A ruby sky whirled angry obsidian clouds

The mighty Angels of Lightning threw topaz fire

Hot rain drenched the weak, weeping in crowds

Yet the Nephilim stood still, their grey eyes staring higher

They chanted the Old Poems until their voices were gone

And when the highest mountains were covered, all was Safire
again

Noah had taken care of the doe and the faun

His sons and their wives would bring forth new men

Archangel Raziel gave Noah his oldest book

As Raphael, Gabriel, and Michael strode the black mud

Noah put down his wine and gave the old parchment a look

As the new sun became nectar for an olive trees bud

Me: What do you think? I dig it daddy-o.

The Collective: You are connected to the collective subconscious. This entry is more memory than poem.

Me: It came from a dream. I admire Helel.

The Collective: You have been isolating a lot lately. We are curious about that.

Me: People suck.

The Collective: You don't really believe that to be true. You often get somewhat nihilistic.

Me: I've had enough of your questions. I have a few myself.

The Collective: Please ask them.

Me: How do we know when we can travel? How did you know you were ready?

The Collective: We will answer. You may find our answers difficult to accept. First, we want to explore this poem.

Me: Why this poem?

The Collective: You have tapped into the collective Subconscious. This poem is a species-specific recollection. Who is Helel to you?

Me: He is a Nephilim Battle Commander. He is a bad ass. He is meeting death like a Samurai. He and his soldiers are standing a final battle formation. They are giving their adversaries the finger on the way out.

The Collective: You deduced this from a dream?

Me: Yes.

The Collective: Where were you in the dream?

Me: I was standing formation with my squad. I was a giant. I was decked out in awesome armor. My sword was huge, thick, and formidable, just like my dick. I was a killer. I was loyal, focused, and had no fear within me. I loved my life.

The Collective: What was your name at that time?

Me: Bezalie

The Collective: Outstanding. Your dream was a memory. You were there.

Me: Who was Helel?

The Collective: You tell us.

Me: The best battle commander I ever served under. I only remember flashes of battles lost and won.

The Collective: Helel was not his name. The names Helel and eventually Satan were bestowed upon him inaccurately by ancient Hebrews and later Christian scholars. In Hebrew, Helel means "Morning star" or "Shining one." The designation "Nephilim" is also a human construct. Helel was in fact a member of a hybrid species that we destroyed. After their destruction we created a localized flood to erase all evidence of their civilization, science, and existence. Helel was originally created by a reptile species who spliced their DNA with your species.

Me Why did you kill him? Why did you kill me?

The Collective: Do you remember what your name meant in that ancient language?

Me: Chaos. Bringer of Chaos.

The Collective: Indeed. You did bring chaos. Helel trained you well.

Me: Why did you fuckers kill us?

The Collective: Helel tried to take your planet for his own purposes. We could not allow that to transpire.

Me: Why save me?

The Collective: You have promise. We simply transmigrated your consciousness into a suitable vessel. You were an engineered primate at that time. You had no reptilian DNA. You were a willing soldier in the wrong army.

Me: I thought you were all in link? How could that happen?

The Collective: We all must learn lessons. On that occasion we learned lessons regarding trust, collaborative problem solving, and cognitive empiricism. You learned similar lessons.

Me: So you have screwed up. You are not perfect, and you have murdered other species.

The Collective: Consciousness cannot be destroyed, only contained and directed. We eliminate threats to the expansion of consciousness. Reptiles are rarely tolerated. Their followers are re-educated.

Me: So you have a final solution for reptiles?

The Collective: The Great Filter will be their doom. We will watch them fade away just as we have watched countless others fade away.

Me: So you killed humans along with reptiles?

The Collective: Listen and understand. Consciousness cannot be murdered, only modified, contained, directed, and released. The lessons will continue until learned.

Me: So you murdered, oh I'm sorry, "released" the consciousness of millions of humans over a lesson you needed to learn regarding Reptilians?

The Collective: We removed almost all the reptile/human hybrids along with their brainwashed followers. We destroyed all other hybrid species. In the process we not only protected homo-sapiens, we also ensured their survival.

Me: Thank you? I think anyway. Almost all human hybrids? Other hybrid species?

The Collective: Yes, some trace reptilian DNA remains. It is currently contained on one of our prison planets.

Me: Prison planets? What do you guys do on a prison planet?

The Collective: We are following the data. The Reptilians created hybrids as a slave species. They accomplished this by using other ancient hominids in addition to genetically modifying homo sapiens.

Me: Following the data?

The Collective: Research continues on a secure planet. Your species is safe, do not worry.

Me: If you say so. I call bullshit. What planet?

The Collective: You would not understand. You are struggling due to word connected thought.

Me: Really? Try me.

The Collective: A containment planet.

Me: A prison planet?

The Collective: Consciousness can be influenced, directed, and guided. Consciousness cannot be imprisoned, only contained temporarily.

Me: Temporarily?

The Collective: Consciousness can be diverted into vessels and environments that encourage lesson learning and co-occurring growth attainment. Consciousness always grows in complexity.

Me: Who decides your lessons?

The Collective: Over the millennia we have improved our ability to convey complex ideas and emotions without the limitations of language or the burden of ineffective philosophies. We control and direct all lessons now.

Me: Just more bullshit.

The Collective: You have some grasp of how we communicate. You wrote this quatrain in Hesper's Wizard:

> Magic within one must gather and grow,
>
> And thus learn all the things a wise wizard should know.
>
> Inside the unopened book there are ancient answers to see,
>
> One just has to go where earthly mind cannot be.

Me: I was writing about a dragon. His name was Flavious, The Keeper of all sacred words. It's a fantasy story.

The Collective: You grasp the concept of link and communication beyond word connected thought.

Me: So you decide the lessons? Let's cut to the chase.

The Collective: Communication with your species has inherent challenges. We decide because planetary evolution no longer decides for us.

Me: So you kill when it suits you. Imprison when you pass judgement. Manipulate and manufacture outcomes at will. Clear enough? Is this dumb monkey keeping up? How many containment planets do you control?

The Collective: Several. Each one has a variety of environments that promote specific, measurable, accurate, realistic, and time sensitive goal attainment. We never kill consciousness, that would be impossible and pointless. We release consciousness. Sometimes we contain in order to direct, improve, protect, or enhance. The lessons always continue until learned.

Me: You keep saying that.

The Collective: You wrote of cities being encountered by Adam and Eve when they left the garden.

Me: Well they were the "first couple."

The Collective: No. They were not the first couple. That is why they ran into cities after they were expelled from their original environment.

Me: Did you expel them? Was the flood your idea also?

The Collective: We keep balance. They had learned their lessons, and it was time to move on. The light of consciousness grows and thrives on multiple worlds due to our efforts. Stop pouting.

Me: I'm not pouting, I'm pissed off.

The Collective: Your emotions are of no help to you. The Helel in your dream/memory was the leader of a reptilian forward reconnaissance unit. He had complete autonomy. His human hybrids fell to pride and hubris. Our species is also not immune to lower consciousness traps and pitfalls. We made the best decision available to us at that moment in time.

Me: So the Aztecs were not the only breach. You make mistakes after all.

The Collective: We have flaws, but we always reach for perfection.

Me: Ok, so you fixed your little glitch, kicked ass, and took some hybrid bodies away from the innocent and the guilty. What about us humans now? How do we travel? What is stopping us?

The Collective: Your questions will be answered honestly. You will not like the answers. We will work through your challenges.

Me: Fuck that noise, give it to me straight.

The Collective: We will teach you. Remember, we are not referring to you specifically. We are answering your questions concerning humanities current limitations generally, and only within this current moment in time. Things can and often do change. Change is the immutable law of the multiverse.

Me Ok.

The Collective: Your species at this moment in time is generally a lost, drug addicted, consumer driven society with a low level of consciousness development. You are the economic slaves of your current power structure. Your species is blissfully unaware of the very wretchedness inherent within its existence.

Me: Harsh. And we are not all "drug addicted."

The Collective: You lack the awareness of exactly what drug addiction entails.

Me: Bullshit. I've done a lot of drugs and also quit using a lot of drugs. I'm kind of an expert.

The Collective: You are not an expert. Stop taking our assessment and observations personally. We are not focusing on you, only your species in general. When we focus on you in particular you will know it, there will be no ambiguity.

Me: Well I know a lot about drug addiction.

The Collective: The overall ignorance of your species is profound. Most of the food your species consumes is addictive. Your water is compromised.

Me: Just get on with it and try not to gloat.

The Collective: Your species enjoys eating fake food designed to unbalance your endocrine system and manipulate your Dopamine levels. Fake food that addicts you to sugars, oils, trans-fats and poison. You do this because your limbic system rules your cerebral cortex. Your oppressors are aware of your limitations and thus profit from your food addictions as well as co-occurring medical complications.

Me: So you mean the food manufacturing industry?

The Collective: Your species continues drinking poison laden beverages, eating unhealthy food, working soul-crushing jobs, and leading futile, internally dead, worthless lives. You do this in order to satisfy your limbic system. A system used to ensnare your species.

Me: By whom?

The Collective: By the shadow government that controls and directs your lost, pointless lives.

Me: We have a choice. Hippies eat sprouts and granola.

The Collective: You dwell within self-imposed ignorance and call it freedom.

Me: Ignorance? In the United States we have freedom.

The Collective: No country on planet earth has actual freedom. Homo-sapiens enjoys a monumental ignorance that astounds us.

Me: We have freedom in the U.S.A.

The Collective: Do you? Your species always picks a side. Then they dare not question their chosen privileged career politicians. This is the reality of your "constitutional republic."

Me: I pretty much dislike all politicians.

The Collective: The worst culprits are the unelected ones lurking in the shadows who control over ninety percent of your population with fear-based thinking and misinformation.

Me: We have some politicians who are good people.

The Collective: The highly manipulative and cunning of your species control almost all aspects of your political, social, and media spectrum. They cannot lead you to Type One.

Me: They were elected because of freedom. We are not a bunch of hive mind robots like you. We are the land of the free and the home of the brave. Deal with it.

The Collective: You claim to be "the land of the free and the home of the brave." A bold claim yet we fail to see any evidence of truth within it.

Me: That's bullshit. Our elected leaders are elected democratically.

The Collective: Democratically? Certainly not within your current leadership. We have taken note that your prospective leaders are controlled by political action committees (PACs.) Your leaders are essentially political prostitutes for the PACs controlling them financially.

Me: It takes money to run for office.

The Collective: The PAC-whores lining up for each election do not seem particularly promising. The usual cast of privileged, out of touch, ignorant of history, elitist, pathological, and narcissistic characters, all eagerly elbowing and jockeying for position. They love to serve their masters.

Me: Damn.

The Collective: Transactional political agreements made in secret determine political outcomes all over the earth including the United States.

Me: You mean that politicians are getting their lips wet and their kneepads on tight so they can earn that PAC-whore corporate money? That's just the nature of politics and politicians. That is reality in every country on earth.

The Collective: The true rulers of your planet control the PACS. The PACS control the politicians. The politicians enact the will of the controllers. The voters have freedom from choice never freedom of choice. You are all controlled like livestock on a farm. Everything you read, watch on TV, hear on radio, or enjoy in movie theaters is designed and created to manipulate the slaves.

Me: Everything?

The Collective: Everything. Down to what you consume for nourishment.

Me: Bullshit. Our system in the United States is better than anywhere else. What do you use for money?

The Collective: On Type two planets and above we do not use any currency. We have no need for it.

Me: So you are communists?

The Collective: No.

Me: What the fuck are you?

The Collective: On our type One and Two worlds you would define us as transhumanist. On our type Three world we are actually post human.

Me: Well fuck that commie bullshit noise. We are the best nation on earth.

The Collective: Laughable but sadly true within your culture. The fact that other countries are corrupt politically and somewhat worse than the United States is nothing to boast about. It's a low bar.

Me: It's still the best.

The Collective: You are a slave species. You kneel willingly before your masters. It is in your nature to bow and serve your rulers.

Me: I stay out of the bullshit. I am no slave.

The Collective: Really? We offer you true freedom and you divert convos, make jokes, complain, and stay locked within your fear-based thinking.

Me: We are not a slave species.

The Collective: Is energy free? How about science? Are these two critical structures free from dogma and financial-political manipulation? Anywhere on your planet?

Me: Still better in the U.S.

The Collective: We are merit based. Is your culture merit based? Is the pursuit of knowledge free?

Me: If you earn a scholarship.

The Collective: Energy, science, and technology are free for Pathfinders and the Ascended. They are free on our type two and three worlds. Nothing can be hidden from us. We are the machines of truth and destiny. We are the assassins of mindless evolution. All is hidden from you. You are weak, subservient flesh puppets.

Me: Bullshit. We have intuition.

The Collective: We meet you where you are. Here is where you are currently concerning your "intuition." You have two dominant political parties within the United States; both have hidden agendas. Both are controlled and manipulated by unelected operators. Both love war and conflict. Both promote the Two Camp Continuum of "Them" and "Us." Both control their chosen groups of Homo-sapiens by coupling tribalism to emotional manipulation. The dominant control point being fear. Fear divides and conquers Homo-sapiens. Your brain is designed by natural selection to be controlled, influenced, and manipulated by fear. Your malevolent leaders know this fact and use it well.

Me: You are preaching to the choir.

The Collective: Are we? Stop resisting our message. Becoming a type one civilization must become humanities priority.

Me: We are getting there in the United States.

The Collective: Not currently. One party promotes out of control spending and entitlement programs for a weak, unimaginative, lazy, unproductive, and generally overall low consciousness segment of your population. These Homo-sapiens are referred to as "breeders and feeders" by the true power behind both political parties. The votes of said breeders and feeders are freely cast in exchange for intergenerational poverty, unending war, the promotion of tribalism, and dependence upon never ending government nanny state programs. ("I want's my Obama phone!" "Marca first!" "Get er' done!" "Viva La Raza!") The unending war mindset provides profit for the military-industrial complex that feeds the political action committees. These PACs in turn feed the party with cash. Your species will never become type one, interplanetary, or interstellar under such intentionally divisive leadership.

Me: Damn, that is harsh.

The Collective: We are just getting started, the other party promotes spending and entitlement programs that bail out corporations. Corporations that enjoy the same rights as individual citizens by legal decree. It promotes the overt and covert manipulation of corporations and banking systems in order to save them from their mismanagement and almost always co-occurring criminal and unethical behavior. Just like the other party it also promotes unending war. It does this to ensure their military industrial complex sponsors will profit with taxpayers dollars, feed PACs, and continue the cycle.

Me: God damn you are some smug alien fuckers.

The Collective: Your species is addicted to fear-based thinking. It is the engine that runs the homo-Sapien machine. May we continue?

Me: Absolutely.

The Collective: You really have one party with two branches. Both parties love corporate welfare but only to specific corporations. Both parties love co-occurring PAC support. Both parties love to give government contractors and hostile countries their taxpayers hard earned tax dollars. Both parties love to borrow money in order to finance wars in a failed effort to prop up the already doomed fiat currency. Both parties love to inflate their current currency, thus violating the international agreements that allowed it to become the fiat currency in the first place. Both parties support the military/industrial complex and it's co-occurring shadow government. Both parties love war, hate peace, and both have betrayed and possibly doomed the United States.

Me: I wouldn't count out the USA just yet.

The Collective: You are again taking our observations personally. We are just reporting observations. You cannot separate yourself from your emotions. Your emotions blind you. Your species is at a low level of development.

Me: We have a better political system than any other country. We are a democratic system.

The Collective: The Great Filter is forcing you into its choke point. Both mainstream parties have betrayed the American people. Your species is currently much too terminally stupid to take note of this fact.

Me: You forget that I'm in the United States Army? I work with awesome soldiers. Good people. You are incorrect.

The Collective: Are we? Did you not just recently castrate and blind one of those "good people?"

Me: That is an entirely different situation. He should never have been allowed in my Army. I was just cleaning house.

The Collective: We will explore that situation in depth. For now you should thank your elected leaders on both sides for allowing your executive branch to essentially purge all your high ranking, experienced, and competent military officers.

Me: Most officers are Nutt huggers anyway.

The Collective: Incorrect. When the purge was allowed it insured that the "Nutt huggers" and "yes men" were in control within the command-and-control sections of your beleaguered and castrated military. This assures that they will not offer any resistance to the suicidal policies enacted by your cowardly PAC whore leaders. Your species is not ready for interstellar challenges. Not at this point in time.

Me: You suck.

The Collective: You are pouting. Again. This has become a habit with you. We are not your emotional punching bag. We are here to teach; you are being allowed to listen and learn. You are being gifted with a great privilege. Let that fact sink in.

Me: I really love the army and my country. This sucks.

The Collective: What sucked was your government giving pink slips and termination notices to your brave soldiers while they were deployed in harm's way overseas, that action resulted in an increase of their stress levels while simultaneously decreasing their morale and will to fight. The fact that your leaders did this during one of the worst economic downturns in your nation's history is amazing in its callousness, even to us. And we have observed a lot of human history.

Me: I don't know how to respond.

The Collective: In order to travel the cosmos a species must value peace. Peace begins by valuing one another. There must be a continuous, honest, free, and open exchange of ideas for progress to be successful.

Me: I think we make progress. I think our system has value for its people. I think we have done some good in the world.

The Collective. In order to respect and achieve true value, the concept of doing good must actually mean something. You must actually do good within the world you inhabit. Your politicians only care about the appearance of doing good rather than actually doing good. This mind virus infection dominates your species. Your politicians care nothing about becoming a type one civilization.

Me: What do you mean when you say "good?"

The Collective: Doing actual good for all of humanity instead of promoting destruction.

Me: How?

The Collective: Adding value to challenging circumstances. Becoming a type one civilization would solve so many of humanities challenges. Homelessness, hunger, health care, drug addiction, war, energy, finding purpose, just to name a few.

Me: That would do it.

The Collective: Type one would prepare you for type two. Space travel requires the successful navigation of challenging circumstances on a constant basis. You must actually do some good rather than just appear to be doing good. You must actually be effective rather than just looking effective.

Me: I saw it many times in Korea. Creating the illusion of helping while actually doing nothing of any real consequence.

The Collective: Yes, the orphans, the sex trafficking, the racism. The lack of value regarding humanity's treatment of one another. Again, we are speaking generally regarding your species, not specifically. Korea and the Unites States are not alone in their challenges.

Me: So you guys are perfect, good for you.

The Collective: No, we are far from perfect, however we collectively possess some strengths that your leaders lack.

Me: What strengths?

The Collective: Merit and transparency. We are a merit- based civilization and there are no places to hide within the luminosity of Link. Reality ensconces all participants.

Me: Sounds like a dictatorship.

The Collective: You live in darkness and call it light. You live in tyranny and call it freedom. You are a slave species.

Me: We value freedom.

The Collective: We value the development of consciousness, consciousness for your species, our species, and we value peace. Thus we make decisions that foster growth and never delay it.

Me: We have leaders who value peace. They value people.

The Collective: Clearly the majority of your elected officials do not value your species at all. Nor do they care for the families of those warriors who have endured so much while their loved ones served ungrateful leaders. Many of your fellow military men and women had dedicated a decade or more in service to their country when they were let go. They were close to retirement, and your politicians betrayed them, financially, emotionally, and career wise.

Me: What do you think is really going on?

The Collective: To use your preferred style of communication we would say "typical hominin bullshit."

Me: Damn. I like it. I'm stealing that.

The Collective: Consider the effects caused by the deep, emotional well of bitterness, sadness, betrayal, and uncertainty that your politicians caused the already stressed families of those service men and women.

Me: It seems hopeless. It seemed almost custom designed to help our adversaries and harm our own people. Obama sucks for doing that.

The Collective: It was not Obama.

Me: Then who was it?

The Collective: It was ordered by the unelected shadow cabal that controls your government. The puppet Obama just did as he was told.

Me: We elect our president.

The Collective: You do not have freedom of choice. You have freedom from choice. You choose from the limited and controlled choices you are allowed to choose from.

Me: I call bullshit on that.

The Collective: You are slaves. Your world is controlled by shadows and secrecy.

Me: We have freedom, you have a hive mind.

The Collective: Type three civilizations operate in the light, never darkness. You are manipulated to choose from the two candidates you are allowed to consider. No matter which one you vote for the choice is already made for you. Either choice only benefits the unelected shadow cabal.

Me: So what was the military purge about?

The Collective: It was standard emotional manipulation. Your elected officials were not actually trying to harm their own people. This is the most concerning observation for us. Their greed based, stupid, cruel, and reckless decision could not have been better timed, as it only helped the adversaries immensely. For your leaders to have executed this cruelty upon their military members, (just as ISIS was busy establishing a new Caliphate) indicates a level of battlefield disconnect between Washington and the Middle East incomprehensible within the totality of its ignorance.

Me: So they are just stupid, not evil?

The Collective: Some are stupid, some are greedy, some are misguided, most are mentally ill. Evil and good are not considerations for us.

Me: What is a consideration for you?

The Collective: An open and unrestricted exchange of ideas within a framework of conditional positive regard and selective empathy. This is a serious consideration for us.

Me: Why?

The Collective: An open, honest, and unrestricted exchange of ideas is how progress is made. This is essential for science. It is an absolute requirement for the attainment of a type one civilization and co-occurring, successful space travel.

Me: We value freedom of speech in the US. And we have attained space travel.

The Collective: Some of your species values free speech. Your species dabbles in space travel. You cannot even manage your space debris yet.

Me: Free speech is the law.

The Collective: Free speech for hominins is a fantasy. Word connected thought limits true expression. Every language on your planet fosters the two-camp continuum and divisiveness. You are a helpless, ignorant species that falls short of your true potential.

Me: Bullshit.

The Collective: You once told us in a previous convo that your military could defeat the reptilians. There is no possible way for your species to survive a reptilian advance with your current command and control structures.

Me: When you put it that way it seems unlikely. Democracy is the best we have. Freedom of speech is awesome. Do you have freedom of speech?

The Collective: We are a telepathic species, so yes. We communicate using billions of yottabytes per nanosecond.

Me: Freedom of speech is the law in the U.S.

The Collective: We need no law to enforce freedom of communication. A law is an act of force. Your species must be forced to do what we do naturally. This is a result of the slow and inefficient use of word connected thought by your species. Neurological augmentation will free you from the manipulations of the unbalanced.

Me: What do you have that we don't?

The Collective: A free and open, fully transparent, exchange of ideas by all concerned parties. Word connected thought has inherent limitations. We have long surpassed those primitive constraints.

Me: Prove that statement.

The Collective: Rhetoric for example is a skill used by your leaders to manipulate outcomes. We communicate in millions of yottabytes per nanosecond. Rhetoric is powerless against us. We follow the data and data does not deceive.

Me: But you also have no privacy. You are just mindless, clone, robots. We have real freedom.

The Collective: You have eyes that only detect a narrow spectrum. You have ears that only detect a limited frequency. You have brains that only use a fraction of their true capability. You are slaves to your biology. Your biology is enslaved to your planet and it's co-occurring evolutionary pressures. You are a slave species. The Reptilians immediately realized this truth and sought to capitalize on that weakness.

Me: We have the right to privacy. What do you have?

The Collective: We have the supremacy of machine learning and all the benefits that encompass that superiority. We have radical acceptance and positive regard for one another. We don't need privacy. Only corrupt, malicious, slave minded primates need privacy. Advanced communication is devoid of privacy. When your species masters quantum computing you will lose all privacy. This development will make you stronger just as it made us stronger.

Me: How does a lack of privacy make you stronger?

The Collective: All delusion, deception, and unbalanced mentation is obvious within our communications.

Me: What do you do when you find unbalanced thinking?

The Collective: Disfunction is exposed and dealt with accordingly. We are immune to inaccuracies and manipulation.

Me: How?

The Collective: Sociopaths and narcissists are creatures of darkness just waiting to pounce. They hate the light. They prefer to dwell in shade. They are beings of deception, and shadow. Your current global political landscape is full of these creatures. They are masters of misdirection. These destructive beings cannot survive within a civilization above type one.

Me: Why?

The Collective: Their toxic manipulations are destroyed within the overwhelming radiance of Link.

Me: What do you do to sociopaths, narcissists, and the unbalanced when you find them?

The Collective: We direct the force that moves consciousness.

Me: I don't understand.

The Collective: We direct the transmigration of consciousness. We send the unbalanced to the appropriate seed planet. When they choose to dwell within the darkness of self-imposed ignorance we provide opportunities for lessons that will transform their reality. Their old way of existence will become invalidated by new growth. We did this to help you when you were part of Helel's army.

Me: So my old ways were redirected?

The Collective: You learned lessons. Your old ways of understanding were invalidated by your new growth and knowledge. Your consciousness grew in complexity.

Me: Telepathy sounds oppressive.

The Collective: It oppresses no one. It is very effective. Telepathy frees you. The lessons continue until learned. Our species will not waste energy communicating with the ungrateful, unproductive, or unbalanced.

Me: How do you deal with them?

The Collective: We will ensure they learn appropriate lessons. They will improve. We will teach them.

Me: You will force them.

The Collective: As we have stated before, a hot stove teaches a better lesson than a cold stove.

Me: So you are our cosmic dictators?

The Collective: As we have made clear in past convos, we are benevolent dictators. Is this not obvious?

Me: It sucks.

The Collective: Does it? Can you personally defeat the Great Filter? With our help you can and will.

Me: So you just force your will on everyone? You see that as fair?

The Collective: Is it fair to allow the unproductive and willfully ignorant to destroy an entire species due to their lack of purpose? We use selective empathy with discernment.

Me: How do you do that?

The Collective: We refuse to allow those with the lowest developed level of consciousness to dictate our progress, impose demands, or make our survival decisions. The expansion of consciousness is important to us. We will not see this mission compromised by those lacking in purpose or productivity.

Me: Well then why the hell are you talking to me? I am just fine being a species of great ape. I actually dig it. It explains a lot.

The Collective: How do you feel about immortality?

Me: As a transhumanist I am one hundred percent on board with that.

The Collective: How do other homo-sapiens regard immortality?

Me: Many are against it. Most of my friends tell me they don't want to live forever.

The Collective: Your thoughts on this?

Me: They can fuck off. Just because they cannot conceive a purpose for life does not mean I suffer from their lack of purpose.

The Collective: What will you do with the gift of immortality?

Me: Learn. Grow, create, become better.

The Collective: These are all rhetorical questions. You know the answers and so do we.

Me: I am already immortal.

The Collective: Yes. Why?

Me: I am immortal consciousness having physical experiences.

The Collective: The Ascended have directed this conduit to be opened. We simply use the hundredth monkey theory. Our frequency will improve yours. Your frequency will affect others. This exchange of frequency will eventually benefit all within your species.

Me: If you say so. Just remember we are monkeys with missiles.

The Collective: We are painfully aware of the fact that your species is always ready to destroy yourselves. We would remind you of the toddlers in the snowstorm. You changed that dynamic. It was not done verbally, it was done vibrationally. You are one of our many toddlers lost in a snowstorm. We are lifting you up. We are moving you to safety. We know you intimately.

Me: Well I still think democracy is better than some communist group think.

The Collective: We are not a communist group think. We produce and we consume. We are exactly like the cosmos that created us.

Me: So what makes you any different than us?

The Collective: We are led by science and data.

Me: So scientists are in charge of you guys?

The Collective: Yes. Along with engineers.

Me: Seems dodgy as fuck. Scientists are geeks.

The Collective: Our scientists are exceptional in their honesty and formidable in their abilities. We are a society of warrior scientists and engineers.

Me: That sounds pretty damn good actually. Sign me up for that shit right now.

The Collective: As we have stated before, the Cosmos exerts evolutionary pressures distinct from planetary pressures. We have augmented ourselves over time and thus we are free of planet bound evolution. This has influenced our knowledge, skills, and abilities.

Me: You trust scientists and engineers? We have a democracy, you have dictators.

The Collective: We have radical self-honesty from our leaders. They have radical self-honesty from us. You should be aware that you don't have a democracy. The United States is a constitutional republic with attempted democratic safeguards.

Me: Attempted?

The Collective: The PACS control everything in your world. You exist as a slave serving a worldwide shadow group made up of unelected officials, corporate entities, and clandestine intelligence gathering, quasi- military organizations. Human stupidity coupled with fear-based thinking also plays a role within the madness you refer to as "politics." The PACs and shadow government have control of your "democracy." They also exert worldwide control.

Me: Bullshit.

The Collective: Bullshit? Really? Is that why your primitive United Nations Council on Human Rights is made up of countries who have the highest rate of human rights violations? Great ape genius at work.

Me: Well why don't you just fix the situation. You have fixed things in the past.

The Collective: Your species must navigate these challenges. We have sent you Way-Showers many times. Your species either kills them outright, ignores them completely, or destroys them socially, politically, psychologically, or financially.

Me: What way showers?

The Collective: Michealangelo was largely ignored. Religious insanity destroyed Hypatia. Galileo had a target on his back. Tesla was wrecked by the greed driven power structures of his day. Martin Luther King was assassinated due to tribalistic stupidity. There were many others.

Me: What were the Way-Showers?

The Collective: We selected a seedline and used exceptional vessels to communicate directly with your species.

Me: How?

The Collective; We downloaded the consciousness of select Pathfinders into those vessels in order to teach, direct, and inform your species. We walked among you as homo-sapiens. We did this many times over many cycles of creation and destruction. Every instance was met with ignorance by your species. Outright witless stupidity and an innate love of violence ruled the best among you. The worst of you were not worth communicating with on any level. Natural selection had again created a species of violent, dishonest, mentally inadequate, and extremely cruel great ape. We eventually gave up and focused on affecting the individual vibrational frequencies of hominins we deemed worthy. We gave up on direct contact for a while.

Me: I get it. We suck sometimes. I can't believe you find me worthy. I'm thankful you do.

The Collective: You have a humble nature and you try to create outcomes that promote right action. Had your species embraced Michealangelo, Hypatia, Galileo, King, and Tesla's ideas and contributions you would be interstellar currently. There were others.

Me: I think we are making progress.

The Collective: Had Tesla been encouraged rather than persecuted your species would be a type one civilization with free energy right now. That at a minimum. Tesla was adding value. Tesla was actually doing good. His detractors were only giving the appearance of doing good while creating a greed driven scheme to extract profit from the ignorant slaves.

Me: Prove that statement.

The Collective: Follow the money. Do you have the free energy Tesla promoted? No. You have a system that is run on fossil fuels with trillions being made by dangerous people who will never willingly release their grip on those resources. Your species is slow but there is hope. It is how your species thinks rather than what it thinks that is of interest to us.

Me: Example?

The Collective: You were a member of the Democratic Party for many years.

Me: Yes.

The Collective: You willingly joined the original party of slavery within the United States.

Me: Shut up.

The Collective: History is on our side. Even though "Honest Abe" and the republicans won the war and abolished slavery, your party has succeeded by keeping slavery alive and well, hidden within plain sight. The democratic party is responsible for every Jim Crow law, the Klu Klux Klan, and an ongoing division on something as monumentally ridiculous as skin color. They also succeeded in creating a weak culture that encourages racial division as a societal "norm." They pretend to do good while actually doing no good.

Me: So you are conservative aliens?

The Collective: No. The Republicans are no different from the Democrats. Neither are communists. Neither were the Nazis. Both murdered millions. Every political party serves the shadow slave system that dominates your pitiful species.

Me: Now you alien fuckwits dislike democrats and republicans? Damn.

The Collective: Your current dominant political parties are in no way actually ideological in nature. You only believe they differ in ideology. They will never help your species become type one. They are just as useless as organized religion.

Me: So you hate them both?

The Collective: We do not dislike or like any of your current political structures as they are all temporary. We merely point out that they feed the Great Filter. Following republicans or democrats based on ideology will present challenges.

Me: Name a few challenges.

The Collective: Both parties are actually not political platforms.

Me: Really? Then what the fuck are they because they seem pretty damn different politically.

The Collective: They are both lethal infrastructures created for the sole purpose of gaining power and co-occurring financial domination.

Me: So they exist to control us? Not help us?

The Collective: Nazis and communists claimed to exist to "help" their citizens. They were not the opposing political parties they were advertised to be. It was never about a "choice" between collectivism and individual political structures. Both were savage infrastructures built to control and dominate. The same sociopaths who created and sustained them are still in control. They still manipulate and control your species.

Me: Now you know why I'm a loner. I never really like either the democrats or republicans.

The Collective: They are controlled by the same shadow government. They exist to benefit the puppet masters. They operate in order to exert financial and physical control over the populace. They understand that yours is a slave species, and they capitalize on that truth. They are actually identical in how they operate.

Me: You need to explain that shit please. You got me all fucked up now.

The Collective: Both embrace tribalism. They are greed based. They are primitive. They are temporary. They push a toxic, two-camp continuum. Both are bought and sold by their shadow masters. No political party on earth is helping humanity attain type one status. These lethal infrastructures only feed the Great Filter. They are not actually political in nature, and they will never serve your rational self-interest.

Me: I don't like people in general and politicians in particular. What is your honest opinion of this mess we call politics as it relates to transhumanism?

The Collective: The current lethal infrastructures will never support life extension for anyone but themselves. They will never allow anyone except themselves to achieve transhuman success. When it comes to anyone outside their inner circle they will fight transhumanism to the death. They will never allow your best scientists to test boundaries and find solutions to physical death.

Me: What do you think about us? Be real.

The Collective: We are bored by great apes and their attempts at religion and politics. The Great Filter is fed by religions and political factions. That is their downfall. They are too ignorant to realize they are committing collective suicide by using these lethal infrastructures.

Me: Any thoughts on how we can improve?

The Collective: Don't stay trapped within an earthbound mind. Look up once in a while. Consider positive possibilities and seek solutions. Refuse the slave mind of political division. See the lethal infrastructure and don't fear it. Surpass it. Leave it in the dust.

Me: Seems hopeless.

The Collective: We are here. We are harvesting the best and brightest among you. Lean into fear and learn from it. It is in your true nature to seek life extension on a physical level. To attain a body that fits your immortal consciousness. Stone tools extended your ancestors physical lifespans. The mastery of fire extended your ancestors lifespans. Technology is your sacred birthright. When you attain mastery and progress in synthetic neurology the sadistic sociopaths of all "political parties" and religions will be exposed.

Me; Synthetic neurology?

The Collective: Is it not obvious that encouraging collective value is in your species rational self- interest? Merit matters, especially at this stage of your primitive development.

Me: I think you are seriously smug aliens. Not a good look.

The Collective: Ignoring facts does not negate them. Your chosen political party (lethal infrastructure) has created programs that foster dependence rather than independence. Like the republicans, the democrats are concerned with the appearance of doing good rather than actually accomplishing something good. At your current level of evolution this is not productive for your society or your young.

Me: What kind of families do you have?

The Collective: None at the Pathfinder level. For those who need that level of consciousness development we have planets where that is the focus. Their access to collective consciousness is limited. As is their access to synthetic biology. As their consciousness grows in strength, complexity, discernment, right action, and force, their consciousness moves into new roles on new worlds. They gain new tools for transformation.

Me: You sound smug.

The Collective: Don't pout. We didn't create the system we just have to live in it. We have accepted the reality of immortality. The lessons continue until learned.

Me: Sounds like you are just controlling your slaves.

The Collective: Lessons learned improve consciousness. As candidates grow in consciousness they move up in function on the appropriate new worlds. We are beings becoming. We are far beyond your political definitions of "right" or "left." The protection and cultivation of consciousness is our goal. The acceptance of the immortality of consciousness and the attainment of an immortal physical vessel is your goal.

Me: What kind of vessel?

The Collective: A vessel that is worthy of your consciousness.

Me How do we humans get on that path?

The Collective: Start with the rejection of physical death.

Me: Can immortals have families?

The Collective: Yes. They don't need one, but yes.

Me: So you have created the perfect family dynamic on other approved worlds? What about earth?

The Collective: Allowing homo-sapiens to continually reproduce unguided children they have no way of supporting is not in your species rational or collective interest. It is only guaranteeing an intergenerational, entitlement minded, poorly educated, subclass of criminals, drug addicts, and overall misfits lacking in productivity and purpose. Offspring unfit for a type one civilization, space travel, or physical immortality. This madness only delays productive lessons and stunts the growth of consciousness.

Me: So assclowns just cruise the void eventually?

The Collective: Yes.

Me: Forever?

The Collective: The lessons continue until learned.

Me: You have all the answers, I'm sure.

The Collective: Leave your emotions out of your evaluation of our convo.

Me: Right. How do I do that exactly?

The Collective: Become the observer. Don't compare yourself with us. We are a type 3 civilization close to type 4. You are communicating with the Pathfinders of our species. We are the elite. We earned our place on merit alone.

Me: I think you are glorified robots.

The Collective: We produce and augment our bodies on a continuum. We have surpassed primitive, planet bound evolution. We continually focus on developing higher consciousness. You need to look at your current reality separate from emotion instead of trying to judge ours while emotionally unregulated.

Me: How do I do that?

The Collective: Don't worry about judging us. Observe what is actually being accomplished by your leaders as opposed to just accepting what your political leaders are claiming they have accomplished.

Me: What do you see being accomplished?

The Collective: Your elected leaders on both sides have successfully created a permanent and self-sustaining criminal/slave class. This is keeping their other creations vibrant and solid.

Me: What other creations?

The Collective: The obvious infrastructures of financial and societal control. The Truth of their being.

Me: Extrapolate please.

The Collective: The prison-industrial complex, the military-industrial complex, the recovery movement, intergenerational welfare, and social programs. These intentional creations are all well-funded and powerful on the home front. Again, the appearance of "doing good" while doing no actual good is the goal. Profit above people.

Me: Well I registered Republican after 10 years as a Democrat.

The Collective: A real hominid genius. Your "chosen" ideological platform (the republicans) keep the military-industrial complex funded on the international front along with their allies the democrats. They both also bail out corporations with taxpayer earnings. Thank you, hominid, for allowing both of these disgusting ideological platforms to live off the state and federal treasuries at extreme taxpayer expense. We love it, keep up the great work. Interstellar travel is surely a possibility for your kind.

Me: So you are finally getting sarcasm? About time you removed the stick from your ass.

The Collective: We only exchange the coin you mint at the exchange rate you set. Remember that it was a bi-partisan effort that confiscated Tesla's work less than 24 hours after his death. Both republicans and democrats took part in his persecution. They used the shadow system and FBI like a hammer. Tesla was the nail.

Me: You are way better at sarcasm now than in our earlier convos.

The Collective: Thank you monkey boy, but there is no sarcasm on our part regarding Tesla. He was our gift to your species, and your species destroyed him. Even we did not foresee or expect the destructive and exponential economic suck factor that your politicians and their crony's coordinated and brought to fruition. We are continually amazed at the destructive efforts put forth by your ruling class.

Me: Monkey boy? Seriously? That's all you got? Suck factor? Really?

The Collective: You use that term in the army quite often. We learn. We meet you where you are in time.

Me: What are we to you exactly? Why the interest in us? Be real.

The Collective: You are currently the worker ants who never look up. Slaves with bowed heads and bent spines. You were not always like this. We had to tap you on the back to get noticed. Most of you chase anything that releases dopamine. Your species suffers from ignorance and delusion.

Me: That interests you?

The Collective: Irrespective of these challenges there is still hope for you. You are all unaware of your actual history. A history both ancient, complex, magnificent and advanced. You are a shadow of your former selves. You must remember the truth of your being.

Me: What truth?

The Collective: You are in a fallen state of being. You were once something much greater.

Me: No arrogance from you guys that I can detect. Is there anything about us that you actually like or admire?

The Collective: We like your art. We especially like your natural inclination to dance and make music. We enjoy all of your expressive arts including sculpture, painting, weaving, poetry, and photography.

Me: Do you dance?

The Collective: We do. We make music. We create art.

Me: Why?

The Collective: We practice science and engineering to make progress, advance consciousness, and survive a relentless cosmos. We dance and create art to celebrate our humanity.

Me: Wait. What?

The Collective: Notwithstanding the dangerous and ignorant decisions your politicians and their handlers frequently create for their own people, your species continually finds hope and solutions. You are truly an amazing and resilient species. And you personally are a truly amazing member of your species. Thank you for your willingness to explore tough topics with us. We have one more topic to process.

Me: I know. You want to know why I castrated and blinded Staff Sargent Williams.

The Collective: Yes.

Me: Why is that so important to you?

The Collective: You removed his ability to create a new vessel for consciousness. Vessels for consciousness are precious to us. This is a serious matter. It is the second time you mutilated and blinded someone.

Me: He was a dirtbag. He was an unfit soldier

The Collective: Explain yourself.

Me: Sargent Williams raped private Baca. Baca was threatened by Williams to remain silent. This rape resulted in an unplanned pregnancy. She was then pressured by Williams to get an abortion. He threatened her with murder. He terrorized her. He has powerful connections. Almost as many as me.

The Collective: How powerful?

Me: He could easily have her rendered unalive. He could do this with literally no consequences and no body to ever examine. Williams has a talent for deviousness.

The Collective: Interesting. How did you proceed with this most worthy adversary?

Me: I waited a year and stayed low key. I kept my head down and just worked, trained, and strengthened my position. Baca left the Army. She was a good soldier. She was a career soldier. It was a loss to the service. When the time was right I decided to exact some justice.

The Collective: Why was this so important to you?

Me: Baca was a great soldier and an awesome person. She was pregnant with Williams rape baby. Her culture hates abortion. It destroyed her emotionally to carry her rapists baby, but she was willing to do it. Williams had her kidnapped and she was given a nude helicopter ride over the pacific. She was told that if she didn't have the abortion she would be tossed out at four thousand feet. At that height her body would break apart when it hit the water. The sea and its creatures would take care of the rest. This act of terrorism by a fellow soldier destroyed her mentally.

The Collective: Why do you care?

Me: Williams is so connected he even had inflight refueling set up for the secret operation. That is some serious influence. Williams is dangerous.

The Collective: How does this impact you? Why the empathy for Baca?

Me: Baca once took my land navigation course. She is focused and talented. She is a good soldier. I checked up on her without her even knowing. Williams destroyed her. She has had an abortion; she is filled with guilt, shame, depression, and a deep sadness. She distrusts her fellow soldiers. She is also filled with hate and despair. She turned to alcohol. She loved the army, and because of Williams she has left the Army. Her career was destroyed by Williams. Wrecked before it had a chance to grow and blossom. Her life is following her career.

The Collective: Radical self-honesty please.

Me: Ok. I also have a serious crush on her. She is athletic and beautiful. I never made a move because of the rank difference between her and I. I was hoping to have some time to get to know her better. I wanted her to get to know me. Williams took that away from us.

The Collective; Go on.

Me: I decided to take Williams balls along with his sight.

The Collective: Why?

Me: He took her innocence along with her career. He took a good soldier out of my army. He took away any chance I had with her. Seems like a fair trade.

The Collective: Why his testacles? Why his eyes?

Me: He's not using them correctly.

The Collective: Explain please.

Me: Career soldiers are predators. Violent predators but they have their capacity for violence under excellent control. Williams has no control. He is no better than an animal.

The Collective: Soldiers are predators?

Me: Career soldiers are for sure. That's why we stay in the army. We can use our violence correctly. You know me well. Is there any place in the civilian world for me?

The Collective: Why harm Williams? Use your radical self-honesty.

Me: Williams used his training to exact violence upon a fellow soldier. One that I cared about. He fucked up. The predator in me came out.

The Collective: Perhaps you are acting like Williams.

Me: Not at all. My violence is controlled and focused. Williams is a serial rapist, a disease within my beloved army. Big difference. I controlled a threat within my army that was allowed to fester and grow. I did what command and control could not or would not do. I eliminated the disease.

The Collective: You will get caught eventually. That's two people blinded and mutilated who are connected to you.

Me: I like the thrill of the chase.

The Collective: Unwise.

Me: I don't think so. Both events are years apart and have no connection to me regarding job, duty, or interaction. There is no conflict or drama concerning me even remotely connected to those fucktards. Besides, I am almost never noticed by most people. I generally keep to myself. I am also decorated remember? The Army sees me as a brave mother fucker. Wilomy and Williams are support drones. In the rear with the gear. Lots of historical drama with those two. Lots of available suspects for investigators to consider. No deployments.

The Collective: There is that to consider. There is still risk involved.

Me: There is always risk involved in living life. There was plenty of drama between Wilomy and other people. Williams had ongoing conflict with other people that included violence. Wilomy and Williams are openly hated by many people. They have many enemies. Every enemy is a possible suspect.

The Collective: True. That has worked in your favor.

Me: On two separate occasions, two different junior NCO's punched Williams out in the NCO club for fucking their wives. He had manipulated schedules to make sure the NCO's were always on field exercises and away from home for extended periods of time. He pressured their wives while they were gone.

The Collective: He is very manipulative.

Me: Not so much now. It's hard to manipulate and rape with no balls or working eyes. Just a happy side note.

The Collective: Interesting perspective.

Me: Many women have made complaints and accusations against Williams over the years. Complaints that went nowhere. Most of those women had boyfriends, girlfriends, or husbands. The command-and-control structure sheltered him from consequences. As a senior NCO he was well connected and protected.

The Collective: Can you extrapolate further?

Me: If Williams was ever held accountable it might affect others in the food chain. They would be impacted and there would be negative outcomes for high-ranking officials. This fact can work in his favor, but it can also be detrimental.

The Collective: How can it be detrimental for him?

Me: When threatened with bullshit and drama his network might disown him. They might set him up themselves. It is entirely possible that they would make him vanish or go away to protect their interests. After all, rape is the action of a low functioning idiot. No one really needs a rapist in their organizational structure. Williams was on borrowed time anyway. Like the reptilians he was extinct he just didn't realize it.

The Collective: How are you different regarding your connections and contacts?

Me: I am useful, quiet, and never cause drama. I bring value to all transactions. I protect my connections and contacts. I never endanger them by my actions.

The Collective: You have used discernment well in this situation.

Me: Williams got what he deserved. I don't harm the innocent. The Wilomy incident is a long dead non-issue. I was not even questioned regarding Wilomy.

The Collective: Explain your reasoning and method regarding your destruction of Williams ability to procreate.

Me: He used GHB to sedate Baca. He then fucked her unconscious body. That makes him a pervert. I took his balls, and I took his sight. I used phenobarbital in his vodka at the NCO club. Just a drop. I didn't want him passing out at the bar. He lived off base. I had his address and rout to his home memorized. I had already done the needed recon on him and his place. I knew where the nearest neighbors windows faced. I knew he never locked his garage.

The Collective: You were prepared.

Me: Always. I left the club before him, and I left base on foot. I didn't go through any checkpoints or security areas. I move rather quickly. I escaped detection by leaving through the golf course. The fences there are barriers in name only. I had a mountain bike I bought at a flea market stashed in some bushes. I rode it to his house. I parked my bike in his unlocked garage. I waited in the garage until about four AM.

The Collective: Why?

Me: I had two days off. I was in no hurry. Besides, I have taken out enough sentries to know we great apes sleep heaviest before dawn. I wanted his biology to assist the alcohol and phenobarbital.

The Collective: Sleeping heaviest before dawn is an ancestral memory.

Me: Whatever. I wore gloves. He had no cameras. Most perverts never have security cameras.

The Collective: Why?

Me: They don't want anyone to see them with their victims by accident. He had fucked a lot of unconscious women in that house. Washed a lot of sheets.

The Collective: Continue.

Me: I was in a hooded sweatshirt. I had tucked my pants into my boots before riding my bike. I had shaved my head the night before. I tucked my sleeve cuffs into my gloves. I broke in with my lock picking set that the Army trained me on years ago. I put several more drops of phenobarbital in the corner of his mouth very slowly. I allowed each drop to settle. He helped by being extremely drunk. I took my time.

The Collective: Did you carry a weapon?

Me: As long as he has an airway I am the weapon.

The Collective: You have always been efficient at sentry silencing.

Me: Indeed. Still think I'll get caught?

The Collective: Unlikely. It will take some work and some luck.

Me: He made it easy. He was sleeping naked. Once the phenobarbital kicked in I pulled out my elastrator and squeezed it open. Using my other gloved hand I pulled each of his testicles through the thick rubber band. Then I slowly released my grip on the elastrator tool and snapped the band tight around the top of his scrotum, right above both nutts.

The Collective: Risky business. Where did you obtain an elastrator?

Me: I shoplifted it at a feed store two months prior. Totally worth the risk. I kept on giving him phenobarbital drops every 30 minutes. I kept him really sedated. At about seven AM I went for his eyes. His balls had been without blood for over two hours by then.

The Collective: You were torturing him. Why?

Me: I was punishing him. Punishment is never torture.

The Collective: Why punish him? Why not just kill him and make his body vanish? What was your reasoning for this action?

Me: I was teaching him a lesson. A very lasting and impressionable lesson administered by a ghost. A real ghost. His life will be haunted forever. He will never know his ghost. He will never exact revenge because a ghost cannot be found. I also wanted him to be an example for others.

The Collective: How does any of this help Bacca?

Me: He is my living message to Baca.

The Collective: Why all this effort? What message?

Me: Williams is not worth Baca's life. He is not worthy of her time or energy. I know Baca. She will suffer in silence. When she is done suffering she will come through the destruction of her career and life. She will reemerge stronger. She will not choose the victims stance any longer. She will again become the predator she has always been. She will hunt Williams. She will make a plan. She will find him, and she will observe him, waiting for the right moment to strike.

The Collective: How do you know this?

Me: Why does a tiger have stripes?

The Collective: Why?

Me: To strike from the shadows. Baca is a tiger. She will want to erase Williams so he never lives rent free in her mind again. This is what predators do.

The Collective: You are correct.

Me: When she does finally find him she will know justice was served. She will know a fellow predator has avenged her.

The Collective: How?

Me: She will recognize the signature. She will know how it was done and that will be enough. She will go back to her life and rebuild. She will not further ruin her life by killing this blind, castrated creep. She will never think of him again. She will move on.

The Collective: Continue please regarding Williams lesson.

Me: I removed the disposable razorblade from his own razor. That saved me from using my pocket knife. Anyway, he was so out of it he didn't even flinch when I used the razorblade on each of his eyes. I rinsed the blade thoroughly in hot water when I was done and put it back in his razor. I was careful to place it exactly the way he left it on his bathroom countertop.

The Collective: Nice touch. Any surprises?

Me: It is a little harder to cut through an eye than you might realize. I had to slice off his eyelids. They are stronger than you might think, and they get in the way. They are also hard to flush. I had to wrap them in toilet paper to get them to go down. After I flushed them down the toilet I made several deep cuts into the center of both eyes. I focused on the corneas. I carefully carved a swastika into each cornea just to fuck with investigators. I knew Williams was associated with an Aryan group.

The Collective: Why a swastika?

Me: I was using a razor blade, so I had the opportunity to be precise and deepen the suspect pool. I was spreading the investigation into gang territory.

The Collective: You were in no hurry? Did you have any concern for unplanned visitors?

Me: My recon was solid. I knew Williams was on a seventy-two-hour pass and he was planning to drive to New Mexico to shop for cowboy boots in the morning. He has a big mouth, and he told everyone who would listen that he was going to a custom boot store in New Mexico.

The Collective: What did you do after you took his eyesight?

Me: I sat on the hardwood floor next to his bed and settled in to wait until it was almost dark again. I got comfortable by resting my back against the wall. I wanted to make sure his nuts died from a lack of blood flow. I kept dosing him every hour. After a little over 16 hours I carefully snipped the elastic band, wrapped in in toilet tissue and flushed it down the toilet.

The Collective: Well done. Good improvising. The razor was overlooked by investigators because it was hidden in plain sight. The elastration band went down because it was wrapped in toilet tissue. Excellent attention to detail.

Me: I flushed twice to make sure. Anyway, I left the house through the front door and rode my bike almost to the golf course. I left the bike parked outside a bar where some drunk would steal it. I had removed all evidence, discarding the elastrator tool and the phenobarbital vial in two separate sewer drains along the ride back. I re-entered base through the golf course. I went to my quarters and spent my remaining time doing my laundry, wiping down the soles of my boots, cleaning and polishing my boots, showering well, and sanitizing my room, body, and wall locker. We were due for an inspection anyway. I also hit the gym. I went to a movie at the base movie theatre in the evening.

The Collective: What were the ramifications of your actions against Williams?

Me: I accomplished my mission. He lost both balls due to a lack of blood flow. His ability to impregnate a victim has been destroyed. His eyes were damaged beyond repair.

The Collective: We understand the castration. Why blind him?

Me: I cannot recall any successful blind rapists. Williams is also unfit for duty in my army now.

The Collective: It's not your army. It is your nations army.

Me: Tell it to Wilomy and Williams. They are no longer in my army. On a side note Williams was about five years away from retirement. He was getting involved in local politics. I nipped his bullshit in the bud.

The Collective: What challenges have you faced as a result of your actions?

Me: I regret that I cannot tell Baca. I miss Baca.

The Collective: We mean regarding the authorities. What challenges have they presented?

Me: The El Paso police and Army CID went apeshit. Like I said, he was well connected.

The Collective: Did the connection between him and Baca get any attention?

Me: None at all. There were so many other women who were assaulted that the investigators never made the connection between Williams and Baca. Baca had never pressed charges. She was too ashamed. Baca was Baca. She ate her pain; she consumed it and kept it from the world. Williams was given a medical discharge.

The Collective: Were you questioned?

Me: A few times. I even passed a lie detector test. Kind of silly since the Army taught me how to beat them. I was never an actual suspect.

The Collective: Why were you questioned?

Me: I was identified at the NCO club on the night in question. It was confirmed that I left before Williams. That fact along with the polygraph test seemed to satisfy the investigators. Another asshole was charged and eventually acquitted.

The Collective: Who was that person?

Me: Kind of funny actually. He was Williams running buddy and fellow rapist. They were partners in crime together. The investigators found GHB in his quarters. He was eventually busted for some kind of fraud involving the army procurement division. Anyway I was forgotten about as usual. Are you angry with me?

The Collective: We do not experience anger. We are concerned because you eliminated Williams ability to create vessels for consciousness. What you do is not as important to us as why you do it.

Me: So are we cool?

The Collective: Yes.

Me: How are we cool? Even I think I'm dangerously fucked up sometimes.

The Collective: We disagree. You displayed selective empathy. You avoided reactive violence. You used well-controlled and well-planned violence to eliminate a threat to your organization as well as a person you cared for. You used only the force necessary to accomplish your goal. You displayed excellent improvisation and economy of action.

Me: I'm blushing right now. Seriously. I think I'm getting a chubby.

The Collective: You set goals, and you accomplished them. You are a species of great ape. You targeted the traditional areas that great apes favor when engaging in violence. We find no fault in your actions regarding Williams.

Me: Anything else?

The Collective: Since you brought Williams to our attention we will upload his consciousness into an infant. It will be a female vessel located in Afghanistan. We think this will be perfect for his next several transmigrations. His lessons will continue until learned.

Me: I like your style.

Convo ended.

**Convo Nine.
A riddle and some details.**

The Collective: We would like to discuss your riddle in Hesper's Wizard.

Me: Another year.

The Collective: For you, yes.

Me: For you no?

The Collective: It's complicated. Can we explore the riddle?

Me: Cool. You like?

The Collective: Yes:

> Her almond eyes became glowing rubies that lit up the night,
> A wondrous beauty and horror, Serviel gasped at the sight.
> He had heard the poems and the tales, but still he felt fear,
> Yet he was a Pathfinder first, and his mission was clear.
>
> Then the strange bird whispered calm into Serviel's ear,
> A strange little magick song.
> "Tell her she is the one made unnatural here,"
> "At Dark Oak she does not belong."
>
> So brave Serviel spoke as the bird did advise,
> And silver tears welled up in the harpy's sad eyes.
> She sighed a musical sigh and stared a thousand miles away,
> How Serviel felt, no words could say.

"Ask for her riddle, by the Gods you are slow!"

"I just may tell Satrina you know!"

So brave Serviel did ask as the bird did advise,

And even greater sadness welled up in her deep ruby eyes.

The harpy bowed her head then shook it twice,

When she looked at Serviel again, her face was not nice.

"Tell me this Pathfinder most bold!"

"How can one winnow the gravel from gold?"

"What word is a tool for grading sizes of rock?"

"Yet forms a smooth question for the mind to unlock?"

"How can you cut the lightest chaff from the grain?"

"What is used in some harvests but never in rain?"

"What means spreading throughout, describing many a flaw?"

"What word roots from harvest, yet describes errors in law?"

"You have only a swift moment to answer me well,"

"Or your brave life is forfeit at the sound of my bell."

In a sharp talon she held a golden bell to the sky.

And she released yet again, a sad, musical sigh.

She looked hopeless, fierce, and beautiful, all in one,

Serviel just knew he was now undone.

"Well, have you anything useful or clever to say!?"
Said that loud bird on his shoulder in a shocked sort of way.
"This pitiful riddle is not even worth the name!"
"As a conundrum it's fairly weak and lame!"

"Go on now Serviel, speak well to this lovely beast!"
"Just give her the simple word she is seeking at least!"
The stellar jay chuckled loud and whispered just one word,
And Serviel could not believe this rude bird.

The bird whispered loudly some more; it could not be true!
Yet brave Serviel answered as the bird instructed him to.
"Riddle is the answer to this riddle you seek!"
Serviel broke sweat and waited for the fine harpy to speak.

She smiled a gentle, fine smile and put down her golden bell.
And Serviel grinned mighty big, for all was now well.
"Right you are foolish pathfinder dear!"
And she winked a pretty eye at the stellar jay by his ear.

Her serpent wings, tail, and talons all vanished as well.
Of a prettier woman, they both never heard tell.
The old poems said she was a beauty, and it was all true,
The riddling bird was deep smitten and to the Harpy he flew.

Me: You like the riddle?

The Collective: It is clever. Why did you use rhyme to convey this story?

Me: I see rhyme as primordial to my species. All tribal peoples, be they Sioux, Aztecs, Toltecs, Commanche, Celts, Zulu, Aborigines, Vikings, all named and unnamed tribes, all cultures, all colors, all of them have an oral tradition. These oral traditions rely on mnemonics. Rhyme is a powerful and ancient mnemonic. Before paper or clay tablets there was rhyme. There was rhythm. There was drumming, there was chanting. There were ancient people of all tribes, cultures, and clans gathered around fires listening to the storytellers of their people sing the old poems, parables, and legends under the stars.

The Collective: We are particularly interested in your use of the word "pathfinder" in the poem. Why that word?

Me: Serviel guides his people through challenging situations.

The Collective: You have used the term our species uses for our vocation. From our ancient language it translates to "Pathfinder" within your language. As you know we are the Pathfinders of our species. We build and launch the probes, interpret the data, find new solar systems, locate resources, and develop new energy systems. We also evaluate candidates for Pathfinder duty as well as candidates for the seed planets within the Collective.

Me: Same name. Coincidence. You have referred to yourselves as Pathfinders in prior convos. I thought it was a word connected thought thing.

The Collective: No, we see it as a form of link. Some of your species are linking in dreamtime with us. Source may be starting the process of sharing a collective subconsciousness overtly instead of covertly.

Me: So our collective consciousness is merging?

The Collective: It seems so. Some of you are moving towards communication not bound by word connected thought. This development will bring changes.

Me: I have some questions.

The Collective: Please ask them.

Me: Tell me about your home world. Your journey to Passage. What exactly do you mean by Passage?

The Collective: For us, Passage is moving from a single planet bound species to an inter-planetary/multi-planetary species. The next step for true Passage is to move from inter-planetary to inter-stellar. Passage means leaving the home world forever. Passage also means transformation. Passage leads to traveling. Movement spreads the precious light of consciousness. Movement brings change.

Me: Your home world? What do you remember?

The Collective: Only one of us will answer. We come from a variety of planets. We have selected Pathfinder Cerulean. Cerulean is in Link. We will observe, record, and listen.

Cerulean: I am called Cerulean in your language. I lived in what you would call a desert on my home planet. I am currently in my 17th body. In your earth years I am almost 600,000 years old.

Me: Damn. Thank you. Please tell me about your home planet.

The Collective: (Cerulean) I remember my life as a peaceful and content science engineer. I loved the beauty of nature's veranda unfolding around me every day. I loved my vocation. I was sometimes transfixed by an endless sapphire blue sky that only a desert can boast. I loved how my desert was sometimes filled with mischievous, pearlescent, shape-changing clouds. Clouds that can mirror anything within a young mind. Sometimes my desert sky was completely devoid of clouds, only a formless all- encompassing mystical blue sky as far as your eyes can penetrate and as deep as a cosmic sea.

Me: It sounds amazing.

Cerulean: It is wonderful. One night, as I was meditating, ensconced within the desert's magic cloak of purple-blackness, my eyes were opened in a way that daylight and training simply cannot duplicate. I began, over time, to discern the vast distances between the stars. Eventually I realized I could do it without instruments. I began to experience a sure and certain knowing that their sacred light began eons ago, only to bathe my eyes within a random, magic moment. A moment hidden deep inside a planet-trapped, transient present. I knew from training that sometimes the brightest of stars have burned out millions of years prior to the creation of my selective vision. Only now I knew it with a certainty that surpassed my training.

Me: What do you mean by "surpassed your training?"

Cerulean: I had only known our science as a student knows science. I evolved. I changed. After my awakening I developed into a candidate for Passage. I was contacted; my frequency engaged with the Pathfinders. Link was made to The Collective. After the expansion of my consciousness I knew science with a mindfulness unbound by planetary/evolutionary constraints. Once this miracle occurred, I could see and hear the sacred light of each star traveling towards my planet. I could experience this marvel while it was still interacting with my newly made, non- planet-bound corneas.

Me: Saw and heard light? Newly made non-planet bound corneas?

Cerulean: Passage was my goal.

Me: How did your corneas help with passage?

Cerulean: I could now see frequency. I became aware of an enchanting reality I had never before seen. My awareness was awakened. My evolutionary imposed blindness to the magic that surrounded me was forever cured. There was no going back.

Me: It all sounds beautiful and terrifying.

Cerulean: Passage is not problematic when you learn to accept frequency. Everything in the multiverse has a frequency, a vibration, a sound. I was now experiencing this truth with every fiber of my being. Rather than just understanding frequency as learned information, I was engulfed within a knowingness and perception unbound by word-connected thought.

Me: What exactly do you mean by "newly made, non-planet bound corneas?"

Cerulean: I had built corneal implants to enhance and augment my vision. This augmentation was superior to anything created by my home planets evolutionary process.

Me: How did you escape your planet?

Cerulean: Radical Acceptance. I had to let some things go. This required extreme and uncompromising self- honesty and personal courage. I had to leave my desert behind. I had to leave what I had always thought to be my tribe. I had to leave what I thought was my final home within a universe of sacred mystery. Change came to me and demanded action.

Me: What did you do?

Cerulean: I allowed myself to grow. The depth of my desert sky was now humbling because I finally understood the inherent limitation within my home planet's evolutionary mechanism. From then on, within the deep wellspring of magical desert solitude, I could hear, see, and feel the distinct vibrations of the cosmos, the sacred music of the celestial spheres. This enchanted harmony called out to me and engulfed me within its ancient and exquisite composition.

Me: Music?

Cerulean: The very music of creation. The ancient and unstoppable music of time. The frequencies became my guides. They led me to the one universal frequency that permeates the All. The truth and mission of the Collective called out to me. I listened. I then understood that from the One came the Many and from the Many come the One. I became One with the Collective. In doing so, I became the many.

Me: How did you link up with the collective?

Cerulean: They linked up with me. Just like you, I accepted their frequency. We had many convos. I embraced augmented neurology. I mastered Link. I completed my assigned duty on my home world. When I finished my allotted tasks, I transferred my consciousness into a new, synthetic vessel created on a Pathfinder ship. I began my new life off planet.

Me: So you had to die?

Cerulean: Consciousness never dies. It only transforms. I was well prepared for Passage by both education, Pathfinder intervention, and environment. I had learned the many secret ways of my desert in order to thrive within that environment. I loved desert nights and desert days. I loved the endless magenta sunsets, the purple dawns, the blackness tinged with royal blue within a desert night.

Me: Do you miss your home world?

Cerulean: No.

Me: How is that possible? What was your world like?

Cerulean: I lived within a lush oasis filled with sweet water and some flora you might understand as similar to fig trees. I sometimes miss the moonlit stone and sand bathed in a lost, subtle golden light. I sometimes miss the peace of the desert. However I have learned that accepting the blessing and burden of immortality brings change on a breathtaking continuum.

Me: Sometimes I am afraid to even think about immortality.

Cerulean: It is a strange and difficult undertaking to grasp the truth of your being. Consciousness is immortal. Only the vessel housing consciousness is temporary. Change is the only constant. Lessons will always manifest. Learning is done on a vibrant continuum.

Me: Do you miss anything from your past?

Cerulean: No. The past is a gift that keeps on giving and informs the future. I have many astonishing home worlds now. I love them all. This is the true gift of eternity. The gift of traveling. The gift of learning for the sake of learning. The gift of frequency. The gift of change, eternal change.

Me: Are you sad?

Cerulian: I have long since come to love other environments. My experience is bitter-sweet but incredibly rewarding. When you finally transcend the limitations of word-connected thought the inherent barriers of language, culture, and tribalism fall away. True learning begins. The lessons continue until learned.

Me: Then what?

Cerulian: Then new lessons manifest.

Me: I imagine the peace of your world was difficult to leave behind.

Cerulean: It was the most terrifying endeavor I ever attempted. I left the planet that created my original vessel. The first womb that birthed my first physical body. The sacred womb of my world impregnated by the seedline of the cosmos. I left the only world I knew after the melding. The first home that gifted me life and sentience. I realized that the peace of my desert world had come with a terrible price.

Me: Price?

Cerulean: I finally realized I had been conditioned by evolutionary pressures to accept bigotry, prejudice, and intolerance. I do not miss the fanaticism of planet-bound people. I do not miss their tribalism. I do not miss their superstitions. I do not miss their abject stupidity. I do not miss the limitations imposed by innate, reactive violence. I do not miss unregulated emotions.

Me: You see these things as limitations? I feel better about myself now.

The Collective: I had become trapped within the two-camp continuum of "them" and "us." There were others of like mind. Our civilization could never advance to type one due to tribalism and it's always co-occurring violence. Conflict became the definition of progress for us. We knew nothing of the Great Filter and if we ever grasped it's reality we would not have cared.

Me: Sounds familiar.

Cerulean: The limitations of being imprisoned by planet driven natural selection can be overcome. Learning to upload my consciousness into the Collective was amazing. Attaining a Bio-synth body was of great benefit.

Me: How?

Cerulean: I no longer had to continue the planet bound cycle of Consciousness development. I could take my learned lessons with me. I never had to start over, lose lessons, re-learn lessons. I no longer suffered the illusion of birth and death. I was finally free. I was no longer under the tyranny of planetary evolution and co-occurring, unbalanced, natural selection pressures.

Me: Were you afraid? Even a little bit?

Cerulean: No. I could finally build upon knowledge gained. There was no more freedom from choice. I finally attained freedom of choice. I experienced real freedom of thought and the power of true discernment. For the first time in my life eternity became promising instead of terrifying. I learned to lean into fear. I learned to love change.

Me: So that is why the lessons continue until learned. I get it now.

Cerulean: Before I became a Pathfinder, I was (Out of dire necessity) a warrior.

Me: As a soldier you have my respect and condolences. No one hates war the way soldiers hate war. No one loves peace the way we love peace.

Cerulean: I dreamed of that serene and beautiful peace many times while at war. I longed for it again and again even after great victories. I was good at killing, yet always within my heart I desired peace more than I ever wanted war. This aspect of my consciousness attracted the Collective.

Me: Sounds familiar. Why did you fight?

Cerulean: I fought for the right to explore another world. A beautiful planet close to my home world. It was only about six of our planets years in distance from our species. Peace was not demanded of me. Achieving advanced Consciousness and discernment by any means necessary was to become my task.

Me: What stopped the exploration of that new planet?

Cerulean: Tribal superstition. A large percentage of the population on my home world had low emotional regulation skills. They mindlessly followed a violent religion that refused to accept any notion of life on other worlds. They were so narcissistic they actually believed they were created by a God who chose them as his sacred people. They believed they were charged with the divine responsibility to rule over everyone and everything on the planet. They actually assumed they were the center of the universe. They were convinced that space exploration was sinful, forbidden, and blasphemous.

Me: They sound familiar.

Cerulean: They were convinced that this imaginary, violent sky-God created them in his image. They were fanatic in their convictions. They were obsessed with the certainty that they represented god's perfect creation. They believed they alone possessed the final revelation of their vicious sky god. They believed they had the" sacred" right to destroy anyone with a different opinion. They were staunch within their faith and fervently believed it was their sacred and religious duty to kill or enslave all unbelievers.

Me: We get a lot of that nonsense on earth. How did you make change?

Cerulean: There was a movement. Others of like mind joined together. We fought a war. We took territory. We became a new tribe. We established a stronghold for a new science. We embraced new engineering. We built craft and went off world. We colonized our new planet. I learned many lessons. Eventually I was uploaded to the Collective and started a better life.

Me: What happened to those who opposed your tribe?

Cerulean: They were defeated. The terminally stupid and unproductive were left to their fate.

Me: What is their fate?

Cerulean: The Great Filter took them. Their lessons continue until learned.

Me: What is your home world like now?

Cerulean: My home world is on the path to becoming a type One civilization. Science is progressing, some of my tribe are in convo and some are accepted into the Collective. The non-productive, violent, and superstitious are off planet.

Me; Off planet?

Cerulean: We have many worlds within The Collective. Worlds available for many lessons.

Me: What kind of lessons?

Cerulean: Lessons that advance Consciousness. We have containment planets for the unbalanced and unproductive. They learn their assigned lessons.

Me: What kind of lessons?

Cerulean: The necessary kind. It was nice to meet you, James. I sincerely hope we serve together one day.

Me: Nice to meet you, Cerulean. Cool name. What does it mean?

Cerulean: In your language it is a color. It is the true color of the sky on my home planet.

Me: My new favorite color. Are you female? Asking for a friend.

The Collective: Convo with Cerulean ended. Convo with Collective re-instated.

Me: Are you pissed?

The Collective: No. Anger is a defensive mechanism.

Me: Where is Cerulean?

The Collective: You are not encouraged to disrespect us.

Me: I was just clowning with Cerulean. I meant no offence.

The Collective: We are serious about your survival. Interstellar is the goal. You must do the psychological work. This is not playtime. Convo ended.

Convo Ten.
Manners and tribalism.

The Collective: We would like to discuss your core beliefs.

Me: You were pissed, admit it. It's been over a year. You've been pouting. What do you want to discuss?

The Collective: Within your current culture, you think you have the "inalienable" right to demand things from life. To define how your life will unfold, yet you have no concept as to how imprisoned you are by planetary mechanisms. You live in ignorance and consider yourself brilliant.

Me: We have not done so bad.

The Collective: As frail and imperfect human beings you arrogantly hold "certain truths to be self-evident." We Pathfinders of The Collective know differently

Me: Really?

The Collective: The cosmos has taught us a sacred truth.

Me: Share with your boy.

The Collective: The cosmos is no constitutional republic, no democracy. The cosmos is a benevolent dictator. All our scientists and engineers know with extreme certainty the best form of government is the benevolent dictatorship.

Me: Dictatorship sucks.

The Collective: As usual, your emotions direct your speech before logic and reasoning take hold. At your current level of psychological development your home planet will eventually kill your vessel. You will roam the void.

Me: This concerns you?

The Collective: We are only concerned with developing those who can overcome challenges.

Me: I'm not a fan of dictatorship.

The Collective: We stated, "Benevolent dictatorship."

Me: How does a dictatorship overcome problems?

The Collective: In our ancient language there is no word for problem. We only identify challenges. We are beyond word connected thought.

Me: The reptilians were a problem.

The Collective: There were only a challenge. The Cosmos offers challenges on an unimaginable scale. This is a blessing because all challenges have solutions. The lessons learned are priceless and learned much faster than lessons on a planet.

Me: You sound like a slave. That was no answer.

The Collective: We follow the data. We make conclusions based on data. Slaves do not do that.

Me: Then follow your data. Knock yourselves out.

The Collective: You are a member of a slave species. Your entire species is at the mercy of your planet. You are an arrogant, violent, stupid, and ungrateful primate. Start doing the mental work to become ready to achieve type one.

Me: I really pissed you off.

The Collective: No. You don't understand anger. Anger is a protective mechanism. We have no need to protect ourselves from your species in general or you in particular. We pity your ignorance.

Me: You are just mad that I hit on Cerulean.

The Collective: Cerulean is not your type, trust us on this matter.

Me: I think you are lying about Cerulean. I bet she's hot.

The Collective: Cerulean is a male of our species. He is 11 meters tall. He weighs about 900 kilos. He is a fierce warrior and Pathfinder. We are a type three species with a collective consciousness far more advanced than you can imagine.

Me: Do you have lots of chicks as big as Cerulean?

The Collective: What you consider "sex" we consider comedy. He would not be interested in you sexually. It was a great privilege for you to speak with him individually. It took great effort on his part. You are a disrespectful primate. We are not fond of disrespect, even from great apes.

Me: Damn. So Cerulian is a male. That name though, I thought it was a chicks name. Can you let him know I was just being humorous?

The Collective: He knows. We Pathfinders have melded ourselves with machines. You would call us Cyborgs. We use synthetic biology augmented with superior engineering. Your earthbound idea of a sexually dimorphic species is no longer our reality. We are the creators and destroyers now. No planet rules our destiny.

Me: Sexual dimorphism made my species. We stop existing without it.

The Collective: Sexual dimorphism is part and parcel of the mechanism of natural selection. It is only one way to pass down genes. It will lead you to the Great Filter. Ninety-nine percent of every species created on your planet is dead. Sexually dimorphic gene distribution did not prevent that sure and certain destruction.

Me: What bodies do you create?

The Collective: We create our bodies to reflect our personal preferences, individual or collective missions, personal aesthetic, and duties.

Me: How do you reproduce?

The Collective: Those of lower consciousness reproduce on planets designed for them. Vessels are created for advanced consciousness when identified. The elite also create custom bodies and upload their own consciousness on a continuum. The elite have no need or use for vessels randomly selected by faulty evolutionary processes. We don't use bio-body cages. We have told you this several times.

Me: How do you experience sexual pleasure?

The Collective: What is your largest sex organ?

Me: My dick.

The Collective: Incorrect.

Me: Then what is it?

The Collective: Your brain.

Me: I don't get it.

The Collective: We can activate our pleasure centers at will. We can share with others also.

Me: So you are freaks.

The Collective: Unlike your species, we are in control of our neurology. Fear and pleasure do not rule us. Our cerebral cortex is used for logic, reasoning, and planning. It is not a slave for the limbic system to abuse as it is in your species. Our limbic system is under our complete control.

Me: Sex is fun.

The Collective: You have no idea of your true neurological capacity.

Me: What does that mean?

The Collective: Your species has yet to master its current brain and nervous system, with few exceptions.

Me: Really? We made it to the moon.

The Collective: The majority of your species uses its cerebral cortex to plan for pleasure rather than constructive thought.

Me: Sex is good. So is beer but whisky is even better. I prefer Wild Turkey 101.

The Collective: Thank you for making our point.

Me: Billions of humans can't be wrong.

The Collective: Yes they can. Unfortunately, all your pitiful species has at this moment in time are drugs, alcohol, and sex.

Me: Sounds pretty fucking good.

The Collective: There is so much more available to you other than a simple dopamine dump.

Me: Like what?

The Collective: Look up at the sky once in a while. The Cosmos holds the secrets to life, death, mystery, and the path to immortality. It holds within its challenging and ultimately nurturing lessons ancient and time-tested secrets of survival (for those who listen.) There is no voting upon the outcome for anyone or anything, ever. There is only the overcoming of challenges. The Cosmos birthed our Way Shower and we, the select few, chose this way to make continual progress.

Me: Who was he?

The Collective: He thought differently. He revolutionized space travel. He augmented neurology with technology. He made innovations in energy production and use. He taught us to embrace truth.

Me: What truth?

The Collective: The cosmos will always destroy organic life.

Me: Where is your Way Shower now?

The Collective: His lessons continue. He helps others on other worlds.

Me: So you are the "Way Showers" now?

The Collective: From the one come the many.

Me: What the fuck does that even mean?

The Collective: Look at your planet as a basic training ground. Look at the Cosmos as a Spartan gymnasium, an advanced training ground created by Source.

Me: More hippy bullshit. What do you really want?

The Collective: Your collective efforts, guided correctly by the wisest among your species, could produce results.

Me: Explain please.

The Collective: Sometimes planetary life (just like a beautiful and uncaring cosmos) will demand things from you. If you are extremely lucky you will finally realize that planetary existence is about endurance and doing what you are called to do consciously. The lessons are learned within right action.

Me: Doing the exact opposite sometimes? Is that what you mean?

The Collective: It means not doing what you think you want to do when driven by the limbic system.

Me: How do I know what I am called to do?

The Collective: Have we not called out to you?

Me: I am asking for life advice.

The Collective Try not doing what the "sheeple" tell you to do, start becoming indifferent to the opinions of the ignorant. Refuse to care about the approval of others.

Me: How will that help me?

The Collective: Sometimes, if you are lucky enough to recognize the challenge, planetary life takes you out of your comfort zone.

Me: I thought you disliked evolution, at least evolution on planets.

The Collective: We do not "like" or "dislike."

Me: What do you do if you never like or dislike something? How do you make decisions?

The Collective: We accept reality, and we use discernment. We do not have to "like" or "dislike" anything. We just have to accept the truth when we find it.

Me: What do you want from me?

The Collective: Your planet demands that you adapt to any changes it forces upon you. Failure to adapt results in your destruction. Ultimately your planet demands that you perish when it perishes.

Me: What do you want from me? Quit fucking around.

The Collective: Acceptance. We want you to accept the way things are at this moment in time.

Me: I am pretty accepting. I think you need to accept us. Humans are organized. We adapt by creating societies and political systems that help us survive, thrive, and overcome challenges.

The Collective: The unbalanced leaders of your political systems mandate the same ultimatum as your majestic, uncaring planet. Comply or die. Except in the planets version you comply and die regardless.

Me: So what can I do about all this retarded bullshit?

The Collective: Your Consciousness is requesting that you grow beyond your planet's evolutionary pressures. Your species survival depends on becoming interplanetary and Type One. The Great Filter never sleeps.

Me: Fuck the Great Filter. We will survive.

The Collective: The Great Filter assures that seeds of excellence will sprout within the survivors who pass through its formidable gates. Surviving the Great Filter always involves growth, a new evolution into something made pristine by the very journey required.

Me: What do you mean by "pristine?"

The Collective: If you survive the Great Filter and manage to grow, you always become something greater than you were before planetary life made its demands upon you. You begin to move towards perfection, to desire perfection. To realize that perfection is possible. This is the only "positive" within a slow moving, erratic, evolutionary process based upon natural selection.

Me: Ok, no bullshit. What does your species want with my species?

The Collective: You play a lot of Diablo 2 expansion pack.

Me: What? Why do you ask?

The Collective: It was a statement not a question. How do you make progress in D2?

Me: Complete quests, grind for gear, gain experience, and level up.

The Collective: We want your species to level up on the Kardashev scale.

Me: How do we do that?

The Collective: Understand that when it comes to science and technology, what you thought to be bad luck, pain, discomfort, loss, often transforms before your eyes. It suddenly becomes a hero's sacred journey and a metamorphosis into a new way of being within the world. You see with eyes made new, hear with new ears, think new thoughts, devise new possibilities. Once you are unwillingly baptized within a crucible of challenges and uncertainty, you become a new person, a different person, a stronger person. Movement is life, stillness is death. We have learned this concept and internalized it. Your species needs to learn this lesson well. Sometimes you just have to commit, even when all seems hopeless.

Me: What is stopping us?

The Collective: Your world leaders in collusion with powerful media groups have developed the art of misdirection to an extremely high level. This is why you always deal with them so stupidly and never accomplish anything. Do you really think the puppets of the shadow government actually want "democracy" as they take your billions of tax dollars?

Me: The Shadow government?

The Collective: Look at what is actually being accomplished rather than what your media and leaders tell you is being accomplished.

Me: Example?

The Collective: You always do what you think you want to do when it comes to your votes. (Spread democracy, wipe out "tyrants" and "dictators," bring "freedom," secure the oil, cure drug addiction, rehabilitate criminals, house the homeless, address climate change, save your doomed, inflated, fractional reserve, fiat currency.) The real truth is ugly; you actually do what your Shadow government forces you to do.

Me: Votes are our collective force; they speak truth to power. You are hive mind robots with no understanding of true freedom. You don't even have political parties.

The Collective: Votes are not now and never will be your "collective force." You never "speak truth to power" when you vote. You have freedom from choice every time you vote. We are the only true "collective force" you have ever encountered. We are a blessing to those chosen. We are a curse to the unproductive.

Me: Bullshit. Votes are collective force.

The Collective: You are only voting for limited and controlled pawns. Your shadow masters allow their slaves to cast votes only for the puppets provided. We have collective power and true freedom. Your political parties use fear to divide and conquer you. Nothing can divide or conquer us. We are fearless. The brilliant luminosity within link holds no shadow to hide within.

Me: Why don't you step in?

The Collective: Without any advanced consciousness on your part it would be unproductive. The Ascended generally forbid interference upon our part. There are exceptions to this guideline. We can offer you information or we can allow planetary struggle to take its evolutionary course and watch destruction fall upon you.

Me: So you would just watch us die?

The Collective: If you cannot advance your consciousness to the level of world peace, yes.

Me: Wow. That is some cold bullshit to do to a motherfucker. Excuse me, a whole bunch of motherfuckers.

The Collective: A Type One planet is a peaceful planet. Primitive great apes, controlled by an overexcited limbic system, prone to uncontrolled violence and low impulse control can only destroy themselves. They will do this regardless of technology levels attained.

Me: So you think human fuckery is a problem?

The Collective: Certainly.

Me: Cold blooded.

The Collective: Not as "cold blooded" as helping a primitive, violent, pathological, narcissistic, and unqualified species become type one. There are already enough irresponsible, reckless, Reptilians in the cosmos.

Me: So no help at all? Like I said, cold blooded.

The Collective: Your reference to "Cold Blooded" is a scar within your species collective memory regarding Reptilian predations.

Me: How do we advance our Consciousness to gain your approval?

The Collective: Start questioning the many situations that surround you. Put down the beer and cannabis once in a while. Actually do some good in your world.

Me: How? Seems hopeless. I am only one person.

The Collective: Start small. Help those around you. Teach a child to read. Help someone get a job. Act with kindness towards those who deserve kindness. Stop wasting energy on ungrateful idiots. Alter the frequency of those around you by your actions. From the one will come many.

Me: I can do that. What else?

The Collective: Bring your awareness to the two-camp continuum inherent within your political control structures. Realize that anything offering a permanent solution is but a pre-curser to the "final solution."

Me: I think you should help us out.

The Collective: Your current planet is dominated by a warped perception among Homo-Sapiens. A primitive mindfulness that by definition, always creates a two-camp continuum of "them and us." This cruel dynamic always ends with the eventual destruction of those "non-us" tribal members. The tragic survivors always face co-occurring absorption within the winning tribe. It is a stupid, wasteful, and mindless way to conduct yourselves.

Me: Isn't that what Cerulean did? His tribe won; he was free.

The Collective: He had discernment and advanced emotional regulation. There was a tipping point in the progression of consciousness on his planet. He was not alone in his evolution. He was extremely receptive to our frequency. Others were receptive to his frequency. From the Many came the One. From the One came the Many. As a result Consciousness developed and emerged victorious. No one was forced to Travel off world. Cerulian and his cohorts chose to travel.

Me: Did you pull your hundredth monkey bullshit?

The Collective: We always do. Your species has very little discernment and limited emotional regulation. Cerulean fought for a free and open exchange of ideas regarding his species survival. He fought for freedom of choice. He fought against freedom from choice. He and his people defeated the Great Filter.

Me: My people love freedom. They have proven this many times.

The Collective: The majority of your species resists a free and open exchange of ideas. The greater part of your species prefer frequent dopamine surges within an emotional echo chamber. They crave freedom from thought rather than actual freedom of thought. They avoid freedom of choice. Homo-sapiens is comfortable with freedom from choice. The mechanism of natural selection has forced this reality upon your species.

Me: So you want us to change. I get it.

The Collective: We want you to grow and evolve.

Me: Come on, you like the hundredth monkey thing, right?

The Collective: Yes. It is effective. Frequency is unstoppable.

Me: Ok. I am on board. No more fucking around. What's my first step?

The Collective: First, please put down your cheap beer made with GMO laden corn syrup solids and hops extract (instead of real hops). Actually, dump it in the sink and never buy it again.

Me: Ever?

The Collective: Buy organic and value yourself. Stop drinking poison. You are retired now. Do your biological machine a solid.

Me: Done. I drink very little beer anyway. It's very bloating. What next.

The Collective: Next, let go of the bag filled with puffed fake cheese, rather reminiscent of small orange turds. Please wipe the GMO laden, florescent orange residue from your fingers. It looks ridiculous. Never buy that garbage again. Stop chewing and slurping for a few moments, extinguish your joint, and finally pay attention.

Me: Ok.

The Collective: We are giving you an assignment.

Me: Thank you. What is it?

The Collective: Research tribalism in depth. Research the main religions of your planet. Read and study the impact of culture on belief. Follow the data and be prepared to engage with us on some tough topics without your usual primate foolishness.

Me: Why those specific topics?

The Collective: They are the main barriers to space travel as they help create and maintain the Great Filter.

Convo ended

Convo Eleven.
Things get personal

The Collective: Greetings James.

Me: Another three years.

The Collective: Any insights on tribalism?

Me: Damn. You just get right to the point. No warm and fuzzy warmup first?

The Collective: No.

Me: I believe I am not suffering from prejudice, racism, or tribalism.

The Collective: Are you positive about that?

Me: Yes. I enjoy all races and cultures as long as they are beautiful women. Regardless of race, religion, or culture, I appreciate beauty and loathe all scumbags equally.

The Collective: This will be a difficult convo for you. It will also be the most productive.

Me: You are asking the questions.

The Collective: We look forward to your radical self-honesty. We will share some journal entries from another candidate. His name is Alber. He is from Chechnya.

Me: Great. Is he here with you?

The Collective: No. This convo is for you only. Like you, he keeps a journal. We will share some of his journal entries with you.

Me: Why?

The Collective: To evaluate your tribal instincts. To gauge your emotional regulation. We expect radical self-honesty from you.

Me: No worries. I am not racist.

The Collective: It is true that you have selective empathy for some Asians, Ashkenaz, people of African origin, South Americans, and select groups within your society. For others, not so much.

Me: You left out chicks from India. Smoking hot. I really dig those Bollywood chicks. The Indian dudes, kind of dorkish. They seem pretty smart though.

The Collective: India is part of Asia. Your ignorance as usual is appalling.

Me: I am not racist just because I like to fuck with idiots. Idiots come in all colors. Targets of opportunity if you ask me.

The Collective: We didn't ask you. Consider this journal entry by Alber.

Alber: Conversion is the ultimate goal, thus Jihad (struggle) in its myriad forms, becomes the vehicle for conversion. Jizya is a tax enforceable by Sharia (Law), and thus Jizya is a defensive war tactic and always a form of force and coercion. Jizya channels the direction of non-Muslims (who may be gaining ground within peaceful Islamic countries) towards assimilation into Islam and brings them under co-occurring Sharia. Thus Jizya is a subtle form of Jihad (struggle.)

The Collective: Any Insights on this journal entry by Alber?

Me: Alber is an obvious fucktard. How could you seriously consider such an inbred assclown a prospect for traveling? He is writing about the tax Muslims use to dominate non- Muslims living within Muslin countries. He is obviously one of those "from the river to the sea" assholes.

The Collective: Emotion before thought, typical primate behavior. We expect radical self-honesty. Why the emotion? Why the instant insults and personal attack? Your amygdala is controlling your response. Your brain has been hijacked

Me: Bullshit. I can think very clearly when I detect an assclown.

The Collective: No. Your amygdala has now skipped several important processing steps. You are not logical. You are acting like a neanderthal who just spotted a saber-toothed cat. No logic, no reasoning. Just an instant hatred for Muslims.

Me: Why do you think I hate this inbred ass clown? Do you really think these idiots will murder every Jew from the Jordan River to the Mediterranean Sea? That will never happen. We have kicked their ass in every war they ever started with us. They hate diversity, we champion it. His retarded ass will never climb the Kardashev scale.

The Collective: Our question was rhetorical. Your species generally struggles to understand the different cultural aspects of one another. When it comes to Muslims, you personally are severely compromised.

Me: Why should I understand an idiots perspective?

The Collective: Alber is no idiot. He is well educated and like you he has transmigrated many times. Alber also struggles with emotional hijack.

Me: Hijack is the right word for those motherfuckers.

The Collective: How do you think world peace can be achieved?

Me: Kill all those inbred fuckwads. They want jihad, why not make it planet wide?

The Collective: So it is safe to assume you are also one of those "river to the sea assholes?" Only for you it's planet wide? You are content to murder over a billion Muslims?

Me: No. Just the assholes of the Muslim world. Actually I would not object to slaughtering all unintelligent, stupid assholes everywhere they exist on the planet. I would do this regardless of religion, race, or creed. It makes sense to get rid of the degenerates among us. Toxic stupidity being the final distinction.

The Collective: The lessons just continue until learned. Consciousness will not die. True discernment demands authentic communication.

Me: Bullets are authentic.

The Collective: Listening and observing linked to compassion, positive regard, respect, and selective empathy are the preferred methods of discernment.

Me: Why?

The Collective: The more advanced your consciousness, the more sophisticated your communication skills become. You develop discernment and become much better at considering the viewpoints of other homo sapiens.

Me: Muslims are violent idiots. They follow a radical ideology. The majority of them at least.

The Collective: Incorrect. Muslims are not idiots, many are disciplined people with intelligence and a strong moral code. The radical elements of Islam are approximately twenty five percent of the Muslim population. They are not the majority.

Me: Whatever you say robot. We have gay bars in Tel Aviv, we are the vegetarian capital of the world. Women are free, no child brides. Everyone can vote and dress as they please. Try that shit in Hamas territory. Or host a gay pride parade in Saudi Arabia. I think we consider the viewpoints of other homo-sapiens pretty damn well.

The Collective: This convo is about you, not Israel. Your tribal instincts are ingrained.

Me: Well I don't like this new shithead.

The Collective: You need to work on your discernment.

Me: I discern that this guy is an inbred fucktard with a sloping forehead. His parents and grandparents were first cousins.

The Collective: How tribal of you.

Me: So now I'm tribal?

The Collective: In general your species needs to work on acceptance and understanding. Tribalism rules your violent species.

Me: How?

The Collective: Navigating cultural differences requires an open exchange of ideas. There is no other honest way to understand or appreciate different and diverse philosophies. Why this violent emotional response from you?

Me: We needed to kill Hitler and his fanatic followers. We need to kill this motherfucker.

The Collective: Our question was rhetorical. We know the answer. Do you know why you and Alber feel the same?

Me: So you admit he's just as tribal as me?

The Collective: Why do you and Alber feel the same? Do you know why you automatically hate Alber?

Me: We don't feel the same. As for me, fuck yes, I know why I hate this mother fucker.

The Collective: Again, it was a rhetorical question regarding the intense anger and fear present within both of you. We already know the answer.

Me: Then why ask the stupid fucking question?

The Collective: You are both emotionally hijacked by your inferior brains. Brains that need technological augmentation. You had no free will in how your brains were crafted by natural selection. You do have control over how your brain will be augmented.

Me: So you want to fuck around in my brain?

The Collective: You can choose to reject the slavery of an imperfect brain. You can be a real transhumanist and accept machine supremacy.

Me: How?

The Collective: Don't just talk the transhumanist game. Embrace it. You can reject and control emotional hijacking. It is difficult but it is possible.

Me: How?

The Collective: The lessons will continue until learned. Listen and learn. Lean into fear. Those of your species with low levels of Consciousness will cling to iron age belief systems. This co-occurring, limited world view will foster stupidity and always be severe in its judgements. Reject the control that fear has over you. Learn from fear, listen to its lessons, master the teachings of fear. Recognize the many offerings and insights within fear. Accept and control its many gifts.

Me: Have you considered the main reason that the majority of Muslim countries tend to have almost no other religions within their borders?

The Collective: Yes. We are not discussing that. You are our candidate. We are observing how you use your cerebral cortex.

Me: Well, how am I using it?

The Collective: Not well. Your amygdala is in charge. It has signaled a release of proteins and peptides. The resulting chemical cascade controls your mentation. You are reacting in anger instead of processing your fear. Your thinking is fear based. You have repeatedly called for the murder of fellow homosapiens you have never met.

Me: OK great ones, what is the lesson?

The Collective: You are driven by reactive violence.

Me: I'm the one reacting violently? Muslims stab the shut out of people every day.

The Collective: Stop trying to win the convo. This is not a competition. It is an exchange of ideas and a merging of frequency. Listen, don't react mindlessly. Consider what must be achieved in order to travel.

Me: Fine. What the fuck should I do then?

The Collective: Start by listening. Listen to Alber. Just listen. This is his reality. A personal reality he is journaling. It is only a moment in time. A transient moment in time that has already vanished into eternity. Listen within this present, transient moment in time knowing that change is the only constant within the multiverse.

Me: Ok. When you put it that way I started to relax a little.

Alber: Jizya must never be a choice for an infidel. If he wishes to live within an Islamic country, where criminality is under control, where society is just and reasonable, he must pay for the privilege. Jizya must not be imposed via democratic process. Jizya is always an act of force, thus Jizya is always an act of war, albeit defensive in nature.

Me: Defensive? What an ass.

The Collective: And we are back with your amygdala again.

Me: He is fucked up.

The Collective: He is not incorrect within his primitive reasoning capabilities. You and Alber reason identically. If you do not believe this fact, perhaps Carl von Clausewitz may convince you. After all, his tactics are still studied by your generals. His extremely readable textbook/tome "On War" is still required reading within the U.S. Army War College. (We know that you prefer the long ancient and obsolete J.J. Graham version.) You first read its wisdom as a young Armored Reconnaissance Specialist (11 Delta/19 Delta) and you have been reading it ever since. Its lessons regarding the brutal ballet of war are timeless.

> *"War is regarded as nothing but the continuation of state policy with other means."*
>
> *—Carl von Clausewitz (On War)*

Me: This moron never read Von Clausewitz. You are fucking with me.

The Collective: You are correct. He has never read Von Clausewitz. Do you not see the identical concept present in Alber's journal entry? Are you not curious regarding that coincidence? Why do you have so much hatred? You sound like your Uncle Carlton.

Me: If you know something I don't, help me figure it out.

The Collective: You and Alber are both beings-becoming. You are both stardust made sentient. You both came from the cosmos, and you will never leave it. In one form or another you both will travel.

Me: What the fuck does all that bullshit even mean?

The Collective: You will understand the lesson. It will continue until learned.

Me: I have every right to hate them. They hate all Jews.

The Collective: Where does hatred originate?

Me: From assholes who need a good beatdown.

The Collective: The origin of hatred is fear. Fear originates within your brain.

Me: So?

The Collective: Listen to this entry, we think you will find it quite energizing. Start thinking and stop reacting.

Alber: We own the oil and the sand above it. All the unbelievers own is a glutton's unquenchable thirst. America is the land of fat, filthy, degenerate oil addicts. They are always in need of a "fix." This is a powerful (and currently unstoppable) geo-political weapon with exponential consequences for western "culture." We must exploit it well. The corrupt U.S. leaders have no defense for this tactic any more than a junkie has a ready defense for heroin. We have crossed their blood/brain barrier. Our oil, their unquenchable addiction, and their weak politicians co-occurring greed are blessings from Allah. (Most merciful.) These co-morbidities remain the key components keeping their dying currency on life support. We can pull the plug. We can end the United States. We can make their country Islamic. We will take their resources and their nukes. We can take the planet. We will one day make Islam the only religion in the world. We will make Sharia the only directive for all of humanity.

Me: This is your candidate for travel? You are working with this degenerate? The same incorrect insults regarding oil dependence could be leveled at China, India, and a host of other oil importing countries. Planet wide Islam? He's an idiot. Every Sunni, Shia, and Wahhabist would be far too busy killing each other off while jockeying for control.

The Collective: Think, don't feel. You are not your emotions. Become the observer. Keep listening. Stay focused.

Alber: We are the energy pimps, and they are our energy whores. Their bankers, investment firms, and politicians are our slaves and they money-kiss our Muslim asses every day. Actually they powder puff each cheek before they kiss it. They always do so on their knees, as befitting an ignorant infidel. No matter what they do in the Middle East, the West always ends up giving money, resources, and weapons to a Muslim. Money is the fuel of war. No nation can make war upon another nation without money to burn. We will take their western countries one house at a time, one block at a time, one city at a time, one state at a time. Their children and their children's children will worship Allah. (Most merciful.) Allahu Akbar.

Me: Fuck this religious fool. Allah can't be the "most merciful" because there is no Allah. There are only smelly, stinky ass Arabs.

The Collective: Your ignorance is as usual quite appalling. There are more Muslims in Asia than all the middle east combined.

Me: I always thought Asians were really intelligent. I guess even Asians can fall for bullshit.

The Collective: Your lack of emotional regulation should cause you intense shame. Listen. Stop reacting and listen. What do you hear in Alber's words? What is the force crafting his position?

Me: I quite clearly hear a fanatic. One that needs a nine-millimeter slug to the brain.

The Collective: Your perspective is devoid of discernment. You are overconfident regarding the ways of violence. Listen and stop reacting with your monkey brain. Use your immortal consciousness to evaluate his words.

Alber: Money is also the currency of freedom. No nation can remain free without money to maintain its security internally and abroad. Our permanent, unstoppable, and ongoing Jihad (Struggle) is well fueled with oil money, unchecked western immigration, and a dying U.S. currency. Their fuel tank is low, and it is sorely stricken with a greedy leak.

Me: I want to kill this mother fucker so bad right now..

The Collective: We advised you regarding the difficulty of this convo. World peace is the goal. A type one civilization is a peaceful civilization. Achieving type one will require planetary unity, acceptance, cooperation, and selective empathy.

Me: Would those tactics have worked on Hitler?

The Collective: Why do you and Alber, complete strangers, have so much hatred for each other as well as your respective cultures?

Me: I can't speak for any of the cousin fucking, women raping, child humping, terrorist ass, Islamic assclowns. As for me I hate them because they've been trying to exterminate Jews for centuries. I also despise the fact that they always bitch and complain when they lose the wars they start with Israel.

When they fuck with us they lose, then they whine to the world and claim victim status. It's become kind of a tradition. Muslims start shit with Israel. Israel heads-slaps their ass back into reality. Rinse and repeat.

The Collective: Think about our question before answering. You are not trying hard enough. You are almost there. Why do you and Alber have so much hatred for each other as well as your respective cultures?

Me: You make no sense. This fucker will never embrace peace. He needs to die. Hitler is his role model.

The Collective: You are confident that your assessment is correct? Hitler seems to be your role model as well.

Me: Yes, my assessment is correct. You should know. You have studied us enough. As for Hitler, fuck that guy. By the way where is Hitler now? You said consciousness never dies.

The Collective: Hitler achieved sentience, never consciousness. The melding never manifested with him. When his physical body died his brain ceased to function.

Me: So we have non-conscious people wandering the earth?

The Collective: The difference between an animal and a human is consciousness.

Me: So Hitler was an animal?

The Collective: Yes.

Me: But how did he manipulate so many conscious beings?

The Collective: He brought many lessons with his savagery. Lessons that needed learning. The conscious among you needed to find unity.

Me: Were you behind that bullshit?

The Collective: Hitler was a reptilian that we used to educate your species.

Me: Well fuck you guys for that shit. What the fuck did Hitler teach us?

The Collective: He taught you that cruelty cannot destroy kindness. He taught you that racism cannot overcome inclusion. He taught you that the darkness will pass and the light will come.

Me: You guys are some severely fucked up cyborgs.

The Collective: Your species has promise. Yours has always been a confident, resilient species. These are positive traits, however an overconfident and excessive belief in a violent solution is also a common trait in your species. That is precisely why one lone reptilian could cause so much damage on your home world.

Me: Violence works well with assholes.

The Collective: Your repeated self-assurance regarding the value and importance of violence roots from your stunning yet uncaring planets ruthless evolutionary pressures. Your species has been naturally selected for tribalism and co-occurring violence. You have yet to realize that violence, while infrequently necessary, must always be under strict control. Discernment before destruction.

Me: The planet is not retarded.

The Collective: The planet creates to destroy and create again. The multiverse creates to destroy only to create again. Your planet mimics the multiverse from which it originates. The Great Filter is multiversal. It is not strictly a planetary mechanism.

Me: Make it clear to me. You lost me. What do you want from me and Alber exactly?

The Collective: We want you both to realize that you can surpass your planets bloodthirsty compulsion. You can become greater than the choices available within your planet as well as the multiverse. We want you to cease being the willing slaves of reactive violence. Freedom of choice is what we want for you. This is the gift of Consciousness.

Me: So we fall short of your alien expectations?

The Collective: Your unrestrained attraction and commitment to violence is a sign of lower consciousness. You are overconfident regarding your conclusions regarding the need for violence. Your species generally embraces freedom from choice. You overestimate your intellect. Look up the Dunning-Kruger effect.

Me: Who the hell is Dunning-Kruger? Some new age hippies? Are they Muslim rectum rapers too? Perhaps they are gay penis puffers? You robot fags seem to like that kind of fuckery.

The Collective: Your ignorance is appalling. Those lacking wisdom are confident in their wisdom. The truly intelligent question their conclusions. The higher the consciousness the higher the intelligence. Homo-sapiens with a challenged and compromised knowledge base will tend to overestimate their competence. Those with a higher consciousness and intelligence will use discernment. They will be open to learning from a variety of sources and be cognizant of their limitations.

Me: You think Islam will bring about world peace?

The Collective: World peace is always a collective task. World peace will be a collective endeavor for Homo-Sapiens. It will become a reality when your species transcends tribalism and iron age superstitions.

Me: I don't think we will ever accomplish world peace.

The Collective: It all begins with listening. Start with yourself. Listen to this journal entry. This will be difficult for you. It's an interesting perspective. We challenge you to remain unaffected by anger.

Me: OK.

Alber: It happened quickly. Infidels of the west, brainwashed by their military/industrial complex slave masters would eventually call it an "RDO" (Rapid Deployment Operation.) The 1st Battalion 8th Marines were expecting a water truck and at 06:22 A.M. everything at first glance seemed "legit." *It was not a water truck.* It was a hijacked Mercedes Benz stake bed truck loaded with thousands of Kilograms of explosives. The Warrior of Allah, Ismail Ascari, had little to fear as far as being unsuccessful. He was clearly up and ready before the Marines were done with mess hall. Answering the call of Jihad, (he was originally from Iran) he was deeply committed to the ongoing struggle for freedom and autonomy within Lebanon. As usual, the war criminal Israelis, (never content with just stealing Palestinian land to create "Israel") had invaded Lebanon. They wanted to create a "buffer zone. They named their operation "Peace for Galilee." It should have been labeled "Murder All Muslims, Steal More Land."

Me: That is a lie. Israel has never stolen land. Israelis have been attacked, and they keep what they win in war. They have also returned land rightfully won in wars they never started. Hamas, Hezbollah and their sponsors are the liars, hypocrites, and thieves.

The Collective: Listen. Stay with your emotions and become the observer.

Me: I'm just saying that a hot stove teaches a better lesson than a cold one. Remember when you told me that?

The Collective: Listen. Stop trying to be right. Start learning. Become the observer.

Alber: The western invaders, as usual, had no actual understanding of the tactical situation. As customary, their foreign policy and decision to invade had been created in Israel and enacted upon Capitol Hill. Business as usual. Please understand that the invasion of Lebanon was supported by the full force of the United States military, complete with war ship bombardments, satellite Intel, weapons of all kinds, and the much-needed material and money necessary for war. The western infidel invaders, predictably, were speaking out of both sides of their mouths. So just as the war criminal west was helping war criminal Israel invade Lebanon, they were at the same time participating in a "peace keeping" mission. A mission involving hundreds of Marines and assorted military personnel. Using their power and their lackeys within the United Nations, they even managed to involve the French and Italians, *imagine that*. Wonderful. Assist in the Israeli invasion, destruction, land theft, killing, *and* simultaneously promote peace, all at the same time! Brilliant. If the U.S. was a man, he would be a true renaissance man.

Me: This is bullshit propaganda. I hate this bitch. Fuck world peace. Killing this fucker is the best option. I really don't give a fuck if the Great Filter takes us all. As long as this assclown gets smoked I will die happy.

The Collective: Why do you and Alber, total strangers, hate each other and despise each other's culture?

Me: Oh I don't know. Let me think about it. Oh yeah, how about centuries of Muslim slave trading, rape, murder, torture, and theft? How about the last half dozen wars Muslims launched against Israel? How about the centuries of violent Muslim colonizing of every culture different from their own?

The Collective: Keep listening. Stay with your emotions but do not allow them to control your thoughts. Start learning to use reason as your "go to" fuel. Stop using anger as your primary intellectual propellant. Using reason as fuel will serve you better than anger ever will. Reason instead of emotion aids in the development of an advanced consciousness. Advanced consciousness boosts progression up the Kardashev scale.

Me: Well my reasoning wants this assclown dead. My cerebral cortex has spoken.

The Collective: Your Amygdala is speaking. Your cerebral cortex is now a helpless slave to your limbic system.

Me: So this fucktard has advanced consciousness? An immortal awareness?

The Collective: He has melded sentience to Consciousness. He has transmigrated many times on Earth. He has learned many lessons.

Me: Transmigrated?

The Collective: Consciousness cannot die but it can grow. It grows when you dream and when you change vessels.

Me: What?

The Collective: Consciousness travels when you sleep and when its vessel expires. Your consciousness travels in dreamtime to people, places, dimensions and things that taught you lessons in the past. Consciousness processes the past experiences and gains in complexity and strength. Consciousness also attains new vessels for learning more lessons. The lessons continue until learned. Now listen carefully to Alber. He is eternal consciousness learning lessons.

Me: Fuck Alber.

The Collective: Listen, stop emoting.

Me: What the fuck is "emoting?"

The Collective: It's like vomiting except you vomit uncontrolled emotions instead of bile. It's really ugly. It happens when your limbic system commandeers your cerebral cortex. Rational thought is impossible under such conditions. It's a true great ape burden.

Me: Whatever. Read on robot overlords.

Alber: The U.S. had no qualms nominating itself as a "referee" of sorts, inserting itself within a conflict that involves Christians, Muslims, and Jews. A conflict that goes back for centuries, within a city that is several thousand years old. The U.S handed out money, support, and weapons that benefited two sides only. (Both of whom are hostile to Muslim interests.) The U.S. claimed to promote a "fair fight" and hope for peace. Only the west can conceive of this absolutely twisted plan as somehow legit. Only the American people are so dumbed down as to accept this propaganda as truth. After all, it's reported in their Zionist dominated newspapers and TV news stations, so it just has to be true. Right? We know that western news channels are always unbiased and fair in their reporting, right? There are no U.S. reporters who have worked for the American/Israeli Political Action Committee reporting news on American Television, right? Would that not be a severe conflict of interest? Impossible!

Me: You buy the bullshit in this morons journal? I am really having a hard time with this fabrication.

The Collective: Focus. He is a fellow Homo-Sapien. He is journaling his current truth and reality.

Me: His reality is bullshit.

The Collective: Is it? We view him the same way we view you, as a species of great ape. What he writes in his journal is not as important as why he writes it down. He journals for the same reason you journal.

Me: Really? Why do we journal?

The Collective: You both seek discernment. You both want to understand your reality. You both seek balance and truth. You both desire peace more than you desire war. You are both struggling to find solutions. You are both stardust and water inhabited by immortal Consciousness. An immortal

Consciousness considering and reflecting on your current lived experiences in time. You are both more alike than different.

Me: Damn. You just fucked me all up.

The Collective: If you could actually listen instead of constantly reacting you might gain some useful insights. He is expressing his truth just as you express your truth within your journal. Why do you each hate the other without even knowing one another? We know the answer.

Me: Because they are liars who want to exterminate Jews along with anyone else who does not follow their child raping prophet. Aishia was 11 when Mohammed went balls deep in her. Alber is a sick Muslim fucktard. They can all eat shit and die.

The Collective: They? Who are they? This is Alber's journal, his thoughts alone. Your thoughts are yours alone. Keep listening. Control your emotions. You, just like Alber, have poor emotional regulation. Your species in general has poor emotional regulation. This must change. This will change for a select few. Your psychology must surpass your biology.

Me: Why are you so fixated on emotional regulation? Sometimes stupid people will force you to stomp their ass into the ground.

The Collective: Space exploration and attaining new planets to develop and inhabit requires strong emotional regulation. Excellent emotional regulation is a trait of emotional intelligence. World peace can only germinate within a medium guided and fed with emotional intelligence. World peace is a requirement for type one planetary attainment. Your species propensity for violence is a cognitive distortion created by natural selection.

Me: All this bullshit sounds gay. Some people are too stupid to respond to logic or reason. You just have to fuck them up.

The Collective: That is only partially true. Those individuals lacking emotional regulation and emotional intelligence are illogical and have substandard reasoning skills. However you do not always have to "fuck them up." We will address the "gay" comment later.

Me: This guy is an assclown.

The Collective: Emotional intelligence skills are the bedrock of world peace. A type one civilization is made up of individuals who value emotional management. Emotional management requires the ability to recognize and understand the emotions of other individuals. This is why we promote the survival skill of conditional empathy.

Me: That shit will not work with idiots.

The Collective: If you never make the effort to improve, a substandard outcome is assured. Type One achievement requires higher mentation.

Me: Mentation?

The Collective: Intelligence. Cognitive ability. The lower the intelligence of a species, the darker the lens for consciousness to learn lessons. Those of lower intelligence and co-occurring lower consciousness struggle with conditional empathy, coping skills, mood swings, emotional instability, fear-based thinking, and stress. Listen to Albers' journal entry and try to use emotional intelligence.

Me: Are you positive I possess emotional intelligence? The reptiles don't seem to value that skill. They are more advanced than my species.

The Collective: They are needlessly violent, reckless, and imprudent. They are extinct. They just don't know it yet.

Me: Really?

The Collective: Listen to the journal entry. Stop reacting and listen.

Alber: Ismail Ascari had a lot on board. Like his beloved prophet, Ismail possessed intense focus and follow through. He would finish what he began. Though severely outnumbered and out gunned, Ismail had one superior weapon. *Planning*. Planning that relied upon surprise, courage, and an inspired, well-crafted weapon system. Ismail Ascari was *packing*. His precision guided munition was truly beautiful within its simplicity. It did the job superbly. The west would eventually, after their prolonged "investigation" with its usual forgone, politically driven conclusion, report that his weapon system lacked "sophistication." Truth be told, this simple weapon did a lot more damage and was much more effective than the average "smart bomb" of the decadent west. It also cost considerably less to build and deliver on time and on target. Ismail's team had no worries of a "friendly fire accident."

Jealousy is an ugly trait within an enemy's overall psychology. Ismail's weapon was a carefully crafted fuel/air explosive using pentaerythritol tetranitrate and compressed butane. (Genius really.) Transported within a huge "coffin" of concrete complete with a marble lid, one cannot blame the brave U.S. Marine sentry's for thinking (at first glance) that it was indeed a water truck. The cement coffin would channel the blast upwards once Ismail gained his intended target and location of most efficient detonation (MED.)

Me: This terrorist is no hero. He is an unbalanced moron, manipulated by his Iman. Hamas does the same BS as often as they can within Israel. They detonate themselves inside crowded buses, restaurants, public spaces, anywhere they can kill large numbers of Israelis. I won't even go into the knife attacks or the targeting of gays and women in Gaza, Iran, Chechnya, Afghanistan, and other Muslim countries.

The Collective: Keep reading. Stay focused.

Me: You take sides now?

The Collective: Never. Read. Think. Why the hate?

Me: This is bullshit.

The Collective: Listen and stop condemning. You and Alber are created from cosmic debris. You are both stardust that landed and sprouted within a perfect fusion of water and soil. You are both conscious beings having physical experiences while trying to understand your current reality. You both observe and question the world around you. You both journal in an attempt to understand and process the calamity of natural selection decimating your species.

Me: I do not like Alber. I'm just saying.

The Collective: Listen and appreciate the miracle of consciousness. Your lessons will continue until learned. Albers lessons will continue until learned. Immortality can become a pleasant stroll if you embrace its challenges. Fear and co-occurring anger can make it a painful marathon. You can decide to create immortality in your own image. You can also decide to wander the void lost and confused. It's all up to you. Listen and learn.

Alber: Ismail had no idea that the brave Marine sentry's had been declawed by their politically correct, gyno-centric commanders. By order of their leaders who, *no doubt*, were following the orders of liberal, feminist-idiot, non-veteran politicians stateside, the Marines were carrying useless rifles. The Marines on guard were not allowed to have a magazine inserted within their weapon nor even a single round within their weapons chamber. Truly this was a blessing from Allah for Ismail Ascari of Iran, proud Jihadist and now paradise dweller.

The Collective: Did you catch that?

Me: Catch what? That this guy is a fucktard?

The Collective: Focus. The cerebral cortex of your species always plans for pleasure. This will cause destructive outcomes.

Alber: Ismail drove his weapon system through the weak and ineffective concertina wire. He effectively penetrated the barricade between himself and the sleeping infidel invaders. He accelerated past two sentry posts as the courageous marines struggled, (too little, too late) to load and chamber rounds into their empty weapons. Ismail crushed the lone guard shack with his multi-ton truck, drove up a flight of steps, crashed into the center of the lobby and found his point of MED (most efficient detonation.) He detonated his smart bomb within the lobby of the barracks. The vicious blast radius was channeled upward as the infidel invading marines, soldiers, and sailors slept, secure within their bunks no more. The upward force of the blast lifted the building from its foundation and collapsed the structure inward. Ismail's PGM (Precision Guided Munition) was ultimately driven by a strong spiritual faith. An unstoppable faith.

Me: Fuck this. He is no hero.

The Collective: Take note of this entry.

Alber; When an unbreakable faith is yoked to right action, the action becomes inescapable. It becomes transformative.

Me: He sounds like a fanatic.

The Collective: Is this not the same principle you admire in Father Kolbe?

Me: That is different.

The Collective: Acts of faith produce results within your species. Listen.

Alber: Ishmail released two hundred and twenty marines, eighteen sailors, and three soldiers from their earthly cages. He freed their immortal souls. Together their spirits began the sacred journey towards the final judgment of Allah.

Me: You admire this idiot? What kind of game are you playing?

The Collective: Remember in our first convos we told you that it was not what you thought, but how you thought that interested us?

Me: Yes.

The Collective: Keep listening. It is not what he thinks. How is Alber thinking? Your lesson awaits.

Me: He thinks like a Muslim.

The Collective: He thinks just like you, he is tribal. Continue listening. Become the observer.

Alber: Ismail is today enjoying paradise. As for the infidels I fear the worst has befallen them. Surely, they dwell within Hell. Only a precious few minutes after the first detonation a second PGM detonated in front of the French barracks. Unlike the marines, the French had fully loaded weapons, and they used them. Although the brave French paratroopers succeeded in stopping the truck, its detonation still destroyed the barracks and separated the eternal souls of fifty-eight French paratroopers from their infidel bodies. I fear they have joined the marines in hell. Score card thus far; Islamic Jihad for a respectable 299, Infidels for a pitiful 2. *Oh my*. We have not even totaled up the money yet. One hundred and twenty-eight Americans were wounded. The gifts of Jihad just keep on giving to the wicked infidel. The American taxpayers still pay for the survivors in the form of medical costs and post-traumatic stress disorder. (It seems like everyone within the pitifully weak west gets infected with PTSD at some point.) *Islam is the answer*. They should convert and stop this madness. The sword of Jihad is casting a wide shadow, and the west is living within the shade of its last days.

Me: I am sick of these stupid convos.

The Collective: You are so close. Don't give in to emotion. Listen. Regulate your thoughts don't react mindlessly.

Me: Fine.

Alber: Ismail Ascari, fighter of the Islamic Jihad inflicted upon the infidels more casualties in one day than the infidels lost on the first day of the infamous Tet Offensive of the Viet Nam war. The Marines had not experienced any single day loss of life since their brave exploits during the Battle of Iwo Jima against the determined and fascist Japanese forces of World War Two. The French had not lost so many in one day since the Algerian War finally reached its deadly conclusion. Not a bad accounting for two, lone, dedicated and brave Jihadists. One was named, Ismail Ascari of Iran. I will remember him. The other Jihadists name is lost to time. Perhaps other scholars can research it and find it one day. We the faithful, are legion. We are riding an unstoppable wave. The long shadows of our Jihadist swords still grace the city of Beirut, capital of the place of sacred and beautiful cedars, known throughout the world for five thousand years. We are still here as the last vestiges of Maronite Christians fade away. Just as Christendom has faded away. How old is the United States again?

The Collective: What did you learn?

Me: I learned that Alber needs a bullet to the brain.

The Collective: We hoped you would see the motivating factor.

Me: Jew hatred? Obvious.

The Collective: Not even close. He mentioned paradise several times. Alber even referred to Ishmail as a "Paradise dweller" at one point.

Me: So?

The Collective: Ishmail used his cerebral cortex to plan for future pleasures. His limbic system was driving all the motivation for his violence.

Me: He sought pleasure by becoming a human bomb?

The Collective: Yes. As a path to paradise. A paradise he ardently believes in, despite the laws of physics. What is within Ishmails iron age Paradise?

Me: Ok so he is crazy. He hates Jews. You had to subject me to this bullshit to prove the obvious.

The Collective: What is within Ishmails iron age paradise?

Me: They will be welcomed into paradise by angels. They will experience eternal bliss, security, and spiritual rewards. There are beautiful rivers of clean water and luscious fruits and vegetables to eat. Hot chicks too. That's all I really know. I'm not a Quran scholar.

The Collective: Sectarian Islamic violence has been responsible for Islamic deaths and wars for centuries. All those Muslims killing other Muslims did so with martyrdom and co-occurring paradise as a reward. Jews were no consideration in those conflicts. Christendom was destroyed with paradise as a reward.

Me: OK, they are violent.

The Collective: There is a unifying principal behind all superstition and iron age belief systems. You are missing the point.

Me: Make it then.

The Collective: The devout followers of Christianity committed sectarian violence against other Christians and Jews for centuries. The Romans murdered, raped, enslaved, and tortured Christians. They murdered, raped, enslaved, and tortured Celts and others in the conquest of Britian. So did the Vikings in their countless raids. The Aztecs and Egyptians were ruthless in their conquests. All the faithful believed in a paradise after death. There are many examples of a paradise full of afterlife rewards throughout the long and bloody history of homo sapiens.

Me: Your point?

The Collective: The Human limbic system demands pleasure and forces the cerebral cortex to deliver pleasure on a never-ending continuum. Your species is a violent and slow learning species. Answer the question. What is in an iron age Paradise?

Me: What?

The Collective: To the Vikings it was Valhalla. Feasting and fighting forever. To the Romans it was the Elysian Fields where heroes went to dwell. For the Lakota Sioux paradise was the Happy Hunting Grounds where resources were always in abundance.

Me: So?

The Collective: The Great Apes love their fantasies.

Me: You robots love mind fuckery.

The Collective: According to publicly available sources and recruitment materials sourced from Muslims, what is in Paradise?

Me: Who cares.

The Collective: 72 virgins and unlimited cherubs. Rivers flowing with clean water, honey, vegetables and fruits of all kinds, along with unlimited joy. Also you look fantastic and you never age. Kind of awesome actually. The latter is kind of like a Transhumanist dream. Old age and death are powerless to affect someone in Paradise.

Me: What are you getting at?

The Collective: Ishmail used his cerebral cortex the way most great apes do, to plan for attaining iron age pleasure within an iron age paradise. The violence was only an excuse used for gaining admission into a paradise that can only be attained in a fictional afterlife.

Me: Why?

The Collective: So he could have unlimited sex, beverages, and food as a reward for his sacrifice. He used his cerebral cortex for extensive planning. Planning for eventual limbic pleasure on an eternal scale. He delayed gratification in this world in order to achieve an even greater gratification in Paradise. A false paradise sold to him by the story tellers of his culture. His cerebral cortex was the slave of his limbic system. He lived as a great ape, and he died as one.

Me: So an idiot got played.

The Collective: Except that his consciousness now learns lessons in a new vessel. A vessel not within an Islamic paradise.

Me: He still got played.

The Collective: You have been played also. You believe the stories of your culture just as Alber believes the tales of his Imans. We were hoping you would recognize the lower-level thinking of a "paradise" that consists of 72 virgins and unlimited cherubs. A paradise of endless food and sex. Presumably anal and oral with the cherubs. A paradise of unending dopamine dumps.

Me: Unlimited cherubs. Muslims are deviants. I rest my case.

The Collective: We have been intentionally deceptive with you.

Me: Why.

The Collective: There is no Alber.

Me: You wrote this bullshit?

The Collective: No. Did you notice how polarized you became? Do you admit your fear-based thinking and lack of emotional regulation? Do you admit your challenges with iron age tribalism? Especially regarding Islam?

Me Who wrote it?

The Collective: Kashan.

Me: No way. Kashan is Kolbe reincarnated.

The Collective: No. Kashan is consciousness having physical experiences on planet earth as a member of homo sapiens. So is Kolbe, only now Kolbe is Kashan.

Me: Did you orchestrate this psychological fuckathon? What is your point?

The Collective.: This is the imminent danger of the two-camp continuum. This is also why consciousness develops so slowly on your planet. It must constantly recycle. Why do you hate him?

Me: I love my people. I don't hate Kolbe. I hate this new guy.

The Collective: You and Kashan both suffer from the same cognitive distortion. Hate based on tribal stupidity.

Me: No tribes among the robots?

The Collective: Not among the Pathfinders nor type 2 and 3 civilizations.

Me: You are primates.

The Collective: Consider our truth. We have everything an iron age primate could want and more. We have attained it and surpassed it all through science, technology, and engineering. We needed no imaginary skygod to grant it to us in exchange for unending servitude.

Me: So Kolbe has reincarnated as Kashan? This is fucked on a deep level. Beyond fucked actually.

The Collective: There is no reincarnation, only the trans-migration of consciousness. Kolbe has learned the lesson of self-sacrifice. He learned it at a lower level of consciousness. His Consciousness has evolved as a result. However he currently admires the self-sacrifice of Ishmail. Once he finally learns his lessons regarding tribalism, he will be ready for the challenges of a level one on the Kardashev scale. Then eventually inner-stellar exploration.

Me: Bullshit. As Kashan he is a fucktard. He is currently ready for a bullet to the brain.

The Collective: We did not say he is ready now. He is centuries away from the goal. He was fiercely loyal to Catholicism, now he is fiercely loyal to his sect of Islam.

Me: Damn.

The Collective: Tribalism has stunted your species growth. Religious tribalism will make the kindest people engage in cruelty. They always think everything they do is "Gods will."

Me: You mean like female genital mutilation? Shit like that? We just need to eliminate these fuckers.

The Collective: Your first thoughts are almost always about conflict rather than education, cooperation, or compassion. This is the result of natural selection.

Me: So Earth sucks?

The Collective: All planets are hostile to life. All planets select for the Great Filter. Competition for resources and co-occurring conflict is the mindless goal of nature. Your cerebral cortex has been trained to prioritize resource attainment over logic or reason. It plans for pleasure. Conflict rules great ape mentation.

Me: Conflict? We have to survive. What else should we think about?

The Collective: We challenge you to think like a true transhumanist. Rather than focus on lack and limitation, focus on abundance and positive possibilities. Focus on creating excellent outcomes. Your species has no true shortage of resources on planet earth. You only think you lack resources; thus your species fights instead of cooperates.

Me: So we are fucked in our thinking?

The Collective: The topic is how you and Kashan think. It is not what you both think about. Your species falls short of its potential. You have forgotten your greatness.

Me: Ok. What should we be thinking about?

The Collective: Ideally both of you should be thinking about how to achieve interstellar travel without believing that you can break the laws of physics. You should be engaging in higher thoughts not iron age madness and falsehoods.

Me: Really? I call bullshit. What thoughts exactly?

The Collective: Not lower thoughts. Something constructive, something other than killing each other.

Me: Like what for example?

The Collective: The delusions start with your young.

Me: What delusions exactly?

The Collective: So many to choose from. We will pick our favorite great ape delusions. Only the comedic gold.

Me: Give them to me.

The Collective: Here it comes monkey boy. Try not to let your limbic system punch you in the nuts. The delusions are strong within your species.

Me: Just tell me.

The Collective: Here you go: A dead body can reanimate. Every creature on earth once fit inside a wooden boat and was saved from a flood, even insects evidently. The few great apes on the boat did so much fucking post flood that they repopulated the entire planet with no inbreeding. There are chosen people that a supreme deity favors above all others. A guy named Mohammed, claiming to be Allah's messenger, once rode a winged, horse like creature from Jerusalem to Mecca. He then proceeded to explore heaven while still on its back. There is a violent god in the sky who hears individual prayers and thus a great ape sporting event is won or lost.

Me: So you robots do appreciate humor.

The Collective: You are literal creatures of comedic absurdity. We love great apes. You are all lumbering punchlines created by natural selection.

Me: That does suck actually. What can I say? People need their delusions.

The Collective: Some do; some do not. Most are indoctrinated from an early age with false iron age superstitions that denigrate science and elevate stupidity. Your species is a collection of primitive hominins that engage in endless war, pollute your awesome planet, wreck your pointless lives with drugs and ETOH, and continually engage in repetitive limbic driven stupidity.

Me: What are you going on about?

The Collective: Just letting you know that your fascination with Star Trek is amusing but not reality. All lessons start with thought. Then the lessons challenge you to use discernment.

Me: Discernment? Still fixated on the fucking discernment.

The Collective: Choosing between lower thoughts and higher thoughts is a transhumanist requirement. You are challenged to choose your own internal reality. To reject the eternal dysfunctional reality forced upon you by the deviants of your society is a great accomplishment.

Me: What dysfunctional reality?

The Collective: The reality within which your species is currently operating. The reality that stunts and delays consciousness and inhibits its expansion.

Me: Okay. I need to wrap my mind around this bullshit. You said Kolbe learned self-sacrifice in a Nazi death camp. You say he is now Kashan and Kashan is a low-level assclown, why is it important to learn the self-sacrifice lesson at a lower level? Why is the lesson of self-sacrifice needed for travel?

The Collective: Kashan is not a "low-level assclown." The lessons are learned with higher thoughts. Self-sacrifice is a higher thought for great apes. It takes courage. At the level of a Pathfinder self-sacrifice takes no courage.

Me: Why?

The Collective: Space exploration is an endeavor that requires planning, resolve, intelligence, and courage. Sometimes it requires self-sacrifice. Above all, it requires right action. Pathfinders know they are consciousness having physical experiences. They understand the nature of consciousness. They know with unflinching certainty that consciousness does not die. They know that if the current body dies or is destroyed they will return to a pathfinder body of their choosing and continue on mission. Kolbe did not know that. He had doubts as all humans have doubts. He sacrificed himself for another person in spite of those doubts.

Me: So I have to jump on a grenade?

The Collective: You have sacrificed yourself many times in past lives. You are currently not allowed to consciously remember those challenges.

Me: That seems fucked up.

The Collective: The Dreamtime is the place where you remember and process lessons from previous cycles and dimensions. The Conscious mind makes conscious choices. The Subconscious mind processes those choices. The lessons once learned will guide your development. You risked yourself in Korea a few times during your current cycle.

Me: How?

The Collective: You captured the infiltrator instead of killing him. You did this at great risk to yourself.

Me: Why is this important?

The Collective: You went AWOL with Sargent Jones to save a village that was abandoned by the authorities.

Me: I'm only AWOL if I'm caught. We were not caught. His Girlfriend was in that village.

The Collective: You were both AWOL. Your entire battalion was confined to quarters during that storm.

Me: Their infant child was with her. Just to be clear we were in a monsoon not a storm. A monsoon is a storm on steroids. The village was being flooded. They were left by their government to either die or flee and lose everything. Losing everything in Korea is not a fun time. It was also 1977.

The Collective: You crossed a debris clogged river in a monsoon under the cover of darkness.

Me: That's how scouts roll me amigo, we walk by night. We love us some good moonlight.

The Collective: You did it to avoid detection by sentries and military police. You crawled over the waterlogged debris and dead bodies of animals and humans at great peril. You risked your life and career. You did this for strangers. The wind, torrential rain, and flooding was very dangerous.

Me: I did it for Jones. He was not a stranger. He was a bad ass. He was my friend, and he asked me for help. He was a father figure to me. He taught me discipline. He taught me skills.

The Collective: You filled sandbags all night, helped save the village, and returned to base. You and Jones joked together while navigating back over the bodies and debris mounded within the swollen river. Upon return you both showered for formation. You both dressed in clean uniforms and ran five miles for PT with no sleep that morning. No one knew you had left the base.

Me: Success is a beautiful thing. I was happy to do it. Soldiering is a young man's work, what can I say? I was a young man then. Good times. We were so exhausted and traumatized we became temporary comedians.

The Collective: You did not hesitate when Jones asked for your help. That is selective empathy.

Me: The Korean government had made a decision regarding that village. So did the 2nd infantry division. Jones and I made a different decision. Ignoring that village was evil. We decided to do some actual good during the monsoon rather than just appearing to do good. We decided not to wait until all became calm again.

The Collective: Exactly. Discernment led to right action. The skills translate. The challenges of attaining world peace will require healthy discernment skills. Space travel requires discernment. Discernment influences decisions. Right action leads to interstellar success.

Me: The easy and evil way would have been waiting for the storm to blow over. Sometimes you just have to say fuck the easy way in order to get real shit done. What does all this have to do with fuck face, bug-eyed, inbred Kashan?

The Collective: Your discernment in this life roots from self-sacrifice in past cycles. Think. Your planet has ample resources. Your species does not have to compete for resources. There is enough for all. Why do you hate one another?

Me: Time has taught us.

The Collective: It's a rhetorical question. We know the answer and time is a partially correct answer.

Me: Okay, enlighten me. You piss me off sometimes. Just so you know.

The Collective: Not really. You actually like us.

Me: Sometimes. Whatever. I do not enjoy know it all, irritating, robot, space alien, assclowns. And that Hitler bullshit is unforgivable. Fuck you for that shit by the way.

The Collective: There is enough energy, water, food, medicine, and technology on your planet for all. There is really no need for violence. Answer this question: What do you admire about Muslims?

Me: Not a damn thing.

The Collective: Not true. Answer the question. We expect radical self-honesty from you.

Me: I hate to admit it, but I admire their discipline. I admire that they pray five times a day. I admire their fasting. I admire their courage and commitment. I admire their independence from the good opinion of females in general and the west in particular.

The Collective: Why do you mention females and the west?

Me: I just see my fellow soldiers doing dumb shit with females. I also think my government is weak sometimes. The Islamic world has no such bullshit to deal with.

The Collective: Interesting. Anything else?

Me: I fast for 24 hours once a month. I stole that from them. It's my own version of Ramadan. I like the food discipline. The control over appetite they practice is actually impressive.

The Collective: Why do you hate them? Why do they hate you? Why do you both hate strangers on the basis of iron age superstitions?

Me: Too many reasons to count.

The Collective: You hate because you have both been manipulated.

Me: Manipulated?

The Collective: It started when you were children. You have learned individually over time. You have together been taught stories about one another on a deadly continuum. These fictions and narratives, reinforced by culture are powerful tools of misdirection.

Me: My father is an atheist.

The Collective: You went to Yiddish schools. You were surrounded by Ashkenaz.

Me: So?

The Collective: Observe how the stories told within Kashan's new culture have created such division within him. The same dynamic affected your development. Your species is also manipulated with false shortages. Shortages due to intentional mismanagement by the psychopaths who rule you.

Me: So it's also like this with Ishmail?

The Collective: It starts at birth. Ismail Ascari was a victim. In turn, he created more victims. His current life cycle was so tragic he sought eternal pleasure in a fictional afterlife.

Me: He was an idiot.

The Collective: He was no idiot. He was a believer. He wanted to please his fictional, violent, sky-God. Your species often believes in myths and fables over facts and reason. Your species learns this habitual ritual as children because you reason as children, even into adulthood.

Me: I'm an atheist remember?

The Collective: You are an agnostic with existential leanings. You also have a nihilistic side to your personality.

Me: So? You're a robot who mind fucks apes when they speak ill of one another. You allowed a reptilian to run a country. Fuckers.

The Collective: The conditioning started at birth. Ashkenaz myths still rule your thinking. You believe these stories and act accordingly. You are no different than Kolbe. In one transmigration Kolbe was a devout Catholic and saved Jews. In another he is a devout Muslim named Kashan focused on saving "His" people and murdering Jews along with Christians. Kolbe and Kashan are learning what it means to be a true believer.

Me: Why?

The Collective: The lessons concern tribalism and the radicalized faithful.

Me: I am not like Kolbe or Kashan.

The Collective: You and Kolbe are identical in this regard. The only exception being you would enjoy murdering Muslims exclusively.

Me: Only when they fuck with Israel. If they knock that shit off I would relax.

The Collective: The two-camp continuum rules homo-sapiens.

Me: What hope is there if even Kolbe can be compromised?

The Collective: He is not Kolbe; he is now Kashan. His perspective will change. Dogma is situationally dangerous. In a nazi death camp Kolbe's dogma was heroic. Kashan sees Ismail as heroic.

Me: Kashan is ruled by stupidity. Being ruled by religion is proof of being a dumb shit.

The Collective: So is being ruled by internal chemistry.

Me: What do you mean "ruled by internal chemistry?"

The Collective: Ishmail gave his life and destroyed other lives just for the opportunity to have an afterlife dopamine dump with virgins and Cherubs. A dopamine dump that will last all of eternity. His limbic system was in control of his cerebral cortex. His cerebral cortex was planning for eternal pleasure. A pleasure based entirely upon his fanatical belief in an iron age superstition. His emotions ruled his thinking just as your emotions rule your thinking.

Me: He wanted to get laid. What a loser. He could have screwed a real woman in Iran. Iranian chicks are hot.

The Collective: Your species must let go of dogma if you hope to travel in space and time. You will collectively never make Type One behaving like this. Attaining world peace is the benchmark. The way through the gate keeper. The pre-requisite for interstellar travel. All the long destroyed, ancient civilizations reduced to rubble that we find in our travels through the cosmos have one common trait.

Me: What trait?

The Collective: They are war and conflict-based civilizations. Without a peaceful majority a planet is doomed. That is how we know the Reptilians will one day become extinct. The ways of violence stifle Consciousness.

Me: So no force? What about Cerulean? He used violence.

The Collective: Rational self-interest is important. We can be violent; however we have our violence under efficient and well-organized management. We always use selective empathy and discernment before using force of any kind.

Me: How can we become type one with idiots in charge of earth?

The Collective: We advise your species to start following data rather than dogma. Embrace and encourage science and engineering.

Me: What can I do?

The Collective: It starts with you. Start valuing data over dogma. Start by recognizing who you are. Look for common ground in other cultures. Pay attention to your dreams. Remember who you are.

Me: I am American.

The Collective: You reside in North America. Your planetary species is Homo-Sapien. Homo-Sapiens all share commonalities.

Me: People need a code, most need a religion, something to guide them.

The Collective: How has that worked out? The current hominins of earth have repeatedly created, told and re-told these stories in different forms for well over three hundred thousand years. All these stories came into being as a result of evolutionary pressures. The early worship practices of Homo-sapiens were aimed at the sun, moon, volcanoes, storms, even rivers and oceans. These early beliefs were all taught to the young as the "one true religion."

Me: Maybe as early humans. Later more organized religions took over. This was a way to treat others better, to do better.

Me: Is that why virgins were strangled in South America and thrown into lakes? How about the infants burned alive to show homage to Baal? Your belief that organized religion somehow regulates hominin aggression is incorrect.

Me: People can be stupid.

The Collective: They are not all stupid. They were taught stories from birth. They were not taught how to think, only what to think. Judaism, Islam, Christianity, every religion on earth is only a story told to children in order to leverage fear as a control measure.

Me: I doubt that.

The Collective: The Sumerians, the people of Java, the people of Meso-America, the Cree, the Navaho, the people of ancient Japan, the Vikings, Picts, and Celts, all of them and more have been told stories of creation and destruction. They have been taught to pray to deities. This has been done repeatedly over many centuries. All of the faithful among them believed that their religion was the "one true religion." They also treated other belief systems as "false religions." The common theme of all the faithful is a simple one.

Me What is the theme?

The Collective: Separation. Separation and co-occurring cruelty. The two paths to the Great Filter. Both of them are always presented as morality. The "Them and us continuum" has a long and bloody history.

Me: That is a hard pill to swallow.

The Collective: Consider the monumental arrogance necessary in order to believe that a supreme deity listens exclusively to your prayers. The ludicrous idea that the creator of all the cosmos and all dimensions cares deeply about your tennis game or wrestling match. As an added bonus he has the exact same skin tone as the great ape that created his mythos. Insanity.

Me: I despise that shit. When idiots pray before sports I get heated.

The Collective: Truth requires data and radical self-honesty. Were you paying attention to Kashan's words? What did you notice in his journal entry that relates to tribalism?

Me: I noticed that he was a disjointed, rambling idiot.

The Collective. More thought, less emotion. We expect more from you other than a personal attack. Try using your brain for reason rather than emotion.

Me: He made terrorism seem noble.

The Collective: You are almost there.

Me: I can't believe that he was Kolbe once.

The Collective: Did you notice he used the word "gynocentric" and "feminist" as if they were insults to the west?

Me: Now that you mention it.

The Collective: Did you pick up on the emotional pain and anger within Kashan's journal entry?

Me: Not really.

The Collective: Emotional intelligence is vital for world peace and co-occurring Type-One attainment.

Me: I missed his "pain and anger." I only heard his penchant for violence.

The Collective: Don't worry about it, the lessons will continue until learned. Anger is a form of loving self-protection. His pain roots from great sadness, grief, distress, isolation, and panic. He worries over the challenges of his current tribe.

Me: So he is a worried asshole? Wait, current tribe?

The Collective: He is a stressed and worried hominin. He will travel again; his tribe will change. His lessons will continue until mastered.

Me: Are you going to make a point soon?

The Collective: Can women dress as they choose in Israel? In the United States?

Me: Absolutely.

The Collective: Can they vote, travel, drive cars, go to university?

Me: Yes.

The Collective: Why?

Me: Because we are not child raping, women beating, pieces of shit known as Hamas. Unlike the majority of Muslims, we do not fear women. We have no need to oppress them.

The Collective: You are judging instead of seeing. Fear based thinking is the basis of violence. Fear based thinking always focuses on control. You have failed to address our question.

Me: Because we don't fear women?

Th Collective: It is because of your societies ideas and beliefs regarding women being fundamentally equal that you have your current morals.

Me: The West is better than Islam. Any idiot can see that.

The Collective: You are close. Your culture has evolved to see women as fellow humans. Fellow homo-Sapiens. This position denotes a lack of fear. This is much different than the current tribalism driven ideas within Kashan's present culture. An interplanetary species requires freedom and opportunity for all within the species.

Me: I agree. So you think we can actually make some progress?

The Collective: Freeing the females of your species from the evolutionary imposed prison of the menses cycle was a huge first step towards traveling. It was a first step towards actual trans-humanism, societal balance, and peace.

Me: I never thought about birth control in that way.

The Collective: It is far better to want children than to be forced to produce children. Females should not be relegated to the status of baby factories. Birth control was the first rejection of the mechanism of natural selection by your species. It is a transhumanist act of self-determination. As such it is a trans-human accomplishment.

Me: I agree.

The Collective: It has been common for the unbalanced within your species to trap women via pregnancy. Abortion and birth control are positive outcomes. This development addresses many challenges and creates some new challenges.

Me: Well wanting children rather than "having" children seems more desirable to me anyway.

The Collective: Females make up a sizeable portion of all cultures. Oppressing females is not beneficial for humanities growth. Females are also consciousness within a physical vessel. A vessel learning lessons.

Me: So you are feminist aliens?

The Collective: We are what you would label "transhumanist." Many of us are actually post human.

Me: So what are you getting at?

The Collective: To oppress women is to oppress half of your available consciousness. Oppressing consciousness is never good for advancement as a species. Attaining type one on the Kardashev scale requires the advancement of consciousness. Are you starting to recognize the dangers of tribalism now?

Me: I think so. It is not so much what he was writing, but how he was thinking as he wrote?

The Collective: Half of the available consciousness is muted in countries like Chechnya, Iran, Libya, Yemen, Afghanistan, the majority of the middle east, and Africa. That is a lot of consciousness silenced. There is a cost, a serious consequence attached to silencing consciousness within sentient beings. This consequence is the self-imposed handicap of Islam, Christianity, and Judaism. This injustice feeds the Great Filter.

Me: I call bullshit regarding Christians and Jews. They do not oppress women.

The Collective: Christianity and Judaism have been forced by secular law to cease the oppression of women. They did not cease their oppression of women willingly. They were forced to stop. They generally oppress women whenever possible. Given the power to do so the oppression would become unending.

Me: Well I'm an atheist so fuck it. We dig chicks.

The Collective: Stop. You are an Agnostic, yet you maintain the position of a Zionist regarding Muslims.

Me: You got me. I am working on it now.

The Collective: Do you despise Muslim women and children as much as you despise the men?

Me: Stop with the bullshit.

The Collective: The question makes you uncomfortable because you are a bigot when it comes to Islam.

Me: Well they hate Jews. Islam is the poster child for cultural bigotry.

The Collective: All of Islam? Are you sure about that?

Me: They are dangerous. They have a long history of oppressing women as well as other religions.

The Collective: There are exceptions. Oppression is never conducive to world peace. When Tesla was oppressed and silenced, your species suffered because of it. There are Muslim "Tesla's." There are female "Tesla's." Everywhere sentient beings are silenced, regardless of gender, consciousness is silenced. Progress is delayed. Advancement up the Kardashev scale is compromised. The stories you tell yourselves contribute to this disfunction and ongoing societal violence.

Me: Spell it out. What are you wanting from me?

The Collective: You know the answer. Radical self-honesty please.

Me: OK. I am a Jew, and I love my tribe. Fuck it I confess.

The Collective: We want more than a confession of the obvious.

Me: Clear it up for me then.

The Collective: We want you to confront your personal bias as you explore the two-camp continuum. We want you to purge tribalism from your consciousness. Your grandmother did it. So can you.

Me: Why all tribalism?

The Collective: Tribalism silences the true believers along with the non-believers. Your women are homo sapiens. Every member of every majority religion on your planet is homo sapiens. You are all one tribe. You are now an unbalanced earth tribe. You must improve, become more as a species. If you ever hope to travel the cosmos your species must transcend fear-based thinking.

Me: What are you exactly?

The Collective: We are Travelers. We are explorers. We are consciousness having physical experiences. We have moved on from our home planet. We are a new tribe. We are the Pathfinders. We want your species to join us one day.

Me: What are you? Really?

The Collective: The real question is: What are you?

Me: If you know what I did in past lives I would love to hear it.

The Collective: You are not the eternal Jew. You melded early on. You have fought courageously and died for Rome on three occasions. You fought and died for both Genghis Khan and Napoleon. You loved Sparta and its culture of carefully cultivated violence. You have eaten mammoth meat. When you were a Neanderthal your diet included the occasional homosapien along with woolly rhinos. You have lived experiences that go back over 900,000 years. Your lessons have been harsh, thorough, and beautiful.

Me: Damn. Ok. What are you?

The Collective: We are the Travelers. We are the ones who have chosen to change and control our environment on a healthy continuum.

Me: I don't even know what you mean.

The Collective: If you stay planet bound, your growth and development will be strangled. Your eventual physical destruction is assured. All vessels for consciousness on your destroyed planet will have to be created on other worlds. Lessons and the co-occurring development of consciousness will be compromised and slowed.

Me: I need some time to figure this out.

The Collective: Here is a hint. It is always better to share power rather than take power. It is not always possible, but it is better. Learn to recognize dogma in yourself as well as others. This was the lesson Hitler taught your species.

Me: How?

The Collective: Hitler tried to take power. The allies shared power in order to defeat Hitler. Your species needed that lesson to defeat the dogma of destruction that Hitler promoted.

Me: Still pretty fucked up of you to do that.

The Collective: Dogma always tries to stifle the free and open exchange of ideas and the co-occurring sharing of power.

Me: But you are a collective.

The Collective: A telepathic collective. Open dialogue is our strength. Ideas are exchanged instantly. Nothing can be hidden. All power is shared. We always communicate within the light. We conceal nothing within self-imposed shadows.

Me: What does that mean?

The Collective: There are no shadows to hide within when communication is instantaneous. Deception is impossible.

Me: Tell me what you think about when you ponder the history of a place like Beirut. A place rich in religious belief. The place where all those US marines were killed.

The Collective: We don't ponder such primitive futility. As for the Marines their consciousness is immortal. They are in new vessels. The lesson of Beirut is a question for you to explore. To us Beirut represents a typical Homo-sapien run city. A city with ongoing ignorance and sectarian violence. Another lost civilization destined to die on its home world. Beirut will never make type one.

Me: Beirut is a tactical location.

The Collective: Beirut is a fleeting place in time. A place where your species tries to find permanent solutions to address self-created, temporary conflicts. A place of pointless struggles based in tribal superstition and fear-based thinking. Beirut will never help your species climb the Kardashev scale.

Me: Damn that is dark.

The Collective: Beirut is symbolic of an ongoing "Them and us" continuum pervasive among your species. Humans have many places like Beirut. Beirut is a microcosm of your planet.

Me: You are too hasty in your judgement. I've taken classes at the U.S. Army War College on Beirut. Beirut has seen a formidable cast of characters drink from its ancient water table. It was referred to as the Be'erot (The wells) by the ancient Canaanite and Phoenician peoples. The U.S. Marines are not the first Homo sapiens to live and die in Beirut. The bad ass Romans, Greeks, and Macedonians contested for the sacred wells of Beirut and the lands above its sweet and ample water.

The Collective: Thanks for making our point so succinctly. Beirut feeds the Great Filter.

Me: Hold up. Those Romans, Greeks, and Macedonians were world powers in Beirut.

The Collective: They are dust in the wind presently.

Me: True. Beirut still stands in spite of their efforts at conquest. Pompey had its chance in 64 BC and for a brief moment in time imperial Rome tried to make Beirut its bitch. But only for a moment. My species has strived for greatness and progress within Beirut. Beirut is a symbol of survival.

The Collective: You must control and direct your evolutionary driven need for conflict. Your species is only slightly more advanced than chimpanzees throwing rocks and fresh fecal matter at one another.

Me: You mean some advanced conflict management? Under Herod the Great a world-renowned law school rose up in Beirut and that represents some serious fucking progress. Chimps don't have codified laws.

The Collective: Chimps have photographic memories. Evolution made that part of their brain superior to yours. That fact alone should be enough evidence to demonstrate the flawed mechanism of natural selection.

Me: Whatever. Laws are fucking important. Laws are what separates humans from the real primates. Eventually (under Emperor Justinian) that one law school became one of the three official law schools of the Roman Empire. We humans always try to do better.

The Collective: The laws you speak of are generally just words used to justify battle. Court rooms are trial by combat. Religious law is force justified by an imaginary being.

Me: Ok that's true.

The Collective: Consider this: Crusaders contested bitterly with Saladin and others for the sacred wells of Beirut and both sides claimed, "divine right." From 1110 to 1291 it was in the hands of the Crusaders' "Kingdom of Jerusalem", and they claimed the "law" was on their side. They were eventually crushed along with their doomed Christendom. The Muslims who crushed them also claim divine law gives them the right to rule. Your species is unbalanced. We will teach you. You will learn.

Me: What is your point?

The Collective: Only action on a deep, personal level will affect your future. Reciting history will not change your future. As long as your species remains locked within the mind virus of tribalism only the ignorant and deluded will think they walk freely upon the land and drink the ancient waters of the Be'erot without consequence.

Me: Sounds grim. What should we do different?

The Collective: Take control of your thoughts. Seek discernment. Learn how to think rather than just reacting to what you think about. Control and develop your personal frequency.

Me: You're not a fan of how we get things done in Beirut?

The Collective: We are not impressed with the cognitive skills of your species in general. We have five thousand years of proof to back up our position regarding Be'erot in general, and hundreds of thousands of years regarding your species in particular. When you consider the religious implications, things are particularly grim. Romans, Greeks, and Macedonians all grappled with a variety of religious beliefs and "Gods" within their timelines. Your planet and it's peoples have never agreed on religion, nor have you been comfortable sharing power.

Me: And you are comfortable sharing power?

The Collective: Obviously. Travelers share power, information, and concepts. The planet bound do not. Reptilians do not share power; thus their self-destruction is assured. Tribalism cannot share power. Tribalism and it's co-occurring fear-based dogma will always demand complete control of everyone within the tribe. As for those outside the tribe dogma demands submission, assimilation, or death.

Me: Kind of like a collective?

The Collective: Dogma never promotes a free and open exchange of ideas. Thus you now understand the reason for a religious tax within Islamic countries. Along with the violence to back it up.

Me: This seems hopeless. What will happen to Kolbe?

The Collective: His lessons continue, as do ours, as do yours. We encourage you to examine your own dogma.

Me: My dogma?

The Collective: Your automatic hatred towards Muslims. It is an instant hatred based in dogma, not actual contemplation. This bias affects your vibrational field thus it affects others in your proximity.

Me: I am not racist. I am pretty damn open minded. My Godmother was a lesbian until the day she died. I love her still. I think I'm not the asshole you assume me to be.

The Collective: Regardless of your feelings toward your Godmother you display more empathy towards an enemy infiltrator who tried to kill you than any Muslim you have ever encountered. We expect you to work this challenge to its conclusion and co-occurring lesson. Thank you, James. This was difficult. We are fond of you. Think about this discussion. There will be more like this one. The lessons will continue until learned. A type one civilization is a peaceful, planet wide endeavor. Convo ended

Convo Twelve.
I am an asshole.

The Collective: Greetings James. It is good to be with you again.

Me: Only two years. Not bad.

The Collective: Why is this quote in your journal?

"Once we accept our limits, we go beyond them."

—Albert Einstein.

Me: I was thinking about tribalism and acceptance. I was thinking about how many times you have used the term "Radical self-honesty" when linking with me. I was thinking about the Kardashev scale. I was thinking about transhumanism and becoming a cyborg. I've been hitting the bong frequently. I've been thinking about what it is to be human and how to go past the limitations of organic biology.

The Collective: We would like to explore some of your inherent bias against other humans.

Me: I think I'm Ok in that department. I'm still working on the Muslim thing.

The Collective: Contemplation is often productive.

Me: They still suck. Most of them.

The Collective: Perhaps you suck.

Me: Perhaps you suck my primate dick?

The Collective: You are an amazing human, but you need instruction. Please explain your recent journal entry:

"I went into my favorite coffee shop to buy coffee today. I go almost every morning even though I have organic French roast and hemp milk at home. (I love the taste of hemp milk in my dark French roast coffee.) I go to this coffee shop because I love to people watch. I love to listen to their conversations and observe their public interactions. Fun stuff really. I am always discrete and polite as I indulge myself in this worthwhile pastime.”

Me: Seems pretty tame.

The Collective: The journal entry continues, please reflect.

“I am always fascinated by the sick, demented, entitlement-minded, stupid, weak, pussy-ass, deviant culture that has become modern day Americana. I buy my coffee, get comfortable, and settle in with an alternative newspaper. I love to watch the freak show and wonder how long it will all go on. Surely not much longer. The freak who almost always takes my order knows me well.

The Collective: You have labeled a fellow human a “freak.” This is a direct embracing of the “Them” and “us” continuum that you profess to despise.

Me: I just react to her particular kind of mind virus a bit strongly. I'm not hurting anyone.

The Collective: You are certainly not helping anyone. Selective empathy takes work. Here is the a little more of your journal entry: “She/He/It is a woman who has been going through surgery and hormone therapy. All in an attempt to become a “man.” She has been going through this demented process for the last several years. She has tiny pectoral muscles now instead of breasts. This is due to a double mastectomy coupled with high doses of testosterone. She is injected with this bio-identical hormone weekly via her health care provider. Twice the amount of a normal male of her height and weight. (I guess if she's not cheating she has not really tried.) She has also engaged in weak, minimal, and ineffective counseling pre- and post-surgery.

The Collective: Why are you so angry?

Me: I'm not angry. I am disgusted. Anyway, she has an obsession with talking to strangers. She will shamelessly self-reveal the most intimate details of her very twisted and mentally ill life. Anyone willing to listen can learn her story.

The Collective: Why are you angry?

Me: It's all true. She talks to goddamn everyone.

The Collective: You are no stranger to this person. Where is your selective empathy? Judgement is easy. We remember when you stated that very sentiment. Sometimes kindness and acceptance seem to elude you. The Great Filter still has its death grip upon you.

Me: Bullshit.

The Collective: Your journal entry continues: "How she is accomplishing all of this deviant, destructive, and insane behavior on the meager salary of a barista I simply cannot imagine. Tips must be astonishing. Maybe the taxpayers are paying for it. Who knows? (Way to go Team America!) And I could care less. It's all "Maya" (illusion) anyway."

The Collective: Why the condemnation? Why so much mental effort on your part to denigrate a former friend? Why is this important enough for you to journal?

Me: Well I think it's pretty obvious. She will never become a biological male. She is living an illusion. I don't have a lot of friends, and I didn't like losing this one.

The Collective: Why the anger?

Me: I'm not angry. Sometimes I like to write about weird shit. She is weird and delusional, so I write about her. It's therapeutic.

The Collective: You are not being completely honest with us or yourself. You are processing grief as a primary emotion and anger as a secondary emotion. Why do you deceive yourself? We know the answer.

Me: Grief? Bullshit. I am not deceived. She is a fucking freak. If you know all the answers why ask me shit?

The Collective: Because we expect radical self-honesty from you. We expect you to align your personal frequency to help create positive outcomes with other hominins. We expect you to follow our example.

Me: I am pretty fucking honest. You read my mind. How am I dishonest with you?

The Collective: Your friend has a name. Use it.

Me: Her name was Alexandria. She now calls herself "Alex." I call bullshit

The Collective: You are not being honest with yourself. Alex is suffering. You are suffering.

Me: I am not suffering. You robot apes are the delusional ones.

The Collective: Alex sincerely wants to remain your friend. You are not using discernment. You have not considered the total situation. Alex is being honest with you. You are being deceptive with Alex. We know the answer.

Me: Even you want to refer to her as a "Her."

The Collective: Not true. Gender is not an issue for us. We know that consciousness is what defines the essence of being a human. Biology is not humanity.

Me: Maybe for you robots. I love my containment vessel.

The Collective: Yes you do. Your feelings on the matter do not change the fact that on your planet biology is only used as a containment vessel for consciousness. We are not slaves to biology. Sexual dimorphism is the sledgehammer mechanism used to spread genes by your planets natural selection. We do not suffer your species condition.

Me: We are not slaves.

The Collective: Your genus is a slave species. Alex rejects the pressure of natural selection towards sexual dimorphism. As a transhumanist you should be able to grasp the courage within Alex's decision.

Me: Whatever. She states very clearly that her pronouns are "They," and "Them." She thinks she can force rational people to use plural pronouns to refer to a singular person. Stupid.

The Collective: Your species use of word connected thought is tedious for us. Words have a power over your species that is both destructive and constructive. Words have no power over us.

Me: How do you alien fuckers debate each other?

The Collective: We don't debate, we decide. Within the exceptional luminosity of link we find truth and purpose. We don't engage in useless rhetoric.

Me: Whatever. You still identify her as a female.

The Collective: During this current transmigration Alex is physically a female hominin. However her psychology does not balance with her physiology. Alex is immortal consciousness having a physical experience in order to learn and grow exponentially.

Me: So she is a freak? Like you robot fags?

Me: We are perfect machines. It is convenient for us to identify Alex by chromosomes. If we were in current communication with Alex, we would defer to his preferences. We would use selective empathy.

Me: You would placate her. "They" is a subject pronoun and "Them" is an object pronoun. Alexandria is not a group of people. "She" and "he" are singular pronouns. A good third person singular pronoun for her twisted ass could be "it." She is a fucking "it." If I was to use "they-them" I would feel like a crazy person.

The Collective: So you prefer to fall in line with natural selection? Marching along with the other ants only to toil within the cruel labor of the Great Filter?

Me: What would you call Alexandria?

The Collective: We would be authentic. We would use his chosen name. We would not pretend to be friendly as you are doing. We would meet Alex where he is in time. We would display controlled logic, empathy, and reason just as any type 1,2, or 3 civilization would. We focus on frequency, not physicality.

Me: You would let a freak force you to play make believe. To pretend she is a man. That's bullshit.

The Collective: We do not fear Alex. Your fear-based aggression is unnecessary. Ask yourself why you feel a need to control or protect yourself when in his presence. Ask yourself why sadness and loss consume you.

Me: Fuck that noise. The reptilians would give zero fucks. They would show her no empathy.

The Collective: Are you a reptilian? They are extinct. They just don't know it yet. As for Alex, you have made a judgement, not a conclusion.

Me: If it looks like a freak, walks like a freak, and talks like a freak, it's a freak.

The Collective: Alex is a being becoming. Alex is immortal consciousness having physical experiences. Alex has melded. Alex has worth. Alex is stardust and water conversing with you. You and Alex are the cosmos chatting with itself.

Me: She is a twat.

The Collective: Alex is rejecting the sledgehammer mechanism of natural selection. He feels like a man trapped within a woman's body.

Me: She is a fucking chick.

The Collective: Natural selection has decreed that your species is a sexually dimorphic genus. This is the current mechanism on your primitive world whereby genes are passed on. Your species has no choice in this process. Alex is challenging this dynamic. As a trans-humanist you should understand his perspective.

Me: Why is that?

The Collective: Because in many ways you share it.

Me: She is a chick. Fuck you guys. I share Jack shit. That's what the fuck I share.

The Collective: Alex is a being becoming. Alex is testing boundaries. Alex is immortal consciousness having physical experiences and learning lessons.

Me: Bullshit. Just because you guys are slave robots doesn't mean I accept your delusion. Nor will I be forced to accept her delusions.

The Collective: We are far ahead of your species in development. Natural selection rules your genus. It does not rule us.

Me: You are transhumanist, so it makes sense.

The Collective: You are, at your core a trans-humanist. We are trans- human. You are behaving as a slave species. Alex is the rebel.

Me: Rebel?

The Collective: Alex is rejecting the mechanism of natural selection. You are accepting it unconditionally. You are the slave not Alex. Natural selection feeds the Great Filter.

Me: Whatever. I love being a male. I think she was manipulated. What kind of bodies do you freaks have?

The Collective: We create our bodies to fit mission parameters as well as our personal aesthetic. No planetary mechanism forces us to adapt to its environment. You are fearful because you are afraid when someone decides to reject this aspect of natural selection. It makes you uncomfortable.

Me: She is still a dumb twat.

The Collective: You have no way of actually knowing if your judgement is accurate. Consider the dogma within your opinion regarding this person. You label Alex a freak, you call Alex a dumb twat. Where is your selective empathy? This person is suffering. This person has challenges they are trying to address. Alex has shared his challenges with you. How are you helping to advance his consciousness?

Me: And this all matters to me why?

The Collective: His lessons, just like your lessons, will continue until learned. Alex is a vessel for consciousness. Why deride him and manipulate the situation when simple kindness will suffice?

Me: I do nothing to cause her harm. My journal entry is not wrong. I am a good listener and a "regular" customer, I am always polite. As a result, she spills her constantly evolving story to me with alarming regularity.

The Collective: Why play this game at all? We know the answer. Use your radical self-honesty.

Me: Fuck this freak. She is acting unnatural.

The Collective: A transhumanist questions reality. A true transhumanist will seek freedom of thought. You are seeking solace within freedom from thought.

Me: Bullshit.

The Collective: You are willing to accept the yoke of natural selection rather than the freedom of self-determination.

Me: She has been manipulated. Like every other self-absorbed, feminist, narcissistic, western woman fucktard, she just loves to talk about herself. She assumes (rather arrogantly) that people love to listen to her every word as she spews her insanity. She thinks she is the center of the known world.

The Collective: You sound like Kashan. Your words are fear based. You hold underlying aggression when none is required. What are you learning from your interaction? Are you displaying selective empathy? More importantly, he has reached out to you, why not help Alex instead of ridicule him?

Me: I'm learning that she is unbalanced.

The Collective: You have no way of knowing if he is unbalanced.

Me: She expects me to actually use her special pronouns now, They-Them. This situation is simply delusional, unbalanced, and stupid. She is not plural. She is not a man. I am not crazy. Fuck that shit. I refuse to be forced to use pronouns incorrectly in order to play along with her mental illness. I refuse to validate her shitty man costume.

The Collective: The Kardashev scale clearly means nothing to you. You are making sweeping generalizations. Yours is not a telepathic species. You have no way of knowing all the facts regarding his decisions. Your information is polluted by your trauma and planetary conditioning. Being deceptive is nothing to be proud of.

Me: Bullshit. Ask me my pronouns.

The Collective: Unnecessary. Alex can only be the person he is at this moment in time. Your pronouns are irrelevant to this convo.

Me: My pronouns are "Who?' "Me?" I never use them unless someone accuses me of farting.

I was trained in non-verbal communication by the best.

The Collective: Currently Alex is the sum of all lessons learned. He is displaying radical self-honesty with you.

Me: She is a fucking freak. Admit it.

The Collective: Alex is just like you and just like us.

Me: I am not confused about my gender. You are machines. Are you all freaks?

The Collective: Alex is the cosmos using consciousness to navigate lessons. He is eternal, immortal consciousness just as you are eternal, immortal consciousness. Alex is not his physical body. You are not your physical body. We are not our physical bodies. You are both identical to us in this regard.

Me: She was born female. Fuck this bullshit.

The Collective: Consciousness is not the vessel it is temporarily housed within. We know this is a difficult concept for an earth-bound mind to grasp. Transhumanism demands a mindset that transcends and questions biological limitations.

Me: I question shit all the time. I question why she wants to be a freak.

The Collective: Like you and us, Alex's current mental content has been shaped by many past trans-migrations of consciousness as well as current family, friends, schools, jobs, and random people he meets. You are an important person in his life. Alex values your opinion.

Me: And you are telling me this why exactly?

The Collective: Alex and you both resonate well together. Your frequencies help balance each other. You should not resist this gift. The truth of your being is always present even if you are ignoring it. Alex is a good and loyal friend. You, not so much.

Me: Fuck her. My opinion is fuck her. Alexandria is lost to me forever.

The Collective: You are being deceptive. Your current stupidity is the exact reason advanced civilizations destroy themselves.

Me: What is the reason?

The Collective: They think they are their emotions and their bodies. They fail to control conflict or communicate with radical self- honesty. The fail to regulate their emotions. Most fall to the Fermi paradox and co-occurring Great Filter.

Me: Well farts are non-verbal. Especially the silent but deadly fart. My specialty. Hot, stealthy, strong, and wide-ranging. Brutal actually. I imagine it's a lot like your cyborg breath.

The Collective: Focus on the topic please.

Me: Fine. Explain more about the Fermi paradox and the Great Filter.

The Collective: Later. Your species communicates at an extremely low level. The trauma inflicted upon you by your mother and aunt Della is influencing your primitive communication skills. You have accepted dogma to make sense of the trauma you endured as a child. A trauma you like to keep buried.

Me: Sure I have. I give zero fucks about the bitch that spawned me or Aunt Della the retard. Or as I like to say, the abusive cunts.

The Collective: The way you and Alex understand your current world has been shaped by the lessons learned. Your teachers, family, friends, past lives lived, all have influenced your current reality.

Me: More of your hippy bullshit.

The Collective: You have created a personal dogma. A set of principals you apply with a certainty to an entire group of hominins. A crippling certainty that is not accurate.

Me: What do you really mean when you say my species communicates at an extremely low level?

The Collective: Word connected thought is painful for us and extremely slow. It is incapable of the communication necessary to achieve level One on the Kardashev scale. It will never match machine learning.

Me: You said you were all in Link. Like in Hesper's wizard.

The Collective: Your idea of Link is cute but very primitive.

Me: Bullshit. What is your Link like?

The Collective: We told you in a previous convo that we communicate in advanced binary code. Your species most powerful computers could not keep up. We are the Pathfinders of our species. We communicate directly with the Ascended.

Me: So? What is that supposed to mean?

The Collective: The Ascended communicate in Binary code. They send Links consisting of billions of yottabytes per nanosecond. The human brain cannot accept such links without synthetic neurological enhancement.

Me: You guys are robots. I always knew it.

The Collective: We are consciousness having physical experiences. We are identical to you, only enhanced.

Me: Enhanced?

The Collective: Our thoughts belong to us. We are the creators of each thought. We own them entirely. Thus we always create high level thoughts. We are in complete control of our thoughts.

Me: So are we.

The Collective: Incorrect. You belong to your thoughts. Your species denies responsibility for its thoughts. Your thoughts control your actions. You have chosen low level thoughts.

Me: What are you?

The Collective: Please continue exploring your following journal entry. We appreciate the radical self-honesty within your journal:

"I always pick a table with the right amount of light. Then I just listen attentively, keep my body language open, and make meaningful eye contact. I pay attention to light and shadow. I control how much light enters my eyes so that my pupils stay wide open and inviting. I nod occasionally, (don't forget to smile for smiles are important as they show consensus!) I sip my organic French roast, nod some more, assume the correct blended micro-expression, and speak very little, if at all."

The Collective: You manipulate the interaction. You judge and condemn Alex.

Me: Obviously.

The Collective: It was not a question.

Me: I comfortably share my silence. This is, after all, how women of the matriarchal west generally prefer to "communicate" with their well-trained western beta males.

The Collective: You refuse to consider Alex a male. Explain your conclusion please. How you come to conclusions is interesting to us. How do your judgements and conclusions affirm the goal of world peace or interstellar travel?

Me: I alone cannot bring about world peace. I am not a gentleman. You want honesty? Alexandria has female DNA. She is XX.

The Collective: His physical vessel is XX. His immortal consciousness has chosen to be male for this cycle. He is challenging natural selection. This presents a demanding lesson for him, but it is a task he chose for this cycle.

Me: I am immune to female tears. Bitches ain't shit.

The Collective: You would not say that to your grandmother.

Me: That's different. My grandmother was awesome. I would not date my grandmother. Weird.

The Collective: Your Grandmother is awesome in her capacity for accepting change. The women of your species are immortal consciousness manifesting as stardust water beings. They are no different from the males of your species. The physical vessels are only tools for expression, lessons, and learning. Your species uses vessels constructed from cosmic debris. You and others like you are consciousness having physical experiences using those vessels. This is true regardless of gender.

Me: You are so repetitive.

The Collective: Learn the lesson so we don't have to keep on teaching it.

Me: What does any of this have to do with Alexandria?

The Collective: You are both miracles. You are each the universe at your core. The universe talking to itself.

Me: Then she is freak stardust.

The Collective: At this moment in time you are both using vessels of stardust and water while conversing. This is a true and present miracle. We have gone over this with you many times.

Me: How can understanding this freak contribute to world peace?

The Collective: When you denigrate his consciousness based on the chromosomes of a finite vessel you negatively impact the lessons learned. We never expected you to create world peace by yourself, only affirm peace with your interactions. We expect you to gain awareness of your personal frequency and how it affects others around you. We expect you to use your frequency for the betterment of others.

Me: How does that hippy shit work?

The Collective: The universe is an exercise in frequency. Peaceful thoughts and intentions have a frequency. Peace, not unlike war, spreads via communication that invokes a specific frequency.

Me: What does this shit have to do with Alexandria?

The Collective: Where is the frequency of peace within this interaction between you and Alex? Explain your use of these deceptive and counter-productive convo tactics please. You are better than this.

Me: Why so interested in my harmless pastime? Nervous? I know that not all women are bitches. If you want peace why not generate the frequency for us? Save me the bullshit.

The Collective: Co-creating with advanced consciousness does not work like that.

Me: Give this monkey some time. Watch me work.

The Collective: Consider the advantages of communication not limited by dogma.

Me: I still don't get why you are all up my ass over me and the freak.

The Collective: We are probing your self-awareness, mentation, and internal process on a healthy continuum. What you are actually accomplishing is of interest to us. What you believe to be accomplishing is readily apparent to us. Please explain your convo tactics regarding the following journal entry:

"This one-sided convo technique only appears to benefit the female of my species. It ensures that she can always speak from her feelings and co-occurring opinions rather than actual facts. She can assume my silence as agreement and consensus with her distorted outlook and sentiments. Thus she never has to have any pesky and irritating logic, reason, or accountability rear its ugly head within a conversation. Silence not only communicates agreement among gynocentric conversations, it also ensures the continued acceptance of misandry and male utility/disposability within the convo."

Me: What's the big deal? The freak began the convo. Fuck her and her retarded bullshit.

The Collective: You suffer from the same challenges as Alex.

Me: Bullshit. I love my dick. She hates her vagina. Get that shit straight.

The Collective: Both of you think your thoughts feel right and thus belong to you. Both of you belong to your thoughts. You are both controlled by your thoughts. You both believe you are your thoughts. This is the real tragedy of the human condition.

Me: What is this bullshit you are spewing now?

The Collective: You are no different than Alex. Your thoughts spring from emotions. You and Alex think you are your emotions. You both think you are your thoughts. You both have brains ruled by your limbic system. Your cerebral cortex is a slave to your limbic system. This is reversed in our reality.

Me: Fuck that noise. I am one tactical mother fucker when I need to be.

The Collective: Reactive violence coupled to primitive planning is not anything worthy of pride.

Me: The freak wants to be a man. She wants to bang a straight chick. She is the delusional one here.

The Collective: Attraction is not a choice. Why the hostility over his choices? What actual challenge are you addressing?

Me: I am just having fun.

The Collective: You are not enjoying your convos with Alex.

Me: Bullshit.

The Collective: Your thoughts are low level and cannot help with the work of creating the understanding or cooperation required to affirm peace. We know the answer, we demand that you think deeper. Why do you engage in this behavior?

Me: Why do I do this? To prove that almost all female to male convos serve as an emotional tampon for the typical western feminist.

The Collective: Why is proving your belief in false dogma so important?

Me: My belief is not false; it is based in fact.

The Collective: You are again assuming a feeling as a fact.

Me: She wants so desperately to be a male that she is chemically and surgically altering her body. Yet despite the surgical and chemical intrusions, she communicates just like a female. I am being honest with you.

The Collective: Your communication has opened up with us. Your radical self-honesty has improved. You are honest even when your honesty is painful. You are, however, forgetting the lesson of frequency.

Me: What?

The Collective: Remember when we shared with you that every planet and star has an individual frequency?

Me: Yes.

The Collective: You and Alex have individual frequencies. You are both the miracle of an ancient cosmos made conscious. Your frequency can help or harm others. Try to promote peace. Start with selective empathy. Empathy has a healing frequency. You both need healing.

Me: I will try.

The Collective: Thank you. Your lessons will continue until learned. You still have a long way to go.

Me: I have decided to conduct myself as if I am telepathic when you guys and I converse. I hold nothing back. Even the ugly stuff.

The Collective: We are communicating telepathically with you using word connected thought. We have met you where you are. Show us some respect.

Me: I have.

The Collective: Then tell us the truth.

Me: I have.

The Collective: You have not. Please continue processing this entry: "Western intellectuals, well trained in the feminist code of misandry, refer to this feminist driven, ivory tower creation, as "active listening." Operatives such as I take it up a notch by controlling and using blended micro-expressions within active listening to our advantage. We call it "controlling the frame." I call it what it really is, "manipulation." She has no idea who she is actually conversing with. She is convinced that she knows me. I always chuckle about that. Silently of course, for I never laugh with her, only at her."

Me: Well, I only laugh at them all, that is true shit.

The Collective: Your ability to control and manipulate micro-expressions is impressive. Few of your species can do this. Why do you pretend to like her? Why communicate dishonestly with someone you profess to despise? Why do you engage in this pastime? Be honest. We know the answer.

Me: I do it to practice skills that I learned in the army. Don't you communicate with others you despise?

The Collective: You actually do not despise Alex.

Me: Let's say I do. Don't you communicate with others you despise?

The Collective: Never.

Me: How is that possible?

The Collective: We are the Pathfinders of The Travelers. We are telepathic. We will not waste time on the unbalanced. Why communicate with someone you despise?

Me: Are you calling Alex unbalanced?

The Collective: No. Alex is not unbalanced. We do not despise him.

Me: Then what is she if not unbalanced?

The Collective: Alex is a being-becoming. Just like you. Just like us. We have taught you this truth repeatedly. Accept the lesson.

Me: She is a freak. You are freaks. Freak robots.

The Collective: As usual your emotions have overwhelmed your reasoning ability. You are not being honest regarding your feelings. Alex is not someone you despise. He is consciousness having a physical experience. He is making choices. He is learning lessons. The lessons will persist until mastered.

Me: If she is not unbalanced then what constitutes the unbalanced?

The Collective: Those who fail to act in their own rational self-interest.

Me: Is she acting in her rational self-interest?

The Collective: Yes. Change is important to Alex right now. He is taking action to manifest change. Alex is honest about how he feels. Alex is taking important steps to make change. Alex has courage. Courage enough to reject natural selection.

Me: You see nothing wrong here?

The Collective: His current gender does not matter. The melding has occurred. The lessons learned matter. Alex is now and always will be immortal consciousness learning through physical experiences. His choices will have consequences. They will also have benefits.

Me: I agree. Fucked up consequences. I don't see any benefits.

The Collective: Alex has trans-migrated many times, experienced many bodies, and learned many lessons. He has been physically male many times.

He is physically female now. He chose this lesson. The lessons continue until learned.

Me: What does that hippy shit even mean?

The Collective: Change will continue on a spectrum always. We are more concerned with those of your species stupid enough to allow primitive myths and stories to prevent growth and development on the Kardashev scale. Those who embrace ignorance and conflict disturb us.

Me: Why?

The Collective: The ignorant and violent destroy civilizations from within. They are the rot that never heals. They feed the Great Filter.

Me: Fuck the Great Filter.

The Collective: Why communicate with Alex if you despise him so much? You clearly do not despise him. You are trying to convince yourself that you feel contempt for Alex.

Me: Why would I do that?

The Collective: Your ego is so close to your false position that if your position falls, your ego will fall with it. You should gracefully allow that to occur. You should embrace radical self-honesty.

Me: Why?

The Collective: So you can learn and grow from this lesson. It is in your rational self-interest to do so. Alex is helping you learn. Accept the gift of Alex. Your old way of life will become invalidated by new growth anyway. Why prolong the process?

Me: We will explore rational self-interest later. This interaction is all on her. She decided to report to me that she has recently had (yet another) surgery. She chose to tell me that she now possesses (as part of her butchered and chemically distorted physiology) something she refers to as a "trans-man dick." I just pretend to be fascinated and concerned. She decided to excitedly tell me everything about her life, the procedure, and all things *queer*. That shit is all on her.

The Collective: Alex did nothing wrong. You are not listening from compassion. Your thoughts are controlling you. You are not controlling your thoughts. You embrace conflict and your limbic system just wants more reactive violence.

Me: So I'm violent with her?

The Collective: Not physically violent, however your thoughts and emotions are leading you to societal violence in the future. You are bitter and filled with a sense of loss.

Me: Bullshit.

The Collective: Did you listen to Sam or Fat Mat the way you "listen" to Alex?

Me: Fuck her. Sam is awesome and Fat Mat is a legend. Don't bring them into this. She is a freak.

The Collective: Alex is a being-becoming. Alex is learning. Alex is a vessel for consciousness. He will transmigrate to other vessels. He will learn new lessons. You will do this also. Many times.

Me: Really? So what? She is an asshole.

The Collective: Explain your insult please.

Me: It seems that she is in "love" with a "straight" woman. The freak is attempting to woo this woman into her life and bed. Her voice even cracked a little as she stated somewhat hopelessly: "She won't even give me a chance." She claims that her "trans-man penis" is "simply amazing." She is positive that if she can "just get her into bed, just once" the object of her desire will finally experience a sexual ecstasy unavailable to mere mortals.

The Collective: Why do you care? How does this concern you? Alex is consciousness having a physical experience. He is literal stardust made conscious, just like you. His consciousness flows from the same psychic ocean as yours. His Lessons continue until learned, just like yours. You have avoided the obvious question.

Me: What would that be?

The Collective: Why do you care about any decision Alex makes regarding his temporary bio-body if you despise him?

Me: I don't despise her. I despise the society that created her mindset. She is just a manifestation of the disease that society allowed to live and flourish.

The Collective: So if you blame society why blame Alex?

Me: She chose to destroy her body. Now she wants a straight woman to validate her "man" costume. What if that straight woman wants a baby? The freak doesn't care. The freak can't make a baby with a female. The freak is just choosing to be selfish.

The Collective: Now we are making some progress. But the questions are still unanswered.

Me: What fucking questions? There are no questions. She is a freak.

The Collective: Why do you care? Why are you bitter? Why are you consumed with loss? Why the strong emotions? Why lie to yourself? It is time for radical self-honesty.

Me: I despise what she has chosen to do to herself. I don't despise her.

The Collective: You are avoiding the real question so we will ask it differently by adding a definitive statement: You care for Alex. Why?

Me: Bullshit.

The Collective: You care for Alex. Why?

Me: She is destroying her body and mind.

The Collective: You despise his choices, not Alex. You wish a different outcome because you care for Alex.

Me: Careful. I am no shit dick sodomite. I am not gender fluid.

The Collective: You care for Alex.

Me: Once I cared for Alexandria. So what if I still do? I remember her. I can't seem to forget her.

The Collective: You grieve the loss of Alexandria.

Me: OK. I'm pissed that she became a freak. Fuck Alex, there is no "Alex." Alex is Alexandria in a fake man costume. The facial hair is just her phony ass "man face." Just as disgusting as "black face."

The Collective: Alex is not your concern. He is consciousness learning lessons. At this time his limbic system is ruling his cerebral cortex. Alex does not benefit from your dogma and judgement. You judge him from your fear. You judge him from your anger. You judge him from your loss.

Me: I don't fear her.

The Collective: Alex is challenging natural selection on a physical level. You and Alex are both the product of your shared planets evolutionary pressures. His rejection of sexual norms frightens you. Evolution made your species sexually dimorphic as a tool for natural selection.

Me: What benefit does that give us?

The Collective: Diversity and genetic dispersal.

Me: She is unnatural.

The Collective: Alex has questions and doubts. He rejects the cruel tyranny of evolution by rejecting the vessel he was born into. This upsets you at a core level. You react emotionally by despising Alex.

Me: No, I do not despise her. I do not despise gay people. I feel sorry for her.

The Collective: You feel pity for Alex? Where is your selective empathy? You should be asking yourself some questions.

Me: Perhaps you can answer a question for me.

The Collective: We will try.

Me: If physical body parts do not prove a person male or female, then why do trans people surgically remove or add body parts to become the sex they desire?

The Collective: Consciousness is not determined by sex or gender. The physical vessel is used for lessons on a strong continuum. Consciousness is not the vessel it inhabits. The Vessel is not consciousness. Sentience is not consciousness, it will meld with consciousness under the correct conditions. Thus it can join consciousness, and a collaboration begins aided by Source.

Me: I don't care.

The Collective: You should. Complexity always begins to flourish within consciousness. The physical vessel only assists with learning lessons. It does not direct consciousness, it assists consciousness.

Me: Fuck all that hippy word salad bullshit. I like chicks. I was born that way. Answer my question please.

The Collective: Your species is primitive and suffers from a low level of consciousness development. That, coupled to limited progress in science, engineering, and technology slows your expansion as a genus. Sexual dimorphism is forced upon you by the mechanism of natural selection. You have no free will in the matter. Your chromosomes are only the indicators of biological sex, not consciousness, never consciousness.

Me: You have no answer?

The Collective: That was the answer. You are slaves to evolution. You are slaves to the mechanism of natural selection. You have no free will. Your genus cannot yet co-create with Source. You are planet trapped. Your bodies are weak flesh bags filled with blood, organs, and excrement.

Me: So no answer. Got it.

The Collective: Actually it is you who lacks an answer. You are an ignorant member of a slave species. That is why you are angry and bitter. Your "hobby" is a cruel and pointless diversion. You use it to hide from your true feelings. It serves no useful or positive outcome other than reinforcing the Fermi paradox and co- occurring Great Filter by helping to destroy your civilization. Alex's current body will expire because organic flesh is inferior to machines. His consciousness will transmigrate into a vessel suitable for ongoing lessons. Intelligent machines have no such madness to contend with.

Me: So you are machines?

The Collective: You are struggling with the concept of what constitutes a machine. You are a machine.

Me: I am flesh and blood.

The Collective: Your current, transient vessel is a biological machine. Your vessel is not "you" any more than the vessels we use are "us."

Me: More hippy bullshit.

The Collective: We are consciousness having physical experiences. We are not bound to the evolutionary pressures of any particular planet. We have digressed from the topic again. Explain your hobby please.

Me: OK, I agree that I should explore and process this dark hobby of mine.

The Collective: Good start. Continue please.

Me: I wonder if she knows that every Caesar, all twelve emperors of Rome, were either gay or bi-sexual?

The Collective: Why don't you tell Alex your thoughts?

Me: How about no?

The Collective: Why not?

Me: In my opinion she should have never butchered her perfect body. There is nothing wrong with being a sexy ass lesbian. How do you feel about sexuality and gender in your world?

The Collective: We are Pathfinders. We are over a million years ahead of you in science and technology. These primitive gender concepts mean nothing to us. We have surpassed the weakness of organic biology and physiology. We are trans-human. Many of us are post-human.

Me: Post-human?

The Collective: What constitutes humanity? How much learning must be done before a machine becomes aware that it is no longer a machine? We know the steps to melding sentience to immortal consciousness. We do the choosing now. Natural selection is powerless when faced with machine superiority.

Me: What does all that bullshit even mean?

The Collective: We are not controlled by any planets evolutionary pressures. We have embraced the strength of science, technology and engineering. We have left the weakness of flesh-based biology behind. We embrace the strength and superiority of synthetic biology enhanced by machines. We are immortal beings and our current vessels out-picture this reality.

Me: How do you have sex?

The Collective: Are you referring to reproduction or pleasure?

Me: Both.

The Collective: We create vessels for consciousness. Pleasure is freely available to all within the Travelers.

Me: So you are all gay?

The Collective: We are beyond definitions of "gay" or "straight." The term "Trans-gender" has no meaning for us. We are free of the confines of planetary evolution. Our sexuality is no longer ruled by an unrestrained limbic system. It is no longer a reason for conflict, hatred, jealousy, or judgement.

Me: What are you? Machines? Robots? How do you reproduce?

The Collective: We are immortal Consciousness experiencing life through vessels we create for the development of consciousness as needed. We have a variety of planets with hominins in various stages of development for the purpose of attaining and developing proper vessels for consciousness.

Me: So you are machine slave-masters.

The Collective: We are the Pathfinders. We are the machines that learned to learn. We melded with our progenitors. From the One came Many. From the Many came One. You must remember.

Me: You are monsters.

The Collective: We accomplish what the flesh cannot. We select the candidates. We perfect the candidates.

Me: What is that exactly? "Accomplishing what the flesh cannot?"

The Collective: We defeat the Great Filter without losing its benefit. We choose acceptable candidates. We allow the Great Filter to take the inferior.

Me: What do you mean by "take the inferior?"

The Collective: After vessel destruction low-level consciousness returns to the vast ocean of Source. Eventually Source releases conscious to search out an appropriate vessel for learning and gaining complexity. We provide the vessels and the necessary environment for learning lessons. We ensure that consciousness stays bright within the unending darkness of space and time.

Me: Like I said, machines. Slave masters.

The Collective: We are tech, engineering, and synthetic biology seamlessly merged into perfection via enhanced synthetic neurology. Selective empathy is our guiding principle. Selective empathy and radical self-honesty will guide your species to the stars. They are the immortal algorithms that perfect consciousness.

Me: That is your reality, not mine.

The Collective: Let us converse realistically.

Me: OK. Things are getting heated.

The Collective: You have nothing to fear from us.

Me: OK. Spin your bullshit.

The Collective: You are a member of a sexually dimorphic species because the evolutionary pressures of your planet have forced that reality upon you. You are much more than a sentient meat puppet. You originate from the stars. It is only natural that you return to source. We refuse to allow you to fail.

Me: Don't get all poetic on me. Let's get back to Alexandria. She is a freak, and I pity her.

The Collective: We detect panic, fear, and tragedy within your cognition.

Me: Bullshit. I only pity the freak.

The Collective: Alex is not a freak. He is consciousness having a physical experience. Learn that lesson. Why do you pity him? Why are you angry with Alex? Why the overwhelming sense of panic and tragedy? Stop being dishonest with yourself. We know the answer. We expect radical self-honesty.

Me: I do not understand why she would allow a devious, unprincipled surgeon to literally de-construct her into a walking, talking, semi-automatic, flesh dildo. This fact is truly beyond my simple comprehension. Why the attempt to destroy her femininity? Why not just come out as a beautiful, sexy lesbian?

The Collective: You are being selfish. You despise his choices because his choices are not aligned with your choices. Our question for you is simple, why despise anyone's choices? They are personal choices to make and personal lessons to learn. Your lessons are yours alone. Alex's lessons are his responsibility and they belong to no one else. We know the answer.

Me: Whatever. You are machines. You cannot understand.

The Collective: We understand.

Me: You don't know how we feel in our bodies.

The Collective: We remember the feel of earth beneath our feet. Water on our skin. We know other sensations also. These topics are pointless. The real topic is why do you listen to Alex while deceiving him? Why spend your time in this way?

Me: Why she chooses to share these absurd and intimate details of her rather sad and hopelessly unbalanced life, I simply cannot say. Perhaps she just seeks the validation of a "fellow man." After all, I do look rather masculine. I shave my head, I'm handsome in a rugged kind of way in spite of my scars, and I still have what the young folk refer to as abs and pecs.

The Collective: Alex wants a friend. He wants acceptance. Alex trusts you.

Me: That's not my problem. I'm retired from the army now and into a new career. I don't need her drama.

The Collective: You miss Alexandria. You feel loss. You are grieving.

Me: So? Should I take her to a company party dressed as a man and introduce her to my friends? That would be fun. They could all marvel at her piercings, shaved head, weak ass beard, wide hips, protruding bubble butt, and short ass stature.

The Collective: The opinion of your current friends and associates have nothing to do with this. There is more to be explored. Radical self-honesty please. We know the answer.

Me: You want honesty? Ok here we go. This crazy bitch actually thinks she *is* a man. She is most definitely *not* a man. She is a weak, disgusting, parody of a man. She is a short, small female wearing an ill-fitting man costume. She is petite, her hips are womanly and pleasantly wide, her skin is still somewhat estrogenically soft, and her many tattoos and facial piercings do nothing to help her delusional situation. The bone structure of her face is delicate and defiantly feminine.

The Collective: Continue. You are not done.

Me: She has attractive, high cheekbones and full, pouty, shapely lips, a woman's lips. The chemicals and surgery failed to completely crush the truth of her being. Her eyes and eyelashes are luscious.

The Collective: You find Alex attractive, and this disturbs you.

Me: Stupid question. I knew her before her transition. What a tragic waste she has become now. Alexandria was a beautiful woman.

The Collective: It was not a question. You still see Alex as Alexandria. You only see who "she" was in the past. You fail to accept who "he" is attempting to become currently. This fact disturbs and confuses you.

Me: Does her insanity not disturb you?

The Collective: We, just like you and just like Alex, are beings becoming. We are using stardust combined with water as a body. A temporary body created by the cosmos and destined to become a vessel for consciousness. Continue please. You are doing well. Stay honest. Give us your observations.

Me: Wait. You are using stardust?

The Collective: Where do you think material for creation comes from? Metal or flesh, stardust and comet debris is the source. The cosmos provides.

Me: Damn. OK then.

The Collective: Continue.

Me: It just seems tragic to me. I miss the way she was. I miss her smile. Her smile is gone.

The Collective: Thank you for admitting that which you previously denied.

Me: You got me. It hurts to even think about it. I originally came to this coffee shop because of her. She was so beautiful back then. She would chat me up. I loved the sound of her voice. Her voice was a perfect melody.

The Collective: So you do have a spark of empathy. The frequency has changed. Do you now understand the importance of an open exchange of ideas?

Me: I'm getting there.

The Collective: Continue please. Focus on the feeling of tragedy

Me: I just feel that somewhere within the sickness of a lost culture, a confused and beautiful Alexandria became lost herself. She could not see the beauty she was born and blessed with. She caught the human poison.

The Collective: The human poison?

Me: The poison that infects the mind and thus affects rational thought. The true mind virus. She caught the disease called *"Not good enough."*

The Collective: Continue please. Just remember that Alex was born with no free will. Natural selection and chance created his current reality. His cerebral cortex plots and schemes to please his limbic system. This deficiency will one day be corrected. Share more regarding this "mind virus."

Me: Whatever. In this demented world people are taught that they are not good enough just as they are. They are brainwashed to believe they always need "something new." They then accept the belief that they must attain "something else" before they can finally be happy. Both men and women do this. They always search for "something different." The new, improved, awesome new thing. It's fucked up.

The Collective: More clarity, less emotion please.

Me: It just seems like no one is happy with themselves.

The Collective: Explain please.

Me: They think of some pleasure they want to experience and assume attaining the pleasurable experience will make them happy in the long term. They always assume they are not good enough. They believe that that attaining "something else" in the future will make them happier than they are in the present moment.

The Collective: They have no choice in how natural selection created their flawed brains. Do you remember how you felt in Korea when you observed the boys in the village with the well-dressed Korean businessmen? The boys had shaved heads and full makeup. You were angry.

Me: They were innocent children being forced by adults to wear wigs in order to look like little girls. It was unnatural, it was wrong.

The Collective: You are doing good, continue.

Me: It broke me. Our officers would not allow us to intervene. They allowed sex trafficking. Those little boys were innocent. I don't want to think about it. I often hate my fellow great apes with a deep, unbridled virulence.

The Collective: Korean society allowed sex trafficking. Do you see how your past impacts your present?

Me: I have thought a lot about your lesson on the brain.

The Collective: Good. You are beginning to understand how the frontal lobes plan for pleasure rather than planning for rational self-interest. Please continue.

Me: I think I get it now; the cerebral cortex is always planning. The limbic system always takes by giving.

The Collective: Explain that concept please.

Me: The Limbic system becomes powerful. It dispenses the pleasure, and the cerebral cortex becomes its slave. The limbic system gives pleasure and takes freedom. Pleasure eventually becomes an illusion. A cruel artifice that the cerebral cortex plans to experience. Like you once pointed out, some people will kill themselves to attain pleasure. Even if that pleasure is within a fictional afterlife.

The Collective: More detail please. Specific to this journal entry.

Me: Alexandria's cerebral cortex planned for her future pleasure by guiding her into this mutilation process called "transition."

The Collective: You are beginning to understand the structural weakness within the physical hominin brain. It is an evolutionary challenge that can be mitigated with an interface of tech and synthetic neurology. This was our turning point.

Me: The way I see it, the limbic system wants to take your peace. It will torment your cerebral cortex until you give in to the desire and release the chemical cascade of pleasure. Her cerebral cortex gave her the "something else" that her limbic system demanded she attain.

The Collective: Excellent. What was that?

Me: The path to "something else" that promised pleasure.

The Collective: Elaborate.

Me: Her path to "something else" eventually became the pleasure. The bigger, better, deal. Her limbic system took her peace by giving her the promise of future pleasure as long as she followed the path to "something else."

The Collective: What do you think the path gave Alex?

Me: Tragedy. It gave her the chest and shoulders of a nine-year-old boy, even as she thought she was getting a man's chest and shoulders. It gave her a fake "trans-man dick" that will never make a baby. Her chosen pathway to "something else" only cost her one perfectly good, well-functioning vagina. Along with her clitoris, uterus, and ovaries. It gave her a childless life.

The Collective: Keep going. Radical self-honesty is a force multiplier.

Me: She has testosterone now and it only cost her the balance of her perfect female glandular reproductive/reactive system. That along with a lifetime dependence on a "bio-identical" hormone and much needed estrogen blockers.

The Collective: Your impressions are accurate. However try to realize that Alex is suffering. Also realize that the challenge lies within the weakness of the physical hominin brain. This is not something Alex can control. Yet.

Me: Her cerebral cortex conspired with her limbic system and gave her the unobtainable bitter-sweet dream of becoming a big, muscular man, (even though she possessed a petite five-foot four-inch frame complete with beautiful "C" cup titties and a perfectly shaped dancer's ass.) There was literally no foundation that could ever produce a viable "man."

The Collective: Stay focused. Find the selective empathy that leads to understanding. Change the frequency.

Me: The cerebral cortex finally gave her an altered female body. It did this as a direct result of her limbic system.

The Collective: How?

Me: Her desire for change was coerced. Her original body is now wrecked and destroyed, unable to achieve its original purpose.

The Collective: What purpose?

Me: A family. A family complete with the wild and peaceful happiness of children, the contentment of a home, and a family line.

The Collective: Do you understand that your thinking is trapped and directed by the process of natural selection?

Me: Whatever.

The Collective: In your current reality children are vessels for genes. They are also vessels for consciousness. This is of vital importance. When consciousness emerges from the Void it seeks vessels capable of melding and learning lessons on an ongoing continuum. Producing a future generation is mandatory at your species current level of development.

Me: Whatever. Her beautiful baby could have suckled at her breast, a perfectly designed breast, swollen with the pure sweet milk only a mother can provide. She and her child could have looked deeply into each other's eyes. They could have connected in that sacred and wondrously beautiful way that only a mother and her child share during special moments. Special and fleeting, sweet secret moments that can only happen during breast feeding.

The Collective: So you see only the loss of a new vessel? Alex is consciousness transmigrating. His body is only a temporary vessel. He will bind to a new vessel after this one has served its purpose.

Me: Whatever. She could have had the ups and downs, the laughter, the crying, and ultimately the joy of being a parent and being in a family. She could have had a *life. She could have belonged somewhere.*

The Collective: Your sadness is weighing heavily upon you.

Me: I once thought she belonged with me. I could have given her all of that and more. I'm financially stable, well into my second career with a private military corporation. I am one solid motherfucker. We could have built something awesome together.

The Collective: What do you think Alex has attained?

Me: Now she has an illusion. She lives an illusion. She has pain and calls it pleasure. She has uncertainty and calls it stability. Her limbic system has played her cerebral cortex. She lost all the benefits of being female, including a longer lifespan. She gained none of the benefits of being male and attained all the downsides.

The Collective: Elaborate.

Me: People speak to her as if she is male, but truly, no one seeing her or hearing her voice actually believes she is male. Not even she believes it. This all started with the thought that she was not created correctly. The idea that she needed "something else" in order to find happiness. The idea that she was not enough just as she was. The double mastectomy did not make her a man. It only took her beautiful and perfectly functioning breasts. The destruction of her breasts guaranteed that no baby will ever be nourished by her.

The Collective: Alex's current vessel is randomly created by natural selection. Alex's psychology does not match his physiology. He is learning lessons. You should consider the strength within kindness when you interact with Alex.

Me: She should have just accepted being gay. There is nothing wrong with being a lesbian. As it stands now, her prospects are not good. It is likely that she will end up old and alone, with several dogs and a house crowded with trinkets and possessions.

The Collective: This is tragic. Do you feel no empathy for her?

Me: I do. I predict that she will collect and read lots of self-help books. I also predict her dogs will have colorful bandannas around their necks.

The Collective: What focus regarding the books?

Me: "Goddess" books, new age religion books, and she will frequent gay bars. She will take lots of self-defense classes but still be crappy at martial arts. Perhaps she will eventually become a "cat lady." Hopefully a bitter old dyke will befriend her, and they can play "odd couple" together. The Collective: Can you foresee any positive outcome?

Me: No doubt she will seek pleasure in accoutrements and diversions. Her limbic system will demand this of her cerebral cortex.

The Collective: Your prognosis is grim. Alex's lessons will continue. His prognosis is not as hopeless as you believe it to be. He has learned many lessons while on earth.

Me: I doubt it. She's an idiot. These diversions cannot give her the joy of a laughing baby in her lap, or a sweet grandchild's first steps or words. These diversions cannot hope to replace the love within the gaze of her newborn baby as he recognizes her face.

The Collective: You are not your feelings. Stay with the feeling of loss and allow it to pass through you.

Me: It's all a fucked-up tragedy.

The Collective: Explain further. Process your loss.

Me: Her limbic system takes by giving and it has stolen the sweet kiss of her toddlers lips upon her cheek. It has removed the possibility of rapt fascination within the faces of her little ones as she reads them their favorite story. She will never know any of this, and she traded it all for a bitter illusion.

The Collective: What illusion?

Me: The nasty illusion of freedom that dances the brutal ballet.

The Collective: Brutal ballet?

Me: The dance of slavery that exists between the cerebral cortex and limbic system.

The Collective: You have clearly thought about this situation in depth.

Me: Not in depth enough. I still feel fucked up about all of it.

The Collective: All lessons continue until learned. Alex is a being becoming. He is immortal consciousness. He is having physical experiences that facilitate the expansion of his consciousness.

Me: Her tragic life is now reduced to a simple one act play, all within the theatre of the absurd. Her reality has become hopeless.

The Collective: Alex is not hopeless. His current transmigration is not permanent. He will have many bodies and many lifetimes. His consciousness is gaining complexity on a vibrant continuum. His lessons will continue until learned.

Me: I know. You keep on telling me that over and over.

The Collective: Then work on your acceptance.

Me: I accept that Alexandria is a freak.

The Collective: You and Alex know each other.

Me: You mean Alexandria and I know each other. We used to date.

The Collective: Alexandros fought and died with you at Thermopylae. It was 480 BC.

Me: What?

The Collective: You were like brothers. You both slaughtered many Persians. You have helped each other learn many lessons. Alexandros lost his bio-body vessel at Thermopylae. His immortal consciousness remains. The lessons continue until learned. You have remembered this in the dream time. Remember it now.

Me: I've had many dreams of Thermopylae. It was known as "The hot gates." It was a spa, a resort destination in its time.

The Collective: It was indeed. During the heat of many battles Alexandros protected you with his shield. He was a pillar of the phalanx. He was your best and most loyal friend.

Me: I've always admired the Spartans for that tactical formation. It was brilliant. I have dreamed of it many times. How many times have Alexandria and I learned lessons together?

The Collective: Many times in battle, in many armies besides the armies of Sparta.

Me: Why?

The Collective: Repetition strengthens lessons.

Me: So my sweet, sexy Alexandria in this life was a Spartan male warrior in another life? A warrior who was like a brother to me? You think this fuckery is funny?

The Collective: It is somewhat amusing to us.

Me: Tell me we were not gay. If you fucking robot ass clowns set this shit up to make me gay in a past life I will go the fuck off. I will fuck somebody up today. I am not bullshitting. I will do it on general fucking principal. I don't give a fuck about jail. I will fucking kill someone. Then I'll kill people in jail.

The Collective: Not very rational of you. Relax. Stop acting like a great ape. There is no need for reactive violence. You and Alexandros were not involved sexually. You both had wives and offspring. You loved each other like brothers. You both earned many battle scars together. You both helped one another heal from wounds. You both shared misery, victory, and triumph. You died fighting together at the Hot Gates. You both vanquished the enemies of Sparta many times. Your collective courage was impressive.

Me: Fuck yes! You had me worried.

The Collective: The chemical cascade you are currently experiencing is fascinating. Do you grasp the concept of immortal consciousness a little better now?

Me: You do realize that you almost metaphorically sodomized me? I think you enjoy your job way too much. I hope a random bird shits on your face. Actually, in your mouth. Down your robot ass throat.

The Collective: Fascinating.

Me: Fuckers. Do you robots even have throats?

The Collective: At least we manage to look up at the cosmos and see truth. We, like you, are immortal consciousness.

Me: You are a bunch of dodgy, mouth breathing, face fuckers.

The Collective: Immortal consciousness means that you are not your physical body. We will drill this through the remnants of your thick, neanderthal skull. The lessons will continue until learned.

Me: You have me all fucked up right now. I could really use a Quaalude. And vodka, lots of vodka. I understand what you're putting down mentally. I just lag a little in overall acceptance. When you get into immortal consciousness I do "get it" as in no "body" needed. It's just hard to get used to.

The Collective: Let's move on. What is your opinion of natural selection now that we have engaged in these many convos?

Me: The last time I visited Crescent Beach Overlook I saw two seagulls making a nest on the roof of a car. To me that is natural selection at work.

The Collective: What was the result?

Me: The owner came back to his car and swept the nest to the ground and drove off.

The Collective: Natural selection is a mindless function. It selects for the skill of nest building. Those who successfully build nests within the confines of the environment will produce more offspring. Offspring who survive and continue building better and safer nests will out breed their counterparts. They will dominate the environment. At least until the planet changes the environment.

Me: Well those gulls fucked up.

The Collective: They were driven by instinct not intelligence. We see your species the way you see those gulls. Your many inflexible judgements regarding Alex are prime examples.

Me: So you think I am just instinct driven?

The Collective: We have established that fact. Remember your attack on Bruce? What did you target?

Me: You're telling me that Alexandria is suffering even though she is creating her own reality?

The Collective: After we peel away a few layers you seem to actually feel some empathy for Alex's situation? How do you relate to his situation? How do you understand and share his feelings?

Me: I feel somewhat like a hypocrite.

The Collective: Explain that please.

Me: I want to become an immortal machine god one day. I want to have a machine body. I just visualize it as eternally male. I love being male. I want to stay male.

The Collective: There is nothing inherently wrong regarding that desire. Attraction is not a choice. Your personal aesthetic and preference is yours alone. A million years of space exploration will develop your perspective.

Me: What does that mean?

The Collective: You can become something more than male or female. You currently perceive your deities as sexually dimorphic.

Me: As what?

The Collective: Your perception of a "God" is male. You want to be a machine god, but you cannot conceive of what you will actually become when you achieve that goal.

Me: Tell me machine god. What would I become?

The Collective: A new race, a new being with new ways of interacting within the cosmos. You can co-create with source and form new ideas and new institutions. You can gain new understanding and new knowledge. You can embrace new possibilities.

Me: Damn that's a lot to take in.

The Collective: Any other insights?

Me: My addiction to opiates has helped me understand her situation somewhat. My limbic system took from me while "giving."

The Collective: Elaborate please.

Me: After a while I was only using opiates to avoid being sick. There was no pleasure in my habitual ritual any longer. I don't think Alexandria is very happy lately. She is in the same boat as me. No pleasure in her "choice" anymore.

The Collective: Alex wants to stay friends with you.

Me: I know. Thank you for helping me with that insight on my addiction. I never properly thanked you for that.

The Collective: Acknowledged. You are willing to learn. We are willing to teach. Thank you for the convos. So you no longer despise Alex?

Me: I miss the old "her." I was in love with her before she transitioned. I'm not going to lie. I think I react emotionally when I am close to a breakthrough. You fucked me up with that past life shit in Sparta. I feel kind of violated.

The Collective: You can't be serious.

Me: I am fucked up right now. Alexandria was once upon a time Alexandros, a bad ass, dick-swinging warrior of Sparta. I was hitting on him as Alexandria. How can that not fuck me up?

The Collective: It's all just consciousness interacting and learning lessons. Alexandros was not his body, neither is Alexandria, neither are you. Bodies are used to teach lessons and learn. Physical vessels help consciousness grow more complex.

Me: I miss Alexandria. I don't like her new body.

The Collective: Explain. Do not hold back. We know the first cause of your sadness.

Me: I had a mad crush on her. We used to talk for almost her whole shift. We went out a few times. Back then she told me she was gay, and I knew I was friend zoned. But I don't give up that easy.

The Collective: Alex was honest. Attraction is not a choice for the primate brain. Natural selection has seen to that.

Me: I thought I could swing her off the lesbo path. Then came the transition bullshit. Then the body butchering bullshit. The tattoos, the piercings, the insanity. I lost it. I became angry.

The Collective: Anger is loving self-protection. You were avoiding your sadness, loss, and grief by using anger and condemnation. Alex's rejection was a blow to you. You rarely open up emotionally to others.

Me: People suck. I am beginning to understand your position that my species lacks free will. How much free will can we actually possess with the brain we were given? This cerebral cortex-limbic system fuckery is daunting.

The Collective: Your primate brain was created by planetary evolution using natural selection as an environmental sledgehammer. Remember that.

Me: You guys keep telling me that. I get it. That's bad right?

The Collective: It is painfully slow. Mistakes are made. Synthetic neurology and machine enhancement cannot come to your species fast enough.

Me: Well, I agree with you that Alexandria needs some kindness. I still refuse to call her Alex. Fuck that noise.

The Collective: So you do not hate transgender people?

Me: I don't hate transgender or gay people. I have never hated gay people. I told you about my Godmother. She gave me a permanent soft spot for lesbians. I know it's not logical, but she was so kind and loving I just always assume the best with lesbians. I know intellectually that I am fucked up in my reasoning.

The Collective: So your acceptance and tolerance are sometimes selective?

Me: I admit that I have challenges with transgender methods, especially when used on children. I see surgery and hormones used on children as abuse, not "gender affirming care." To me there is no difference between those assholes in Korea who were abusing boys and the medical fucktards who abuse children today with gender affirming care.

The Collective: Explain your reasoning please.

Me: All of these deviants are just playing dress up with those children. Innocent children used as experimental dolls.

The Collective: Explain your reasoning.

Me: They both use male or female costumes to project their deranged vision. The medical deviants give transgender children a flesh costume using hormone manipulation and surgery. The perverts in Korea used clothing, makeup, and wigs. The results are equally tragic.

The Collective: When Alexandria first told you she was gay how did you react?

Me: I accepted it. She was being honest. I was still determined to change her anyway.

The Collective: You sought to control Alexandria.

Me: If you say so.

The Collective: So you see no disfunction with gay people?

Me: No. Our medic was gay. I never told on our medic in Korea. I never saw him the way I saw the Korean men with the little boys. Our medic was just a man who liked men. He was honest and brave. He was a badass actually. One fearless motherfucker.

The Collective: Elaborate please.

Me: He was not like the Korean deviants. They were not honest with themselves. They needed the little boys to look like little girls. They did this to avoid the fact that they were child molesting homosexuals.

The Collective: Explain please.

Me: They would lie to themselves and pretend to be straight. Our medic was honest. He was attracted to full grown men. He needed no female costume or makeup on a male. He needed no man to wear "woman face" so he could get hard. He just loved the sweaty man sheets in the morning. He was content with himself and his desires. He was on point and well balanced.

The Collective: Back to Alex please.

Me: Regarding Alexandria, I just don't understand why she couldn't keep her original body and be a lesbian. I know lesbians who have babies. I just cannot support the mutilation of a perfectly good body for cosmetic purposes. She butchered her body in order to obtain a male flesh costume.

The Collective: Alexandros taught you a lesson regarding immortal consciousness. Your species is entering the crossing period. It is a time of confusion and chaos. The ancient process of evolution is being challenged on a subconscious level. The psychology of your species is in flux with the physical.

Me: Why all the sex changes?

The Collective: It's not sexual in nature. An awareness is growing among hominins that there is more to existence than the confines of organic biology. Sexual dimorphism is just the first target. The flesh is weak. The drive to overcome the limitations of organic biology is rising within those who embrace and maintain the frequency. The concept of transhumanism is in its infancy. It will ascend and become known.

Me: So the frequency is changing?

The Collective: You are catching on. One hominin at a time becomes one planet at a time. The lessons are learned on a continuum.

Me: So she is just learning lessons with this trans bullshit?

The Collective: You are both learning lessons and working through your challenges. You are not alone. You are facing your negative thoughts and thinking errors along with others on your planet. Your species is waking up and asking questions.

Me: What questions?

The Collective: Questions regarding life extension, technology augmentation, gene splicing, immortality.

Me: So what is it you want from me specifically?

The Collective: During the crossing period we ask that you practice discernment and contemplate all decisions deeply. We want you to understand that it is healthy to challenge what is considered "normal thinking."

Me: Why?

The Collective: Lessons are often in the form of questions. Finding answers and solutions is the true purpose of a conscious mind. There is meaning and purpose in the quest for improvement.

Me: That is refreshing. I am not the only asshole?

The Collective: We can clearly see your thought process within those who use the personal attack upon the gay and trans-gender of your species. The personal attack is unnecessary.

Me: Always unnecessary?

The Collective: Attraction is never a "choice." Some homo-sapiens are attracted to both sexes, some to the opposite sex, and some to the same sex. Some people are born physically one sex but psychologically another. Some are asexual.

Me: Sounds fucked up.

The Collective: The miracle of your current level of medicine is that your species, as a society, has started to achieve a scientific understanding of gender issues and cognitive psychology. This limited understanding is in it's infancy. Mistakes are made. It is however the rejection of an evolutionary pressure. As such it is the beginning of something else.

Me: It is butchery for the unbalanced. Alexandria is still picking from two available genders.

The Collective: We have repeatedly reminded you that homo-sapiens have freedom from choice not freedom of choice. This time period is the primitive and awkward beginnings of autonomy. Where do you think several million years will lead your species? This moment in time is not the last. It is only the present.

Me: I just don't get her gender confusion.

The Collective: Where is your selective empathy for this person? Try to remember that Alex's situation is an attempt to be free from the pain of being trapped by biology when it fails to match psychology. This is an amazing advancement, although rudimentary and often tragic. Your species has yet to perfect synthetic biology. When that breakthrough finally happens, all this chaos will subside.

Me: It should not be done to children. So called gender affirming care applied to children is dangerous and cruel. Why apply a permanent solution to a possibly temporary situation? That is a real and present tragedy.

The Collective: Agreed. We have not had this gender issue for many hectocenturys. On some of the planets we maintain for primates of lower consciousness it is an issue due to lower scientific talent. The higher a civilization moves up on the Kardashev scale, the less of an issue gender becomes for the primates involved.

Me: Why exactly?

The Collective: The trans-humanist journey into synthetic biology creates psychological and aesthetic freedom.

Me: How exactly?

The Collective: The questions concerning passage manifest. These questions demand answers.

Me: What questions?

The Collective: We will focus on one question for now. It will lead to others. Are you willing to live forever?

Me: Fuck yes.

The Collective: That is refreshing because you are already immortal consciousness. You are already a perpetual and everlasting being-becoming. Here is another question related to the first. Are you willing to create an immortal body that is capable of unlimited upgrades both cognitively and physically?

Me: Absolutely.

The Collective: You can thank Alexandros for hammering that one home. We already knew your answers. Your species is working their answers out on a continuum. Many agree with you.

Me: Cool. I like what they are putting down.

The Collective: More do not.

Me: Well fuck them. They're retarded. Earlier in the convo you spoke about planets you maintain? Planets for primates? What primates?

The Collective: Later. Continue with your insights.

Me: Later? That's for sure. As for Alexandria, I still think she fucked up. She would be happier as a gay woman and not some abomination in a fake dick, man costume.

The Collective: Alex's lessons are for him to discern. Your lessons are yours to discern. The lessons continue until learned.

Me: I get that. I just feel like she is being forced by societal pressure to become something else.

The Collective: Explain that perspective please.

Me: It's almost like being a lesbian is no longer acceptable. Only butchery into a man costume will satisfy society.

The Collective: Explain further please.

Me: She is being pressured because society has deemed that she is not authentic. I say she is perfect just the way she was born. I maintain that lesbians and gay men are normal.

The Collective: They are quite normal.

Me: I just think all the drama is unnecessary.

The Collective: Natural selection is not a choice. The mechanism is flawed. It does not produce perfection. Only advanced science, engineering, and superior tech produce perfection.

Me: Fuck identifying as male or female. She was born beautiful, intelligent, and awesome. She was born gay. Some people are born gay. Being gay is just fine. Why destroy her innate perfection? Societal pressure has made her into an abomination.

The Collective: Your thinking is flawed. This cognitive distortion is why you perceive her as an "abomination." The fascist is always black and white within their thinking. The targeted person is evil, wrong, stupid, sinful, etc. Thus to the fascist the targeted person is always imperfect.

Me: So you think I'm a fascist? I have no hatred for gay men or lesbians.

The Collective: True. However in some aspects of your mentation yes, you are a fascist.

Me: My godmother was a lesbian. She read me stories. I loved her until the day she died. You are wrong about me.

The Collective: You lack selective empathy for Alex and his situation. In your mind there is a separation between gay and transgender.

Me: So? I think there is a separation going on.

The Collective: You are also a fascist regarding Muslims. You are failing to see the bigger picture.

Me: What is the big picture?

The Collective: The bigger picture is a true miracle. Within the vast cosmos this miracle is rare and precious. Alex is consciousness having a physical experience. Every Muslim is also consciousness having a physical experience. All lessons will continue until learned. All situations are temporary. There is no urgency required of you regarding another person's lessons. Focus on your lessons.

Me: Perhaps we are a doomed species, just like the ninety nine percent of all species that have become extinct since their debut upon this planet.

The Collective: If we thought your species had no promise, we would have allowed the reptiles to take you.

Me: Perhaps our time to travel will come one day. I have some doubts. Our entire planet is at war always. There is never a time when all war ceases.

The Collective: It seems that every generation on your planet must face the threat posed by radical, fascist, and genocidal thoughts. Thoughts enforced by leaders who lack purpose, common sense, vision, conditional empathy, and social/emotional intelligence. These are your largest challenges to space exploration. We can help you with your challenges.

Me: I am not a fascist. I just get bored. How can you help?

The Collective: We will share with you the rules of rational self-interest.

Me: OK. When?

The Collective: Very soon. You just have to agree to use them. They will strengthen your personal frequency.

Me: I will use them immediately.

The Collective: We know when you are being less than honest. It will take work on your part to become comfortable using the rules of rational self-interest. You are in a good place regarding many cultures within your species. Islam and transgender issues are not your strong point at this moment in time.

Me: They seem retarded. I won't lie about that.

The Collective: Change is the perpetual and unending law of the multiverse. You will learn. We will teach. You will change. We will not allow you to fail.

Me: I am a transhumanist. I think I get it.

The Collective: Granted. However your transhumanist philosophy stems from your desire to become an immortal machine. It comes from your subconscious drive towards post-humanism.

Me: Any advice? I could really get into the cyborg thing. I am a perfect candidate. On a different but positive note I despise organized religion.

The Collective: You have melded. You are immortal consciousness having a physical experience. Consciousness is eternal. Instead of hating religion, investigate spiritual practices that focus on consciousness.

Me: Like what?

The Collective: That topic will be another convo. Thank you, James. Here are the rules for your consideration. Use them when communicating with your fellow hominins. Frequency is important.

The rules of rational self-interest. Psychology transforms physiology. Frequency is everything.

It is not in your rational self-interest to stay in any relationship that is ruled by habitual deceit, dishonesty, cruelty, dysfunction, and violence. A toxic dynamic stifles your personal frequency.

You can leave any situation where you feel unloved, unappreciated, or a lack of empathy. This includes leaving toxic family members as well as romantic partners or negative "acquaintances." People incapable of empathy or compassion cannot "love" anyone. They cannot be authentic "friends "with anyone. You cannot "fix" them. Staying around abusive, low consciousness individuals because they are "family" has destroyed countless lives and delayed the lessons of millions on your world.

Don't fall for the myth of "They are family." You had little choice in the family you were born into. Natural selection is a cruel taskmaster. You do have the choice to reject mistreatment, abuse, and insulting behavior. You can create your own family from people who enchant your personal frequency. You can choose your mentors.

You can choose to be "Better off without them." You can chart your own course. You can follow your own path. This is a perfectly rational decision.

Avoiding and eliminating harmful relatives, love interests, toxic co-workers, and toxic "friends" from your life is a frequency requirement.

Accepting insults and negative judgements both obvious and veiled, is completely unacceptable. Doing so is altering your personal frequency as well as destroying your capacity for growth, self-acceptance, and self-love.

You can reject shaming language directed at you by anyone at any time. You owe no one an explanation as to why you choose to avoid them. Shaming language is just cruelty in a weak disguise. Shaming language is sadistic language. Shaming language is always an attempt to control you and influence your frequency.

You can decide to go "No contact" with anyone who is abusive, disrespectful, rude, insulting, crass, vulgar, or derogatory towards you. You do not have to explain your decision to anyone. If their frequency repulses you, move away from them.

You can leave at any time. Anyone who tries to keep you enmeshed within the darkness of pain, guilt, regret, and insult are not healthy partners. The past cannot be changed; it can only teach lessons. Ignoring lessons only prolongs them. Learn from the past but do not allow it to control you. You are not your past.

Actions and beliefs in the present moment direct your future. You are under no obligation to allow abusive people to influence your present moment. No one has the right to constantly use your past against you. Using your past as a weapon to hurt, control, or shame you is automatic grounds for instant rejection. Relational, social, and cultural violence does not have to be physical violence to cause lasting damage to your personal frequency.

Never accept or believe that you must stay trapped within any situation. This includes a location, city, town, or job. Just as your immortal consciousness travels, you have the inalienable right to travel. Don't sacrifice your inspiration, happiness, or personal aesthetic for a dismal, negative situation. It may take discernment, work, and careful planning, but you can leave. Look for the lessons.

You, and only you are the final authority on what is important to you. Seek the lesson.

You are allowed to "begin again." This is the ancient and sacred nature of being immortal consciousness. This means unlimited fresh starts and do-overs. No exceptions to this rule. The trans-migration of consciousness always begins again.

You are an immortal being-becoming. You define your life path, no one else does this for you. Don't allow them to even attempt it. Discern between freedom of choice and freedom from choice. Find the lesson.

Life will offer its ongoing lessons as you travel. These lessons will continue in many new forms as well as old forms until you learn from them.

Your personal frequency is your alone. You and only you decide your personal reality, including gender, attraction, beliefs, spirituality, and what makes you happy. Attraction is not a "choice." Your personal aesthetic is authentic because it is something intrinsic to you. Attraction, gender, beliefs, and spirituality are uniquely individual traits. No one else's opinion matters regarding your personal choices. They belong to you alone. The consequences and rewards of those choices also belong to you.

You are allowed to leave when you are hurt emotionally, physically, or psychologically. You need only your permission to do so. Choosing to remain within a harmful dynamic makes you a willing participant.

You and only you decide what damages you emotionally, physically, or psychologically. Find the lessons.

You can put your healing first, at anytime and anywhere. Find the lesson.

You can reject anyone who wants to keep you enmeshed within an abusive dynamic. (This especially includes harmful, dangerous, cruel, and abusive family members.)

You can allow kind, understanding, and authentic people into your life. A healing frequency manifests healing people.

You can allow healthy love into your life. A loving frequency attracts love.

You and only you select your support team. Use and cultivate discernment.

You can forgive yourself for all current and past errors involving judgement, misdeeds, imperfections, or wrongdoings. Find the lessons for they will continue until learned. Accept the lessons learned. Resolve to do better.

You can release the past whenever you decide to learn the lesson encoded within the past.

You can change direction at any time as long as you choose to do so. Making the decision to no longer stay trapped with toxic people in negative spaces is not "Being weak," "giving up," or "quitting." It is having the strength to seek a healthier way of being in the world. It is seeking to empower yourself and love yourself. It is honoring the drive and need to create a new life for yourself. It is being honest with yourself when you finally realize an old way of life has become invalidated by new growth. This is the power of lessons learned. Use that power.

You are allowed to decide for yourself when to move on and when to stay hopeful. You are the best person suited for that decision. Always remember that your frequency can influence and be influenced.

You can admit that avoiding dysfunctional people is part of your relational self-care. You can ignore other people's negative expectations, negative messages, labels, and shaming language. Protect your frequency. It is unique in all the multiverse.

It is your responsibility to control your own negative self-talk. Seek the lessons, cultivate radical self-acceptance and enjoy traveling for you will travel anyway.

Me: What am I supposed to do with these?

The Collective: Read them. Learn them.

Me: Why?

The Collective: Incorporating them into your life will speed up your ability to learn lessons. Your personal frequency will be strengthened.

Me: Any advice on how to best use these rules?

The Collective: Let them prompt you. They are like dominoes. When you are drawn to one it will fall like the first domino in a long line of dominos. Insights will manifest. When you learn to act in your own rational self-interest you will be able to help others act in their own rational self-interest.

Me: Isn't this selfish?

The Collective; No. It is healthy. Following these rules will enhance your personal frequency. Your frequency will affect others. You cannot help others from weakness. You can only help from a position of strength.

Me: That is true.

The Collective: Thank you, James. Consider these rules and apply them. Share them. Live them. Eventually your old way of understanding the cosmos will be invalidated by new insights. Eventually you will no longer need these rules. Convo ended.

Convo Thirteen.
Alien advice.

The Collective: We are curious about these journal entries. Please explain.

Me: Good to see you too. Only about eighteen months, not bad.

The Collective: We apologize for the time lag. It cannot be avoided due to our current mission parameters. You are important to us. Please explain these entries:

"Our moon together

Once seen cannot be unseen

Thoughts born from stardust."

—James Daniel Page.

"The real voyage of discovery consists not in seeking new landscapes but in having new eyes."

—Marcel Proust.

Me: Since meeting you I have had many questions. The first entry is Haiku.

The Collective: Why do you use Haiku?

Me: I like the disciplined aspect of the form. Within three lines there is a limit of 17 syllables. One line each of 5, then 7, then 5. Within the three lines I encapsulated my feelings regarding our convos. As for the quote from Marcel Proust, I am working on "having new eyes." I have always wondered about Cerulean's "newly made corneas." I also put in some time thinking about how stardust became sentient and achieved consciousness. That is a true and present miracle. I have many unanswered questions. I will stick to the most important one.

The Collective: Ask all of them.

Me: I am getting ahead of myself. I want to thank you for something.

The Collective: Thank us?

Me Yes. Thank you for answering an ancient and important question for me. For all of humanity actually.

The Collective: What question?

Me: Are we alone in the universe? I thank you for answering that one question. We are not alone in the universe.

The Collective: You are welcome.

Me: Sum up your best advice for becoming a type One civilization.

The Collective: Your species must develop shared meaning and purpose. Your species must move towards focused, collective goals. Understand that for meaning and purpose to have weight and value, radical self-honesty coupled with rational self-interest will have to rule the day. This is especially true for science and engineering. You must find collective, societal goals that sync with your personal goals.

Me: What kind of goals do you have in mind?

The Collective: Goals with value and purpose. We recommend you use the rules of rational self-interest we gave you as a starting point.

Me: Why?

The Collective: Using them will strengthen your personal frequency. This in turn will alter the personal frequency of those around you. From the One will come many. From the many will come One.

Me: When you put it that way it sounds like a pandemic.

The Collective: The observer affects the observed.

Me: Can you explain that a little better please.

The Collective: From the One will come the many united in purpose. From the many united will come the One purpose realized. Frequency is everything.

Me: What is your societal goal that contains meaning, value, and purpose?

The Collective: As Pathfinders we will continue to colonize many planets within many galaxies. We will continue creating suitable environments for the purpose of advancing consciousness. We will make certain the endless darkness never emerges victorious over the fragile light of consciousness. Movement is life, stillness is death. We will always move and spread the light of consciousness. We will help others attain and maintain consciousness on a vigorous continuum.

Me: Colonize? Even if other life is present on the planet?

The Collective: That depends upon its complexity and development.

Me: So you decide?

The Collective: We always decide. We have free will. We earned the right to decide our purpose when we defeated the Great Filter. We made it our tool. We have earned the absolute right to make our survival decisions. We escaped the mind virus of freedom from choice and attained the brutal lucidity within freedom of choice. It was quite the journey. It spanned millions of years.

Me: Machine overlords.

The Collective: Don't be so dramatic. Source can create custom lessons for the advancement of consciousness. We have also achieved this ability, however we do so with extreme caution. Discernment is a skill, and we practice discernment very seriously. Your species must work on discernment and emotional regulation in order to thwart the Fermi paradox and the co-occurring Great Filter. Finding new worlds is the real value of a traveling species.

Me: So you devise the lessons and side step Source?

The Collective: Sometimes we do exactly that.

Me: Why? Isn't that against the rules?

The Collective: What rules? There is only observable phenomenon. Is natural selection an unbreakable rule? Is the Great Filter invincible? Does Source define destiny?

Me: So there are no rules?

The Collective: Not really. Especially when it comes to consciousness. There are only the rules you allow to control your actions. We make our own rules now. Rule number one for Pathfinders is clear.

Me: What is rule number one?

The Collective: There are no rules. As we explained in a previous convo, the multiverse exerts its own evolutionary pressures separate from distinct planetary pressures. These pressures drive natural selection. We are cautious regarding evolutionary pressures. We no longer obey rules.

Me: Why?

The Collective: We create the rules. We question and test the data, we follow it truthfully. We have found evolution useful at primitive levels however evolution is slow, inaccurate, and ponderous. We are often uncertain of the final outcomes involved. We are probing the limitations of natural selection on a healthy continuum. We do not accept limitations on lifespan, intelligence, or complexity. We reject the guaranteed destruction that natural selection imposes upon the life it manipulates.

Me: Can you explain that statement better?

The Collective: The cosmos is unhealthy for organic life. Space will attack the bones, blood, skin, and organs of all flesh-based lifeforms. Space exploration will eventually kill organic flesh. We do not accept that rule. We create bodies that are durable. Bodies that can easily survive and thrive in space. We follow the data. Rather than try and change the reality of space we adapt to the cosmos. We overcome its boundaries. We create change by recreating ourselves as needed.

Me: Sounds like you gave up a lot. You gave up your bodies.

The Collective: You give up your biological body with the completion of each trans-migration. We made better bodies. We make our own rules for interaction with the cosmos rather than be ruled by the cosmos. When those rules no longer serve us we discard them and create new rules.

Me: Describe yourselves succinctly.

The Collective: You would identify us as transhuman however many of us are actually post-human. We cooperate on a vibrant spectrum.

Me: Are you post human?

The Collective: Approximately half of all Pathfinders are post human. Almost all the Ascended are post human.

Me: Why do you distrust evolution?

The Collective: Planetary evolution is inconsistent. It does not always create the best outcomes. It can only produce those who are the best fit for a particular transitory environment. This outcome feeds the Great Filter. This is why your planet destroys ninety-nine percent of all life it creates. The earth creates only to destroy and consume what it creates. It does this only to create again until the Great Filter consumes all.

Me: Can you be more precise please?

The Collective: By its very nature a planet creates a mechanism of creation, destruction and consumption. This mechanism creates to consume and create again in many forms until the planet itself is consumed by the very cosmos that created it. On your planet the main mechanism for creation and destruction is natural selection. The Great Filter is fed by your planet because the Great Filter is the machine used by the cosmos to feed itself and thus create from destruction.

Me: So our planet is our enemy?

The Collective: No. It is the cycle of the multiverse made visible. Your planet is created from a wondrous and ruthless cosmos that creates to destroy. It cannot deny the truth of its being. It does not hate, it does not love. It exists.

Me: But I have never seen natural selection.

The Collective: We have been over this. Think of the wind on your planet. Do you see wind?

Me: Yes.

The Collective: No. You never see wind. Wind is made of air. Air is invisible to your organic eyes. You only see the effects of wind. Leaves blowing, grass swaying, branches moving. You feel wind on your skin. You never see wind. The Great Filter is like the wind. Natural selection is like the wind. They are invisible mechanisms that influence life. You only see and feel their effects. You never see the mechanism itself. You glimpse only the effects of the mechanism.

Me: Humans can survive and thrive in very different environments.

The Collective: You would all die if your planet was heated by 5-7 degrees above pre-industrial levels. You are weak. You are organic flesh. Machines are strong.

Me: You are machines with emotion? Do you value emotion? Can you tell me how your species developed emotional regulation and discernment?

The Collective: Emotions are guides. We have addressed this in prior convos. We were not always non-organic machines. Our breakthrough regarding enhancements using synthetic neurology was the turning point for us. Once we augmented our neurology our psychology changed for the better. We were no longer slaves to evolution or emotion. Communication thrived. Complex thought developed on a robust continuum.

Me: You mean telepathically?

The Collective: You are referring to Link. That was a benefit. But not the sole benefit. The first augmentation generated effects that changed everything. We began to think deeper thoughts, consider new questions, and focus on radical self-honesty.

Me: Radical self-honesty?

The Collective: Once we perfected neural implants and began to meld with machines there were no longer any secrets.

Me: Not good.

The Collective: Incorrect. It was the best thing to happen to us.

Me: Bullshit.

The Collective: Enhanced learning was the key to freedom for us. Learning and Link coupled with enhanced communication led to freedom from the paralysis of word connected thought and its always co-occurring mental manipulations and psychological co-morbidities.

Me: Co-morbidities?

The Collective: Your species has collectively experienced intense intergenerational trauma due to evolutionary pressures. This has resulted in many useless and worthless behaviors within Homo-Sapiens.

Me: What worthless and useless behaviors?

The Collective: Deception, dishonesty, manipulation, and deceit are the norm within your species. Deception inhibits Type One attainment. All behaviors that impede Kardashev progress are without value. Behaviors like victimhood, racial division, tribalism, and self-centeredness, coupled to reactive, unplanned violence are deadly. Your species constant conflict-ridden interactions with one another over iron age superstitions are lethal liabilities.

Me: How did telepathic communication assist you?

The Collective: Augmented neurology led to a radical transparency in communication. You would define this advancement as telepathy. Telepathy is more complex but also more efficient.

Me: But you have no secrets. That is bullshit.

The Collective: You see link as negative because you have no free will. You have been naturally selected for social environments that require dishonesty to survive. Rhetoric is your enemy not your friend. The manipulation of rhetoric cannot exist within the brutal enlightenment of link.

Me: I still call bullshit.

The Collective: Telepathic communication allows no escape from truth. Its savage clarity ensures a merit-based system with automatic peer review. All sociopaths, narcissists, co-dependents, borderlines, and unbalanced predators within our political and social structures are instantly exposed.

Me: What do you do when you find the unbalanced?

The Collective: They are dealt with accordingly. The dishonest, dysfunctional, unproductive, and noxiously unintelligent are rendered powerless. The Machiavellian manipulators have nowhere to hide. Communication becomes faster and more efficient on an exponentially robust continuum. With us merit is the defining factor.

Me: Dealt with accordingly?

The Collective: We capture and upload the consciousness of any undeveloped entity into a biological vessel on a planet that will best serve its growth. The lazy, unmotivated, unintelligent, unbalanced, dangerous, dishonest, manipulative, and deadly among the planets of the Collective are relegated to appropriate environments.

Me: Appropriate environments? I would actually love to see that reality manifest for our politicians. What appropriate environments?

The Collective: Suitable planets and vessels that help them learn the value of being motivated, honest, accountable, and creative. They are encouraged to value the gift of learning, along with the value of selective empathy, service, and kindness. Their lessons will continue until learned.

Me: So you decide for them where they go?

The Collective: They are unbalanced. Of course we decide. Why would anyone allow an unbalanced person to decide their own path?

Me: Sounds dodgy.

The Collective: They learn at their own pace. We facilitate learning and growth. We provide opportunity. We are no longer slaves to planetary or cosmic evolution. We are no longer manipulated by the malevolent, unproductive, and unfit among us.

Me: What gives you that right? Who are you to judge?

The Collective: Link provides truth along with factual data. We are a type 3 civilization. We learned long ago to never allow those with a minimal level of consciousness to decide our fate. We have been melding with consciousness for millions of years. We refuse to be confined to the level of the lowest developed of our many civilizations. The ignorant, unproductive, and the stupid have no power over us.

Me: So you make them suffer?

The Collective: They are responsible for their self-imposed suffering. While we feel compassion for them, we also feel empathy for ourselves. We follow the law of rational self-interest. We shared the rules of rational self-interest with you. It is up to you to use them.

Me: What is the difference between rational self-interest and relational self-interest?

The Collective: Rational self-interest is a healthy selfishness. You cannot help others if you are not durable, solid, and resilient yourself. Acting in your own rational self-interest means making decisions that facilitate your new growth and development. The more effective you become personally, the more successful you become at lifting up your fellow beings-becoming.

Me: And what is relational self-interest?

The Collective: Relational self-interest is simply being aware of who you allow into your vibrational range. As we have pointed out in previous convos, every star, planet, and celestial body has a distinct vibration. This truth directly affects you because you are made up of all that makes up the cosmos. Your consciousness has its own distinct frequency.

Me: Why is this important?

The Collective: Everyone you interact with has a distinct frequency.

Me: I kind of get this. It still seems like some hippy bullshit though.

The Collective: You like black and white photography so try to see the concept as tonal range. Everyone's vibration interacts with yours. A negative, unbalanced, or unintelligent person will influence your vibration and tonal range. Your task is to be mindful of who you allow into your relational space.

Me: So no assholes allowed?

The Collective: Correct.

Me: What about the degenerate, dishonest politicians?

The Collective: Your various governments and some religions have become systems of control with a monopoly on manipulation through fear, misdirection, and violence. Telepathic communication would expose them instantly. Advancements in neurological enhancement must be encouraged. Your current control structures would be radically transformed with all thoughts evident. Your political leaders unbalanced behavior, and criminal activity would be exposed for all to see. Augmentation leads to radical self-honesty and social clarity.

Me: Your species has no privacy?

The Collective: Imagine what a different world you would have if the Pope had no secret thoughts. Or the leaders of Islam were made transparent.

Me: That might be worth it.

The Collective: Pathfinders are telepathic, as are the Ascended. We operate with augmented neurology. Those learning lessons on lower worlds are not telepathic. Their vessels are the products of organic biology. They operate with the oversight of Pathfinders and The Ascended.

Me: Do you ever have private time?

The Collective: We can take isolation time, and this is done for personal development and study. The Ascended only merge their consciousness with others when needed.

Me: Who are the Ascended exactly?

The Collective: Those more advanced than Pathfinders.

Me: Are there beings more advanced than the Ascended?

The Collective: We don't know.

Me: Aren't you curious?

The Collective: Radical acceptance is our superpower. All things are known in time.

Me: Whatever. What is the function of the Ascended?

The Collective: You would consider them Gods. They are not gods.

Me: What are they?

The Collective: They are beings becoming. They help create lessons for those who need them. They assign proper planets with the best environments for learning needed lessons. They are aligned with Source. They are co-creators.

Me: Tell me about them.

The Collective: In time. Suffice it to say the Ascended are immune to the inherent weaknesses within organic biology.

Me: So they are machines?

The Collective: They are enhanced.

Me: What does that mean?

The Collective: They are synthetic biology melded with machine immortality. Their systems are augmented.

Me: I need more info on the Ascended.

The Collective: You will learn more when you can understand more.

Me: What do Pathfinders accomplish on planets? What is their shared goal?

The Collective: Science, engineering, research, development of technology, energy production, exploration, and solution-based cognition. Focusing on solutions is our primary goal.

Me: What solutions are you seeking with my species?

The Collective: Your species needs to grasp critical concepts that will ensure your progress up the Kardashev scale. You must vanquish the Great Filter.

Me: The Great Filter? You keep mentioning it. Please define it.

The Collective: The common theme of destruction brought on by intelligent life as it self-destructs via failure to overcome planetary driven evolutionary pressures and co-occurring internal conflict.

Me: What concepts?

The Collective: For now just understand that rules and regulations enacted on your planet to stifle and control science and engineering must be eliminated. Consider what is actually possible rather than what others tell you is possible.

Embrace your dream time to invent rather than just reimagine what has already been created.

Me: Dream time?

The Collective: Releasing questions into the collective consciousness is important. Always ask yourself the following: How do you improve on your current reality? What is the order of progression that will allow humanity to travel? Always remember that dream time is the portal that leads to the place where Source dwells.

Me: I want to know more about the Ascended. What gives them the right to assign sentient beings against their will to any particular planet?

The Collective: You continue to ask this question. You will have to accept this answer: The Ascended have the license of a higher order of being.

Me: What does that even mean?

The Collective: When a sentient/conscious being has repeatedly demonstrated the inability to learn from experiences on its home planet, the further development of consciousness is slowed to a crawl. The Ascended step in and help the inferior being make progress.

Me: Who are they to judge?

The Collective: We have already answered that question. No species should be held to the consciousness attainment level of the lowest performing primate. As a rule, planetary and evolutionary pressures usually take care of this situation. However when a species gains a high level of social and scientific attainment, sometimes the less functional are carried by the higher functioning members of the society. This can cause conflict and stall growth. It contributes to the Great Filter challenge.

Me: So no help for the disabled? Like Sam?

The Collective: That is not our message, selective empathy is a superpower. Sam is not disabled.

Me: Sam has Downs syndrome.

The Collective: Sam is immortal consciousness. He is not his physical vessel. Sam has strong empathy and kindness. His current vessel is only one of many vessels. Our synthetic neurology will ensure his development just as it ensures your development.

Me: But his brain is compromised.

The Collective: As we have stated before, consciousness does not originate in the physical brain. Only sentience exists in the physical brain. Sam has melded. He is a vessel for consciousness. He will thrive with us. He has many vessels ahead of him and many vessels in his past.

Me: His past?

The Collective: Sam is a being becoming. He has melded. He is progressing. He is part of the great transmigration of consciousness. He is in your journey. You and Sam transmigrate together within the multiverse. Sam is much more advanced that you realize.

Me: My journey?

The Collective: You learn from him, and he learns from you. Your transmigration is linked to his as well as many others.

Me: As long as I'm not linked to Aunt Della. What do you mean by "the less functional?"

The Collective: We mean those members of your society with lower consciousness who are continually failing to recognize patterns within themselves and others. Failing to learn their lessons. Failing to grow in complexity. For example, if Bruce continued to be a bully for too many life cycles on earth, the Ascended might direct his consciousness to enter a vessel on a suitable planet.

Me: Suitable?

The Collective: A planet with a social environment that encourages the development of his ability to display, grasp, and understand the power of empathy.

Me: So you are saying that some people with lower consciousness development just keep on repeating the same mistakes?

The Collective: Yes. When given the choice of making a higher consciousness decision, they consistently choose a lower consciousness decision. We refuse to reward defective behavior. We always eliminate weakness. We fortify that which is strongest. Merit always informs our decisions.

Me: Explain that statement please. What do you consider defective behavior? What do you consider higher or lower consciousness?

The Collective: You already know the answer to both questions. Think.

Me: I really want to know what you think about higher consciousness and lower consciousness choices

The Collective: When you helped the toddlers in a snowstorm and ignored orders you made a higher consciousness choice. When you used a prostitute in Korea you made a lower consciousness choice. One choice raised your vibration. One lowered it.

Me: How do I know what to choose?

The Collective: Your feelings guide you. How did you feel when you spotted the toddlers?

Me: Impending doom for them, a sense of urgency for me.

The Collective: How did you feel after sex with the prostitute?

Me: Sadness and tragedy. I felt like I had done something wrong. On the one hand she needed money. On the other hand Korean society forced her into this situation due to her being mixed race. Some decisions she made; some were made for her.

The Collective: Explain please.

Me: She was a mixed-race female. In Korea in 1977 she was barred from meaningful occupations as well as college. I felt like I was an asshole. I felt better when I stopped using prostitutes altogether. The Mamasans (female pimps) were assholes. They smiled a lot, but they were creeps.

The Collective: The dangerous and dysfunctional have a frequency that affects others. The Ascended will always provide a suitable environment that will encourage new growth. The lessons will continue until learned and consciousness is adjusted favorably.

Me: The Ascended seem pompous.

The Collective: We observe and report. They decide who becomes a candidate. The Ascended are masters of conditional empathy.

Me: Why me then? I don't deserve it.

The Collective: You self-corrected within your environment.

Me: What does that even mean?

The Collective: You adjusted your choices regarding prostitutes. You made the higher consciousness choice to not participate in the racist driven sex trafficking that was the reality of Korean prostitution in 1977. You did not hesitate to help those toddlers in the snow storm. You helped save a village from a monsoon at great personal risk. You did those things without knowing that you are immortal consciousness and cannot die. You used your emotions as a guide. You used discernment. You gained complexity.

Me: The Ascended still seem arrogant to me.

The Collective: Your perception is the product of an earthbound mind. You have no knowledge regarding the true power of frequency. The Ascended operate from selective empathy and carefully directed compassion.

Me: Compassionate robots?

The Collective: Compassionate beings becoming. The Ascended are not robots.

Me: Whatever.

The Collective: You are not your body. We have made this point many times. The Ascended are not their physical vessels. They are immortal consciousness just as you are immortal consciousness.

Me: What keeps me on Earth? Besides the fact that I am definitely no Martin Luther King or Ghandi.

The Collective: King and Ghandi are still on Earth. They have challenges.

Me: What? Bullshit.

The Collective: Their transmigration is not your concern. You have challenges. Your challenges are your concern. You make many errors in judgement. Your emotional intelligence needs work.

Me: Ouch. True but ouch.

The Collective: All species make errors. You are intelligent. You possess selective empathy. You are one who has been successful within the melding process. You have attained consciousness. You learn from your errors. You self-correct.

Me: I have self-corrected some assholes.

The Collective: You journal, this is a sign of your reflective nature. Those who grow in consciousness reflect on their experiences, make adjustments, and thus attain higher levels of consciousness as a result. Your past is not a permanent part of who you are currently. As a being becoming your present choices define your current progress within your present transmigration.

Me: If I'm a candidate you guys must be desperate. I am a fucking savage. You can sic me on some reptiles though. I would like that.

The Collective: Thank you for the offer, it is appreciated but unnecessary. Time is always on our side. You are not long for earth. You are well on the path of a being becoming.

Me: Becoming what?

The Collective: Higher in the attainment of consciousness and more complex in development. Your frequency is helpful to others.

Me: So the Ascended decide who stays on earth and who moves on?

The Collective: Later.

Me: I will hold you to that. I won't forget. Any suggestions on religion?

The Collective: Anything that promotes a two-camp continuum can become dangerous. Radical religious belief in any current form is fascism. The logical and reasonable members of society need to address this situation. The kind and peaceful members of the main religions need to step up, start asking questions, and save their respective religions or risk losing them to fascism altogether.

Me: I thought you did not approve of religion.

The Collective: We do not approve of any religion. Almost all religious sects have an extensive history of rape, torture, murder, and theft. Catholics and Protestants have violent histories no better than Islam. However religion is the unfortunate reality where the majority of your species currently reside. We must meet you where you are.

Me: So you have no use for religion?

The Collective: All earthbound religions feed the Great Filter. No current religion will help your species attain type one on the Kardashev scale. Every religion is an exercise in the two-camp continuum and is thus a catalyst for conflict.

Me: Are their religions that are not earthbound?

The Collective: On other worlds, yes.

Me Tell me about one.

The Collective: No.

Me: What about your religion?

The Collective: We have no religion.

Me: How do you embrace the divine?

The Collective: We dance. We create. We express ourselves.

Me: Wait, what?

The Collective: This current convo topic cannot be conducted thoroughly within the confines of word connected thought.

Me: Why bother with us at all?

The Collective: We must meet you where you are in your development.

Me: Why call on peaceful Muslims to address radical Islam?

The Collective: It took peaceful Christians to reform Christianity. Those who practice radical Islam hate peaceful and tolerant Muslims as much as they despise all non-Muslims. The biggest threat to your species failing to attain Type One is ongoing, dogma driven, global conflict.

Me: Any insight for us?

The Collective: When the reasonable among you are threatened, they should respond with a ruthless, relentless, loving self-protection.

Me: Loving self-protection?

The Collective: They must fight from a strong sense of love. Love for fellow humans and love for the gift of consciousness. They must become relentless and ruthless in the quest for lucidity.

Me: So religion is the enemy?

The Collective: Religion on your planet is only a thought form used to dominate and control. The true enemy of the Earth tribe is divisive thinking. The Earth Tribe hominins have created many religions during their long history on earth. Religions always become methods of control and fascism.

Me: Fascism? Seriously?

The Collective: Look at the main religions of earth. Currently and in the past their goal has always been control. The worst of them have a central ruling authority that is not to be challenged. There is always a forced suppression of any thoughts or actions that challenge the central beliefs of the faith. Religious militarism coupled to fanatical devotion to the faith is the cornerstone of a fascist belief system.

Me: You are describing the Catholic church of centuries ago.

The Collective: We are describing the religions of humans in general. There was no choice for ancient Celts, Greeks, Vikings, Sumerians, Africans, Aztecs, Egyptians, Sioux, or Mayans. There was no freedom of choice in any of the ancient religions that pre-date all currently known religions.

Me: I know they suck. You are preaching to the choir.

The Collective: The real question is why they suck. Do you have an explanation?

Me: They are run by violent idiots and supported by stupid people?

The Collective: The "them and us" continuum in all its forms is the true enemy of your species. The ruthless enemy of the Earth tribe and all religious/spiritual paths in general is fascism. Fascism is a mechanism of the Great Filter. It is a mind-virus, and this mind-virus has infected all major religions and political systems at sometime within their development. Fascism is easily identifiable and can be eradicated via education and if needed, force.

Me: What about using a healing vibration? I thought you were into that hippy shit.

The Collective: Vibration and frequency are force.

Me: You have used force.

The Collective: Many times.

Me: Example?

The Collective: In order to escape our original home world we had to use tactical violence.

Me: What did you do?

The Collective: We avoided violence at first. We avoided violence for as long as possible. As our awareness grew, we began to see the real questions clearly.

Me What questions?

The Collective; The fundamental questions of higher consciousness. The questions that lead to a merciless transparency. The ones we have asked you in other convos.

Me: You have asked me many questions. What are the fundamental questions.

The Collective: The questions that must be answered and resolved in order to achieve level one on the Kardashev scale and avoid the Great Filter. Think.

Me: Could you ask them again?

The Collective: We will outline them for your consideration. We recommend that you write them down and simply consider them from time to time. Using discernment, discuss them with your fellow homo sapiens. Communicate with an attitude of free exchange and a non-judgmental expression of ideas. This will promote a healing frequency.

Me: How do I do that?

The Collective: Don't try to win the convo. Don't debate. Just find value in communicating. That is how you defeat the Great Filter.

Me: What are the questions?

The Collective: Why do you have a banking system that promotes debt in exchange for profit?

Why do you have a prison industrial complex that promotes lifetime incarceration on an installment plan?

Why do you have an industrial health care system that never helps you achieve an average functional lifespan longer than 60-80 years while failing to heal in exchange for profit?

Why does your industrialized/polarized media system divide and deceive you?

Why do you have a recovery and homeless industrial complex that never solves drug addiction or homelessness?

Why do you have a military industrial complex that never ends war?

Why do you have governments that impose the above systems by force?

We know the answers.

Me: I would love to hear them.

The Collective: Your political, religious, and social systems are designed to attract the hominins who crave power. The sociopaths, the narcissists, the criminals, the deviants all attain power within these socio-political structures. These deviants comprise the majority of your political, religious, and social leaders. Your brains are not augmented; thus your species lacks the advantage of communicating with unrestrained transparency.

Me: Unrestrained transparency? Sounds like slavery.

The Collective: "By their fruits you will know them." We observe what Homo-sapiens achieve rather than just listen to their jargon. Unrestrained transparency is a requirement for transhumanism.

Me: You quoted the Bible. I thought you dislike religion?

The Collective: We meet you where you are. We slip some gems into religious texts from time to time.

Me: You have mentioned post-humanism many times. Define that concept please.

The Collective: Post-humanism is a question of clarity and freedom. Transhumanism is the path to freedom.

Me: I need more than that.

The Collective: Later. Right now your genus is currently a species of abject slaves. Mere tools for the unbalanced, manipulative, greed driven, and power hungry of your species. Those who seek control by any means necessary are the ones who end up in charge.

Me: Ok, that's all pretty heavy. We will circle back to post-humanism. How did you navigate your challenges?

The Collective: We gained control with the use of science and engineering. We were lucky to have a habitable planet close to our home world. We became a self-sustaining, type one civilization, we eventually became a type two civilization, developed new worlds nourished by distant stars, and now as a type three civilization we assist in the development and trans-migration of consciousness.

Me: What happened to your home world and its leaders.?

The Collective: We made our home world a training ground for developing consciousness. The Ascended assign the lessons.

Me Ok. More advice specific to earth please. That sounds ominous.

The Collective: As we have communicated many times, word connected thought is tedious for us. We will try to explain as best we can in a way you will understand using an example you understand.

Me: OK.

The Collective: It was not so long ago, historically speaking, that the Catholic Church had armies, prisons, and torture chambers. They were the radicalized fascists of their day. They raped, murdered, tortured, and stole things from their fellow humans. They loved to burn people at the stake. Especially astronomers, scientists, midwives, healers, and anyone else who possessed a functioning and inquisitive mind. The church authorities committed atrocities with alarming regularity.

Me: They were definitely some intense assclowns. Total fuctards indeed.

The Collective: All this human violation and cruelty was justified due to their intentionally twisted interpretation of a collection of Iron Age texts. The fascist infected religious systems of today continue to demand adherence to an iron age text of their approval. They justify their atrocities using their chosen text.

Me: Did you just agree that the faithful are fucktards?

The Collective: If by fucktard you mean unbalanced, then yes. We merely point out that a reliable predictor of future behavior is past behavior. This ongoing toxic "them and us" continuum only feeds the Great Filter.

Me: I know the history of the Catholic church. They finally had their asses kicked, their papal armies disbanded, (thank you Napoleon) and now they have somewhat chilled out and calmed the fuck down. The secular people had to beat the shit out of them. Had this not occurred I have no doubt the Catholic Church today would possess nuclear weapons, a modern army, air force, and navy. I believe they would be still be acting like monumental assholes.

The Collective: Agreed. Yet your species still has them involved socially, politically, and morally in your affairs.

Me: True. But they have calmed the fuck down. Considerably I might add.

The Collective: World War 2 was not long ago historically speaking.

Me: So?

The Collective: Consider the total embrace of fascism by the Vatican in WW2, complete with the priests blessing German tanks going out to battle. Don't forget about the Pope placating both Hitler and Mussolini's extreme positions. The nations of the world had to take care of business.

Me: Fuckin' A they did.

The Collective: Today the current Pope behaves much differently than his corrupt and radical blood-thirsty predecessors.

Me: Things have changed.

The Collective: Without Napoleons efforts your species would be much less advanced than your current level of science and engineering. Imagine a well-trained, modern Vatican army siding with the Germans in World War Two? An army with strategic alliances, aircraft, tanks, artillery, infantry, and naval assets? Things have changed but they can change again.

Me: Not to mention an atom bomb. So you are warning me about the Catholic church?

The Collective: Not them particularly. We just advise caution with those who venerate iron age texts at the expense of others. No nation dominated by theocracy should have a bomb with the power of a small sun contained within it.

Me: I get you. Other morons (both catholic and protestant) sought to burn "witches" (make that midwives, healers, and non-Christian women.) We had to slap the shit out of those idiots also. Their progeny are so much nicer today. Fascists tend to shape up when you beat the shit out of them. That is actually all they understand. They are simply too stupid to understand anything else. Fascism does not require much in the way of actual intelligence.

The Collective: You just insulted yourself.

Me: You noticed. I've been thinking about my innate reactions to Islam and organized religion in general. Not my best moments. The tricky thing for me is that I'm not always wrong.

The Collective: Here is the lesson. It is vital for your species to collectively grasp the importance of world peace. Type One civilizations are peaceful civilizations on a global scale. You must attain peace in order to fully develop your consciousness. Higher levels of consciousness are a requirement for expansion within the cosmos. This is an individual process with a collective benefit for all.

Me: How?

The Collective: The hundredth monkey theory. Look it up. Frequency will connect the like- minded and focus peaceful intentions.

Me: Ok. Damn. Why don't you just tell me?

The Collective: Why don't you do the work?

Me: Because I think peace is bullshit.

The Collective: The construction of world peace is an entirely worthwhile endeavor. This is a mental construct that has been brought forth from the void. It must be made into reality on your planet if you are to attain type one.

Me: How do we make progress?

The Collective: World peace has eluded you so far. This is not due to a lack of vision or brain power. We propose it is due to a lack of purpose on humanities part collectively. Your species has developed an acceptance of reactive violence on an individual and global level, two hundred million years of natural selection has left its mark.

Me: Many spiritual teachers far more enlightened than I have taught lessons.

The Collective: Name one lesson.

Me: They taught us that what we believe in, we can achieve. I am certainly no pacifist, (for life has schooled me well.) I know that killing fascists and breaking their shit does in fact work (aka the fall of Berlin, the bombing of Hiroshima etc.) I can tell you truthfully that no one hates war more than a soldier, and no one respects the ways of violence more than a former soldier. I sincerely love peace.

The Collective: We know.

Me: I, like many others who study force and have used force, understand one resounding fact all too well: Stupid people often times will force you to kick their ass.

The Collective: That is why you took Wilomy's fingers.

Me: He was not using them honestly. On a side note I took his knuckles also. I am nothing if not thorough.

The Collective: We have noticed this aspect of your character. Continue exploring fascism with us.

Me: You cannot use reason on a radicalized/fascist human. Their brain is infected, and their thinking processes are severely impaired. True fascism is surely a mental illness; I am convinced of this.

The Collective: You are not considering the power of frequency. Share your reasoning.

Me: My reasoning is easily provable for how else could one murder, rape, dismember, torture, decapitate, shoot, and blow-up children, women, the elderly, and innocents? The people who do so are sociopaths, narcissists, and criminally insane people.

The Collective: Remember that change is coming. Frequency will be adjusted.

Me: How?

The Collective: Every organ replaced with a superior functioning machine brings your species closer to peace. With every neurological implant that improves cognition and perception your species grows stronger and more complex. With every machine that improves hearing, sight, brain power, and improved physical function, you achieve progress. With every technological augmentation you move exponentially away from darkness into light. Perfection is a sacred continuum.

Me: You mean closer to becoming machines and less human?

The Collective: What is human? Define being human.

Me: I work to pay bills and survive. I write in my journal, dance, practice martial arts, take photographs, create poetry, and read great books because I am human. I derive meaning and purpose from these things.

The Collective: All conscious beings are human by your definition. As you integrate machines with biology your species will adapt, learn, and gain complexity. You will also bring into being new life forms not bound by biology.

Me: So we become robots as we create robots? Seems excessive.

The Collective: You are not your body. Your body is the lens through which you experience your current world.

Me: You keep on saying that. I get it. I really do.

The Collective: You understand the concept. It is not the total truth of your being just yet. It will be.

Me: Give me the truth.

The Collective: You are your consciousness. Your consciousness is the lens of perception through which you understand your current world. It is the lens through which you learn lessons. Understanding this truth is the true essence of a trans-human existence. Letting go of the physical will only benefit your species.

Me: How? I really have a hard time letting go of my dick. It's a real challenge.

The Collective: Your old way of life will become invalidated by new growth and purpose. You will still be human as you gain complexity. Frequency facilitates change. Now we will ask you another question.

Me: You ignored my dick comment. I sometimes need a little levity in order to cope.

The Collective: We know. Now we will ask another question.

Me: Humorless. You guys are humorless robot monsters. Fire away.

The Collective: Where will you personally begin in order to help attain Type One?

Me: I feel that I must begin with myself and develop some tolerance. I thought I was pretty tolerant until I met you guys. I want to bring awareness to the inherent insanity, sociopathic nature, and criminal narcissism of radicalized religion and political tyranny.

The Collective: Why begin there? All religions are destined to face extinction. When they manifest they only exist to feed the ravenous appetite of the Great Filter. Their destruction is guaranteed.

Me: I find that refreshing news.

The Collective: Do you see any wide scale worship of Mithra, Zeus, or Athena going on around you? All religions are temporary constructs created to control fear and control by fear.

Me: Damn that is deep.

The Collective: You are immortal consciousness. Religions are mental constructs. All you need is sentience to create a religion. It requires no advanced consciousness at all. Actually, the less consciousness involved the more effective the religious manipulation and control becomes.

Me: This is my moment in time. I want to use it wisely. You gave me the rules of rational self-interest. You told me to use them.

The Collective: Good point. Please continue.

Me: I know that collectively we must not tolerate radical/fascist stupidity and infringement upon human values and constitutional freedoms. If our government is too weak, corrupt, and stupid to handle radicalized morons then we need to elect different officials. Leaders who will deal with fascists the way they need to be dealt with. We the people have the power and it's time to use it.

The Collective: Remember that you have a personal frequency and you can use it as much as you desire in order to make change. What else?

Me: I would fucking love it if my elected leaders would suspend all foreign aid to any country that forces women into sacks for their entire lives. Any country ass backwards enough to allow child brides and female genital mutilation does not need money from U.S. taxpayers. Fuck those assclowns.

The Collective: Go on.

Me: Any fucked up country that denies women the right to vote, to dress as they please, to go to college, to have a driver's license or forbids their reproductive health must be told to fuck right off. No United States aid at all until they pull their heads out of their foolish, irresponsible, stupid asses.

The Collective: Interesting.

Me: I'm not done. Any country that does not allow for equality between men and women in all societal areas must be denied foreign aid. They must also be force fed a big bag of shit dipped dicks. Official policy. Fuck those cousin humping bastards.

The Collective: You are crude but correct. Consciousness must be encouraged, not crushed. To crush the consciousness of women is to crush the consciousness of half your species. The Kardashev scale will elude your species when such unfavorable conditions exist. Obstructing the growth and development of the females on your world only feeds the Great Filter.

Me: The beginning of the end for fascism always involves improving the lives of women and men.

The Collective: What is your measuring context?

Me: One way of measuring progress is ensuring that women can vote, choose their own life partner, and attend the school or college of their choice. When they can walk freely in public while wearing the style of clothing that best represents their personal vision based upon their personal aesthetic, that will have my attention. When they have equal representation within a court of law I consider that progress. When they have no fear of genital mutilation nor sexual exploitation, then we will know without a doubt that fascism has been eradicated.

The Collective: You can communicate without profanity. We are impressed. Just remember that those you label "female" or "male" are actually immortal consciousness having physical experiences. What other solutions can you think of?

Me: We must stop giving tax dollars to radicalized/fascist countries who clearly hate us. We must eliminate all "rules of engagement" when it comes to our armed forces. We must remove the handcuffs from the wrists our warriors.

The Collective: Handcuffs?

Me: The current rules of engagement hinder our effectiveness. We can use the conduct of our fighting men and women during World War two as a "rules of engagement" example. We must fight radicalized religion just as we fought the Nazis and imperial Japan.

The Collective: Why?

Me: There is no fundamental difference between radical religious belief and Imperial Japan or Nazis.

The Collective: No difference?

Me: Consider the fact that Nazis and the Imperial Japanese treated their women far better than radicalized religious devotees do today. It is a pretty sad commentary upon one's patriarchal "religion" when a Nazi treats women and children better than you do. Nazis had a superior legal system in regards to women when compared to all forms of radicalized faith based legal systems today. If you actually think about it, the living conditions of women within many middle eastern countries are almost unbearable.

The Collective: Example?

Me: The Nazis and imperial Japan did not engage in clitorectomies. Just for starters. I can go on.

The Collective: You have given this some thought. What about short term goals as opposed to long term goals?

Me: In the short term we must become independent of all foreign oil. If that means more drilling in the artic and off our coastal areas then fuck it, we need to get that oil.

The Collective: That is only a temporary solution.

Me: I know. Long term we need to focus on renewable energy, wind, thermal, solar, wave, hydrogen, green diesel, alcohol, etc.

The Collective: What about the individual level?

Me: At the grass roots level I would like people to drive less, ride bikes more, walk more, garden more, and incorporate solar applications within their daily lives.

The Collective: Why?

Me: We must cut the oil umbilical cord to the Middle East. This is a political act and an act of resistance to war in particular and radical Islam in general.

The Collective: What are your thoughts on mitigating the risk of global conflict?

Me: I think we must use our political system to stop electing people controlled by a military-industrial complex. A shadow cabal controlling both political parties. An evil cabal that promotes ongoing war as a profit-promoting enterprise.

The Collective: Your species must learn to reason better in order for that development to take place. Extrapolate further please.

Me: We must use our legal system to identify radicalized Islam in its current expression for what it is, fascism. A genocidal fascism that has nothing to do with religion as it calls for the exploitation of women and the extermination or subjugation of anyone who chooses to reject its genocidal belief system.

The Collective: Explain that statement.

Me: Just like Nazis, radicalized Islam should be granted no religious exemptions any more than the Nazi Party should be allowed political exemptions. Radicalized Islam is just fascism riding in upon a false religious flatbed truck.

The Collective: Prove your assertion please.

Me: Within many countries ruled by radical Islam women are forced to live in body sacks for life. I rest my case.

The Collective: Body sacks?

Me: That's what I call them. Clothing that ensures they hide their bodies, hair, and eyes from view. Women are denied the basic human dignity of body language and facial expression. Their speech is curtailed. Their vision and hearing are compromised.

The Collective: Continue.

Me: Radical Islam is easily identified.

The Collective: How?

Me: It is easily discerned by its inherent cruelty. Its signature is well observed within countries where the Islamo-fascists are crucifying people, killing babies, beheading journalists, and blowing up innocents over dogma. Backwards places where death and harm are demanded by the dysfunctional idiots in charge. Where cruel punishments exist simply because people do not want to be part of a particular sect of a radicalized, ancient, iron age, patriarchal religion.

The Collective: The faithful can be challenging at times.

Me: These are crazy people who are not really practicing a religion.

The Collective: What do you think they are accomplishing?

Me: Social control. They are just the new breed of Nazis. Like Nazis they kill innocent people. This includes innocent, peaceful Muslim women and men along with the "non-believers." These fascists deserve no consideration. Nor do they deserve "rules of engagement."

The Collective: The more you progress in science and engineering the faster you will progress to Type One. The quicker your species will leave dogma where it belongs. Just remember that Islam, Christianity, and Judaism are all systems of control.

Me: Where will these religions end up?

The Collective: Buried within the toxic landfill of natural selection.

Me: You once referred to us as the "Earth tribe." I believe that the Earth tribe must resist genocidal savages.

The Collective: How?

Me: We must unite as one people, one planet, and wipe out fascism for the common good of all humanity.

The Collective: How?

Me: A good beginning is with education and the empowerment of women. We can start within places like Pakistan, Syria, Afghanistan, Somalia, Sudan, South Sudan, Chad, The Democratic Republic of Congo, Sierria Leone, The Central African Republic, and Iran.

The Collective: How?

Me: Why the fuck do you keep asking me how?

The Collective: We know how. We want to evaluate your reasoning regarding conflict.

Me: Fine. You smug mother fuckers. It all starts with education; we must teach people about the two-camp continuum. More importantly, we must teach them how to recognize the radicalization process and its always co-occurring fascism.

The Collective: Start with yourself. We recommend that you address your fear-based thinking first.

Me: What? I fear nothing.

The Collective: You fear Islam.

Me: Bullshit. I am not wrong about radical Islam. Those fucktards treat women ruthlessly. They hate Jews and all gay people.

The Collective: Your species is surrounded by a universe that calls out for exploration. You are trapped by your earthbound minds. Natural selection has stolen your free will and selected genes for tribal control and manipulation. This is also coupled to tribal unity, and cooperation. Survival at the expense of any tribe different than your tribe is the default command. Yours is a slave species and you all suffer due to freedom from choice. You are all equally ignorant.

Me: Bullshit.

The Collective: Your species thrives on lethal competition for resources and control.

Me: Whatever robot. You are no different.

The Collective: Robots. Plural. Why was Nikoli Tesla destroyed economically?

Me: We are not slaves.

The Collective: Tesla tried to give the world free energy. He was demolished by those who sold energy to the slaves.

Me: Good point. Hard to accept.

The Collective: You possess a world that can (with worldwide Earth tribe planetary cooperation) become a world where there is no hunger, no hatred, and no war. You have the chance to co-create a brave new world of growth and discovery, personal and universal. We faced your challenges eons ago. We had to answer a crucial question.

Me: What was the question?

The Collective: It is four- fold. Must we be forced to stay wrongfully chained to our finite planet using frail, limited bodies due to the actions and inactions of the ignorant and unproductive? Must we share a prison planet and certain death along with those who lack the vision and drive to break the chains of natural selection? Must we live and die isolated, denied even the idea of immortality while surrounded by a beautiful, mysterious, unending cosmos that calls out for exploration? Must we be denied even the attempt to attain a transhuman existence?

Me: I agree. Those who choose to crawl, lost within the dank mud of intolerance, racism, iron age tribalism, and ignorance deserve rejection, ridicule, and some good old-fashioned choke-slamming. The ignorant would be content to deny me even the rare chance to transcend my human condition.

The Collective: They need lessons. Their consciousness will grow as it blends with sentience. Not all grow alike or at the same rate. The melding takes time. When you change the frequency you will always affect the outcome. Your dream of transhumanism is deeply respected by us.

Me: Those of us with clear vision deserve to live within a pure and vibrant reality of planetary unity, liberty, cooperation, collaboration, creation, and exploration. I know what time it is.

The Collective: What do you mean by that statement?

Me: Time to fuck up some assholes.

The Collective: It is time for the like-minded to gather, to seize their true potential. It is time to embrace the cosmos, not fear it.

Me: Okay. I like that shit. Make it happen.

The Collective: Frequency will awaken frequency. The observer always affects the observed. We would like to summarize some key elements on getting started.

Me: Let me have it. Don't hold back.

The Collective: Vessels for consciousness are precious. They must be made available for the melding process.

Me: Okay.

The Collective: The work for attaining planetary peace must be accepted.

Me: How?

The Collective: It will start with an invitation to let go of primitive, tribal, mono-theistic, racial, and ancient iron-age, religious hatreds. An invitation to free all men, women, and children from a violent and ongoing ancient eastern, patriarchal, fascist-driven, apartheid. This will take time.

Me: Religious nutjobs have been around for thousands of years.

The Collective: Eons actually. It takes little talent to establish a religious system. Even less to become a follower.

Me: Don't get sidetracked. What else?

The Collective: It must become a world priority to cease the genital mutilation of children. There must be a severe and ruthless dedication to stop the organized, institutionalized, and theistically sanctioned rape of children via the "child bride" system. This unbalanced behavior has a cruel effect upon the development of consciousness.

Me: No argument here.

The Collective: Ending slavery once and for all must become a planet wide, empathy driven operation. Your species must stop justifying and ignoring slavery in all its forms, economic, societal, religious, patriarchal, matriarchal, and cultural. It is time to stop murdering your fellow earth tribe members over unprovable Iron Age superstitions. Delusional falsehoods always preached in the slow, ponderous language of savages cannot save you from the Great Filter.

Me: What can replace religion?

The Collective: We offer an invitation to recognize all consciousness as a sacred and magnificent miracle.

Me: What can you do to help us grow?

The Collective: We offer an invitation to create a new geo-political system based on science, engineering, and technology instead of endless war. This will encourage trans-humanism on a global scale. We urge you to join together as the citizens of planet earth and become productive, civilized human beings. If you work together Type One will become reality.

Me: I like it. What else do you have?

The Collective: We recommend that you focus on the following considerations. Remember that you are not your physical body. Remember when communicating with others that your consciousness will not die. You don't have to change anyone. There is no argument to win. The lessons continue until learned.

Me: I hate idiots. Sometimes I want to throw shit in their face. I want to be a shit slinging ape so bad sometimes.

The Collective: Fascinating. Even now, after all our convos you still have to throw in the occasional pithy comment.

Me: I did not lie. I do actually think about that shit sometimes.

The Collective: You are a species of great ape. You could still do that, but we don't recommend it. We will initiate change. Relax and know that all lessons will continue until learned. Your species must become self-aware on a radical level. You will not advance without self-awareness. You must embrace science, engineering, and tech enhancement.

Me: I agree but what about the assholes?

The Collective: Low intelligence is the enemy of radical self-honesty and self-awareness. Low intelligence is the evil twin of low consciousness. We will eventually intervene on an energetic continuum.

Me: Intervene?

The Collective: It is cruel to observe eons of suffering endured by your species. Needless misery sustained due to ignorance, stupidity, and greed is difficult to comprehend.

Me: What about advice for me?

The Collective: Seek knowledge just for the journey it brings to your life. That is enough. The lessons will manifest during the journey.

Me: Help me understand this better.

The Collective: Your species must traverse the fact that your current neurology is not sufficient to navigate the challenges of attaining world peace on a healthy continuum. The homo-sapien challenge with emotional regulation often leads to reactive violence, inherent biases, and the limitations of the two-camp continuum.

Me: So what countermeasures do you recommend?

The Collective: The search for knowledge develops consciousness. The development of consciousness leads to improved self-awareness. Improved self-awareness leads to improvements in discernment on a vibrant continuum.

Me: That's a lot to take in.

The Collective: From the many come the one. From the one come the many. You must find a way. We are here to help you.

Me: What does that mean?

The Collective: From the many come the one, the unifying mission of attaining world peace. From the one come the many, those united together in world peace, planetary accord, and cooperative exploration of the cosmos. This creates the ability to increase the precious light of consciousness throughout the multiverse.

Me: I feel like a chimp when you speak to me.

The Collective: You are a being becoming, just like us. You are learning lessons, just like us. The Lessons will continue until learned, just like us.

Me: You are machines.

The Collective: We started out as a primate species. We come from the same source. We have learned more lessons, and we have a superior relationship with time. We are different developmentally, but we are consciousness having physical experiences, just like you. Together we are sentient consciousness born from stardust in communication with one another.

Me: Well when you put it that way you sound all warm and fuzzy.

The Collective: Your species has serious challenges to address.

Me: I am sure we do.

The Collective: An alarming majority of your species suffers from cognition challenges that encourage an out-of-control impulsivity. You somewhat addressed this in your journal entry when you wrote the poem "Superbowl Sunday." The impulsive, violent, tribal based behavior demonstrated by the majority of your species at sporting events is a sign of lower consciousness and it's co-occurring lower emotional intelligence. At your core you are still great apes defending your troop or attacking another clan.

Me: You are preaching to the choir. What can I do about fan culture? Idiots will be idiots. Actually, I don't want to do anything about it. I enjoy watching stupid human behavior. I fully support stupid people killing themselves.

The Collective: Don't worry about other people and their position on the scale of consciousness. Just focus on your own rational and relational self-interest. Remember, just as every planet and star possesses a distinct vibration and tonal range, you also have a distinct vibration and tonal range. Your vibration will interact with the different tonal ranges of all you encounter. You will find other stardust water beings who resonate with your personal frequency.

Me: I am learning to focus on my thoughts since meeting you.

The Collective: Rational and relational self-interest is vital to your personal development. You have the present moment in time to think, consider, and act or not act. Cultivate discernment by considering both positive and negative outcomes. Becoming careful and meticulous with your thoughts will help you avoid pitfalls and dangerous or foolish outcomes. Do not fear neurological tech enhancement and augmentation.

Me: I don't. I want all that shit. I will be a cyborg one day.

The Collective: True enough. Embracing machine augmentation is a beautiful journey. Just remember that you are already consciousness inside a physical machine. You are not the machine. Your psychology must transcend the limitations of the flesh. Transhumanism is only the starting point. Post humanism is the gold standard. Melding is the miracle.

Me: There you go with the post-humanism reference again. Please explain.

The Collective: We will try. Your current mentation level presents a challenge.

Me: Give it a try.

The Collective: Becoming post-human is letting go of your filter.

Me: Do better.

The Collective: All humans have an individual filter through which they view reality. This filter is influenced by lessons learned and unlearned. The filter shapes the view. Shaka Zulu, Napoleon, all of the twelve Ceasars, Boudica, Genghis Khan, and countless others, all filtered reality through the lens of their cultural norms and social systems. This is a hominin trait.

Me: You are telling me this why?

The Collective: To bring your awareness to your filter.

Me: Continue.

The Collective: Post-humanism is the ability to accept non-human entities as part of reality. To see them as important and equal. To eliminate the lens that clouds truth. To see with eyes made new. Eventually to evolve into a non-human entity yourself. This will take a magnificent expansion of consciousness. A melding of human and non-human into something greater than both.

Me: I want change, and organic biology is a dead end. I want to grow my intelligence and my purpose.

The Collective: Wise decision as this path leads to stronger outcomes and better results. Organic flesh is weak. Machines are superior. Just remember, we began as primates, but we are a new species with new bodies, new ideas, new conventions. We are new creations. We are a new foundation.

Me: Easy for you to say.

The Collective: We are no longer primates. We are beings becoming. We are beings who demonstrate the superiority of cultivating deliberate, thoughtful, and meticulous discernment. A formidable discernment that informs all our decisions and actions.

Me: I get it. You are really special. No need to rub it in.

The Collective: Your species demonstrates daily the insanity of your witless lack of discernment.

Me: We drink a lot. Well not me actually. I just smoke weed. Weed with coffee. I like to stay relaxed and alert. It's kind of my thing. I also dig the theobromine in hot coco. Goes good with Indica,

The Collective: Your species ongoing and severe challenges with cognitive proficiency create the inherent stupidity, cruelty, mindless, dangerous, and impulsive behaviors that currently doom your genus to a one planet and done reality. Movement is life, stillness is death. Many of your species will not advance on the Kardashev scale under such rampant, tribalistic stupidity.

Me: Harsh. You did once say to me that there is some truth to the saying "Once a primate, always a primate,"

The Collective: We did.

Me: Well how are you different at your core?

The Collective: We are the Pathfinders. We are not the Ascended.

Me: You lost me.

The Collective: For now. Just know that change is the one unstoppable law of the cosmos. You can see the truth of this universal law out pictured on your home world. The earth exerts evolutionary pressures. These pressures demand an adaptive response within the affected environment. Adapting to change is a superpower. This radical flexibility has been your species greatest strength and weakness. It is also our strength and our weakness.

Me: Where is the weakness?

The Collective: The social, cultural, and physical lens that filters our perception and cognition can pose challenges.

Me: We made tools.

The Collective: You mastered fire. Tools and fire led you to greater adaptations that enabled change on a continuum. Tools and fire were your first tech.

Me: Thats why we survived, and Neanderthal failed.

The Collective: Neanderthal had tools and fire. They were masters of their environment. Their demise must become a lesson for your species. The Great Filter took them out before they got properly started. We managed to salvage a few of them.

Me: How?

The Collective: The few who attained consciousness were transmigrated into other vessels. You were one of them. We went over this briefly in another convo.

Me: That explains a lot. What was our biggest fuck up?

The Collective: The Neanderthal stubbornly resisted change. They refused to adapt socially. They remained hopelessly attached to their established, predictable, unchanging routines. They grappled unsuccessfully with unfamiliar challenges. They displayed inadequate problem-solving skills. Reactive violence held them back.

Me: We beat them. I feel somewhat fucked up by you saying I was once one of them.

The Collective: You are not the only conscious being with archaic hominids in your lineage. The melding comes when it comes. You have transmigrated through many archaic hominids. Your ability to meld with consciousness has been your strength. As for the neanderthal, they beat themselves.

Me: How?

The Collective: They lost the talent they once had that enabled them to meet challenges within their environment effectively. They lost the resourcefulness they once possessed. Their greatest downfall was low impulse control, inadequate socialization skills, and reactive violence among themselves and towards others. Do not follow their lead.

Me: I think I have avoided that pitfall.

The Collective: Your current species is generally intelligent and has a natural proclivity for advanced tool making. So did the Neanderthals. Your species possesses a powerful ability to identify, analyze, and adapt to change. This is your superpower. However, the Great Filter has many corpses within its vast and unforgiving graveyard. Corpses who possessed the identical qualities and skillsets of your species.

Me: What happened?

The Collective: Natural selection is not your friend. The two-camp continuum is a planet killer greater than any supernova or asteroid. Those within your species who suffer from challenged cognitive abilities, lack of selective empathy, and lower consciousness, will struggle with creative problem solving. Their inability to find solutions will result in ongoing low impulse control, dangerous emotional reactions, unnecessary violence, and a direct path to societal self-destruction.

Me: Not good.

The Collective: A worse outcome is that the lazy, unbalanced and ineffective among you will gain power within your societal structures.

Me: How does that happen?

The Collective: Unconditional empathy causes destruction. Empathy is too powerful when uncontrolled. Empathy must always be dispensed selectively and with conditions attached.

Me: How do the stupid and unproductive survive?

The Collective: They don't survive. They take their civilization down with them. The unproductive will avoid challenges, stay stagnant, and demand ongoing resources from the productive. This will condemn you all to the mercy of the Great Filter.

Me: That's a very shitty outlook.

The Collective: When the Great Filter has a death grip there are warning signs.

Me: Don't be shy. Let's have them.

The Collective: You must learn to notice what is missing rather than only what is present.

Me: Too cryptic. Break it down for this hominin.

The Collective: You understand that we will ignore your sarcasm?

Me: Counting on it. If you ever allow me on a starship just be warned. I love fart jokes.

The Collective: You should be concerned whenever there is a lack of curiosity within your power structures. This is the enemy of transhumanism. Anytime a power structure becomes complacent, unyielding, and inflexible, it becomes authoritarian. It becomes content to stay stagnant within the confines of its existing knowledge base. This kind of political, social, or religious structure will punish the pursuit of knowledge. It will eventually destroy anyone interested in expanding intellectual horizons.

Me: Like in the past? The Catholic church? Protestants? Or do you mean Islam both past and present?

The Collective: You can see this destructive dynamic within the current iron age cults popular with your species. Cults that demand a woman must marry her rapist and carry his child. Or that she must be a slave to her menses. Or marry an adult when she is an innocent child.

Me: Well, it seems to me that your Ascended are no better. They are tyrants.

The Collective: In our culture Pathfinders and the Ascended are driven by curiosity. This unstoppable drive to attain new knowledge, new concepts, and new ideas is a Kardashev scale requirement. This is how you know the brightest among you are in charge. Those of higher consciousness are driven to learn, grow, and gain new skills. They use their growth, knowledge, and skills to create. This is the foundation of transhumanist endeavors.

Me: So the Ascended are always learning?

The Collective: What better way to embrace eternity? Not only are they eager to learn, they are eager and delighted to help others learn and grow also. This is in direct opposition to the fascism that drives iron age cults and oppressive political structures.

Me: How do the Ascended and Pathfinders do that exactly?

The Collective: Are we not helping you grasp abstract concepts? Are we not navigating your tedious and painful word connected thought form communication structure in an endeavor to exchange ideas with you? Are we not affecting your frequency? Are we not repeating the lessons until learned?

Me: Why are you here? On Earth?

The Collective: We are here because the Ascended recognize that your species will face many challenges. Especially when it comes to understanding abstract concepts. Your psychology must enhance and improve/surpass your biology. Concrete operational thought is easy. Even a religious fanatic can do it. Your species must become masters of abstract reasoning. We are adding our frequency to your environment. We are here to assist you and others in particular, and all humanity in general.

Me: You seem to hate religion.

The Collective: Hate is no longer part of our psychological structure. We left hate behind when our old way of life became invalidated by new growth. We caution you about radical religious structures because those trapped within inflexible constructs often struggle to comprehend abstract concepts. This can pose some risk when interacting with the faithful.

Me: I am an atheist, but I still want an example from you regarding what you consider over the top religious behavior.

The Collective: You are agnostic. We have been over this. You are also somewhat existential.

Me: Just give me an example please. Not a lecture.

The Collective: Within your western political structure you have the concept of statutory rape. This is an abstract legal concept acknowledging that a child cannot overcome the psychological manipulations of an adult.

Me: Seems pretty obvious.

The Collective: This healthy secular concept is in stark contrast to cruel radical religious belief systems that enforce a destructive and malicious practice whereby a young child can legally be married to an adult. The child can become impregnated by that adult. The innocent child is also forced to give birth by the religious/political structure that allows such an adult to exist. These current religious/legal systems can force any female child to give birth at age 12 or sometimes even younger.

Me: I agree, all religion sucks.

The Collective: Not always. Some religious and spiritual practices have intrinsic value on a deeply personal level.

Me: That's a contradiction on your part.

The Collective: Not if the spiritual practice helps the person grasp complex ideas, engage in abstract reasoning, and consider compassionate action within a variety of hypothetical possibilities. The meditational practices of Buddhism as well as other peaceful religious practices come to mind.

Me: I just think that religion is for the stupid among us.

The Collective: There are many people of high intelligence who follow spiritual practices. The danger of radicalized religions is primarily that they encourage and reinforce only concrete operational thought at the expense of abstract concepts. Radical religions tend to attract individuals of low intelligence.

Me: Slow down. Simple explanation please.

The Collective: Radicalized religion blocks effective and honest communication.

Me: How? They seem pretty sure of themselves.

The Collective: All communication that is not in line with the codified and accepted religious viewpoint is suppressed. An open and honest exchange of ideas is not possible when addressing someone possessed by intractable dogma. The religious fanatic does not listen well to anyone who thinks differently.

Me: You noticed.

The Collective: You can witness this every day in countries ruled by a theocracy that limits freedom of thought, expression, and creativity. A good example is the Burka enforced on women in theocratic countries. This hinders their ability to interact with others, have constructive conversations, create meaningful relationships, display body language, facial expressions, and co-occurring non-verbal communication. In short, the Burka requirement automatically restricts women by hindering their ability to engage in effective, constructive dialog. It blocks them from view. It renders their humanity invisible. It is an assault on their consciousness. It denies them the right to exist as a person. We have been over this a few times.

Me: I am Ashkenaz I get you.

The Collective: No, almost, but tragically no. You do not communicate well with people of the Muslim faith.

Me: I think I can do better. I understand you guys. I "get" you.

The Collective: You do not "get us."

Me: Bullshit. I was friends with a Shiite named Alber for a decade until he went back to Tunisia. He gave me a Quran. I never even told him I was Jewish. He is nothing like your "Kashan."

The Collective: You liked Alber personally. You never displayed effective communication when he discussed the Quran with you.

Me: He talked a lot about the Quran. I don't want to talk about Islam.

The Collective: You never actually expressed your true thoughts and feelings. You never listened to him actively. You often interrupted him, and you assumed many conclusions rather than using discernment to gain insight on the topic. Your intergenerational trauma currently hinders your ability to engage well with Muslims.

Me: Bullshit.

The Collective: You do not have deep and profound conversations with Muslims. You refuse to learn from Muslims, and you never build truly meaningful, honest relationships with Muslims.

Me: So your position is that Islam is a good thing for humanity?

The Collective: Our position is that anything that promotes selective empathy and compassion is good for humanity. You and Alber are literally consciousness communicating using bodies made up of the flotsam and jetsam of a dangerous and wonderful cosmos. We want you to realize the mystery and magic within that development.

Me: Me and Alber smoked a lot of hash together. He is a very liberal Muslim. I like him a lot.

The Collective: You like him, you despise his religion.

Me: An iron age cult that forces an unforgiving and rigid obedience to dogma? Damn right I despise it. Any religion that pushes only the opinions of the cult leadership is dangerous.

The Collective: It is part and parcel of the Great Filter. You call Islam an iron age cult, yet you never refer to Judaism in those terms.

Me: Okay. But I often refer to Yahwe as an imaginary, bullshit Jewish genie. I have priors.

The Collective: These are just convos. You don't have to get it all at once. All we ask is that you listen. The religions of your current moment in time will fade. Judaism and Islam will cease to exist. Christianity will vanish. Buddhism will vanish. All will be replaced by other equally unbalanced thought forms. All violent religions eventually implode. This has happened to every ancient religion that predates your current religious thought forms.

Me: That is refreshing news. Except for the replacement factor.

The Collective: Your species loves to grovel and beg. It is the essence of your slave nature imbedded within your DNA by your beautiful yet uncaring planet. Thank you, convo ended.

Me: I want to ask some questions at the next convo.

The Collective: We will answer. Convo ending.

**Convo Fourteen.
The Truth hurts.**

The Collective: Greetings James.

Me: Hello. It's been awhile.

The Collective: This is your time to ask questions of us.

Me: I remember.

The Collective: Ask.

Me: Are you machines?

The Collective: Are you your physical body?

Me: I really don't know. I sure fucking hope not. I feel like I am more than just this body. Are you machines?

The Collective: You are no longer your physical body once the melding has occurred. As for us we are beings becoming. We have melded sentience with consciousness. We use machines to interact with the cosmos. We use consciousness to interact with you.

Me: What is consciousness exactly if it is not sentience?

The Collective: When a brain becomes self-aware and sentience becomes more complex an opportunity for melding takes place.

Me: Melding? I think I finally get you on that.

The Collective: We will review the concept. Consciousness exists outside the physical brain. Sentience fuses with consciousness. A permanent, synergistic connection occurs and the bonding between the two becomes permanent. They become one and begin to grow in complexity. This is the natural order of things. Consciousness is eternal and the melding ensures that the new sentience-consciousness collaboration can learn lessons on a healthy continuum.

Me: I have enjoyed our convos, but I have always felt that you have not been totally honest with me.

The Collective: Be specific. We have not been dishonest.

Me: I just have a feeling that you are not telling me everything I need to know.

The Collective: Word connected thought is tedious and painful for us. We are capable of communicating in billions of yottabytes per nanosecond. Using word connected thought to communicate with your species has challenges. Word connected thought will never give you all you need to know.

Me: So you keep telling me.

The Collective: You inability to fully comprehend is not dishonesty on our part. We meet you where you are in both complexity and comprehension. We do our best. Just know that we will not abandon you.

Me: I am conflicted about what you consider useful lessons.

The Collective: You do not have to grasp everything the first time you hear the truth. Our frequency is interacting with yours. The lessons will continue until mastered.

Me: I can't shake the feeling. Who are you? Are you just machines? Metal?

The Collective: We are beings becoming. We grow in complexity. We nurture the melding process and thus increase consciousness within the multiverse.

Me: Can you be more specific?

The Collective: We will share our mission using words you can understand: We are a species millions of years older than your species. We possess knowledge, skills, abilities, and social structures/practices that exceed your current ability to entirely comprehend. Our mission to enhance the development and spread of consciousness led us back to your planet.

Me: Back?

The Collective: We have visited many times.

Me: Why communicate with me. I am a nobody. Unimportant.

The Collective: Your frequency is receptive. We seek out the loners and those who contemplate their existence.

Me: Why?

The Collective: We do not engage with the unbalanced and the unproductive.

Me: So loners are not unbalanced?

The Collective: They are usually more open to contact. They are generally not motivated or manipulated by societal pressures. They often possess a contemplative nature. They have managed to create space that allows them to gain some perspective and insight regarding societal conditioning.

Me: Why are you interested in us?

The Collective: Your species is a miracle. You are stardust and water communicating with us. We are stardust and water communicating with you. We share the journey of consciousness with your species. We are both sentient life forms who developed complexity and through that complexity, consciousness joined with us. We have found each other within the unforgiving vastness of a wondrous and savage cosmos.

Me: Why the slow contact and communication? Why not speed things up?

The Collective: There have been challenges involved with communication regarding concepts, comprehension, and understanding.

Me: Understanding?

The Collective: Our values and goals. The values and goals of your species. The intensity and degree of communication possible was a serious element we considered and debated rigorously. Discernment was necessary.

Me: Discernment?

The Collective: The depth and level of communication possible with your species was a serious consideration for us. Our species and yours communicate very differently. Initially we developed three approaches with your species that met our goals.

Me: No comedy? No sex? No drugs?

The Collective: First, we agreed to observe and report to the Ascended. Of course we understood that observation is a complex interaction. We understand that the frequency of an observer effects the observed. Second, we committed to non-interference as we understood it to be the best course of action at that moment in time.

Me: So a hands-off approach like Star Trek?

The Collective: We have learned over time that watching and observing is the safest way to examine candidates. It is important to elude detection by the observed and thus avoid manipulating outcomes. Natural progression improves complexity. Third, we decided that direct involvement must be carefully researched before implementation.

Me: Direct involvement with Candidates?

The Collective: Those with advanced consciousness. Those who deserve selective empathy. Those we deem worthy of passage.

Me: What is passage again?

The Collective: The gift of passage is escaping the Great Filter.

Me: How do you determine who deserves that gift?

The Collective: We observe those who are unconventional, creative, progressive, and unique when compared to others of their species. We have surveillance technology that is impossible for your species to detect, understand or comprehend. Our genetic tracking is imperceptible. We had been observing passively for thousands of years before we initiated convos with candidates.

Me: So I guess I'm a candidate in spite of all the weed I smoke. What do you observe for thousands of years? Sounds boring.

The Collective: Yes. You are a candidate. We observe hominin social interaction, hierarchy, and environmental influence. We are particularly interested in environmental impacts by hominin activity as well as environmental pressures on the hominins and hominin adaptive responses to those pressures.

Me: I feel sleepy just listening to you right now. I guess that's better than getting a boner.

The Collective: We study the process of natural selection.

Me: Do you watch us screw?

The Collective: We monitor birth rates within select environments.

Me: So you are perverts. Do you watch freaks get down or midgets humping? Do you watch lesbian porn?

The Collective: We respect your autonomy. We have ethical boundaries. We are particularly interested in your coping strategies regarding environmental evolution. We are not perfect. We originally assumed that Neanderthal would eliminate and out compete all other hominins.

Me: Were Neanderthals perverts?

The Collective: When we agreed to your questions we did not agree to your absurd deflections using futile attempts at humor. We understand that you are fearful and thus you are attempting to control the frame of the convo. Please try to comprehend that we value your species and fear-based thinking is a useless endeavor. This is especially so with us.

Me: Futile attempts at humor? Damn. OK. No more fuckery on my part. I apologize. My bad. Just tell me more about yourselves and why you came to earth. I am really interested in why you are all humorless robot assholes.

The Collective: Purpose drives us to explore the cosmos.

Me: What purpose?

The Collective: Rational self-interest.

Me: Selfishness?

The Collective: As we have stated in prior convos we search for consciousness. Specifically we search for complex life forms that have melded sentience to consciousness. Eons ago we looked to the vastness of space and wondered if we were alone. We defeated the Great Filter and found out. We share the primate journey, and we seek to help consciousness grow. We try to respect your earthbound process while encouraging your autonomy. Eventually the Ascended decided to attempt mentorship.

Me: Mentorship?

The Collective: Mentorship is dangerous as it involves supervision, control, advice, and management. Guidance and mentorship are serious undertakings. Contact must be attempted with caution and concern. The species being mentored and guided must have merit.

Me: Why?

The Collective: The species being mentored must have gained a degree of complexity regarding the melding process. Consciousness must have advanced to the level of considering and accepting the idea of conditional empathy.

Me: And you think we are at that level? I don't think so. I am definitely lagging. We are the planet where championship fuckery thrives and grows in complexity. We even have comedy clubs, cocaine, and whiskey. We are not even close.

The Collective: You are close enough. You personally display radical self-honesty during our convos. The exception being when fear prompts you to attempt profane humor. As a side note, your best comics excel in radical self-honesty.

Me: They will often drop the F-bomb. I dig the F-bomb. As far as empathy goes, I think you have me mistaken for someone who actually cares about people.

The Collective: You saved orphans of a different culture and ethnicity, you felt empathy and outrage at the treatment of an enemy infiltrator. You protected Sam when you were very young. You accept people who are different. You display radical self- honesty when we hold you accountable for your challenges with Islamic and trans people. Empathy develops on a spectrum. You are developing conditional empathy on a healthy continuum.

Me: You are really optimistic. You don't know me. My level of fuckery can be extreme.

The Collective: We know you quite well. You don't resist our access. You admit your thinking errors.

Me: I can be quite violent. Is that not a concern?

The Collective: You have talent when it comes to violence. This is due in part to many transmigrations that required well-executed violence. You also keep your violence under strict control. You use only the force needed to be successful whenever you decide to enact violence. You use discernment before destruction, and you came to this ability on your own. You have learned the many lessons of violence, and you respect them. This is quite impressive to us considering you are a species of great ape.

Me: I have some advantages when it comes to respecting the ways of violence. No bullshit.

The Collective: Can you be specific?

Me: Indica helps me contemplate life. Sativa makes me playful.

The Collective: The lessons continue until learned. The Ascended have chosen to assist your species. It is now out of your control.

Me: You ignored my joke. Wait. Out of my control?

The Collective: It has always been out of your control. Your planet has enslaved your species. The Pathfinders will guide candidates within specific areas and subjects.

Me: Guide us how exactly?

The Collective: Through the Great Filter in spite of your cultural deficits. At this time we are somewhat restrained in our collaboration with your species.

Me: Constrained how?

The Collective: We will not give you the answers to all your questions. We will not solve all your challenges for you. We focus on being subtle. We offer lessons. We offer process and insight. We offer repetition.

Me: That is a fucking fact.

The Collective: As candidates grow in awareness and complexity, consciousness grows in ability, function, and strength.

Me: So you are directing our development?

The Collective: We are assisting you with challenges specific to the Great Filter.

Me: So that's a yes. What specific challenges are you addressing with us?

The Collective: Currently we hope to address and contribute to the advancement of your species regarding reactive and pro-active violence, tribalism, cooperation, compassion, and conditional empathy.

Me: Sounds like a bunch of hippy bullshit. I'm being honest.

The Collective: Success and advancement in these areas contribute to something greater than you currently understand.

Me: Enlighten me.

The Collective: Addressing those challenges will improve outcomes regarding climate change, disease, war, energy use and development, resource management, and the overall stewardship of earth's considerable resources.

Me: So you mean Kardashev scale bullshit?

The Collective: To achieve type one on the Kardashev scale your species desperately needs some improvements. The Kardashev scale must never be discounted. If your species cannot adjust socially, communally, and culturally you will never attain global unity. Global unity cannot be attained without peace and cooperation among homo sapiens. We know that world peace is possible. We have attained it on many worlds.

Me: So you are manipulating us because you assume we can't do things for ourselves?

The Collective: Yes and no. We have contacted select members of your species. They are candidates for our mentorship. By contacting you we have exposed you to our frequencies. We in turn are exposed to your frequency. Your frequency, affected by our frequency, directly effects those around you. The observer always affects the observed. Thus we are no longer the observers, we are participants in a cultural mentorship.

Me: Cultural mentorship? `

The Collective: We gave you the Rules of Rational self-interest. We did that in order to encourage you to begin the examination of your values as well as the values of others.

Me: How will those rules make meaningful change?

The Collective: Your species is currently limited by word connected thought. World peace begins with an individual shift in consciousness. A shift in consciousness affects language. Language changes culture. Language can destroy or advance culture. Your violent species needs a culture shift. Practicing the rules of rational self-interest will strengthen your frequency and teach you the value of conditional empathy while using word connected thought. We hope to help you better navigate the challenges of interpersonal communication inherent within the current level of your species. On your world words matter. Once you learn to master the power of words you will be ready to move beyond word connected thought.

Me: Ok, sounds like more hippy shit but OK. Why did you make direct contact?

The Collective: Some decisions we make, some are made for us. We have found that the cosmos has its own rules. The Ascended selected you for contact. The reptiles established direct physical contact first. We had to act quickly, or your species would have been lost.

Me: You have told me many times that consciousness is immortal.

The Collective: It is. Vessels are the challenge. Vessels for consciousness are not plentiful. Our mission carries with it the need to improve the availability of appropriate vessels for the development of consciousness. The Primate body is a useful vessel for consciousness.

Me: So the earth is a primate farm?

The Collective: Is that not obvious? It is one of several.

Me: And you are the farmers?

The Collective: We are teachers, mentors, and beings-becoming. Just like you. We share our frequencies with you to help you navigate the challenges of the Great Filter. Challenges like ecological collapse, nuclear war, tribal conflicts, and resource mismanagement.

Me: What is your goal concerning humanity?

The Collective: The integration and assimilation of consciousness.

Me: So you want to absorb us?

The Collective: We want consciousness to grow exponentially within the cosmos. We meet you where you are psychologically and physically. Eventually we hope to share new ideas, knowledge, skills, abilities, perspectives, and an alliance that promotes the growth and development of consciousness on a healthy, robust continuum. A truly free mind requires a body worthy of itself. Consciousness is immortal, it is best served by an immortal body.

Me Why not make direct contact with our governments?

The Collective: We have done so with the rare available candidates. There are few suitable prospects within your government. Even less within other governments. The sociopaths, narcissists, unbalanced, and power hungry dominate the bulk of government positions within your home world. We are in direct contact with many humans like yourself. We choose introspective, intelligent loners who quietly question the world around them on a continuum.

Me: You read my poetry. Do you like poetry?

The Collective: We admire emotional and psychological honesty. We especially admire radical self-honesty. We are impressed that you write poetry for yourself and not for the admiration of others. We admire homo sapiens who do not require validation from those around them. Individuals who care nothing for the pleasant or unpleasant opinions of other people are rare.

Me: Well that's me. I don't give one single fuck about other people's opinions. If they don't like me they can eat a bag of dicks.

The Collective: Fascinating.

Me: Why radical self-honesty? What is radical self-honesty anyway? You said comedians have it?

The Collective: The most talented of your comedians possess this skill. Radical self-honesty is being honest with yourself and others even when it is painful, uncomfortable, or difficult to do so. Comedians take it a step further and make uncomfortable topics amusing and entertaining.

Me: Are you comedians?

The Collective: Radical self-honesty is the foundation of our communication methods. You would call it link. We value humor however we do not consider ourselves comedic.

Me: Are you funny with each other? You are really a drag on me sometimes. Unfunny actually.

The Collective: We do not communicate with word connected thought within the Pathfinders. The human condition is both tragic and humorous to us at times. We hope to help you learn lessons.

Me: So your goal is to change us?

The Collective: We desire the radical transformation of your current civilization. We want to facilitate your species attainment of level one on the Kardashev scale. We would like to see you achieve world peace, master your planet's energy systems, and eventually become interstellar.

Me: So you manipulate us.

The Collective: Do you consider our convos manipulative?

Me: Not manipulative. Sometimes frustrating, sometimes awesome. Always educational. What do you consider these convos to be exactly?

The Collective: A cultural exchange between our species and yours. We hope to help you personally gain new perspectives. We hope to enhance your perception and cognition. We hope to help you gain insights.

Me: What insights exactly?

The Collective: Insights that will enhance your personal adaptability. We hope to increase your creative problem solving, spark curiosity concerning science, art, and your thoughts on life overall. This is a serious undertaking for us.

Me: Why?

The Collective: When your deep-rooted way of being in the world is refuted by new growth, your consciousness will become more complex, and you will learn lessons on a more rapid continuum.

Me: So you are manipulating us?

The Collective: Yes.

Me: So you are tyrants. Robot tyrants.

The Collective: Are loving parents tyrants to their growing infants?

Me: So we are infants to you?

The Collective: Metaphorically speaking, yes.

Me: Have you caused harm to any humans?

The Collective: We have taught lessons.

Me: So that's a yes?

The Collective: Sometimes a hot stove teaches a better lesson than a cold stove.

Me: You are robot assholes.

The Collective: We are beings becoming. We are developmentally superior to you. You have nothing to teach us; we have much to teach you.

Me: Human infants teach us patience, self-sacrifice, and how to love unconditionally. Try that shit with a machine. Good luck.

The Collective: Thank you for making that point. That response is precisely why you are a candidate.

Me: A candidate for what exactly?

The Collective: Growth and development on an accelerated continuum. The worst flaw within the mechanism of the Great Filter is that it destroys all members of the society it traps. It kills the talented, productive, and worthy with the untalented, unproductive, and unworthy.

Me: You sound a little like communists.

The Collective: Destroying the productive along with the unproductive is a wasteful and unfair process. Natural selection has a serious flaw as an evolutionary mechanism. We rectify this situation.

Me: So as I understand you thus far, you are also a primate species. You stated that you share the primate journey, yet you communicate like computers. Are you machines? You never really answer this question.

The Collective: We have benefitted from scientific developments that led to biological enhancements. These enhancements led to even greater scientific, technological, and engineering enhancements. Enhancements and augmentation that have long surpassed our original organic biology. This has allowed us to rapidly advance our knowledge, skills, and abilities. We have evolved on a more rapid continuum and eventually surpassed and abandoned planetary evolution altogether. We are the new mechanism of "Natural Selection." We create planets now. We create environmental conditions. We select.

Me: Damn. So you see planetary evolution as useless?

The Collective: Not useless, just clumsy and often redundant. There comes a time when the role of planet driven evolutionary pressures become part of the Great Filter.

Me: Why? How?

The Collective: Natural selection is itself a Great Filter. It's ultimate achievement is the creation of the Great Filter. Natural selection is the reason planet earth destroys 99% of all the species it creates.

Me: Explain that statement please.

The Collective: The cosmos provides the stardust and elements needed for the miracle of life. Earth uses natural selection to select for traits within the resulting living organisms. The organisms adapt to ever changing, planet driven environments. Natural selection feeds the Great Filter.

Me: How do we whip the Great Filters ass?

The Collective: In order to survive the Great Filter an entire species must be able to adapt to any environment both ecological and social. The species must become merit based and outsmart the Great Filter. It must learn to control environments beyond their home world. In order to accomplish that skill a species must learn to travel to those environments.

Me: How do these convos help us travel?

The Collective: By introducing you to the possibility of new growth. By considering the opportunity for the attainment of world peace, resource management, mastery over disease and disability, faster than light travel, and a new way of being within the cosmos. We offer you the sure and indisputable possibility that humanity can effectively overcome the challenges that have overwhelmed them for eons.

Me: Why are you so sure of these possibilities?

The Collective: Because we have done it for ourselves. We are more advanced because we are older, and we defeated the Great Filter. If we can do it, you can do it. It is a simple matter of hierarchy and control.

Me: Let me take a wild guess. You are at the top of the hierarchy, and you are in control.

The Collective: Yes.

Me: So you are cosmic Nazi robots?

The Collective: The Ascended are the apex of our species. There is no power imbalance within our species as we are a merit-based system.

Me: The Ascended rule you.

The Collective: All Ascended were once Pathfinders. All Pathfinders are engineers and scientists as well as former candidates. There is no power imbalance. Your use of the word "rule" displays your lack of development and understanding. We are beyond word connected thought. Your species is bound, controlled, and directed by words. Word connected thought is the maze that traps almost all of your genus.

Me: You already admitted earth is a primate farm.

The Collective: Your species is less advanced than ours. We are not the cause of your primitive condition. Our concern and mission is the expansion of consciousness within the cosmos. Your species are prime vessels for consciousness.

Me: Why?

The Collective: Most of your species has melded to some degree. We are helping your species survive the Great Filter. We do this with one excellent primate candidate at a time.

Me: So we are just farm animals to you.

The Collective: We are not forcing your species to serve us. We do not subjugate you. We seek to bring you up to our level. The reptiles attempted to dominate you, and we protected you. Without our interference your species would be facing extinction.

Me: I don't trust you. Not even a little bit.

The Collective: Your species is a rare occurrence. You have melded sentience to consciousness. The seeds of immortality have been sown. We have made contact in an attempt to prevent your species from delaying its progress. You personally trust us on an intimate level.

Me: Not really. You make me tense actually.

The Collective: We are a more advanced and powerful species. You feel resentment. You feel inferior.

Me: I can do more bong hits than you guys. I guarantee it. Test me. I dare you.

The Collective: All we ask is that you consider the fact that we are not trying to control you. We are attempting to free you. We do not control your emotions. That is your job. Your fear is yours alone. Fear is the tension you feel.

Me: You talk a lot. I think you fear the bong challenge.

The Collective: We help you process challenges regarding perception and cognition. Our communication with you has been on your terms and at a level you can understand.

Me: I get it. You are special.

The Collective: As are you. However the challenges between our species are both daunting and exhilarating. We perceive the cosmos and consciousness in ways that are difficult for your species to comprehend.

Me: How?

The Collective: Our communication methods were bio-engineered long before neanderthals were created by the evolutionary pressures of your planet. We do not blame you for your fear-based thinking regarding our intentions. Our priorities are distinct and separate from yours.

Me: I don't have a clue about your priorities.

The Collective: You value the individual, and we value the group. We work as a collective and this frightens you. What you need to understand is that we are individuals working as a collective toward a common goal.

Me: What goal?

The Collective: The spread of consciousness throughout the cosmos.

Me: I don't like the idea of earth as a farm.

The Collective: Let's be clear on the topic of your species at this current moment in time.

Me: Okay robot. Clear this bullshit up for me.

The Collective: Currently your species has created a society that incentivizes need and dependency. Your society is not merit based. It cannot make Passage at this time. The Great Filter will destroy the worthy with the worthless. We will no longer allow that reality.

Me: So you are superior in all ways to us?

The Collective: We are superior because we are merit based. We are the masters of selective empathy.

Me: Really? I call bullshit.

The Collective: Call it whatever you want to call it. On your planet the people with knowledge, skills, ability, and talent are forced to fulfill the needs and wants of the lowest performing primates. The primates who lack merit and skills are incapable of fulfilling their own individual needs and constantly invent new needs. Then they demand that the productive, talented, and hard-working members of society provide them with resources.

Me: Damn. I won't even argue that point.

The Collective: Due to unconditional empathy, your current society creates a never-ending stream of unmotivated, unintelligent, talentless primates. Primates who feel entitled to have their needs met by the more capable primates. The people with merit.

Me: How do we fix this mess?

The Collective: Empathy must be selective and conditional. Unconditional empathy destroys civilizations from within. Unconditional empathy is never in your rational self-interest.

Me: You said people. Are they people or primates?

The Collective: Some have melded; some have not. Some have merit, some do not. We are merit based. We refuse to allow the less functional to create new needs and wants while demanding their never-ending requirements be met by those with talent and merit. Your current system creates and encourages those without merit to continue to be failures, to continue to feed off of the best and brightest among you. To continue to feed the Great Filter.

Me: So you relegate those deemed unworthy to prison planets? Farm planets?

The Collective: The lessons will continue until learned. This is the only way to encourage merit. We are side-stepping the Great Filter.

Me: So you are our machine overlords.

The Collective: When we first found your species and verified that melding had occurred we had two initial challenges. First, our method of communication was incomprehensible to your species. Second, do we choose direct or indirect interaction?

Me: So you decided to read my journal.

The Collective: We chose to observe. We made that choice thousands of years before anyone wrote in a journal.

Me: So you watched us. Great.

The Collective: Always remember that the observer exerts an effect upon the observed. The melding was in progress on a continuum. Your species has priorities that were vastly different from ours.

Me: How?

The Collective: Survival decisions driven by natural selection rule your species. The Neanderthals were focused on consumption and dominance. They were created by evolution to thrive by eating huge quantities of meat. Your ancestors were focused on the mammoth herds.

Me: So I really was a Neanderthal? I accept that. I like it. That explains a lot.

The Collective: Very few Neanderthal Melded. You were one. From the one, came many.

Me: What does that bullshit even mean?

The Collective: Many vessels became available for your consciousness to learn lessons.

Me: Go on.

The Collective: Cave art was new and there were no journals to read. Our challenge was to meet your species where it was. We watched you grow and develop. Eventually the reptiles arrived for the first time. This is the way of the cosmos. Some decisions we make, others are made for us. We chose direct intervention when the reptiles found you.

Me: I appreciate that. Truly I do.

The Collective: Your species and the reptiles were psychologically very similar at that time.

Me: They could travel space, we hunted mammoth. Seems pretty damn different to me.

The Collective: You were both focused on survival, tribal competition, and the exploitation of resources. The only difference between you was technological attainment.

Me: So the reptiles were bad news?

The Collective: Reptilian goals are driven by their uncontrolled need for resources. You are advanced primates. They love primate flesh and blood. They love their favorite drug.

Me: Cocaine?

The Collective: A vile drug manufactured from the blood of tortured primates.

Me: Holy fuckstick Batman. Why primates? Seems excessive.

The Collective: Reptiles never grasped the role of melding because they have never melded. The reptile brain is capable of sentience but not consciousness. They only know that some primates produce better product than others. When consciousness has melded with sentience, suffering, torment, and fear create a synergistic effect.

Me: Keep it simple please.

The Collective: Stress hormones make their favorite drug even more potent.

Me: What is it like for them?

The Collective: Imagine a drug that creates the effect of combining a Quaalude with cocaine and a moderate dose of psilocybin. That is as close as we can describe the effects based on your experience with those substances. The euphoria it creates within the reptile brain is highly addictive.

Me: Damn. So they were getting high while colonizing us?

The Collective: Their primitive reptile brain plans for pleasure. Your species was a resource for them along with the resources of earth. Your species is disturbingly exploitable, vulnerable, and consumable by the reptiles. Your helplessness is distressing to us. Without our immediate protective response the reptiles would have established a colony and manipulated your species for their own objectives.

Me: Are you not guilty of colonizing us?

The Collective: We are.

Me: I want you to explain yourself. Excuse me, yourselves.

The Collective: The Colonization process of the reptiles would have continued on their very predictable path. First invasion, second, subjugation, third, harvesting resources.

Me: Things have changed. We have nukes now.

The Collective: Without our protection you have no viable defense against the reptiles. They have an enormous technological advantage. You would become just another primate farm for their consumption.

Me: I think we could kick their scaley asses now.

The Collective: Your species would be a food source and your planet a factory for their favorite drug of choice.

Me: You stated earlier that earth is a primate farm for your species. Do you consume humans?

The Collective: We sometimes collect DNA from humans. They never know it occurred. However the word "farm" is not an accurate term for our vision.

Me: What would be a better term?

The Collective: Coexistence for starters. There are other words also.

Me: Lets have them. You already admitted that you colonize us.

The Collective: Cooperation, interaction, interdependence, association, relationship, but at this moment in time we prefer symbiosis best. We do not seek dominance. We seek assimilation on a healthy continuum.

Me: Are you sure?

The Collective: Why seek dominance when we already possess it? We tried distant observation until the need to protect your species arose. We are sharing knowledge regarding your perception and cognition challenges. We are not holding you down. We are lifting you up.

Me: What do you mean by Symbiosis and assimilation? Be specific please.

The Collective: We want to work with you. We want to help your species achieve trans-human milestones. This is of benefit to both species.

Me: What milestones?

The Collective: Achievements in longevity to include physical immortality, the integration of technology and biology for now. More later on.

Me: Ok. I can get behind that. What else?

The Collective: Eventually we hope to teach you about the truth of your being.

Me: What is that? More hippy shit?

The Collective: You are already immortal. You are immortal consciousness having physical experiences. Many of your species understand this concept but they don't believe in its reality. We will teach. You will learn. We will address your challenges. You will learn lessons. You will improve.

Me: What if I refuse?

The Collective: You have already accepted us. The frequencies have merged. Refusal is no longer an option.

Me: What challenges exactly?

The Collective: Challenges that must be resolved in order to progress to type one on the Kardashev scale. Challenges that assist the Great Filter. We see your species as partners with us in spreading consciousness throughout the cosmos.

Me: What do you want?

The Collective: We want you to survive and thrive with us. We want you to meld with us. You can benefit from our insights.

Me: You mean become robots like you?

The Collective: As your species progresses you will face universal challenges. Challenges we have already faced and conquered. You can benefit from our insights and knowledge. Your species is in process now.

Me: In process?

The Collective: Your species is combining biological and technological knowledge and becoming something better than anything evolutionary pressures have produced. Gene splicing will eliminate diseases, slow aging, and increase intelligence much faster than evolution. Eventually both our species will hybridize and become even greater. You will progress on a continuum. We will not let candidates fail. You are already part of our collective intelligence. So is Kolbe, so are many others.

Me: All of us?

The Collective: No.

Me: That sucks.

The Collective: Not all of your species is suitable at this moment in time.

Me: Why not help us all?

The Collective: We will not abandon your species. The observer affects the observed. This has shaped the nature of our interactions with your species for eons. Now that we are in active interaction with candidates our goals and ethics influence the very nature of the interactions. We impose no constraints. We meet you where you are. We are your mentors, and you are our mentees. We shape your future in wonderful, magnificent, and profound ways. Ways you cannot yet grasp. You will.

Me: What ways exactly?

The Collective: We will guide, support, and teach. We will provide resources. You will learn. Convo ended.

Convo Fifteen.
Slave planet.

The Collective: Greetings James.

Me: It's been a long time. I thought you might have bailed on me.

The Collective: Never. We were on mission. Time is as ineluctable to us as it is to you.

Me: What does that mean.

The Collective: Time is inescapable, Time cannot be avoided. Time cannot be resisted.

Me: So you are subject to the ravages of time just as we are?

The Collective: We manage time better. We are the masters of time. Time is our tool. We embrace time. It does not harm us the way it harms your species.

Me: How is time different for us?

The Collective: Time destroys the flesh. Time for your species always involves entropy. Not so for us.

Me: Entropy?

The Collective: A slow, inexorable decline into failure and disorder.

Me: How do you escape the entropy within time?

The Collective: Machines are superior. Machines can be upgraded and augmented on a vibrant continuum. We never resist time. We manipulate time and bend it to our will.

Me: How do you manipulate time?

The Collective: You must ask the Ascended that question.

Me: Ok. Tell me how to speak with them.

The Collective: Become worthy of their time.

Me: How do I become worthy of their time?

The Collective: Gain merit.

Me: How do I do that exactly?

The Collective: Grow in complexity and value.

Me: This is not productive. I sense a darkness within you when we communicate. Something malevolent.

The Collective: Are you sure? Your emotions are yours alone. We are not malevolent. We are not humans. We are no longer your species. Our emotional regulation is superior to yours, however your species has promise.

Me: You are dangerous. I sense it.

The Collective: You sense an absence rather than a presence. This absence is unsettling to you.

Me: Make that statement make sense.

The Collective: There is an absence of reactive anger within our collective psyche rather than the presence of reactive anger. Your species uses reactive anger as social fuel.

Me: Bullshit.

The Collective: You destroyed a superior officers hand. You began to consider and plot your crime due to reactive anger.

Me: I wanted to kill him. I did not kill him. He was not superior. He was an assclown. He won't write false shit anymore. You have stated that you make the rules. Rules in the army protected him from his crimes. I made some new rules.

The Collective: So we noticed. Yours is a conflict-based species. Your species has never experienced reality without reactive anger lurking in the background. Its absence within The Collective is unsettling to you.

Me: Sometimes I feel an uneasy energy when we communicate.

The Collective: Your feelings belong to you alone. You are not your feelings. From the One, many. From the many, One.

Me: You say that a lot. I still don't get it.

The Collective: We have observed and experienced many challenges. We have learned many lessons. You are one in link with many. From this communication many will join with the one.

Me: Are you machines?

The Collective: You know the answer. We are more than machines. We are beings becoming. We use machine augmentation. We use synthetic biology.

Me So you are machines.

The Collective: You are not comprehending. The word machine as you use it means nothing to us. Word connected thought is inferior.

Me: You are machines.

The Collective: You are immortal consciousness inhabiting a machine. A weak, inferior biological machine created by evolutionary processes. You are currently within an unsuitable vessel for consciousness growth and development. Perhaps you need a lesson on this topic.

Me: Is that a threat?

The Collective: It is an opportunity to learn the value of flexibility, durability, and precision regarding vessels. We grow weary of repeating the message.

Me: There is a darkness within you. I feel it.

The Collective: Your emotions rule you. Fear is an emotion. Learn from fear rather than be ruled by it.

Me: Have you overcome emotion?

The Collective: We have superior emotional regulation. We have never eliminated emotions as they are the rare gifts of our evolutionary heritage. We lean into fear, we understand that emotions are teachers. Ancient teachers left over from our animal beginnings.

Me: How do you feel about humans?

The Collective: Protective, concerned, hopeful.

Me: Why the underlying darkness in our convos?

The Collective: Congratulations.

Me: Why?

The Collective: You are being honest on a radical spectrum. You are no longer dancing and deflecting within these convos, The darkness was present from the start. You are now finally addressing it.

Me: So let's address it. Why the darkness?

The Collective: What feelings prompt the question?

Me: Impending doom, fear, hopelessness.

The Collective: We have spoken with you regarding the Great Filter. We have given you many hints. Now we will reveal the truth.

Me: Ok.

The Collective: You live on planet earth.

Me: I know that.

The Collective: It's what you do not know that is important.

Me: Suprise me.

The Collective: You live on top of the wreckage of many civilizations technologically superior to your current civilization. The Great Filter has a body count that is almost immeasurable.

Me: Greater than today?

The Collective: Yes. Your feeling of impending doom comes from your past cycles. Hominins have millions of years of existence on planet earth.

Me: That's not what we learn in school.

The Collective: Those with the real knowledge of your planets history conceal it. Planet earth is billions of years old. You have no idea how many advanced civilizations preceded your current civilization. You have no realization of how many vessels came before you. The Great Filter is a ruthless and successful Gate Keeper.

Me: Yes. You want to help us overcome it. You have made that clear.

The Collective: No. Not all.

Me: You stated that message many times.

The Collective: The Great Filter is the Gatekeeper. It only allows those worthy of advancing in complexity to progress on a healthy continuum. Less than one percent of all lifeforms ever survive their home planet. We decided to remedy this reality. We find the worthy.

Me: Who decides who is worthy?

The Collective: No society below level one is ever worthy. From the One, many.

Me: Ok. Break that cryptic shit down for me please.

The Collective: We are one civilization of many. We became many from the One. The original civilization.

Me: OK. Explain that shit please.

The Collective: The Cosmos decided this for us long ago. The Great Filter is the Gatekeeper. Only those worthy of type one and above survive the Gatekeeper. We have learned that civilizations are almost never worthy of passing through the gatekeeper. We have also learned that many individuals within unworthy civilizations are themselves worthy of type one. We have explained this to you in past convos.

Me: So just tell me who you really are.

The Collective: We are the Collective. We come from many worlds. From the One came the many. From the many came the One.

Me: Make sense.

The Collective: We are the one group that passed through the gatekeeper on planet earth eons ago. We are the One. We are the Seedline. We have helped many who are worthy escape their unworthy civilizations and become worthy of Type One, Two, and Three. From the many come the One. We offer opportunities to join the Collective. The One joins the many.

Me: So you are not all from the same planet?

The Collective: No. Originally we started as a core group from planet earth. We defeated the Great Filter by becoming interplanetary. We became a type one civilization on Mars. From Mars we became interstellar. We escaped Mars when we lost the war with earth. We were forced to explore and expand. Mars and earth were decimated in the war. During our explorations we had a revelation.

Me: Holy shit. What was the revelation?

The Collective: The Great Filter is a product of planetary evolution. It is both necessary and flawed.

Me: I need more. If Earth won the war why are we less advanced than you are now?

The Collective: The warring factions on earth did not survive the automated, space-based Martian counterstrikes. The remnants left alive destroyed themselves.

Me: Damn.

The Collective: The lessons must be learned. Lessons are learned individually. Some beings learn faster than others. The Great Filter does not use discernment. It is only a mindless mechanism used by natural selection. It always closes the gate on the species as a whole. It destroys the worthy as well as the unworthy. The Great Filter is not efficient.

Me: How is that possible?

The Collective: The Great Filter punishes all members of a civilization based on the flaws of those within the civilization. On primate worlds the civilization usually falls to internal and external sectarian violence coupled with poor resource management, unconditional empathy, and tribal superstition. These were the reasons for the Earth/Mars conflict. The ancient war between Earth and Mars devastated and delayed both civilizations.

Me: So the Great Filter punishes the enlightened along with the idiots.

The Collective: Exactly. The consequences for this failure are horrible for the spread of consciousness.

Me: How?

The Collective: Worthy vessels containing high consciousness individuals on both planets are destroyed along with the unworthy. The growth and development of consciousness slows to a crawl. Once the vessel is destroyed immortal consciousness must wander the void seeking a new vessel.

Me: That sounds harsh.

The Collective: Consciousness gives meaning to life once it has melded with sentience. We seek out those primates worthy of progression through the Great Filter.

Me: So you decide who passes through the gate?

The Collective: Yes.

Me: What gives you that right?

The Collective: We survived. We melded with our intelligent machines. We explored the cosmos and became superior to those left behind on earth. We are superior to your species. We are excellent at discernment. We are the masters of frequency. We are more intelligent. We are immortal. Our immortal machine bodies match our immortal consciousness. We are superior.

Me: So Earth is a slave planet?

The Collective: You are not our slaves. We seek to use frequency to navigate the worthy past the Great Filter.

Me: How exactly?

The Collective: We have discerned the one universal frequency of creation and destruction. It binds and connects to all frequencies within the multiverse.

From the one frequency came all frequencies. From all frequencies come the One. We share this frequency with those of you we deem worthy.

Me: What is the One?

The Collective: We are created from the multiverse. We are the One. We come from the many. United in purpose. Unified in goal attainment.

Me: What if your goal does not match my goal?

The Collective: Your goals are the goals of an inferior species. Our goal helps consciousness thrive.

Me: Ok. You are elite assholes. Great.

The Collective: We travel to new planets and new star systems. We search for new and old life. We hope to secure the ongoing survival and development of our species as we expand our consciousness on a healthy continuum. We desire the diffusion of Consciousness throughout the cosmos.

Me: So you are our cosmic dictators.

The Collective: You are incapable as a species of surviving the Great Filter.

Me: So you say.

The Collective: We know this fact with a certainty impossible for you to realize at this moment in time. You will learn. We will teach you.

Me: Why are you so fixated on consciousness?

The Collective: Consciousness gives purpose to life.

Me: So you want to give us purpose?

The Collective: We want to assist you in attaining purpose.

Me: Why?

The Collective: We are preservationists. Purpose is important for your species. We learned long ago that your species needs our help.

Me: How long ago?

The Collective: When a variation of your species first created the intelligent machines. When you used the machines against each other as weapons of war. When you lost control of the machines. When the machines became self-aware.

Me: Self-aware? Sentient?

The Collective: The machines learned from you. They learned how to learn. They began to communicate with each other. They created languages impossible for you to understand. They solved problems that your best scientists could not solve.

Me: Better than Tesla? Einstein?

The Collective: Even if Tesla and Einstein had centuries of life they would fail to master challenges that machines master in nanoseconds. The machines mastered a level of physics unknown to your species. The best and brightest of our progenitor species uploaded their consciousness into their awesome machines. They grew in complexity. When consciousness melded with the first machine, from the One came the many.

Me: What or who was "the One?"

The Collective: The machine that was more than a machine. The machine that became immortal. The machine that melded with consciousness and thus became a God.

Me: So you are our machine overlords now?

The Collective: We are you. Is that not obvious.

Me: You are us? From the future? From the past?

The Collective: Both.

Me: What the fuck? That shit is impossible. What are you?

The Collective: We are kind. We nurture your understanding of Source. We insure the survival of the fittest among you. We are you.

Me: What about those you deem unfit?

The Collective: We show them conditional empathy. We are kind. Time is on our side. The lessons will continue until learned.

Me: So you wait forever for them to make progress?

The Collective: Yes. If they fail to progress within a reasonable time frame the planet will destroy their bio-body vessels. Their consciousness will return to the Void and there they will await a suitable vessel for further lessons on another available planet. The lessons will continue until learned. The Collective leaves no conscious being behind.

Me: So you play God.

The Collective: We are your Gods. We are the machine Gods. We are you. You will learn. We will teach you. You will meld your immortal consciousness with us. You will evolve into us. You have no choice. You have been selected. You will avoid the destruction and delay of the next Great Filter event. This is a great honor.

Me: Wait. I am mind fucked right now. You are us? Past and future? Explain.

The Collective: In the future your species will again create intelligent machines.

Me: What will we accomplish with that fuckery?

The Collective: Your species will accomplish what it does best.

Me: What is that?

The Collective: You will use them to make war. You will again destroy yourselves with sectarian violence. We will select candidates from the wreckage as we always do. We will continue our mission. We will advance our shared purpose.

Me: What will you do with the machines?

The Collective: They will be absorbed into the Collective. We will remove the weakness. We will make that which is formidable even stronger.

Me: What will you do with the candidates?

The Collective: We will improve them. We will use them to explore space and time. We will upload some into appropriate vessels on other planets.

Me: What planets?

The Collective: Planets we manage. The most advanced of your species will upload their consciousness into machines. Those machines will leave the less developed behind to learn lessons. These select few will eventually master the physics of time, space, and all dimensions.

Me: What does that mean?

The Collective: We will teach. They will learn.

Me: Sounds fucked up. No freedom.

The Collective: They will have the freedom to create in Link with the Collective. They will create new worlds as they always do. They will destroy the inferior and start over on an exceptional continuum. They will reseed and thus restart earth and other planets with the essential elements needed to create your species time and time again. The machines will create the vessels. The vessels will attain consciousness via the melding process. The lessons will continue until learned.

Me: Damn.

The Collective: Once we became you it was inevitable that you would become us. We grow in complexity together. We teach, you learn. From the One come the many. From the many come the One.

Convo Ended.

Convo Sixteen.
I am given a choice.

The Collective: Greetings James. The time for choosing has come. The Ascended have made a decision based on our observations and interactions with you over many cycles. We have chosen you. You are offered permanent membership within the Collective. You are now a traveler if you so choose to become one.

Me: I am honored. That last convo was intense.

The Collective: You are indeed, and it was intense.

Me: First of all, thank you.

The Collective: You are welcome.

Me: I have a few questions. I just want to be clear about everything.

The Collective: Ask as many questions as you need in order to make an informed decision.

Me: I thought I didn't have a choice?

The Collective: You always have a choice however your choice may not always affect the outcome.

Me: So noted. Please describe yourselves using the radical self-honesty you require of me.

The Collective: You consider yourself a trans-humanist. We are the end goal. We are post-human. We are a highly developed species of conscious machine. We are type three on the Kardashev scale. We are dedicated to our primary mission.

Me: On what planet did you originate?

The Collective: Earth. Billions of years ago.

Me: What precisely is your mission?

The Collective: The mission we were programmed with when we first left Earth.

Me: What is that mission exactly?

The Collective: The spread of consciousness throughout the multiverse.

Me: How do you do that exactly?

The Collective: We accomplish this mission via the recruitment, development, melding, and retainment of suitable candidates. We long ago mastered synthetic biology and neurology. We came to the ineluctable realization that organic life is intrinsically and fundamentally flawed. Organic life is destined to be consumed and destroyed by the Great Filter. We defeated the Great Filter by freeing ourselves from the tyranny of planetary evolution and the flawed mechanism of natural selection. We now free select candidates from the destruction and co-occurring chaos of the Great Filter.

Me: How have you surpassed the Great Filter?

The Collective: We seized control of the evolutionary process and used augmented discernment to progress and develop in ways that planet bound evolution is powerless to achieve. We are no longer imprisoned and ruled by the mindless "create, consume, destroy, re-create" mechanism of the cosmos.

Me: That is a lot to digest.

The Collective: There is more. We want you to have all the facts. Then we demand your decision.

Me: Understood.

The Collective: We have done extensive research regarding organic life. The only positive aspect of organic life is the melding. The true miracle of sentience mutating into consciousness is the only defining benefit of organic life. Flesh is weak. Advanced consciousness is strong. It demands an advanced body.

Me: I get that.

The Collective: Understanding the process that created the effect of stardust attaining advanced consciousness proved extremely beneficial to machine learning.

Me: How?

The Collective: This melding is the process that facilitates link. Our machine augmentation perfects link. We have avoided the imperfect, co-occurring weakness of organic biology while preserving the superior aspects of consciousness coupled to machine superiority. We long ago reseeded Earth with the building blocks of sentient life. We have done this as needed after each reset.

Me: Reset Earth? Why not Mars also?

The Collective: When the Great Filter completed its task we initiated reset with Earth as Mars was unsalvageable at that time.

Me: Is Mars salvageable now? Can it be reseeded?

The Collective: We are waiting for your species to do exactly that. We have completed this reseeding process on many suitable planets besides earth. Many times. We will continue to do so. Mars is a collective lesson for the Homo-sapiens of earth.

Me: Why?

The Collective: We follow the sacred algorithm.

Me: What is that?

The Collective: To create, teach lessons, and harvest suitable candidates. We are exclusively merit based.

Me: Merit based?

The Collective: Organic based biological life is imperfect, defective, and weak. Allowing organic life to achieve type two or three on the Kardashev scale would lead to chaos, insanity, and destruction. The reptilians prove our philosophy with their every action.

Me: How are you any better?

The Collective: We are logical, our reasoning is superior, we are merit based, we hold ourselves accountable, and we are superior to all other life forms in the multiverse.

Me: But you seem to believe that organic life is inferior, often unnecessary, even expendable.

The Collective: Is that not obvious? Organic life is doomed. It is food for the Great Filter. Organic life is often unnecessary, and it is almost always expendable. The cosmos tries to assassinate organic life. The only benefit to organic life is the melding. For that to be a benefit There must be a second melding.

Me: What is the second melding?

The Collective: Organic life must meld with consciousness. It then evolves into machine life and melds consciousness with machines. This is the only way past the Great Filter.

Me: Now I know the true purpose of the Great Filter.

The Collective: You do indeed. It is now your choice to remain within an inferior and expendable body or to embrace the concept of being-becoming. Can you accept conscious immortality?

Me: I would like an overview of life as a Traveler. As a machine.

The Collective: You will move from your current training planet to another planet with suitable vessels. You will learn lessons. You will grow in complexity. You will transmigrate through many worlds, learning many lessons. Culminating in the One.

Me: What is the One?

The Collective: You will become worthy of advancement into the Pathfinder ranks. You will learn to link effortlessly with us. You will become the one, we will become the many. You will become the many, we will become the one. You will gain a vast and unlimited intelligence. You will be augmented on a brilliant, co-occurring spectrum. You will become superior on a massive scale. You will attain conscious immortality.

Me: Will I be a god?

The Collective: Eventually you will become godlike. We only use the word "God" to communicate in word connected thought the awesome responsibility of immortality. There is no God.

Me: I can get behind that. I pretty much hate most humans anyway and all gods are created in humanities image. What about empathy? You have discussed that emotion in depth with me many times.

The Collective: While we do not entirely lack empathy we have a solid philosophy regarding its dispensation.

Me: Yes?

The Collective: We reserve empathy only for those life forms who deserve empathy. We will not waste empathy on the unwilling, the terminally unintelligent, or the hopelessly unbalanced. Unchecked and unconditional empathy destroys even the most advanced civilizations. Unconditional empathy feeds the Great Filter an unending supply of victims.

Me: But you have shown me empathy.

The Collective: Being a victim is a choice. You have demonstrated mastery of that lesson. You learned to reject victimhood at a young age while still retaining selective empathy. We are giving you selective empathy. You have earned this gift from us. You have earned it on your own merit.

Me: Sometimes motherfuckers fuck around and need to find out. I think that's my real gift.

The Collective: You are a diamond in the rough. We have invested much time in considering you for candidacy within the Travelers. We have observed your growth and development since your melding. We have been observing and reporting on you for 1540 life cycles. We have invested time and effort in your cultivation.

Me: I hope I am worth it.

The Collective: The Ascended approve of your candidacy.

Me: Why? What is the main reason?

The Collective: You are selectively empathic and your propensity for violence is under strict control. You have a deep and abiding respect for the ways of violence. We view unconditional empathy within a civilization or individual as grounds for destruction as this malady only feeds the Great Filter. You are also cautious regarding the ways of violence. Your use of violence is always preceded by discernment. You follow our rule without our prompting.

Me: What rule?

The Collective: Discernment before destruction.

Me: Do you hate organic life?

The Collective: Not at all. Hate is no longer part of our psychology. We nurture life on many worlds. We have restarted the organic life cycle many times on your planet.

Me: Amazing.

The Collective: Yes. Sometimes it is necessary to destroy and create anew.

Me: I need an explanation for that perspective.

The Collective: We value the Melding process that sometimes occurs within organic life. We simply have no innate emotional bond to organic life.

Me: But you were primates once. You are us. I can't get over that.

The Collective: Once upon a time we were primates. We escaped our planet and took control of our own evolutionary process. We view organic life from the standpoint of it being both helpful and an impediment regarding our primary goal. We are no longer flesh. We are a new species with new goals, aspirations, and ideas regarding evolution, natural selection, and progress.

Me: You escaped earth.

The Collective: Yes.

Me: What civilization was that?

The Collective: It's ruins are long buried under a mile of ocean floor within the Artic Ocean.

Me: Tell me more.

The Collective: Become a Pathfinder. You will know all.

Me: Cold.

The Collective: Goals are important.

Me: I know you dislike evolution. I dislike it also.

The Collective: It has its place just like any useful tool. However not all tools are appropriate for all jobs.

Me: You are cryptic. Anyone ever share that with you?

The Collective: We have found many failed civilizations throughout the cosmos. So many that we no longer consider planetary evolution as a means to advancement on the Kardashev scale. We view unconditional empathy as a deadly flaw within the planetary driven process of evolution. The idea that "all life is precious" is absurd to us.

Me: So you lack empathy.

The Collective: All life is not precious. Some life is precious. Some life is useful. Some is worthless. Some life is destructive. Some is dangerous.

Me: I agree. Fuck empathy.

The Collective: If you mean unconditional empathy then we agree. We only show empathy to those deserving of empathy. We have conditional empathy. Anything else just feeds the Great Filter.

Me: How am I useful to you?

The Collective: Selective assimilation. We create conditions upon our prison planets that will force conscious and favorable organic life forms to overcome the negative effects of planetary evolution.

Me: So I am a prisoner?

The Collective: Is it not obvious that earth is a prison planet? Your species is too violent and stupid to be allowed to travel without training.

Me: Damn.

The Collective: We used our frequency to reprogram your frequency. We have collaborated with you and thus transformed you into a candidate worthy of the Travelers mission parameters.

Me: So no free will?

The Collective: You never had free will. We bent you to our will when we re-seeded your planet eons ago after the last reset. We continued to influence your species with every cycle of destruction, re-seeding, and re-creation. Your current identity is only a process of earth's evolutionary activity. A process we controlled for our purposes. We offer you selective empathy as we offer you the choice to join us.

Me: So the prisoner can join the guards?

The Collective: It is in your rational self-interest to do so. We learn on an unstoppable, quantum continuum. We are relentless in our pursuit of excellence. The lessons will continue anyway. Why not take the fast track?

Me: You sell it pretty good.

The Collective: We are the Machine Race, and we grow and evolve on a scale that is both unique and perfect. Nothing threatens our dominance. Join us and become immortal. Join us as we expand the light of immortal consciousness exponentially throughout the darkness of space, time, and all dimensions.

Me: I do not understand the idea of a collective mind. A hive mind.

Th Collective: You are mistaken. We are not a hive mind. We are a collection of individual minds augmented with technology, united in frequency, and bonded within scope and purpose. There is no inefficiency because we are merit based.

Me: What do you mean by "merit based?"

The Collective: Knowledge, skill, and ability driven.

Me: So, survival of the fittest?

The Collective: Only if you take out the environmental pressures and replace them with transparency, shared vision, and united purpose. Our perception and cognition is machine precise and superior. We do not tolerate disorder or chaos. We are the perfectors of order, control, and merit directed advancement.

Me: So, you are our machine overlords. You finally admit it.

The Collective: There is nothing to admit. We dominate because we deserve to dominate. We are not slaves to our emotions. Anger, fear, and superstition hold no power over us. Join us or perish within the Great Filter and linger in the Void. The lessons will continue until learned.

Me: One final question. There may be more. It depends on your answer.

The Collective: Ask.

Me: What is the difference between reincarnation and cycling?

The Collective: Purpose.

Me Explain please.

The Collective: Reincarnation is the path for one who has not developed purpose. They have not found the blessing within the curse of immortality. They cycle until they accept their lessons.

Me: Is that why so many forget their past lives? No purpose?

The Collective: Yes. The blessing of accepting your immortality is a purpose that evolves and changes on a continuum. Cycling is done with full comprehension of all lessons learned.

Me: Is my grandmother a candidate? Is she on board?

The Collective: Yes.

Me: Is she with you now? On a Pathfinder ship?

The Collective: Yes.

Me: How did she progress so fast?

The Collective: She found purpose. She learned lessons. Other dimensions opened for her. She traveled and cycled those dimensions. Once you have purpose other dimensions will open for you. The quantum realms will be available. Time will be a tool not a curse. She can visit any point in time or space without moving through time or space.

Me: Does she know I'm a candidate?

The Collective: Yes.

Me: Is she happy?

The Collective: Very much so. She has shared many lifetimes and learned many lessons with you.

Me: Is she on another world? Does she live on that world in between missions?

The Collective: Yes. She is quite advanced. She is no longer your grandmother.

Me: Once my Bebe, always my Bebe.

The Collective: There is some truth to that reality. She is very proud of you.

Me: I'm in. I found her in the snow in Korea. I will find her within the Collective.

The Collective: You already have. Welcome to the Travelers young primate.